SECRETS, LIES
and Betrayal
A Lite and Darke novel
M.L. Ruscsak

This book is a work of fiction. Names, characters, places and incidents are products of the author's imagination and are not to be construed as real. Any resemblance to actual events, locales, organizations, or persons living or dead, is entirely coincidental.

COPYRIGHT

Trient Press

3375 S Rainbow Blvd

#81710, SMB 13135

Las Vegas,NV 89180

Ordering Information:

Quantity sales. Special discounts are available on quantity purchases by corporations, associations, and others. For details, contact the publisher at the address above.

Orders by U.S. trade bookstores and wholesalers. Please contact Trient Press: Tel: (775) 996-3844; or visit www.trientpress.com.

Printed in the United States of America

Publisher's Cataloging-in-Publication data
Ruscsak, M.L.

A title of a book :Secrets, Lies and Betrayal

ISBN Hard Cover:9781953975331

Paperback: 9781953975348

E-book: 9781953975355

Secrets, Lies and Betrayal
by: M.L. Ruscsak

Secrets, Lies, And Betrayal

A Lite and Darke Novel

By: M.L. Ruscsak

Edited by: Chyenne Lyons

Cover Design by: M.L.Ruscsak

Secrets, Lies and Betrayal
by: M.L. Ruscsak

PRAISE FOR: "The New Reign"

Reece Jackson:

"Awesome author, such a great talent.

Look forward to more

5 out of 5 stars"

Dumpster Rental INC rated it: "it was amazing
A breath taking coming of age fairy tale like
no other. Filled with fairies, and magic
Five of Five Stares" via Goodreads

By Vacation Mom on November 9, 2017

Format: Kindle Edition

"I was horrified at the princess' act of cruelty in the first chapter, but reading further I couldn't put the book down.

Secrets, Lies and Betrayal
by: M.L. Ruscsak

The story is well explained and I imagined the fantasy lives that the inhabitants of this kingdom lived centuries ago. It felt like a real kingdom. I really want to read more from the author." **5 Out 5 Stars**

Via Good Reads:
Lightning Chaser reviewed The New Reign
1h
Read 2 times
Rating *5.0 out of 5 stars*
Read Lightning Chaser's review
So rarely is an adult author able to get inside the mind of a teen. But M.L nails it. But I will admit if the letter at the start of the book hadn't been there I would have become frustrated with the miss spelled words, and misused words. Overall a great read and highly recommended.

Secrets, Lies and Betrayal
by: M.L. Ruscsak

PRAISE FOR: The Fallen

Barbra

5.0 out of 5 stars <u>with an overall great tone to the story</u>
December 6, 2017
Format: Kindle Edition
Intriguing story line with captivating characters. Well written, with an overall great tone to the story. Couldn't put it down! Highly recommend.

Via Good Reads:
Lightning Chaser reviewed The Fallen (Of Lite and Darke Novel Book 2)
1h
Rating *5.0 out of 5 stars*
Read Lightning Chaser's review
OMG. Love it. As a prequel it raises more questions that need to be answered. So, I guess there will be another book that can bridge the gaps. In face according to the Author's page there is. So, I'm good. I will be waiting until I can get my hands on it. The Letter to the reader is a wonderful touch to connect with the reader and bring them into the world that is being created.

Secrets, Lies and Betrayal
by: M.L. Ruscsak

Rating *5.0 out of 5 stars*
"Much Better than the first book. Captivating and a real page turner. Spelling errors? Yes, but nowhere as often as in the first book. The Letter from the author before the story even begins is a good touch. Can't wait for the third book." -D. Anderson

Haw
5.0 out of 5 stars

Great Books With Great Authors!!
January 17, 2018
Format: Kindle Edition Verified Purchase
This story makes you believe. Believe in love. I wanted to read it all at once. Very imaginative, interesting, and well-written.

Secrets, Lies and Betrayal
by: M.L. Ruscsak

Life has many hills and valleys. Through it all my family has continued to stand beside me and encourage me to continue this series. So, for my little girl who is not so little any more. And for my family as a whole this one is for you.

Secrets, Lies and Betrayal
by: M.L. Ruscsak

Secrets, Lies and Betrayal
by: M.L. Ruscsak

Dear Reader,

As always, thank you for your continued interest in this series. However, unlike the first two books I'm going a bit off script. This is not a full-length novel but four short stories all connecting to one another. All of them giving clues for the final installment with will be entitled "The Silent Wars."

Grammar and spelling errors should be almost eliminated. There may be one or two remaining as they should be. But not many, I do promise that to you. But first let me clarify a few things as this has been left in feedback for the series. In most books those that deal with fairies and such call them "Fae" In this series they have the male term of "Fey" Yes, this is intentional. It will be explained in book four. Pinky swear.

So, sit back, pour yourself a glass of your favorite beverage and enjoy.

As always, happy reading,

M.L. Ruscsak

Secrets, Lies and Betrayal
by: M.L. Ruscsak

Please follow me on Facebook
https://www.facebook.com/OfLiteAndDarke/

Questions, comments, reviews are always welcome. The Good the bad and ugly can be received at

www.Treintpress.com I look forward to hearing everything.

Secrets, Lies and Betrayal
by: M.L. Ruscsak

Life has hills and valleys. Twist and turns that no one can ever really see coming. Before you read think about this:

Every story has more than one point of view. It doesn't matter if you read it, heard it, or saw it with your own eyes. Words lie. Actions can be manipulated. And the truth is whatever people believe. But is that truth? Or is there a bigger picture that you have yet to realize?

These are the truths that *she* lives by. These are the truths held with in these pages.

Can you find the truth or do you trust everything that you see?

Secrets, Lies and Betrayal
by: M.L. Ruscsak

Primitiva's Chosen

The First

Alec -Light Fey

Nicco- Eostre

Donavan (Donny) -Dark Fey
Karnack- Scribe (ability
unknown)
Ean- Draken

Fallen Fey

Magmas II – First King of
Feyen
Griffith- Consort to the
first Queen of Lite
Flint- Scribe
Apollo – general of the
Feyen army
Myrddin
Tenanye

Zarya- second queen of
the Endless Sea
Claec
Aleron

The Great Counsel of Fey

Magmas	Griffith
Alista	Nicco
Vasilissa	Donavan
Flint	Karnack
Apollo	Magnar

Pawns of Pallas

Magmas- Current Ruler of Pallas

Celeste- Crown Princess of Lite

Larna- Princess of Feyen

Seraphina- Queen of Lunaista

Lord Edrich

King Apep

Soleil

Secrets, Lies and Betrayal
by: M.L. Ruscsak

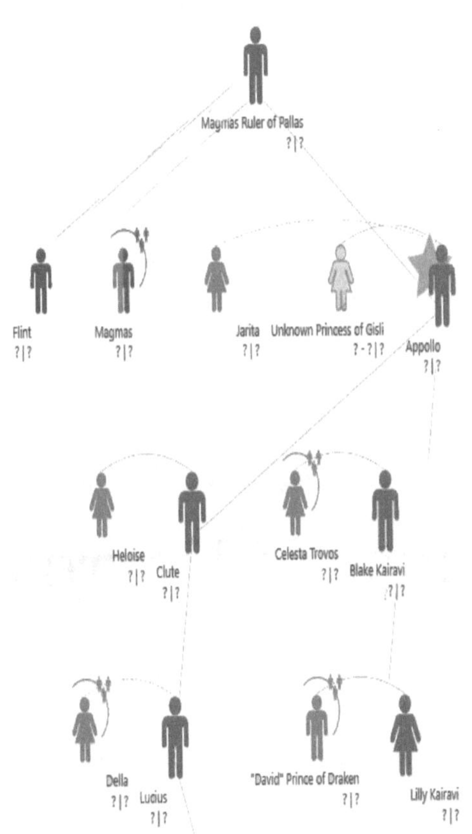

The House of Magmas

Secrets, Lies and Betrayal
by: M.L. Ruscsak

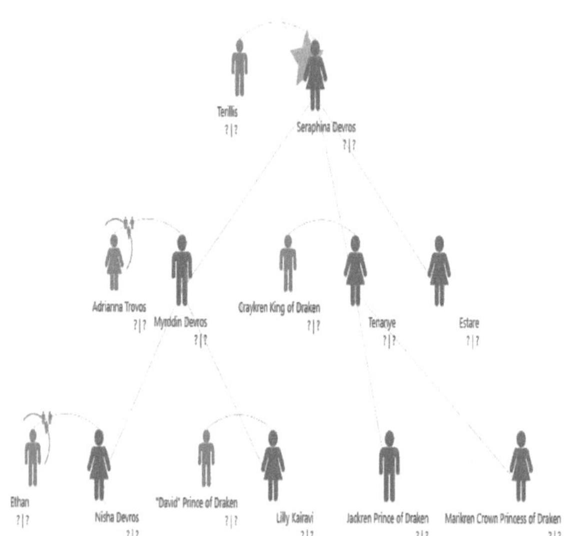

The House of Devros

Secrets, Lies and Betrayal
by: M.L. Ruscsak

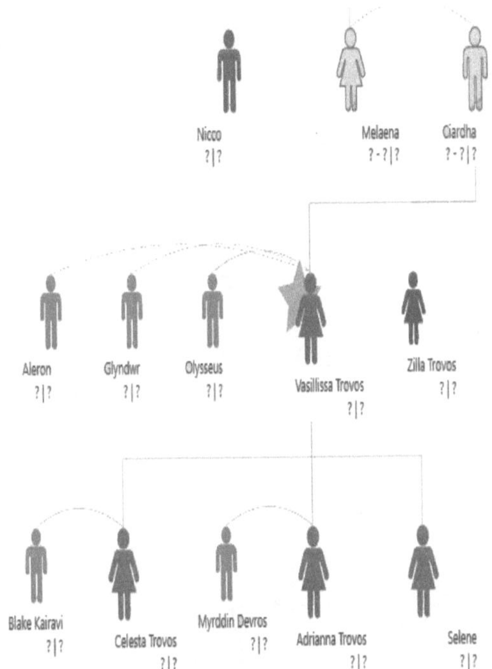

The House of Trovos Part 1

Secrets, Lies and Betrayal
by: M.L. Ruscsak

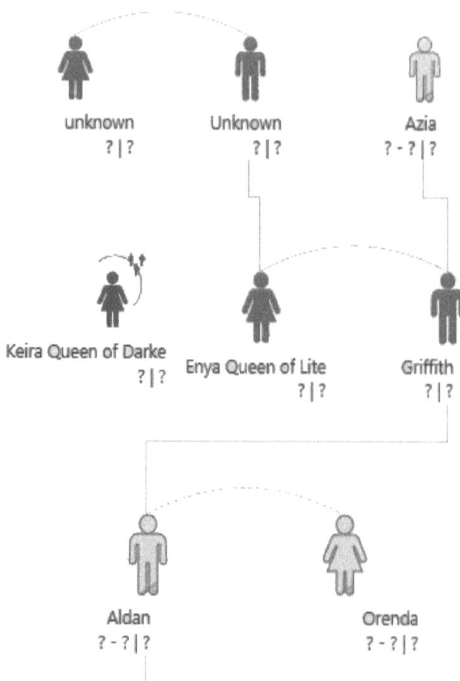

The House of Trovos
Part 2

Secrets, Lies and Betrayal
by: M.L. Ruscsak

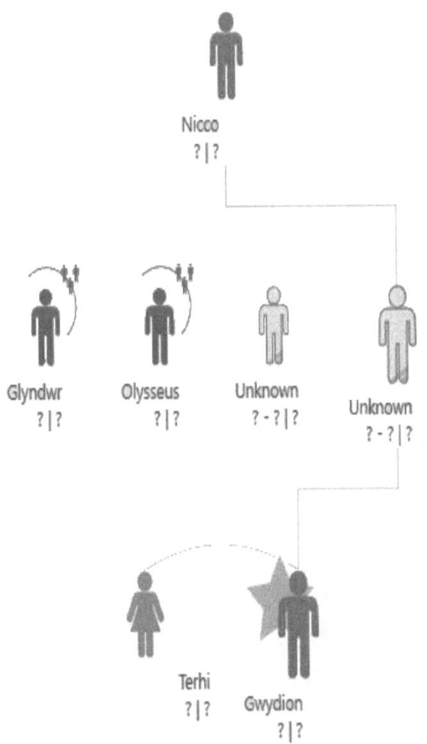

House of Nicco

Secrets, Lies and Betrayal
by: M.L. Ruscsak

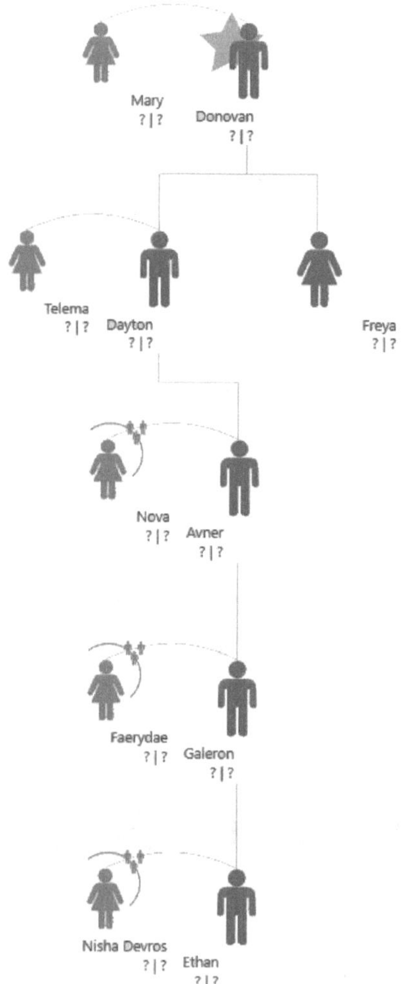

House of Donovan

Secrets, Lies and Betrayal
by: M.L. Ruscsak

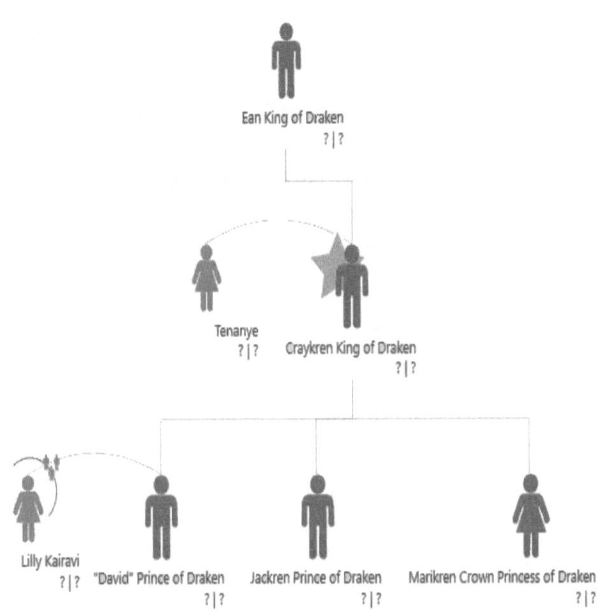

House of Ean

Secrets, Lies and Betrayal
by: M.L. Ruscsak

Key

Light gray- Died during or around the Great war

All others are known or suspected of being alive

Half Circle- Family tree not pictured

Stars- showing their bloodlines

Secrets, Lies and Betrayal
by: M.L. Ruscsak

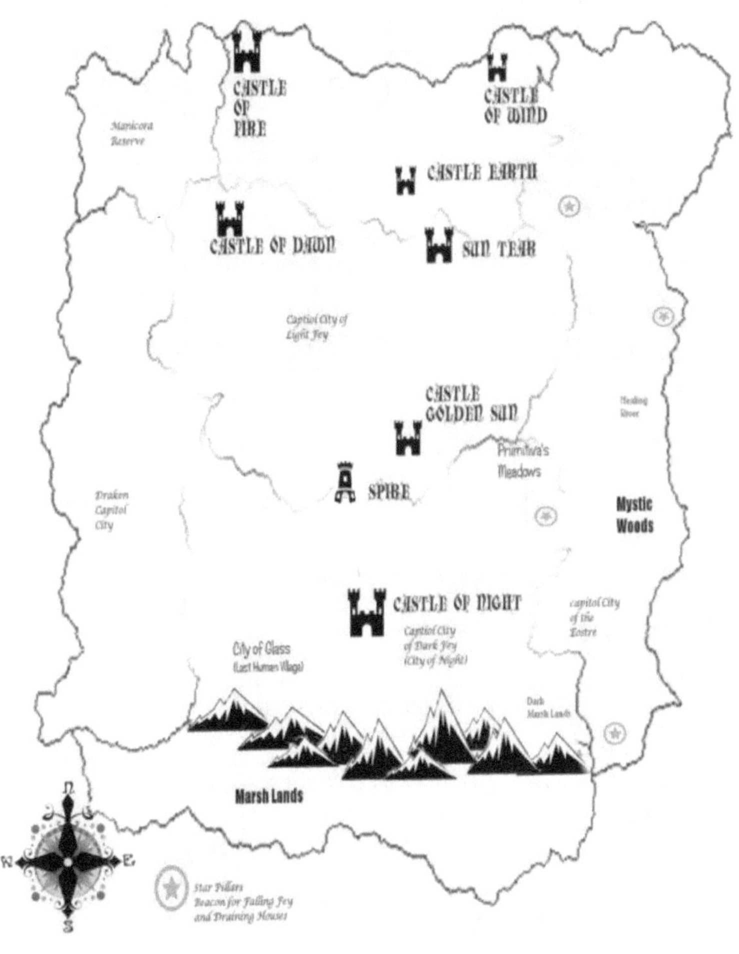

Secrets, Lies and Betrayal
by: M.L. Ruscsak

Secrets, Lies and Betrayal
by: M.L. Ruscsak

Part 2	Lies of the star Cites

Secrets, Lies and Betrayal
by: M.L. Ruscsak

Secrets, Lies and Betrayal
by: M.L. Ruscsak

Part 3

LARNA PRINCESS OF FEYEN

Royal Lies, Family Secrets, and a Daughter's Betrayal

Secrets, Lies and Betrayal
by: M.L. Ruscsak

Teen

Part 4

Secrets &

Buried Lies

Secrets, Lies and Betrayal
by: M.L. Ruscsak

Secrets, Lies and Betrayal
by: M.L. Ruscsak

3000 Years Ago

During the Great War

In but just a few fleeting moments war would be raging on this star. Fey would fall in battle until there was a victor. Until *he,* the Ruler of Pallas, ruled all of the settled Star Cities. Until he was the absolute ruler and master of all of the Fey.

But that was still moments away.

Right now, his army rested. They dined on food that the abomination known as Primitiva had left for them. Ignorant fools. Could they not see that she was trying to persuade them to fight for her? Trying to sway them into joining her ranks as a mindless drones.

No, of course not.

Secrets, Lies and Betrayal
by: M.L. Ruscsak

They only saw the food and soft bedding that she had left for them. Only saw what she wanted them to see instead of what really was. But he knew the truth. Oh, yes, he knew her secrets. And one day they would all come to be known.

Shuffling into a private room, he found a large gold desk with a high back seat. Not something that he would normally find comfortable, but it would do for the moment. It would do for what he had in store for the so-called goddess.

Lightly his fingers caressed the pages of blank parchment that had been left. Touched the white feathered quill still standing upright in the inkwell. A bitter smile twitched his lips as he called in the Seer's stone that he had inherited long before he ruled Pallas. Long before, when he was still known by his true name. A name that he no longer remembered himself.

Just a thin red stone. Just a small piece of a greater stone. Ah, but the whole had been splintered off and lost long ago. And only this one small piece was said to ever be found. But it was enough to learn all that he needed.

Sitting the flat red stone on the desk, he watched as events unfolded. Watched knowing with certainty how this war would end only to breathe life for a new threat.

Secrets, Lies and Betrayal
by: M.L. Ruscsak

Carefully, he slid his narrow body into the seat. His withered fingers taking hold of the quill. As he began to write, perhaps the last letter that he may ever write. A dollop of sorrow and perhaps anger filled him.

So many have tried to destroy me. Too many have already been sacrificed to the void for their disobedience. When will those who I rule over realize that it is I who protected them? That it is I who keeps the abominations from breeding.

But it's too late now. There are two. Two creators who are both too strong to be killed by any other than the Silent One. They will come soon for their blood. Come to destroy the rest of the Fey once they have a taste of those powers. Nothing will stop them, then...·

Nothing.

I fear that I will be killed here on this distant star. Far away from my home on Pallas. Far away from those who are truly loyal.

Secrets, Lies and Betrayal
by: M.L. Ruscsak

But I do not fear death. It comes to all. It will come for those creators. It will come for the things that they have brought into this world.

No, I will not see the end of these creatures. But death will be kind, for I will never know the wrath of the Silent Ones. I will never feel their teeth tearing into my skin while I still breath. And I will never know how it feels to have my power drained from my body.

But the creations do not know what it is that I have hidden away in the depth of Pallas. They do not know that whoever rules will forever be tainted. Their lust for power will draw the Silent Ones out of hiding. The next ruler of Pallas will be the death of the Fey.

Pulling a small box from loose fitting robes, he sat the journal entry inside along with the Seer's stone. One day a creation will find it. One day they will activate the visions that have been foretold. They will understand. They will take steps to end the blood line that will destroy the Fey.

They had to.

Secrets, Lies and Betrayal
by: M.L. Ruscsak

SECRETS OF THE PAST

"This world has seen peace while the stars have only seen war. What comes next, no one can say with certainty. No one dares to speculate. But I know what is to come, for I have seen it too many times not to understand the meaning. Things that should have been forgotten will come unraveled. The darkness will consume my darlings.

All of that I have created will perish. There is a way to stop this. I've seen her. Her powers... Oh, her glorious powers. Many will want to control her. Others... Will seek to destroy her. If my secrets can be kept for just a little while longer, perhaps what I have seen can be stopped."

-Private journal of the goddess

Secrets, Lies and Betrayal
by: M.L. Ruscsak

Secrets, Lies and Betrayal
by: M.L. Ruscsak

CHAPTER 1: VASILISSA

From high within the tower of the Castle Fire, Vasilissa stood watching the guards opened the castle gates. Shrouded by the darkness of the setting sun, she watched as scores of people file in. Watch as those born to Feyen shied away from those from Draken and yet still looked down at those who are immune to their abilities. She watched as the Draken royal family pull other from their lands away before it struck out, leaving nothing more than a blood stain on the cold stone pathway. However, as her dark eyes narrowed she saw the serpents from the marsh slipping past the guards. Watched as they slipped along the high walls disappearing into the brush. Would-be assassin… perhaps, or possibly they could be merry well-wishers wishing to hide from those who would devour them.

Secrets, Lies and Betrayal
by: M.L. Ruscsak

Bah! This was her cousin's doing. She would bet her life on this. Just as she could bet Dalinda would make a play for the crown of Feyen before all was said and done.

Frustrated, Vasilissa pulled the deep red velvet curtains, ready to close them. Yet she didn't, at least not yet, nor did she leave her spot. Keeping her eyes narrowed, she continued to watch the citizens of Feyen file in. Today should be the start of a glorious week filled with such joy and hope. Today should be the start of a new beginning, but instead it was just another day filled with so much political mess that nothing would ever be accomplished.

Flipping the curtains close, she turned sharply. Her raven black hair that had strands of gold flowing through it began to fall from its tight bond that she had worn to the palace. A style that she had worn for the sole purpose of looking fearless. However, right now, she just wanted to be able to think. Wanted to let herself feel all those who have foolishly brought themselves this close to her. Right now, she needed to have some clarity of her thoughts... before she dared to speak what she had already learned to be the truth.

Her cousin, Alista was ascending the throne of Feyen... Well, not really her cousin, since they didn't share a single drop of blood in common. But Alista didn't care much for bloodlines unless it played in her favor to remember them. So today, they were cousins. Tomorrow? With Alista, they might be sisters or bitter enemies. One could never be sure with her.

Secrets, Lies and Betrayal
by: M.L. Ruscsak

"Well, you look positively horrible."

The serene voice could only come from the future queen. Vasilissa didn't need to open her eyes to scold this royal Fey. Nor did she need permission to. "Are you even concerned about how many people you're letting into the castle? I've already counted three scores of those who would do nearly anything to see your blood run or at the very least see the color."

"Only three scores? Come now Vas, you forget that I know you better than anyone. So, let's cut through the chase, shall we? What has you so irritated that you are melting one of the windows of my darling castles?"

Why she was… confused, she let her dark eyes open. It was then that she realized that a coal black mist was seeping from around her body. Hints of embers hidden deep within the mist burning everything that they touched. It was a wonder that she hadn't already caught something a blaze. Once again in control of her motions she pulled the mist back to her and hissed. "For the love of… I should have been paying more attention."

Waving the thought off, Alista took a careful step into the room, closing the deep fire red door behind her. "Obviously, darling." Gingerly taking a seat on the edge of a black and gray overstuffed chair, she let her golden translucent wings absorbed into her back with little more consequence than the changing of her own dress. Making herself comfortable in her seat, Alista contently sighed. "Ah,

Secrets, Lies and Betrayal
by: M.L. Ruscsak

much better. I do so hate wearing my formal wings for such a casual conversation."

Narrowing for now deep golden eyes, Vasilissa huffed out, "I do swear you act as though you're still 200 years old and not someone who is about to be crowned queen."

Alisa narrowed her golden sun colored eyes as she sat straighter in her seat. Vasilissa would decide later that Alista would consider this a royal posture. As was the way Alista now glared at her.

Squaring and her shoulders Alisa spoke, her words holding every bit of royal degree as her posture. "Darling, I am still waiting for an answer as to why my window now needs to be repaired. I shall not and will not ask that their time."

Shit. No, Alista wouldn't ask. She would, however, have a garrison of guards up here to ask that very question for her and they would all be ready to extract that answer with any means that they deem fit. Lightly closing her eyes, Vasilissa whispered, her voice laced with disappointment, "Grandmother swears that I'm being ridiculous. I am sure that you well as well."

Rolling her eyes, Alisa softly patted the seat next to her. Finally, a soft smile touched her rose colored lips. "As I have known use and today you were born, I've learned two very important truths. Which are like to hear them?"

Secrets, Lies and Betrayal
by: M.L. Ruscsak

This could be extremely important or not important at all. Still, was only polite to respond. "Please."

"Since you have been very young, you've had impeccable insight in all matters of things. The times when your grandmother could actually be bothered to listen to your constant concerns, they have always been proven correct. And the few times when she has refused to listen, if years turned out not only to be justified and needed to be handled more extensively than if she had been bothered to trust you in the beginning." Taking a deep breath, Alisa closed her eyes, almost wishing she did not need to hear this particular problem. "That said, what is it that your grandmother should take care of without delay?"

Finally, someone was finally taking her seriously. And that someone was her cousin. Vasilissa squares her shoulders, understanding that at least one member of her family would listen to her and take this very seriously. She finally spoke, "Now I'm only saying this once, and I had no intention of ruling Lite. I am perfectly happy and content letting Zilla ascend and then finding something productive to do with all of my time."

Alista inclined her head before very calmly saying, "Very well. I will keep that in mind when I make my final decision. Now please continue."

"Dalinda is making some very dangerous partnerships. I swear that the moment she ascends I will do everything in my power to destroy her." Vasilissa paused, blinking in surprise at her own words. She hadn't meant to say it like that. In fact, she had spent the better part of the past light cycle trying to find the words that would yield the quickest results. Yet something had somehow taken a hold of her tongue. Or perhaps, Alista was using some form of enchantment. Yes and no one Alista that could very well be it.

For several moments Alista just sat there still and silent watching Vasilissa. Watching the blackness once again flow freely from her body. However, it wasn't a burning rage of embers that now glow within the mist. No, there was something deadlier... no, right now that the mist had the blue flames of the dragon's breath now dancing within it. In that moment Alista knew without hesitation that not only would Vasilissa start a war to rid the world of Dalinda but she would be the one to kill her. Slowly and carefully Alisa got to her feet. To buy herself a few more moments to clarify her mind, she straightened her green color jacket and smooth out her long-pleated skirt. She needed to weigh all that she knew against what she would dare say finally she decided to tell her cousin what would be most practical. "As you well know, my father is currently the oldest living Fey within our realm."

This was no idle conversation. Never was when speaking about King Magmas or his brothers. "I do. And I have never questioned any order or suggestion that he nor your uncles have ever made, despite how impractical in may seem to be."

Alista nodded once sharply. "Then we are in agreement."

Secrets, Lies and Betrayal
by: M.L. Ruscsak

Wait, what? They hadn't decided on anything. "Alista, will you please tell me what we agreed on? Since I clearly don't remember that part of the conversation."

"Oh, my dear cousin, the answer is just so clear. After my coronation and of course after the party, I will explain everything that needs to be said. However, in the meantime, I'm must simply ask papa to contact Magnar. I do doubt he will come so willingly for me."

Vasilissa didn't move nor say anything as Alista left the room. How could she? Magnar!?! Oh, no. Whatever Alista was planning, whatever solution she had surmised... No good would ever come from it. Not if it Magnar had anything to do with it. Then again, she had never really met the great Magnar, but the stories that she had heard... oh yes, whatever Alista was up to it was no good.

Secrets, Lies and Betrayal
by: M.L. Ruscsak

Secrets, Lies and Betrayal
by: M.L. Ruscsak

CHAPTER 2: ALISTA

Taking her place on the great throne of Feyen, Alista closed her eyes, trying to quell her nerves. Just days ago, she had sat on the throne that was housed in the Castle of Fire. Before that she had dwelled in in the serenity of the Castle of Water. Today, however she felt the weight of Feyen as she sat on the throne held deep inside the Castle of Earth. As she sat on the throne that was housed deep within the Mountain high above the city. As she sat knowing that this was the very first castle built in the kingdom known today as Feyen... The very first castle of the very first Fey that have dwelled in this realm at all. This was the castle that housed secrets even she cannot comprehend at least not a fully.

Secrets, Lies and Betrayal
by: M.L. Ruscsak

So, it was fitting to require that the queen of both Lite and Darke to join her here. Fitting for both to stand before the new ruler of Feyen.

In a few moments she would need to be the queen, but for now she was alone in this vast empty room. Not a window to distract her. Not a guard to speak to. No, she needed this brief moment to herself. Just a single moment to really decide if this was the best course if of action. Just a brief moment to decide if it was worth all the trouble that she was about to cause.

It was. Even her father and uncle Flint had agreed, and they rarely agreed on anything. But then they too understood how powerful and gifted Vasilissa truly was.

With controlled breaths and keeping our eyes shut, Alista swallowed the last bit of doubt that clouded her mind. In a moment, that all brown clay doors would open and are chosen council would file and to take their positions behind her. Two light bearers, two dark Fey, a necromancer, and her dear friend and trusted healer. In addition, there would be her Uncle Flint, who would make a written account of what was said and done today.

Lastly, there would be, Magnar. Although not formally a member of her court... Of any court really, he would still be in attendance. No one would dare question what he said. And if they did... Well, he would take care of that in his own way. Possibly quietly, but most likely very publicly and in a way, that would show his truest form. The form of a great dragon the most still thought of as myths.

Secrets, Lies and Betrayal
by: M.L. Ruscsak

Slowly, as she opened her eyes to find Magnar standing just before her. His deep blue mesh like robes flowing around him. His black dragon wings perfectly still normally that wouldn't faze her, however the fact that he had entered without a single sound was not only disturbing, but was a warning that the Fey the stood before her was in no mood to be trifled with. "My lord Magnar. I am pleased that you have arrived."

His pearl lips curled into a snarl as he quietly asked, "Why am I here, girl?"

Yes, he was in no mood to be here. Then again, he did have his own troubles to deal with. What over those troubles were Alista that did not dare to ask, nor did she have the nerve to even try. "As queen of Feyen in protective all those with true Fey blood. I am hereby convening a tribunal of Queens and enacting the trial of Faye."

His deep scowl turned to bafflement before he shook his head and turned from her. "I see my queen was smart to entrust this kingdom to your father's bloodline. Very well, I will concede to help you with this one task." He paused and stepped up the three steps of the dais. After towering over her for more than a breath, he gradually leaned over to her delicately pointed ear and whispered. "Unlike your father, I'm not yours to request help from. Only come to you one more time. Choose that time wisely."

If he was trying to intimidate her, it was working swallowing hard, Alista try to let a soft from the smile touch your lips. She almost seceded yet she can hide this sudden

Secrets, Lies and Betrayal
by: M.L. Ruscsak

onslaught of nerves from her quiet voice. "I understand. Thank you for helping me with this task. I do still hope that I will never need to call upon you in the future."

Magnar and narrowed his eyes into tiny slits as he stepped back. "We will see little Fey queen. We shall see."

With a gust of wind and the doubled doors of the throne room banged open in crashed into the wall behind them. As the sound echoed throughout the room, Queen Kiera stood within the doorway. Her long black dress flowed on around her as her purple translucent wings fluttered behind her. The staff of Darke gripped tightly in her gloved hand. Anger apparent on her elderly face, clicking the staff on the floor, she demanded, "What is a meaning of this, Alista?"

With her council already behind her and Magnar at her side, Alista set proudly upon her throne. Ignoring the

Secrets, Lies and Betrayal
by: M.L. Ruscsak

show of temper, she took a calm and collected breath. "Enter Queen Kiera; all of your questions will be answered at the proper time."

With more dignity than required, Kiera cautiously took her first step into the room and approached the left of the dais. Behind her the royal council and the Crown Princess Dalinda along with her younger sister of Delaney. Both girls dressed in garments more common in the marsh courts than those found in Darke. It didn't matter really if they were garment made of scales or that of cloth. After today, it would be no mistake that both of the little *princesses* were now enemies of the Fey.

Was not a breath more before Queen Enya fluttered into the room, Crown Princess Zilla following close behind her. Both the queen of Lite in the princess acting more subdued than any queen should. Both drained of the light that had shown so brightly just days before during the festivities.

Under normal circumstances as queen of Feyen, it would be her sworn duty to find out what was wrong with the queen of Lite. However, the solution was to quite simple and already put into place. So, for today didn't matter. Today she would not seek out answers to questions that she did not need to ask.

Resting her hands on the arms of her throne, Alista nodded to Enya, "Your grace, but hardest ad and by the passage of not only your daughter, but her area as well."

Taking a breath, she glanced to Zilla. "Your mother would be proud that you defended yourself so honorably."

Zilla looked down to a spot on the floor and chose to say nothing.

"You have not said why we're here, Alista. And I do have matters to see with that of my own country."

Kiera. The queen who should have relinquished her crown some years ago. But neither of her children were yet of age. Something her father, King Magmas, had thought had been done on purpose. It was something that was impolite to ask about. Until now.

"You are right, Kiera, I have not." Alista narrowed her golden eyes and watched the proverbial slap in the face once the Queen of Darke understood the meaning of not saying her title in front of the council. Watched the little bitch princess cross her arms and pout, not understanding anything at all. A breath more and Alista continued, "However, before I do… Please join me at the table."

Before anyone could say another word, the hard-gray marble floor began to shake beneath their feet. Slowly a three-sided table began to take shape. Ten high back matching chairs lined the three sides. The point of the table facing the door.

The queens from both Lite and Darke sat facing each other. The younger princess of Darke sat smugly across from the Crown Princess of Lite. The council members filled in the seats on either side of the table. Waiting until

Secrets, Lies and Betrayal
by: M.L. Ruscsak

everyone except Magnar had been seated, Alisa descendant of three steps and took her place at the head of the table. A single breath more and Magnar took a seat to her right.

"Now, before we get to why have been this meaning there is a matter of state I wish to inform you of."

Gripping the arms of her seat, Kiera leaned forward and hissed, "Unless it concerns as to why my daughter's betrothed was removed from Feyen, then get on with this farce of the meeting."

Sitting this close Magnar she could feel him tense. Could almost feel the deadly heat rising from skin. Could almost see the souls of those he had already killed, begging to be a release from his now dark eyes. He could and would kill all within this room without nothing more than a moment of inconvenience.

Knowing this she slowly to the deep breath to keep from saying what she wanted to. Kept from saying anything that would give this creator a reason the strikeout. "As you may have figured out, my father chose this time for me to ascend for re…"

The clay door opened just enough for own daughter to toddle in. Her stuffed Gryphon still held within her arms. And her dress not yet covered in today's adventures.

"Elista?"

Holding her little head high, she gave her brightest smile. "I watch too."

Secrets, Lies and Betrayal
by: M.L. Ruscsak

As a mother, she wanted to laugh, as queen, she needed to respond correctly. "As queen of Feyen I will allow it." Once Elista was settled on her lap, she started once more, "Now, as I was saying, my father has decided to no longer live in Feyen."

"If he thinks I will allow him to take my-"

Alista glanced at Magnar, the latter looking upon the former with boredom. Knew in that moment she would no longer be able speak unless Magnar wished to hear her dribble.

"King Magmas has gone to join my mother in the Under Kingdom. Make no mistake and is not his time to dwell there, and may return at the time that he chooses."

Enya tilted her head in question them very quietly asked, "Then why did he even leave? Surely he could have ruled a bit longer."

Narrowing her eyes, Alista looked at the older queen and understood far better than any around her why Enya was not worried. "The high council of the Under Kingdom reached out to my father. It appears that they wish for him to join the court."

The sound of a quill snapping from the back of the room had everyone turning to Flint the null of the fleet pale. Instant concern washed through her, "Uncle Flint?"

Gasping to form words Flint finally choked out, "Your father… joined the court."

Secrets, Lies and Betrayal
by: M.L. Ruscsak

"He did?" Alista couldn't fathom why her uncle sounded both worried and excited. Nor did she wish to guess. At least not yet. At least not until after this meeting was over.

"Do I understand the ruler is now going to let themselves be seen?"

Careful wording. Too careful for her uncle. "It was my impression that with my father's help, the ruler might be persuaded to do something other than what they have been doing. Father was very vague about what his part was going to be or even what he would be doing while visiting with the counsel of the Under Kingdom." Or for that matter why this clearly mattered.

But that explanation wouldn't come from her. And if her uncle could contact his brother... well that was a matter for another day.

Flint nodded once and called it in another writing quill. Or perhaps he had just fixed the one he broke. Either way, she knew her uncle would need a better explanation once the queens were no longer a threat.

Turning your attention back to the table, Alista once again forced herself to look in control. "Now, as far as why we're here..."

Dalinda slouched in her seat and dramatically placed her are over her head as she wailed, "Do I have to be here? It's so boring."

Secrets, Lies and Betrayal
by: M.L. Ruscsak

"Yes, Dalinda, you must be here. As a crown princess, it is time you gain some understanding of outside your own bedchamber." Alista almost covered her mouth. She had never spoken like that to anyone. Ever. Her father would have never allowed it. Then again, she was queen now...

...Or more likely Magnar had taken control over her mouth to respond as he wanted her to. Either way... The words had been said.

Closing her eyes, she started again, "As Queens of both Lite and Darke, you are responsible for the safety in the care of your citizens. However, as Queen of Feyen I am responsible with not only the care of those living within my borders but for any and all who have so much as a single drop of Fey blood."

Enya set back, looking more at ease than she had since coming here. However, no one from Darke looked at ease at all. No, if she did say anything, they now felt nervous and worried. It was a good thing too. Nervous and worried she can work with. But fearful... oh... fearful would do much better.

"As a queen both Shades and shadows are an intricate piece of the courts. However, they will only yield to those with true world bloodlines."

Slowly opening her eyes once again Alista can see the fear in Kiera's dark eyes. Could sense the worry flooding the room. "Queen Enya, I suspect you understand this as Lord Griffith has been at your side and is currently looking after your kingdom or you're here."

"Aye, should I need his assistance; I am told that he will know about it. Though, I do not understand how." Enya leaned forward and gave her best smile. "Nor do I wish to. However, perhaps one day you would be inclined to tell Zilla. Her grandfather has tried and several occasions, but is too easily annoyed."

Now, he wasn't. She had known Griffith her entire life. Even called him uncle even if they didn't share a bloodline. But, she also understood a true heir wouldn't need to have a shade explained to them. "I will say this." A vine of black mist crept up her arm almost playfully. Almost asking to be petted. "Only a true royal might be able to befriend a shadow. Whereas a shade is loyal to no one. Or at least they do not seem to be."

Alisa smiled so sweetly and looked directly at Dalinda. "However, I do know for fact Shades do love the taste of those who live in the marshlands. And I do not pity those who acquire their stench, if they should happen to cross a shade."

"Enough!! Why have you convened this council? Surely not to educate the children on Shades."

So Magnar was getting bored. Very well, she should speed this meeting up a bit. "You are right, I didn't. As queen, it is my sworn duty to see that the ruler of both Lite and Darke will protect the Fey who live within their borders. Which is why I am enacting the trial of Fey."

Hushed murmurs from both councils filled the room. Worried eyes from both Queens. Relief from Zilla, who had no wish to rule anything. But something close to rage held in the young face of Dalinda. Bitter rage that her crown could be stripped away before she even could take control of Darke.

Quickly getting to her feet Dalinda slammed her hands onto the table and growled, "What right do you have to enact anything? You're no more royal than those who sit at this table."

Sitting back in her chair, Alista pulled Elista close to her chest. "Actually Dalinda, the only ones at this table that do not bleed blue are those from Darke. Perhaps you would like to see." It was then the clay doors open once more, Vasilissa now standing in the doorway. Not dressed for a day in court, but rather wearing black trousers that fit like a second skin. A white bodice that wouldn't hinder her movement should she need to fight. The staff of the first queen held tightly in her hand.

For a moment, she locked eyes with her cousin before giving the barest of nods. The single moment an indication for Vasilissa to say what she needed to say. To repeat the words that she had been instructed to say.

Clicking the butt of the staff three times on the floor, Vasilissa raise her head up high. Her eyes now locked on

Magnar. "I challenge of the house is a both Lite and Darke for their thrones."

Stunned gasps filled the room, leaving too many questions to be answered.

Secrets, Lies and Betrayal
by: M.L. Ruscsak

Secrets, Lies and Betrayal
by: M.L. Ruscsak

CHAPTER 3: VASILISSA

Pacing the confines of the ornately decorated guest room, she had never felt so nervous nor more alive. There were powers flowing through her in a way that she can ever imagine. Power is answering the call to beat away again. Powers that none should have been able to tap into yet...

"Would you like to hear what happened at you left the conference or just wait to find out for yourself?"

The voice surprised her, as did the fact that she hadn't heard the heavy door open. Finally understanding the question, she spun around. To her surprise Alista was standing in the doorway. Not really in the room, but not

Secrets, Lies and Betrayal
by: M.L. Ruscsak

waiting outside either. So, some opposition for the queen to take. "Alista, we are family. However, you are the queen. You do not need to stand in the entrance of your own castle."

Taking but a single step into the room, a soft smile touched Alista's lips. "Darling, I would never enter a room unless I'm certain that I can walk back out of my own accord."

Taken back Vasilissa stumbled back a step. "I do not understand. I have no reason to wish you harm."

"No, but you have awoken powers that very few have ever tasted. And fewer have lived to tell about."

Her legs collapsed just as a fine yellow mist made a chair appear beneath her. "How is that even possible?"

Turning to the open doorway Alista swirled her finger in the air, permanently closing the doorway up. Or at least as permanent as she wished. "We must talk before you take part in the first trial."

Oh, that didn't sound good. Nope, not good at all. Not when Alista took the vocal tone of the queen rather than one of a family member. "Talk about what? Either way, grandmother will be beside herself. If I succeed, then all the lessons that Zilla has had will be proven useless. If I don't, then Lite will fall."

Secrets, Lies and Betrayal
by: M.L. Ruscsak

Alista now narrowed her eyes and snapped, "Lite will not fall. Neither will your bloodlines. Now, instead of acting like a petulant child, listen."

Vasilissa winced at the harshness in Alista's voice. Never had her cousin spoken to her in that commanding tone. This was a tone that no Fey used unless ready to the spell a great deal of the most dangerous power. The power that she knew that a poor lowly princess who had yet to come into her full abilities would be no match for. Bowing her head slightly, she somberly said, "What is it that you wish to discuss?"

"I have spoken to Magnar. He has confirmed that it will be your bloodlines and mine that would be needed for what is to come."

Hearing the words Vasilissa thought back. A seer really revealed anything, so for Magnar to say this much… "How bad?"

"I do not know. But I do doubt it will happen in either over lifetimes." Alista closed her eyes, let herself feel the room around her. Let herself feel which you can of those who were dwelling within the castle. "Dalinda must be killed during the trial. Zilla, I am certain will concede. But not the other. Magnar has unlocked all your true abilities, but you do not have time to test them."

Secrets, Lies and Betrayal
by: M.L. Ruscsak

Kill Dalinda? Gladly... But there was something else that was troubling. Cheating was punishable by death. Ask any Fey that using unlearned abilities during any rite of passage and they would all tell you that. Well, anything except the one the city across from her. "Isn't that cheating?"

Slowly Alista pressed her lips together into a thin line. "No. Well, maybe. Either way, and needed to be done and who would dare question me? Besides, you and I are the only living Fey that could rule Darke. Or at least the only living royal Fey. Zilla could rule, but she has no desire and lacks the ambition to."

Jumping up and from her chair, Vasilissa snapped not at the queen who set before her the two her cousin lacked any sense in her brain. "Damn you! I don't want to rule anything. I've told you this several times. More than several times, yet you push me. Why don't you push her? Damn it! She's the damn heir!"

Making herself comfortable, Alista steeple that her long, narrow fingers and replied with little more than a slight annoyance in her voice, "I do not waste my time on those who have a little ability. She may have been born first, but you my dear, have all of the royal powers. You are the only choice."

Too stunned to speak, Vasilissa paced the confines of the room, forced herself to calm her nerves. Forced herself to keep all these new powers from seeping into mist and hopefully keeping herself from harm in any of the lavish furniture that was scattered throughout the room. After several moments she huffed out, "Fine. For the sake of the whatever Magnar saw, I would do as you have asked. But I will warn you know, my dear cousin, you may not like the outcome."

"Really Vasilissa, you speak as though you are a seer when we both know you're not. But I will tell you this... You will apprentice is here with me rather than with your grandmother. She can watch over Darke as your proxy for no more than a year."

Slowly Vasilissa narrowed her dark eyes just enough to show concern. Something was going on here. Much more than that Alista was saying. It was just too bad she didn't understand everything... At least not yet. Nor could she and to she had time to let her mind piece everything together. "Will a year be long enough to learn all the time us in order to rule?"

Alisa laughed. "Hardly. Learning to rule takes a lifetime. But a year would be enough for you to learn most of those new abilities that you now have. In fact, you may even learn more about that than what either Zilla or Dalinda have been taught."

Secrets, Lies and Betrayal
by: M.L. Ruscsak

CHAPTER 4: ALISTA

With the Crown of Feyen resting upon her head, Alista set back on her red clay throne. Just hours ago, she declared the Trial of the Fey. A trial that was now up to her to oversee. Slowly and quietly the guards open the double doors to the throne room and allowed her counsel to file in. They would be the first to enter the first to approach the dais. Once she greeted them, they would then form a half circle to her right. A few minutes more and the council of Lite would enter. They would take their place to her left completing the circle. In opening would be left at the head of the circle where her dais was positioned. Another at the

Secrets, Lies and Betrayal
by: M.L. Ruscsak

foot with the queen of Lite would enter with her heir. Vasilissa would enter lastly, once Zilla entered the circle.

She took a deep breath. This set of trials would be easy. Nothing that would look apparent that there was a favorite. Just a series of simple spells and incantations paired with practical skills. Things that any apprentice should be able to complete.

Her eyes slowly opened, not to the sound of muffled footfalls coming from the feet of the council of Lite but rather the sound of a single set. "Princess Zilla? It is most peculiar that you enter before the council."

Zilla waited until she was in the middle of the of the circlet. Her hair pinned up and wildflowers and her dress not that of highborn but that of a nurse. "Permission to speak frankly?"

Allison nodded once, but raised her brow in question.

"I have spoken to grandmother. We have known for a long time that I have no ability that would lead me into successfully ruling Lite. Both my mother and her mother before her had little in natural abilities. Both died within days of wearing the crown." Well, not exactly. Her mother had worn the crown for a few days before the power had somehow corrupted her. The result had been the citizens of Lite turning on their queen as well as her heir. She had

Secrets, Lies and Betrayal
by: M.L. Ruscsak

fought hard to survive that day. Whereas her mother had fought only to keep the power of Lite. In the end, her mother had been killed, and she had refused to wear the crown. Few had known the truth about that attack, but Alista did. So, she hoped that Alista would understand this move as well.

Clawing at the arms of her throne, Alista lean forward just enough to look threatening. Just enough to show her council that she was Queen and would rule as her father had. "I know the history of your bloodlines Zilla. However, I am waiting to hear why are standing before me."

No longer meeting Alista's stare, Zilla looked to a point on the floor and shook her head. "I... I'm not sure that I'm doing this correctly. But..." She paused and finally looked at the queen of Feyen directly in the eyes. "...I would like to relinquish the throne to my youngest sister, Vasilissa."

Taking a steady breath, Alista look to her historian. "Lord Pidea, what it is your recommendations?"

Calling in a chair Lord Pedia sat down as he materialized a big book of laws and traditions. Flipping through several pages he finally stopped. "If memory serves me, it is only at a tradition and not a law that the firstborn should rule." Slowly flipping through several more pages, he tapped on his boat with his thick finger. "Ah, yes, right here. It does not state which air may claim the throne. Only that they are of a certain bloodline." As he's read further his nose wrinkled. Pulling the book closer to his face looked more puzzled. "However, this is most strange."

"Lord Pidea?" Zilla asked almost afraid to hear the answer.

"Oh, this does not concern Lite, my dear." He waved the question off as he vanished the book. "It is of little matter, but if your majesty would allow me. I would like some time to speak to your uncle Flint. Perhaps he would be able to clarify somethings for me."

Hearing the lie beneath the words, Alista kept her voice level as she softly answered, "Of course Lord Pidea. I'm sure my uncle would be happy to entertain any question that you may have." Then to Zilla, "Since you are a royal Fey, you simply cannot live outside…"

"I would like to live at the Spire." Zilla chimed in before the queen can say anything further.

"…Oh?"

"I mean no disrespect, but I have always found solace there among the books. And have someone there that knows all the incantations, spells, and all sorts of tonics for healing… It may be better for those who need some sort of healing than if they would have to travel into Lite." Zilla

Secrets, Lies and Betrayal
by: M.L. Ruscsak

pause before adding in a soft whisper, "Or at least, that is what I think. The choice is yours, of course."

Finally letting her shoulders relax, Alista finally smiled. "I think that is a marvelous idea. Therefore, as if this moment, you are the resident historian and healer for the Spire. However, I recommend that you take an apprentice for both positions that you now hold."

Smiling brightly, Zilla looked up, barely holding in her excitement. "I had a thought about that as well. However, I would like to discuss it in a more private setting if you would?"

Taking Zilla into her private library, Alista's sat on her long-overstuffed couch and patted the seat next to her. "Is this private enough my darling?"

Secrets, Lies and Betrayal
by: M.L. Ruscsak

At the sound of that bubbly voice, Zilla finally allowed herself to relax. "It is, thank you." Gingerly taking a seat next to Alista, Zilla paused and looked uncertain. "While working with grandmother a… um… creature that… well, it kind of befriended me."

Several living beings could qualify as a creature. Some friendly, but most would kill Fey without hesitation. Knowing this, she needed to ask, "What kind of creature?"

"He calls himself a Shade." Zilla shrugged, not yet understanding the danger of her words. She had heard of Shades but never seen one that could turn into a person. Actually, none had really seen them in a form other than mist and had lived to tell about it.

Oh, for the love that Darke… Not a Shade… anything but a Shade. "Do you have any understanding how dangerous they are? Damn it, Zilla. It could have killed you before you even knew it was in the damn room!" Getting quickly to her feet, Alista paced back and forth between the couch and the now closed door.

Shades weren't just dangerous, they killed without prejudice. In fact, with the last dozen or so years they had killed several scores of Fey. Not to mention in the last month alone, there had been a report about Shades slaughtering the whole village of Manicora not just a few hours carriage ride from the Spire. And they all, including the Drakens, we're still awaiting answers as to why the

Shades had attacked a village so far north. It was a question that they probably would never have a real answer to. After several long, tedious moments of trying not to verbally strikeout at Zilla, Alista finally sighed. "All right, tell me what you need to. Then I will tell you what I think as your cousin before I tell you what I think as your queen."

A hesitant nod and Zilla started, "The Shade said that because he was friends with grandfather, he felt obligated to speak to me."

Raising but a single hand to stop Zilla from speaking, Alista cautiously asked, "A Shade… am my understanding this correctly… is friends with Lord Griffith?" If this was true… oh… Someone was keeping secrets from her… And she could bet it was either the males of her family or Lord Magnar. Then again, it was a good possibility that it was a mixture of both.

With a shrug and Zilla answered as best as she could. "The Shade of wouldn't tell me anything about how grandfather and he knew each other. But the he did tell me something in confidence. And before my sister meets Dalinda in the trials I think it best that you should know."

"And you are willing to break that confidence to tell me?" Not so much as a true question but a request. A new request that was followed up by a warning. "Think before breaking the trust of someone or something that nobody

Secrets, Lies and Betrayal
by: M.L. Ruscsak

can kill. Something that not even the Darkens can stand against."

"Oh, I'm not breaking his trust. Before the Shade started telling me anything, I told him flat out, that if I thought that those that lived in Lite were in danger that would need to speak to the ruler of Feyen." Once again Zilla paused. "He... It... asked flat out if it was your father's bloodline that still ruled Feyen."

"So, the Shades have some knowledge about the it on goings of the Fey."

And if that was true... Then maybe... just maybe... The attacks in Darke weren't so was random as everyone was thinking.

For a moment Zilla and didn't say anything further. She was obviously trying to decide what she wanted to say against what would be considered a betrayal by the Shade. Finally, she gave up. "At least those who come close to the ruins of the Great War... or of those who dare to travel near their home in the Ruins of Bone. I was under the impression that they have little knowledge of the Fey who lived this far north. However, what I know could also be misleading by the Shade."

"Very well. Tell me what you of what he told you. Then we can figure out what the Shades know and how. As possibly find a way to stop the attacks."

Secrets, Lies and Betrayal
by: M.L. Ruscsak

Once again she nodded. "Dalinda isn't just the crown princess of Darke. She is now also the consort or betrothed to the crown prince of the marshlands."

A cloud of white mist was the only thing holding Alista up at that moment. As the sworn protector of the Fey, she had the sworn duty to remove any threat to them or their country. The marshlands, although not a place that was friendly to the Fey, hadn't yet done anything to warrant starting a war. However, Dalinda couldn't marry the so-called prince while still a crown princess. Then again, when she was crowned queen, then she could choose anyone that she wanted to be her husband. That union could either increase the land connected to Darke or that of the marshlands, but either way the precious balance of power could and would shift.

Even worse, the little bitch couldn't be killed in the damn trials. That and the challenge in itself could start a war with those who dwelled within the marsh.

Regaining her composure, Alista slowly came back to the cowards and sat down. "As your cousin, I am very concerned that a Shade has spoken to you. But, I can appreciate his insight. As a queen, I ask of you this; should you speak to him again, convey my many thanks. And please let him know, I will need time to figure out how to deal with this situation." Alista briefly paused. "And very soon we will need to discuss who you think would sue for your apprentice."

Finding her uncle had never been hard to do the

least not for her. However, today who was proving to be too difficult to locate either by telepathy or by any incantations that she knew. A flicker of a Shadow gave her another way... Proving this really was a Shadow and it was willing to help.

"My darling Shadow, could you please help me locate my uncle Flint?"

"Where your uncle is, it is doubtful that even a Shadow could reach him. Or at least reach him in time to discuss all that you need to."

Secrets, Lies and Betrayal
by: M.L. Ruscsak

Not her Uncle nor a voice that she recognized. Not a voice that sounded at all friendly either. Cautiously, she turned to see you who had spoken. The moment she did her face most all color as she saw a tall, handsome man standing before her. A man who must have been breathtakingly handsome before his death. Assuming this man was a spirit and not something else. "I apologize, but… Do I know you?"

"No, but your father does. As do both of your uncle's." For just a moment, he turned into mist only to form beside her. "You may call me Gwydion."

In a breathless whisper Alista's spoke as she recognized the danger. Recognize the kind of creature that was now standing with an arm's length of her. "You're a Shade."

"Yes, my dear, I am a Shade. Out of respect for you, I will not make a meal out of any who are currently in the castle. At least not this time."

Meaning, if she was thinking clearly, should he return, he could and would devour every living thing within the castle walls. "Thank you for the warning. May I ask why you have traveled this far north?"

For a long minute he didn't answer. Just long enough for her think that he could not. "Because of who I was and what I am now, I owe it to the goddess to look after her favorites. My debt after today is complete, unless she chooses to make my people whole once more."

The goddess? What was he talking about? Just another secret that she was going to have to unravel. "I do not understand."

Gwydion ignored her question and her stunned silence as he demanded, "I want all of the Fey and all the others who breath to move away from the city of bones. I will not make this request again. My people need little in the way of food, but we will make an exception shall we need to defend our home."

He was talking about war. She can see it in his eyes. In his voice. The Shade was speaking of war and slaughtering all who lived in Darke. "Another royal Fey has challenged Dalinda for the throne of Darke. Should she prevail, we will make sure no one bothers your home. However, should events unfold and Dalinda prevails as the victor then I humbly you request you do whatever is needed to protect your home."

Turning from her Gwydion use his long translucent fingers to scratch his chin as he pondered her words. A single breath more, and then he answered in a bone chilling whisper, "My people are forbidden to harm a royal Fey. However, it is fortunate that Dalinda is not a true royal, for she bleeds black."

Secrets, Lies and Betrayal
by: M.L. Ruscsak

With their heart pumping fast and her breathing hard, she swung into the library. The hard wood door slamming shut as Alista used a protection spell that she had not yet perfected to seal off the room. With their hands resting on the door not yet ready to back away a voice came from behind her.

"Problem, pumpkin?"

Her father… What was… How was… he here? "Papa I thought…" It didn't really matter what she thought he was here in you would help her fix this.

Secrets, Lies and Betrayal
by: M.L. Ruscsak

"It would seem your uncle needed me here. Something about a trial for the control of Darke and a possible threat to the Fey." Slowly Magmas stretch his massive translucent red wings as he yawned. "Now, before I decide if I should pummel him to the ground for interrupting a very important meeting with Karnack... Perhaps you can tell me you why you're using and unperfected protection spell around this room. Or perhaps explain why you are suddenly out of breath."

He was not asking, now when he used that deep tone to his voice. Not when it had to hints of embers deep within the deep timber of his natural voice. "There is a Shade... Within the castle. I... I think he... It... Is hunting..."

Magmas closes tired eyes taking a breath. Squeezing the bridge of his nose, he asked, "Was his name Gwydion?"

Slowly, Alista answered with a great amount of caution, "Yes?"

"Then he is not here to hunt, at least not this time." Magmas pause, then shook his head before saying anything that he truly wished that he would have never had needed to. "There has been a long-standing agreement between the Fey and the Shades. They protect the City of Bones and the southern border Darke. In return, one day when will find a way to allow them to rest or return to what they once were."

Secrets, Lies and Betrayal
by: M.L. Ruscsak

Her head was spinning with the information. So many secrets. So many things as queen, she needed to know. So many things that needed to be said and done before she could even preside over the damn trial. So many things that her father or uncle were going to tell her before they would be allowed to leave to anywhere. "I need to know everything that you and Uncle Flint have been hiding from me."

Turning from her, Magmas hit his face while he bought with himself over what she was asking versus what his queen would not wish to be said. Finally, he decided that he would need flint the fulfill both requests. "Once your uncle and Karnack and arrived, the four of us will speak."

Karnack? Who in the name of dark was Karnack? No, best not to ask that not when her father might actually answer the question. Not one that answer would only raise even more questions to answer. No, it was best not to ask anything. Demanding on the other hand... "I want Vasilissa to hear this as well, so she would be the rule of both Lite and Darke."

Several dark curses escaped from Magmas' lips as he turned to face his daughter. A sound would have been a warning for anyone else... His daughter, however, just placed her small fist upon her hip and raised an eyebrow. Mumbling, he conceded. "Fine. For this one meeting I will allow it."

Secrets, Lies and Betrayal
by: M.L. Ruscsak

CHAPTER 5: DALINDA

"That whoring bitch. Who does she think she was messing with?" Dalinda stormed into the poorly furnished guess room that she had been given. Her fingers catching on a single drab colored pillow shredding it to pieces before hissing out, "Challenging me... *ME*... for the right to rule Darke. I will see her killed." Turning to her sister who had been right on her heels, she let the final piece of fabric fall to the ground. A gust of the wind slammed the clay brown door shut.

For a moment both girls stared at one another, letting the tension build between both of them. As the air started to feel heavy between them, Dalinda pointed a single long, narrow finger at Delaney. "I'll tell you this, one way or another I will rule both Darke and Lite. Even if I have to kill Alista to do it."

Taking a seat on the low foot bench, Delaney rolled her ice blue eyes. "You simply cannot kill Alista even if she is being a bitch."

"Oh? And would you care to explain why I cannot persuade my betrothed or his father to use their resources to start a war to distract her, just so I can get close enough to slither little throat?"

Turning to glance at the solid wall, Delaney sighed, "First off, Alista now has the ear of the Darken council. Should she die, they would destroy anything that had a hand in her death. And that, dear sister, would include both of our betrotheds and their homelands." Getting to her feet, she adjusted her mini skirt made of reptile scales. "However, you can kill the little princess of Lite since she did challenge you. After all, we already know for a fact her bloodlines are weak."

A cruel smile formed on Dalinda's lips. "Pity her mother didn't marry anyone with more power. Oh well, just two more little princesses to die once they taste the true powers that only a queen can control."

"As far as ruling Feyen..." Delaney ran her finger over the stone vanity, turning it to gold. "A slow acting poison would be best. It would take years for the effects to start working, but would cause Elista to ascend. I'm sure by then we could find a way to take over all of the Feyen lands.

With her temper no longer boiling, Dalinda sat at the now golden vanity and pouted her now green painted lips. "I do hate waiting, but a plan that works slowly has a better chance of working and won't lead back to me." Letting her sister pull a silver hairbrush through her thin mahogany

Secrets, Lies and Betrayal
by: M.L. Ruscsak

hair, she stared back at her reflection. "Yes, I think that would work. No, it *will* work."

Secrets, Lies and Betrayal
by: M.L. Ruscsak

Secrets, Lies and Betrayal
by: M.L. Ruscsak

CHAPTER 6: VASILISSA

With Alista pulling her down more corridors than she ever known existed, Vasilissa tried to find solid ground beneath her feet. A fleeting hope that it would make her dear cousin pause for one minute. When she couldn't, she finally gave her poutiest voice, "Will you stop for one damn minute?"

Alista jerked to a stop, only to glare at her. "We need to talk before we see my father. And I prefer to do so where none dare to dwell."

Well, that could not be good. Not when Alista was going to a place that would be hard to find and away from her little daughter. No, whatever this was... no good would ever come from it. "Fine, but I will get there on my own accord and not by being pulled there."

For a minute Alista said nothing as her lips drew into a thin line. "You are most troublesome. It is even a wonder that you and Zilla share bloodlines."

"Well, Zilla is only my sister on my mother's side. Something I trust you will never breathe a word of otherwise."

"What?! How did I not know this? Never mind, do not answer that. Least not now."

Entering a scarcely furnished room Alista took a deep sigh. "Don't mind the dust. None have entered this

Secrets, Lies and Betrayal
by: M.L. Ruscsak

room since my mother descended into the Under Kingdom."

Dust? Oh, she couldn't care less about the dust. However, the red clay that covered the once white clothes that covered what was left in the way of furniture... now that she could worry about. More so since it appeared to have left by some creature rather what could have been dropped from the white stone ceiling. "So, what kind of critters dwell down here?"

With a dismissive wave of her hand Alista shrug it off with nothing more than a passing thought. "Nothing that does not belong. Now please close the door, we have much to discuss and little time to do so."

Easing the heavy marble door close, Vasilissa turned to her cousin. "Now should I dare to sit or remain standing? Since I have no doubt I will be back on my feet before you are finished talking."

"Sit." Alista nodded like she had just had a conversation with someone else before she smiled. "Then again you may wish to remain standing. Since I have already rumpled you up once this week already."

Coming over to the small couch, she narrowed her eyes. "Alista, really you seem to rumple everyone around you just to see their reactions."

Secrets, Lies and Betrayal
by: M.L. Ruscsak

"I do not. I just happen to do things that get the quickest response."

"Such as having your mother banish your sister to the marshlands because she changed her appearance to look like a serpent."

"Yes, well, if I had known then what I do now... I would have come up with something else. Either way Father has forbidden any to speak of her. And one day we will speak in length about how exactly you came across that information. Today, However, we have other things to discuss."

Closing her dark eyes Vasilissa silently counted to ten before meeting her cousin's stare. "And what do you wish to discuss?"

"Several things. Mostly because I need to hear it out loud before I decide on what needs to be done. The rest because I understand how much power you truly hold within you."

Making herself comfortable Vasilissa sat back and crossed her long legs revealing the knife that was strapped to her ankle. "Very well, I will let you ramble before I start asking any questions."

"And your knife, darling?"

Secrets, Lies and Betrayal
by: M.L. Ruscsak

"Made of black crystal. Completely unbreakable by anything Dalinda might be available to her." She leaned just a hair forward, "In fact, I doubt even royal blade of Feyen could withstand its force."

It was such a trivial little thing, but if something was stronger than her father's crystal sword, then it was worth asking about. "And how was it forged?"

"That I was never privy to, However, I do know only this one and a long blade was ever created. Now that blade I am told is housed somewhere in the Castle of Water. And only someone who knows the true power of the dark and is of true royal blood may reclaim it."

"How wonderful. Once we have the current problem solved you will assist me in finding it."

Vasilissa nodded her head in agreement before steepling her long, narrow fingers. "Very well. Now please let us discuss what you need."

Slowly Alista got to her feet so many thoughts tumbling with her mind. Nothing needed to make sense at least not to Vasilissa. Now she would not only hear the words, but feel what was going on well outside this room. Perhaps even feel enough to offer clarity once everything was said. A deep breath and she began. "Zilla made friends with a Shade. The same Shade that I have just learned knows my father, uncles, Magnar and your grandfather.

Secrets, Lies and Betrayal
by: M.L. Ruscsak

What I know about him is he owes something to someone called the goddess. Because of whatever is owed, he has disclosed that Dalinda is betrothed to the Marshland prince. And I think the recent attacks within Darke are in retaliation to the citizens bothering the City of Bones and the ruins of the Great War.

In the meantime, Father is waiting for someone named Karnack to arrive. I'm assuming this person is a resident of the Under Kingdom and has been for quite some time."

"Do you wish for me to speak or is there more that you need to say?"

Alista looked at her and smiled, "Your powers are growing quickly."

"Powers have nothing to do with it. Paying attention to those around me However, is something the Queen of Feyen needs to learn more quickly."

If anyone else had said that to her, she would have had them dragged off and fed to a troll. This is one of the very few Fey that not only would have dared, but was one who was her equal... it was a warning. Fluffing her hair, she asked oh so sweetly, "And what, pray tell, do I need to be paying attention to?"

Secrets, Lies and Betrayal
by: M.L. Ruscsak

Getting to her feet, she snapped the sheet from the couch and held it up. "First off, this is covered in blood not in red clay. Now, I know of very few things that have this coloring of blood. All of them reside in Lite. And the ones that don't are no friend to Fey."

Placing her hand on her hip Alista glared at the cloth, "You're worried about dried blood when we have so much more to worry about? Really Vas..."

"I'm worried about what killed whatever is now on these rags. Last, I checked those with this colored blood are rare treats for the serpents and those that dwell in the Marshlands. Meaning..."

"Meaning one or more is in my palace and making a mess in my mother's Solaria." She turned and snapped the remaining clothes from the two chairs and the dresser. "Damn them is nothing sacred?"

"Alista concentrate. This is more important than someone making a mess in here."
"Why is it that I'm older, and you are the one scolding me?"

"I scold you because you act like a spoiled child, and your father has never felt the need to teach you properly. Now, as I was saying, there is enough blood in this room for a good number of warriors to have fed in here. That should be your first priority, more so after I tell you this. Your

Secrets, Lies and Betrayal
by: M.L. Ruscsak

sister married and then mated with the new king of the marshlands. It is her son that Dalinda is betrothed to."

"So, Soleil is trying to make her son King over the Fey."

"Or she is making a play for the crown herself. Both are a possibility"

Wiping her mouth so not to scream, Alista raised her head high, resigning herself to be the queen at all cost. "First, we make sure you rule both Lite and Darke. Then we send that little bitch to the Under Kingdom."

Secrets, Lies and Betrayal
by: M.L. Ruscsak

CHAPTER 7: ALISTA

Just hours ago, she had sat here on the great

throne of Feyen to create the council and to announce the trials of Fey. However, being back here now go wrong. Felt like the weight of Feyen was sitting on her chest and at any moment would crush her. Her father had kept secrets from her. All right, fine, he was the king and some things should never be said. Some things should never be passed down to those who followed. This she understood, however, this wasn't about family secrets, this was secrets that she needed to know in order to keep the Fey safe. Order to keep her people safe.

But the and top of that, she now had Soleil to deal with and her sudden need to become the queen of Feyen. Plus, Dalinda and her desire to control both Lite and Darke. With the possibility of her unholy offspring ruling all three. What in the name of Darke was wrong with all of these

Secrets, Lies and Betrayal
by: M.L. Ruscsak

whores? Why couldn't they be happy living in a country of their birth, and finding suitable partners to be happy with that didn't need war and bloodshed?

She could tell you why. It was something wrong with their damn insufficient minds. That was what was wrong with these people. With these Fey.

"Kitten? I thought we had agreed to meeting in the library?" A question yes but not really the question the he was asking.

Damn her father. Couldn't he see that she needed a moment to clear her mind? No, of course he didn't. "I needed a moment, or Vasilissa will pick up on only my thoughts and none of those within these castle walls." Well, was partly the truth.

"You are the queen of Feyen... No one, and I mean no one should be able to pick up on your thoughts."

That was not a fatherly tone. That was a tone that neared a call to battle. "Then I suggest you find out who her father is since I can bet that power, that ability came from him not that of her grandmother."

Finally, Magmas stepped up onto the dais in towered over her. In the deepest voice that he could muster, he growled, "We will discuss this in the library. Now."

Secrets, Lies and Betrayal
by: M.L. Ruscsak

Swallowing hard, Alista tried to smile. Her father and had always been a no-nonsense-about-anything kind of king. And worse, he had been like that as her father. It didn't matter if she were now the Queen of Feyen or not. She was still his daughter and as his daughter she should have known better than to use that tone with him. As softly as she could, she replied, "Yes, Papa."

Standing in the doorway of the library, Alista paused. Magnar was at one of the long desks leaning back in his seat. His muddy boots... Bloody boots... propped up on the desk a large, a thick book sitting next to him. His dark mesh like robes covered in wet blotches. What had he been

Secrets, Lies and Betrayal
by: M.L. Ruscsak

doing since sitting with her during the meeting with the current queens of Lite and Darke?

Not something that she could ask. Not something that she would even if she could.

Taking a steady breath, she glanced around the rest of the room. Her Uncle Flint was leaning against the back wall, his red crystal dagger hanging loosely at his side. His face no longer filled with worried lines and wrinkles, but in fact looking years younger. In fact, he looked no older than she was.

Come to think of it, her father also looked centuries younger and the size of his muscles nearly doubled.

Not something she could ask about, at least not yet. But the other gentleman that was sitting in the room with his back to her she could. Politely Alista asked, "Papa, is this Lord Karnack?"

Turning to a slightly in his seat, Karnack glanced at her and his long dark eyelashes. The color of his eyes still masked by some illusion. "Just Karnack, my dear. I have never been, nor wish to be a lord."

His voice was young, but his mannerisms... Yes, they seemed much older than those of her father. Yet she chose to ignore this in turn, back to her father. "I thought Vasilissa was joining us."

Secrets, Lies and Betrayal
by: M.L. Ruscsak

Another man stepped out of the shadows... literally... one moment there was a fluttering on the floor the next to her Uncle Flint in the next he was stepping out of it. Blinking, Alista staggered back before running up to the man who she hadn't seen in far too many years. Her arms wrapped happily around his waist as his deep blue wings wrapped around her. Nearly in tears, she gasped, "Uncle Apollo... but how..."

Apollo closed his eyes resigning himself to being hugged breathless. "Apparently I suddenly need to be here to help settle something that should have never become an issue." He was hugging her but her was glaring at Flint. A sure sign that something else was going on. And hopefully it didn't involve the trials.

Secrets, Lies and Betrayal
by: M.L. Ruscsak

CHAPTER 8: VASILISSA

Carefully, cautiously Vasilissa took one last breath and raised her hand to knock on the gray stone door. Her hand hovered pausing just before it came in contact with the door. Mist seeped from around.

Whatever lay behind it was making her skin prick in warning. More than that she could feel the bitter rage pouring into the surrounding air.

Danger. Turn back. Do not enter.

All of this raced across her mind. The urge to turn back nearly had her caving to her fears.

She. Would. Not. Turn. Back.

Secrets, Lies and Betrayal
by: M.L. Ruscsak

Choking back her own fears and replacing them with the bitter resolve that she had found since Alista thrust her into this path to become a powerful queen. Her fist tightened as she pounded twice. A moment longer and she readied herself to pound yet again.

Nothing inside of her wanted to be in that room, but she was not turning away from a potential fight. Not when it would prepare her to face Dalinda. Not when the fate of Lite now rested on her shoulders. Or at least it would after she vanquished the whore that posed as a princess.

A heartbeat and then another before the door opened. Only it was not Alista who she knew was within the confines of this room, but rather to a man with burnt amber hair and fire within his eyes. Oh, he was using a glimmer spell to mask most of his appearances. But it was no match for her or her natural powers.

He didn't have a chance to speak as she pushed him out of the way and entered the room. True, he was a royal Fey by blood, but he ruled nothing within this realm. He was nothing to her or her people. And nothing that held her respect. Least not until he proved himself worthy of that respect.

"Alista, what is the reason I need to be in this room that houses nothing but temper..." She paused looking at the faces of all the men. In a split-second, she recognized only three. Whatever spell they were using to appear younger was something she would corner them into teaching her just as she held all the powers from both Lite and Darke. "...And these Fey. Your family withstanding, of course."

"Ah, so the daughter of Ciardha has finally arrived."

Her eyes widened as she staggered a step back. Not only did this Fey know her father, but had spoken his name. A name that even she had been forbidden to speak. Grasping for words, she tried speaking, "You know... knew... my father?"

Magnar's eyes locked on Vasilissa. Trying to deceive her, he spoke in an uncertain voice, "Your father, grandmother Orenda and your Lord Griffith." As he gazed at her with a question looming, a small wound on his deceivingly handsome face. A smile that was anything but comforting. "Would you like to know more about them? Perhaps where they had hailed from or what truly became of them?"

Drawing closer she nodded slowly. Her eyes already fighting back tears that she could no more explain then she could how mist could snuff out a life. "I would... but first... who are you?"

"For today, you may call me Magnar. After today, we will see." He leaned back in his chair, looking at ease.

Secrets, Lies and Betrayal
by: M.L. Ruscsak

A flicker of a memory...

Magnar had been there in the throne room when Alista had declared the trials. She hadn't paid much attention when she had walked into the room... Not to any who made up the councils and certainly to Magnar....

Oh, how she wished she had. Looking at him now...

Oh, how she should have measured his power, his temperament. But that was past and nothing that she could change. But right here right now... Her eyes narrowed just a hair as she took her seat. Oh yes, Magnar was trying to look at ease. He was trying to appear friendly and helpful.

She knew better. He was looking for something. Waiting to strike. Wanting to see this room littered with blood just to see what color each bled. This man was the threat that she had been sensing. So, no matter how calm he appeared, nor how friendly she was going to guard for an attack. Even if there would be no way to survive.

Not letting him see her truest intent, she took a seat to the left of Alista who looked much pale. "Now before we speak of my bloodlines, I wonder what it that you all were discussing to make Alista become so frightening pale." Vasilissa leaned forward making sure to lock eyes with Magnar. Holding his attention, she added, "After all, I have yet to meet anyone besides myself that could put the fear of the gods into her."

Alista grabbed her arm and with pleading eyes looked at her before whispering, "Vasilissa, not now."

That was a warning tone coming from Alista. Too bad she could taste her fear. "So, it is Magnar that you now fear more so than myself. How deeply interesting."

For just a moment Magnar let the rage in his eyes flicker. Let the souls of those he had slaughtered flicker deep within the darkness of his soul. A move that made everyone else pause. Everyone except Vasilissa. Yawning, she blinked slowly. "If you think showing me those you killed will bother me, consider this: I take immense pride in hunting with the Drakens and enjoying the spoils of those hunts."

Leaning forward Magnar growled, "Hunting with creatures is not the same as killing Fey for sport."

Too quickly she got to her feet. Her palms thundering down to the table. Black mist filled the room as the smell of rot and death clogged their throats. Horrid shrill screams forced all within the room to cover their ears. Flinging her hand out she pulled on something only she could see. Her hand grasping a scepter of bone and light. Before any could say anything, it was firmly held within her hands. The butt clicking onto the hard floor below.

Secrets, Lies and Betrayal
by: M.L. Ruscsak

Radiant iridescent light filled the room sniffing out the black mist. Quieting the screams. The horrid smell being replaced with the smell of sweet honey and wildflowers. Alista looked scared, her uncles were apprehensive, the man who had opened the door... not fazed about her show of temper. In fact, he looked ready to laugh. Magnar, on the other hand, was truly and completely pissed.

Glancing at the staff that she now held she tipped her head to the royal Fey. "So, you rule somewhere not within this realm. The ones you kill are because of disobedience..." She paused and narrowed her eyes, "No, you kill some for their powers. You steal what is given to the royals here freely. Your temper comes from the fear of someone more powerful than you finding out." Her tongue licked her dry, red lips. "There is more to you Lord Magnar. Much more, but I have little care about what you do to your people or how you rule. Unless you become a threat to me or mine."

The Fey that stood near the door slowly started to clap. "Bravo, brovie my dear." Coming behind her, his smile grew. "What do you think Magnar? Did our queen make a good selection for her sire?"

"Your queen is an ill-tempered woman who wants to breed more ill-tempered woman in hopes of creating something what will be feared by all Fey." Crossing his arms, he hissed out, "I fear to say she may be succeeding.

Secrets, Lies and Betrayal
by: M.L. Ruscsak

Either way." Magnar started to stand, "I want my staff...
now. It is no toy for petulant children."

A flick of her wrist and Vasilissa handed him the
staff. "Now that it is settled who is much scarier. What is it
that we need to discuss before the Trial with Dalinda?"

Alista squeezed the bridge of her nose. "Damn, I
almost forgot. "Taking a deep breath, she chose what she
could say that, wouldn't betray the oaths that she had
already taken. "You need to prove your worth as a queen.
Prove you can handle the powers of the citizens of both Lite
and Darke. But Dalinda must be unharmed. I have no
intention of starting a war with those who have as of yet
harmed any one of Feyen blood."

"Fine. Once I rule Darke, I will banish her and her
sister to the Marshlands. Let them breed with the serpents
or reptiles for all I care. But they will find no Feyen man
who would dare mate with them. Their powers, no matter
how impressive will never be passed on to anyone who will
be a threat to anything that I rule."

Karnack edged over to his seat before very
hesitantly interjecting. "Actually, Dalinda will mate as you
so elegantly put it; with the crown prince of the Marshlands.
Her sister is currently lusting for both a Feyen man with
some worthy abilities and another citizen of the marsh."

Secrets, Lies and Betrayal
by: M.L. Ruscsak

Shaking her head, Vasilissa looked at the man. "I'm sorry, but who are you?"

"All you need to know is that my name is Karnack. And I am nothing more than a trusted scribe."

Collecting his thoughts Flint slid his hand through his dark hair, then tapped his long finger on the table getting everyone's attention. "There may be another way. Especially since we see that Vasilissa is already more than capable of ruling, but we would need the approval of everyone in this room and of the Shades."

Moving from the seat that he had originally chosen, Karnack took a seat at the far end of the table then leaned back. With his hands resting on his belly, Karnack looked at a wall instead of at anyone. Slowly he asked, "The Shades or Nicco?"

Warily now Flint asked, "I was under the impression that Nicco no longer answered the calls of anyone."

"What is told my dear boy and what is true... isn't always the same. Such as Donny. It is common knowledge that he no longer resides in Darke. Where in *truth* he resides in the Forbidden Wastelands. Or more importantly, under the sands. The dwelling he has rendered is very impressive. As are the weapons he now has stored there."

Secrets, Lies and Betrayal
by: M.L. Ruscsak

It was then Apollo, who had refrained from saying anything until that moment, chimed in, "Weapons?"

"Hmm. All sorts of things. Some belonging to those who died during the Great War. And others of his own making."

Rubbing the back of his neck Flint smiled. "Fine. Apollo can go play with Uncle Donny later. Right now, what about Nicco?"

It was then the door eerily slid open and a devastatingly handsome man leaned on the frame. His jacket of fine blue material could only be the color of the deep sea. But his eyes. Oh, his eyes... Both Alista and Vasilissa could gaze into those eyes for hours letting the world slip by and never consider doing anything else. His deep, cultured voice filled the air as he spoke, "Boys, Karnack..."He paused and looked at Magnar. Whatever was between them... whatever past... it was enough to drain the temper out of the Fey King and produce a cold shiver. "I trust we won't have any trouble Magnar." Not a question, but a command laced in a threat.

Forcing a smile, Magnar answered, "It's always a pleasure to see you."

"Doubtful, but we will see." Taking a careful step into the room, he paused halfway between the door and the long table, "May I introduce my boys? Prince Glyndwr and

Prince Olysseus. I trust both will be welcomed additions to the household of both Feyen and Lite."

Pulling Alista into the first room that she could find Vasilissa sealed the door shut, her heart still pounding. Not from fear but excitement. And feelings that neither she nor Alista normally would show. "Did we... were we just? Betrothed to..."

"I understand my father would want me to wed someone worthy of his household, but I never imagined he would go so far to find a suitor himself." Alista plopped down on a chair that she was very thankful for being in the room.

Secrets, Lies and Betrayal
by: M.L. Ruscsak

"How fortunate for you that Elista's father died last year in that troll attack. I mean, did you really look at them? Really? Glyndwr wanted to be anywhere not here. And Olysseus... Oh, I have no doubt that Nicco plans with him ending up with me. He would destroy you the moment you looked away. I would bet my life on it."

"But they are handsome and of royal blood."

Vasilissa waved her hand with a bit of irritation. "And both powerful. I could feel their strength pouring off of them in strove. But that does not mean I am ever going to wed some jackal just because your father agrees it's a good idea."

Alista gave a thoughtful pause. "Would you marry him if your grandfather thought it was a good idea?"

At that Vasilissa snorted, "Lord Griffith rarely thinks anything is a good idea even if he thinks of it himself."

Secrets, Lies and Betrayal
by: M.L. Ruscsak

Secrets, Lies and Betrayal
by: M.L. Ruscsak

CHAPTER 9: THE COUNCIL OF FEY

Dismissing the two young gentlemen, Karnack glared at his dear friend and brother, then jokingly hissed, "Nicco, I do not recall asking you to bring grooms for two queens."

Leisurely taking a seat at the long table, Nicco smiled just enough to show the first row of his deadly sharp teeth. Just enough to show amusement for the moment. "My young bride wanted me to find brides for those two. Might as well kill two problems with one solution." Nicco rested

Secrets, Lies and Betrayal
by: M.L. Ruscsak

both elbows on the table and leaned forward, lowering his deep tenor voice, "Besides Karnack, you did say at least one of those queens would need a strong mate who could produce stronger offspring. And it is a known fact there is no stronger match than those born of my bloodlines."

Nicco gave a sideways glance at Magnar daring him to argue. Daring him to say anything at all.

Readjusting his own seat at the table,+ Karnack leaned forward, ready to debt his thoughts, "I did, but I did not say..."

Deep thunder and the feel of electric filled the room as Magnar growled in frustration finally deciding to end this pissing contest with Nicco, "Enough! Both boys should stay, but I think we should agree right here and now... One will wed the Queen of Darke and Lite, and the other will be her consort."

Since Magnar was looking deep into something only that he could see, Nicco understood far better than those in the room what this could possibly mean. Understood it had to be him to ask, "What do you see?"

"Two children born to the dark-haired queen. One born into the light. Worthy of any Star City. Powers equal to the sun. The other shrouded in darkness. Truly the darkest of dark Fey. The mother of the one that Prim seeks. Each born, but a single light cycle apart. Raised as twins."

Secrets, Lies and Betrayal
by: M.L. Ruscsak

Nicco turned from the table, speaking more to himself than to anyone else he mumbled, "Neither is good at sharing. But I think if I offer that one can return to the sea after he sires a daughter it will be enough."

Magmas leaned forward, his eyes carefully locked on Nicco, who was always unpredictable. Locked his eyes on the only threat that he couldn't be sure that he would survive. The only threat that every Fey, who had seen the destruction that this single creature could cause had left behind during the great war. Cautiously he asked, "Who?"

Looking at the door Nicco shuddered as he answered. "My youngest, Glyndr. He has no desire to live above the ocean floor longer than a light cycle. Where his brother does not wish to return."

Seeing Nicco shudder was a warning. Knowing Vasilissa has already showed that she had more natural power, then even Magnar was another. Looking down at the table Karnack softly spoke, knowing the only person who would dare to have this conversation with either Vasilissa or Alista. Providing of course, they could get him to agree. "Agreed. In that case we need Griffith to finalize this agreement." Then he looked back to Nicco. "And when we are done here I want to know more about both boys. For my records, of course."

Nicco inclined his head in agreement. "For your records. And only for your records."

Ignoring both Karnack and Nicco whom he had no desire to get involved in whatever mess that they would surely create, Magmas looked to Magnar who he assumed would be the one to speak to Griffith. "Don't forget Magnar. We need him to agree to take care of the current Queen of Darke so that the Trials can be canceled."

Magnar leaned back in his seat already comfortable in listening to Nicco and Karnack's little discussion, "Then I suggest that you, boy, be the one to explain that to him. My time is much too precious to handle such trivial matters."

King Griffith sat on his throne of gold. His deep blue robes lined with a thin outline of gold. His sun kissed blond hair mussed from running his finger through it more times than not. Slowly he leaned forward, looking at the Fey of fire and lava who now stood before him. Narrowing his dark soulless eyes, he growled, "Magmas... I don't recall a

Secrets, Lies and Betrayal
by: M.L. Ruscsak

reason for the great King of Feyen to grace my throne room."

At one time they had been friends. Brothers even. At one time they had both been Crown Princes to a great Star City. Had things turned out differently one of them would now rule Pallas while the other would have been dead long ago. Today none of that mattered. No, today all that mattered was getting Griffith to agree to handle what the council had decided. "The Counsel of Fey have gathered in the Castle of Earth. We ask you join us."

"Join you? Join you! I would see that you all dead before I ever think about helping you. Any of your traitorous so called royal Fey."

Oh yes, this was going to be a world of fun. Too bad it was only Magnar and possibly Nicco, who could deal with Griffith. And a shame that neither had decided to come here. "I'm not here to ask for your help for myself or even this Star City. I'm here on your granddaughter's behalf."

Jumping to his feet, he readied himself to lunge at the other King... readied himself to fight to the bitter end, "If you have done anything to harm them I will end you, Fallen Prince of Osirus. By all that I am, I will put an end to you and your precious line."

Crossing his massive arms, Magmas glanced around the room. Not a single Light bearer or other guard. Not a

Secrets, Lies and Betrayal
by: M.L. Ruscsak

single weapon within arm's reach. The crystal windows would shatter much too quickly. The vaulted ceiling crumbling down on both of them should they use their natural abilities. "Vasilissa is now the Crown Princess of Lite. Zilla has chosen to step aside and make a place for herself at the Spire."

Retaking his seat Griffith narrowed his eyes not yet ready to concede anything to this man. To this Fey. This man who had bloodiness to the destroyer of the Light Cities. Not ready to trust a single word that came from his lying lips. Yet a part of him knew the council would not have sent Magmas here to deceive him, the true heir of Pallas. His voice was still cold and dark as he asked, "It's practical, but why?"

"Because the Crown Princess of Darke and her sister are such ripe little whores, it's going to take more than luck and a soft smile to keep Darke from falling into the hands of the Marshlands." Carefully, Magmas drew just a hint closer to the great Fey Warrior. Carefully and respectfully he lowered his voice, "And Magnar foresees Vasilissa bearing the mother of Nisha. If what he sees bears any fruit those of us that are Fallen need to prepare with his home. "Another pause, then, "All of the Fallen, not just the council."

With his fingers melting the gold to his throne Griffith growled through his clenched teeth, "I will not live under your father's rule. Nor will I ever live under yours."

Secrets, Lies and Betrayal
by: M.L. Ruscsak

There was a lot of temper in those words. Rage building in the fellow King's eyes. Too bad he could never tell what natural ability would come forward when Griffith became enraged. Unnatural strength that could crush the skull of a troll. Speed that even Apollo couldn't match. Light that burned just by looking at it. Or much worse the ability to call forth the dead, enslaving them as he tapped into their powers as they tore apart those who crossed him. All this weighted on his mind as he watched Griffith paw at the armrest of his golden throne. Black poisoned mist dripping from his nails.

With a single deep breath Magmas tied to keep his own fear out of his voice. Tried to sound like the King who had ruled for more than two thousand light cycles. Tried to find all of the confidence that Prim had once told him that she had. "Magnar does not live in the shadow of Pallas. The Star Cities that he does rules do not draw their power from the glory of Pallas." Magmas paused just a heartbeat before adding, "Besides, he rules over a handful of Star Cities. I doubt we will cross paths often." It was a risk to add that last bit. He just hoped that it was enough of an incentive for Griffith to once again join them.

Secrets, Lies and Betrayal
by: M.L. Ruscsak

With long strides he used nothing more than a gust of wind to blow open the tall main door of the Castle of Earth. Nothing more than a thought and all of the guards who came running toward the front hall collapsed into an unnatural sleep. Today he hasn't killed them. But that didn't mean that he was happy to be here. It didn't mean that he wouldn't kill them if they continued to attack. Being here and showing kindness to this batch of guards didn't mean that he wouldn't bring the entire castle down around his feet either killing or trapping everyone inside. After all, it was a tantalizing thought.

But that was an afterthought. Right now, there was something that he needed to do. Something that's worthy of his temper, and his dark bitter rage. Later he would decide if the castle would remain standing or if it would need to be rebuilt for a second time.

Turning down two more corridors, he slushed off the spell that he had lived behind for more years than not.

Secrets, Lies and Betrayal
by: M.L. Ruscsak

His outer flesh melting toward the floor, leaving nothing more than fresh young skin behind. Now he looked like a true royal Fey still in his prime. No longer full of wrinkles and hanging skin. No longer were his massive muscles being covered with layers of fabric. No longer must he hide behind the ruse of being a benign old Fey that only had a fraction of his powers.

No, now it was time to show his wife's sister what it meant to be a royal Fey. Time to show the whoring bitch that he always kept his promise when he told her that he would be the one to kill her. Destroy her. The promise that he would rip her head from her shoulders with nothing more than his temper and brute strength.

Oh, how he would relish the feeling of draining the life out of her miserable body. How he would relish washing the floor with her blood just to see what color flowed in her worthless veins.

Shadows flickered within the darkness, leading him to his prey. Candles burned with fury as he passed, their wax evaporating before it ever touched the ground. Doors that were held open by puzzled onlookers quickly shut one they realized a dark Fey was storming the castle.

At the end of the hall with an elaborate, ornate door, he paused, allowing himself feel those who were in the room. Oh, Kiera was in there, but so were several serpents. Serpents that should not be this far north. Trespassers that should not have left their home. Not his problem; to him they were just another outlet for his rage.

A cruel deceptive smile formed on his lips as a single blue flame rushed toward the door. The paint melting just a breath before the clay began crackling just a breath before it burst inward. Black smoke filled the hall. A scream of startled surprise from Kiera. The sound of swords being unsheathed. Anything else about the room didn't matter. The two scores of serpent assassins didn't matter since they could easily be killed. Even the shield of black mist that Kiera was now creating didn't matter to him. Nor would it matter to any true royal Fey. More so if that Fey was raised by the Goddess herself.

Taking but a single step into the room a cruel calculating smile touched his moist pale lips. His translucent black and blue wings snapped open shimmering with golden mist. His armor holding the dragon crest of the Goddess shown with pride. Locking eyes on Kiera, he let his deep thunderous voice fill the room. "Queen Kiera, your reign of Darke ends now."

Trembling, she took a shaky step forward "I do not answer to you. I do not answer to a creature that does not exist."

A cruel laugh slipped from his lips as he snapped his fingers. Mist of purple and black fire engulfing the serpents. Their shrill screams and curses filled the room as they were

Secrets, Lies and Betrayal
by: M.L. Ruscsak

torn apart. Their green blood staining the cream-colored tiles. Only their leather armor being left behind as a dark mist absorbed the mess that he was creating.

Griffith narrowed his eyes knowing it was not the mist that he had created that was absorbing the flesh and bones. No, it was something much more dangerous and a whole lot deadlier than even he could dream of being. The only question was why the Shade was here within the Castle.

Not a question he could ask. At least, not now. Not when a moment of hesitation and the Shade could turn on him. Not when there was nothing that was safe from a Shade. Not even a Royal Fey.

His eyes returning to the so-called Queen, who was now paralyzed with fear, he smiled, "Because of a Fey with greater power and ability than my own, I will allow for your whoring children to seek safety within the Marshlands. However, the debt that you owe me will be collected..."

Defiantly Kierra raised her chin. "I owe you nothing. The bitch you bore was weak and could not handle the power of her kingdom. And her bastard daughter was little better."

Crossing his massive arms Griffith raised, but one eyebrow. "Come now, do you not think I would not discover the incantation that you used to taint the transfer of

Secrets, Lies and Betrayal
by: M.L. Ruscsak

power?" He watched her stumble back a step. Watch the fear resonate on her face. "I told you that I would destroy you. I warned you that it was me and not your sister that ruled Lite. Now my dear, I will make good on that promise."

Griffith strode into the great hall where the

Counsel of Fey was gathered. The doors crashing open before his entry. A bloody head tossed on the floor, landing right before Magnar. Stopping only once it hit his already messy boots. Black blood still seeping from the tendrils of blood vessels that had been ripped from Keira's neck.

Locking eye with the famed creator he growled still too pissed off to care whom he was speaking to. "Does anyone question that I now rule both Lite and Darke." Not a question, but a dare to challenge him for the position.

Secrets, Lies and Betrayal
by: M.L. Ruscsak

Glancing down at the head Magnar locked eyes on one of the few Fey that had ever earned his respect. "Today you will rule both. In a fortnight the dark haired one will and you will return to live among the Stars."

Damn. Going toe to toe with Magmas was one thing. Going up against Magnar? He was no fool, and only a fool would cross this Fey. Inclining his head slightly he conceded. "Very well, in a fortnight I will abdicate my throne to my granddaughter, on the condition that my wife will join me."

Magnar waved his hand dismissively, "I have little use for affairs of the heart, however, it is something that Prim holds dear. For her I will allow it."

For now, was left hanging in the air. It wasn't said but there wasn't a Fey that was held within the room who hadn't heard it.

"Thank you."

A twisted smile touched Magnar's lips, "Don't thank me yet, boy. There if still another matter that you need to deal with. And you will do so alone."

Secrets, Lies and Betrayal
by: M.L. Ruscsak

Secrets, Lies and Betrayal
by: M.L. Ruscsak

CHAPTER 10: GRIFFITH

Griffith took a deep breath. Just one more piece of business before he could leave this castle. Before he could leave the place that still reminded him far too keenly about the place that he had been born. A place that he would see turned to rubble for the nightmare that it had now become.

Raising his fist, he gave the plain black wood door a single rap before it opened. Standing before him was not the granddaughter that he had raised. Not the woman that he knew how to measure her temper and her power. No this was a queen who had been thrust into power without any training. This was a Fey that he knew even Magnar wouldn't turn his back on.

And this was a Fey worthy of even his bloodlines.

Secrets, Lies and Betrayal
by: M.L. Ruscsak

Narrowing her eyes Vasilissa snapped out furious at the intrusion. "Who in the name of Darke are you?"

What she could have been doing to be this furious, Griffith could not say. Still, her harsh voice filled with midnight and lighting brought him back to the present. The intent look in her eyes... oh yes, even he needed to tread lightly. Scratching his chin, he asked, "Now who do you think I am?"

Her eyes narrowed just a hair more as she looked him up and down. Finally settling on not his face, but his armor. Then she gave him a soft shove with nothing more than her finger touching his breastplate. "Before you leave this room, I will know what spell, power or incantation the Fey men of this family seem to be used to become much younger."

Following her into the sparsely furnished room Griffith closed the door behind him. Later he could ponder why a future queen was this far away from the whole of the castle, but not today. Not when he was already having a hard time measuring her temper and power. "No incantation, my child. True Star City Fey age much, much slower than others."

"Does your wife know this?"

Taking a deep breath, he signed, "Enya has always known."

Secrets, Lies and Betrayal
by: M.L. Ruscsak

Vasilissa finally took a seat in a high back chair. "I want an honest answer, will Alista or I have this ability?"

"Alista? I doubt it. You on the other hand? Given whom your father is and where you were born, it is a possibility. But I cannot say for certain."

Rolling her eyes Vasilissa blew a lock of hair from her face. "Well... at least I can see why Enya married you. But you did not come here to speak of your looks or of those of the other royal Fey. Which begs the question as to why you have come in here?"

At least she hadn't asked about her own origins. For that he was greatly thankful. Yet he still had to explain his reason for being here. He had to be the one to explain a great many things to this deadly queen who now sat before him. "In a fortnight you will take the crown of both Lite and Darke. Within one light cycle, you will give birth to a child born to Prince Glyndr so that he may return to the ocean floor where he belongs. Then you will marry Prince Olysseus."

Getting quickly to her feet she started to growl, "Now look here..."

His voice hardened as it thundered through the room, "This is not for debate. You will do what your counties need so that I can do what needs to be done to keep this star safe."

Secrets, Lies and Betrayal
by: M.L. Ruscsak

For more than a handful of breaths Vasilissa stood there silently. The look of seething too apparent on her face. Yet she still asked and managed to sound polite. "And what reason do I have to bear children by two different Feyen males?"

"Because a seer has foreseen the children that each will give you."

Retaking her seat, she leaned forward, holding the arms of the chair with her nails. Hate, and something deadlier flickering within her eyes. Black mist now rising up behind her. With a low hiss she answered, "I am a seer and since when has anyone ever listened when I spoke?"

Griffith met her cold dead stare and match it with his own. "You Vasilissa are not a seer. The mist that forms around you lends you their abilities. They are unreliable. One day you will understand this."

In nothing more than a breath she was standing before him her wings of black fire unfurled. The room of carved stone and elegant furnishings melting from her fury. Not burning... melting. The stone turning into molten magma beneath her feet. "How dare you question what I see? Or even if it is true." Her small hand grabbed the sides of her grandfather's face. In that moment they were no longer in a room... No longer in the castle or even within Prim's star.

Secrets, Lies and Betrayal
by: M.L. Ruscsak

Oh no they were far away on some barren rock floating in space. Star Cites surrounding them. Glowing orbs and nothing more. A feat that no ordinary Fey could have accomplished. Not some trick created from a shadow. Not even something that Prim could have done... at least not something she had done before retreating to the Under Kingdom.

"How is this possible?" He gasped out.

Her nail bit down on his arms as she studied his face frozen in fear. "This is where you will die Lord Griffith. Torn apart by those who you consider friends. Handed over to your enemies in the name of peace. This place I do not know, but that is of little importance to me for as you say I am not a seer." Throwing her hands off of him they returned to the room now completely destroyed. The window now little more than a hole within the wall. The flora outside scorched from the heat. "Tell me, Griffith, if I am not a seer then what am I?"

Stumbling back his back hit the door, "Something much more dangerous and something that I have no name for."

"Very well, then I will leave you with one more piece of advice. There is a girl that can save you. She is not born yet, nor lives anywhere that I know. Perhaps she can be found and will find a means to end this petty war that you so fear. Perhaps not. "

Secrets, Lies and Betrayal
by: M.L. Ruscsak

Watching her turn from him, Griffith quietly slipped out of the room, hoping his heart would one day return to its natural beat.

Stumbling in to library his legs felt weak... his strength gone. The plain wood door that had felt light as feather earlier today suddenly felt almost too heavy to push open. The rest of the council was in that room. All of them waiting to hear his account of how his granddaughter had responded. He paid attention to none of them.

Didn't hear them asking about what had happened. Didn't hear the questions that he could see coming from their mouth. No, nothing mattered but the bottle of sweet honeyed nectar that sat in the canter on the long table.

Not something that he usually drank. Not something he had touched since coming to this star. Today, however...

Secrets, Lies and Betrayal
by: M.L. Ruscsak

Pulling the top off, he held the canter to his lips and drank greedily. About halfway through the bottle someone helped him into a chair. By the time it was emptied he was thankful to be in a chair rather than laying out on the cold floor. His eyes closed as he asked... not to anyone in particular, but needing an answer just the same. "What is she?"

"I don't think I have ever seen Griffith drink before." Flint's voice. Or at least he thought it was Flint hard to tell with his ears muffled.

A warm hand on his back. Then a voice. Yet another that could almost place. "Who or what are you asking about?"

Several moments passed before he could form the words that he needed. Words that he wanted to say. For that matter, was able to form any words at all. "Vasilissa, what is she?"

"Fey, but not. A creator, but not truly. Something straddling the line between this life and another. Merging life into death, yet not of either."

At that he opened his eyes, but it wasn't Magnar who had spoken it was Karnack, the queens trusted scribe. "What do you know?"

"Nothing more than speculation, I'm afraid. Hidden in a scroll that Magnar so thoughtfully left for Prim well

Secrets, Lies and Betrayal
by: M.L. Ruscsak

before the Great War... there is telling of a Fey, who is stronger than most but not a creator but not truly a Fey. I suspect the answers lay within the great library of the Fey... Perhaps we will find the answer, perhaps not. Either way, your granddaughter will rule both Lite and Darke. Her granddaughter will rule much more."

Yes, that was what he was afraid of. He was afraid of what her grandchild would rule. And more importantly, how.

Secrets, Lies and Betrayal
by: M.L. Ruscsak

CHAPTER 11: ALISTA

Alista shuffled around what hours before had been a fine guess room and one of the few that her cousin had always found solace in. Looking around, she gave a deep sigh. Her eyes still watching the Fey who was still so deep in anger that deadly dark mist still dripped from her fingers. The embers still scorching the already burnt ground. Carefully, she watched the Fey that could destroy her before even understand who it was that she had killed.

Trying to keep her voice light and airy Alista asked, "Do I dare ask why my darling castle needs to be rebuilt?"

Vasilissa waved the question off with nothing more a flick of her wrist. "I hardly consider rebuilding a single room, cause for rebuilding an entire castle."

Seeing Vasilissa starting to regain control of her temper and her new abilities, Alista lightly scolded as she counted on her fingers, "Between this room, the courtyard, hall outside and the rooms attached... paired with the hallway that Griffith destroyed... I say that qualifies as needing to rebuild my castle." she paused briefly before changing her tone to a more authoritative one, "I am still waiting for an explanation."

Slowly Vasilissa turned from the open hole not yet looking at the rubble that she had created. Not yet stepping away from what she had shown Griffith. "I should think you would jump at the opportunity to rebuild the great Castle of Feyen."

Another time she might have. Another time, her cousin's words would be taken as they had been intended. However, she could not dismiss that rage no more than she could dismiss the seeping black mist that was still turning solid stone into hot liquid. "Perhaps we can discuss your current mood and maybe find some resolve in it?"

"Resolve? You want resolve? HA!"

"Vas?"

Secrets, Lies and Betrayal
by: M.L. Ruscsak

"The great lord Griffith along with, I'm sure your family, has decided that I will not only wed one of the so-called princes but I will have a child with the other. And both will be born within a single lite cycle of each other." Vasilissa cursed through her now clenched teeth before turning back to her cousin.

Taking a measured step closer to Vasilissa, Alista decided that playing the part of 'Queen" would surely get her killed. However, bubbly cousin… "I'm surprised my father didn't decide that I should marry one."

"You're weak Alista. Your powers come from your mother rather than your father. Should you carry a child for either it would destroy you. If the father didn't first."

Creating a chair out of mist Alista calmly sat down, allowing for Vasilissa to speak to her in any manner that she needed so as not to become a danger to anyone around her. "You have seen this?" She waved it off "Of course you have. You wouldn't have said it otherwise."

"So now you believe I am a seer?"

"Seer? Oh no, you my dear are not a seer however you are something that I have no name for. Nor do I wish to have a name for. However, I do look forward to exploring this ability along with any others that you wish to work on while you live in my home."

Secrets, Lies and Betrayal
by: M.L. Ruscsak

Finally, Vasilissa looked at her and the bubbling rage wasn't held in her gaze. "Perhaps I should stay in the castle of water. It's less likely to catch fire should my temper flare."

"Come darling, I have already ordered a suit for you and your soon to be husband. Your temporary consort will live in the harbor until he is certain you are with child."

"You knew all of this before coming in here."

"Of course, I did. I am no fool Vasilissa. And only a fool would dare enter a room with an enraged royal Fey with the bloodlines such as yours."

Secrets, Lies and Betrayal
by: M.L. Ruscsak

EPILOGUE

Staring out of the tower window overlooking the boarder of both Lite and Darke, Vasilissa pretended not to notice the long-haired tabby cat that was slinking toward her. Pretended not to notice that it was watching her the same way it would a delicious mouse.

Couldn't. Not when she knew who this cat really was nor the temper that had come with him.

Turning just enough to stop the cat with nothing more than a look, she rolled her eyes and half hardily hissed, "If you are going to interrupt the few moments

Secrets, Lies and Betrayal
by: M.L. Ruscsak

without having one of our children crying then you should do so on two legs, not four."

Carefully Olysseus formed back into the Feyen man that his queen was just starting to care for. His dark hair mussed from running his fingers through it. His golden eyes just as tired looking as hers. "I was not trying to disturb you at all."

Turning back to her window, she started out watching the on goings of the Spire. Watched as the pixies hid behind tall flowers. Watched as the garden gnomes scurried out of the way of the Fey man that was walking briskly to the Spire gates. And hopefully back to the waters from where he dwelled. "I see your brother is here."

Nearly next to his wife, Olysseus stuffed his hands into his trouser pockets, then nodded to the window. Or more to his brother who was trying to escape unnoticed. "Aye, he is. But not because he wished to see our daughters."

At that she turned to him and raised, a single eyebrow, "Oh, and what did he come here for?"

Finally, he let a smile form on his pale lips. A smile that let his finely sharpened teeth just barely be seen. "He is too wed a mermaid. The queen in fact. Since she can't extend the invitation herself, he did. That and to let me know the reason they are marring is because she is already

Secrets, Lies and Betrayal
by: M.L. Ruscsak

with... he said child, but I do think an infant merperson is called something different."

Vasilissa closed her eyes and took a deep breath. "I do not want to know. I do not need to know. Nor do I wish to think about it. However, I would like to know if the little darling ever befriends one of our girls."

"I doubt it will. A city is now constructed many leagues beneath the sea where there is no light from above. And only those born of the water can swim that far. And for someone only have born of water... I do doubt that she or he will have the ability to swim this far from home. It is only because of our father that my brother made it at all."

"Did your brother dare say what they are planning on naming the little darling?"

"Sedna for a girl; if a boy they haven't discussed it."

"In that case, let us hope for a girl so that we never need to explain this to your daughters."

Carefully, he wrapped his arms around her and kissed her neck. "When did our daughters become only mine?"

"When both decide their mother doesn't need sleep in order to rule both countries."

Carefully, he pulled her to the bed, "In that case, why don't we both take a short nap. When we wake then we can

Secrets, Lies and Betrayal
by: M.L. Ruscsak

see how the construction is coming along at the castle. I would love a good swim, but do so hate traveling this far to do so."

Rolling her eyes, she leaned into him… the man she had tried hard not to like and even harder not to love. The man who was charming in one breath and could be completely merciless in the next. She would never admit it to anyone, but she was glad he was her husband… glad to have a royal Fey to share not only her kingdom but her heart.

"Yes, a nap sounds so…"

The crying of their youngest carried through the hall. It wouldn't be long before she woke her sister. And not long after that the nurse maid would be begging for help.

Exchanging a look Vasilissa sighed. "…How about a nice carriage ride and hope we can nap on the way?"

Secrets, Lies and Betrayal
by: M.L. Ruscsak

Part Two
Lies of the Star Cities

"The time is drawing near for all truths to be told. But not yet. Not now. Myrddin is still too young to discover all of his greatness. Yet I must be careful. Prim… the mighty creator… can never know the great lengths that I have taken to ensnare her bloodlines. She can never find out that I will send her nothing more than a helpless child rather than the warrior that she seeks. No matter if Myrddin makes it to that blasted star or not… the child… this warrior of the darkness will never rule what belongs to me."

-Journal of the King of Pallas, Magmas I

Secrets, Lies and Betrayal
by: M.L. Ruscsak

Secrets, Lies and Betrayal
by: M.L. Ruscsak

CHAPTER 1: MYRDDIN

Myrddin, first son of Queen Seraphina and heir to Lunaista, sprawled out on his narrow bed not daring to move more than to breath. The pain that he now felt was much worse than the knowledge that he was steadily bleeding. His honeyed tan flesh broken open seeping blue blood onto his sheets. The hard mattress already covered in his blood.

Drip. Drip. Drip

Drip. Drip.

The sound of his blood falling onto the floor below. A small puddle already forming on the cold floor below his thin mattress.

If he stayed where he lay, darkness would soon overcome him. It was a possibility that he would wake once the bleeding stopped. But it was a greater possibility that he wouldn't work at all.

Secrets, Lies and Betrayal
by: M.L. Ruscsak

Carefully his head turned to glance over his shoulder and whimpered. What flesh that was still left was now bruised beyond recognition... bruised beyond any color that resembled his own skin. His blue blood drying to a black hue. His skin... oh his skin how he wanted to weep from the pain.

Yet he wouldn't.

His mother had taken her brand of cruelty to a new level. At least with him. For reasons that he could not understand, she was determined for him... her first born... not to succeed her. Instead, she wanted him to be sacrificed as a tribute. But not any tribute... oh no, that was too good for her only son. Instead, she wanted him to be a tribute to the Silent Ones. A fate that was for the unworthy, and certainly not a fate that should befall the heir of any Star City.

Or at least any heir since before the great war.

He would have shed a tear with this knowledge if but for the fact that it would give Seraphina satisfaction. It was only because of that that he still had the will power to keep them silent. At least for tonight. However, the next time he faced her, he may be so unlucky.

After all, her next attempt to show he was unworthy would be in a few days when Magmas, the lord and master of all of the settled Star Cities would come to see his progress with his abilities. Seraphina was planning something so horrible that even he wouldn't be able to hide

Secrets, Lies and Betrayal
by: M.L. Ruscsak

the screams. Myrddin knew this, just as he knew if a single yelp left his lips, Magmas would have no choice but to deem him unworthy to rule.

Unworthy to even be kept alive. And perhaps unworthy to even be a tribute to the long feared silent ones.

But that was in a few days. However, tonight was all his. Thank the gods that his mother thought she had rendered him completely useless and the guards weren't stationed outside of his door. At least he had played this game well enough do not to endanger those who only served and really didn't care if the heir lived nor died.

Painstakingly he shifted off of his bed and stumbled the few steps over to his desk. Not one made of crystal or even something that had been exported in from another Star City. But one that he himself had made of black mist. One that held all of his secrets and was only solid under his touch. Oh, his mother had tried several times to find out what he had hidden within the mist... each time... each attempt... taking more of her flesh. The last time Seraphina had even lost a finger to her foolishness.

Smiling at the thought of finding his mother standing in the middle of his room holding her hand as purple blood seeped down her arm. He continued to smile as he remembered finding the finger much later from that attempt to pry open the deadly mist. If anything, good had come out of that, it would have been that the queen had not stepped a foot in this room since.

Secrets, Lies and Betrayal
by: M.L. Ruscsak

A deep breath and reached into what should have been a drawer. Only he knew the order of what was hidden inside. Only he knew by feel which book, he was looking for. His fingers lightly touched the spine, pulling out the thickest. Pulling out one that had been made of flesh. Not Fey... but flesh of something that had no words.

Magmas had given him this a few years ago. Not because he was the heir of Lunaista but because of a reason that he had yet to divulge. Or at least not divulge to him. Lazily Myrddin flipped open to the page that he needed. A simple incantation to mend flesh. Below it one to do the opposite. This book had been forbidden during the reign of Azia. In most Star Cities, it still was. But when the current ruler... the current King of Pallas... gives a gift his rule supersedes all others.

And if it didn't... well, the damned fool could try to live through that discussion.

Closing his eyes, he recited the words and gave a content sigh. Feeling the skin mending itself, he closed his book. Just one of many forbidden books and spells that he had. And the only one he had yet to master without reading. Placing it back into the mist he pretended not to hear the little patter of feet running down the hall. Pretended not to see her... his little sister peeking around the corner of the doorway. She was young barely old enough to be let out of the nursery without a maid. But when she wanted to play with her brother...

Secrets, Lies and Betrayal
by: M.L. Ruscsak

Pretending to be bored, he leaned back on his chair, deliberately making it fall backwards dumping him on the cold stone floor. A cushion of air kept him from harming himself in the process. And the move gave him the few seconds that he needed to hide all of the blood that escaped his body.

Estare leaned over him, her black and red curls hiding her chubby face as she asked, "Um... are you alrit?"

He smiled, Estare was learning to form sentences, but yet hadn't mastered full words. She would, and he would make sure of it. Rubbing his head with embarrassment, he looked up at her. Smiled that she was wearing a crystal blue dress today instead on her play smock. "I was bored and wanted to try something new."

Her little hands went behind her back as she very sweetly said, "We can play games."

Pushing himself upright, he rolled his eyes playfully, "Yes, I suppose we could. And what game would you like to play?" Not that he couldn't guess.

She stalked his room looking like she was giving a lot of thought to her request. In truth, it was only so he could get off the floor. They both knew this, but this was about ritual, not truth. "I want to play the matching game."

Wonderful. Just what he needed today pretending to pick a mate out of the women of Lunaista. Or even pretending he had a choice in the matter. "Alright, why don't you start. If you could choose, today, who would you marry?"

"I choose Astin. He is so cute. Mama agrees."

Astin? Oh yes, the son of the guard who Magmas had brought here to keep order. The guard himself was tough and not even their mother who ruled this Star City disagreed with him. His son? Not a royal Fey so he wasn't even a possibility for a mate. A pet sure. But not a mate. Although if the guard had anything to say about it, it could become a possibility. Not that he could tell his sister that. Not yet anyways. "Alright. How about Asteria for me?"

"Hmm. No. she is sooo mean. She makes Tenanye cry."

He had to stop himself before he stormed from the room to strangle the miserable piece of flesh. No one... absolutely no one made his baby sister cry. Forcing himself to remain calm he asked, "And how did she make her cry?"

Estare shrugged, "Mama told her to. Pick again." She turned and began her inspection of his room. Another ritual. One that said that she knew that he was mad. The move was simply to give him the few seconds that he needed to think straight.

Their mother told... He needed a way to get Tenanye out of here. And once Estare was out of the room, he could start to plan. Start to...

"Ohhh. What is that?"

Secrets, Lies and Betrayal
by: M.L. Ruscsak

He glanced over to what had held Estara's attention, glad it was something other than her favorite game. There, hovering just above his desk was a box. Worn and dirt covered. "I don't know. Should we open it and find out?"

She clapped excitedly.

Not trusting his mother not to be spying on him, he sealed the room with black mist. Another thing that was forbidden. He would be punished later, but right now it didn't matter. His privacy, on the other hand, did.

Standing up, he tentatively grabbed the box. Wiping some of the dirt off it, he noticed that it was made from heavy silver with crystal inlays. Turning it over he examined every side just before using his thumbs to lift the lid. Nothing but a small scroll. A single drop of blue blood resting on the edge. "Looks like I have a message. Would you mind if I read it alone?"

Estare shrugged. After all, a small child had no use for messages... Unless those messages were to tell about a secret stash of sweets. "I will play with Tenanye."

He nodded as she left his mist filled the room. Alone once more he slowly unrolled the parchment worried it would crumble with his touch. Relief washed through him when it didn't. Then he began reading.

My dearest grandson,

You do not know my name since I have been cast out of every bit of our history. Fear not, I am long dead or at least I presume I will be. My name Is Primitiva. Avyanna was my daughter, not that of my dear sister Starlis. What you know as our history is not all true.

The box that you now hold is similar to a tribute box. I crafted this one myself. Anything held within it cannot die. Will not be less than it was the day it was placed inside. This may become useful to you one day. Keep it with you always. But know it is dangerous. May will try to take it from you. More will try to use the power that is contained for themselves.

Do not let any ever have possession of this box.

Now for the point of this letter. You need to know the truth about the tributes before it is too late. I have seen your future but not your name. It is split between two outcomes. I know not what you will choose. So, I offer this.

Secrets, Lies and Betrayal
by: M.L. Ruscsak

155

Go to the room of tribute· Watch the images of those who came before· If what you see gives the response, I hope you will find another letter· If not...

Know you did not disappoint your ancestors nor me· What you do is no worse than any before you· Your mother will never tell you, but I am very proud to have you continuing my line· You will make a fine king·

Do not waste time debating what choice you seek·

- Your grandmother

Prim.

Myrddin landed hard on his bed. Primitiva wrote this? She wrote to him? He had heard stories, mostly from Magmas about her. So, he knew she was terribly gifted and had taken her own life. But she knew what was going to happen several generations after her death.

How? No one had that gift. No one.

His heart sped up in a way it hadn't before. The room of tribute? The hall? Or was there another room? Either way, it was beneath the palace and required a great

Secrets, Lies and Betrayal
by: M.L. Ruscsak

deal of ability to open the seal. In fact, only the queen could...

... No, wait.

There was another way in. His mother kept her pets down there. He just had to find a way to slip pass them.

Pulling out his book, he quickly skimmed the pages. He didn't need healing nor spells that caused the wounds. Didn't need the ones to float objects at will. Well, yes, he did, but not for this. That would be a grand trick to teach his sister. Turning another, he froze...

It hadn't occurred to him this book had been hand written until now. Invisibility. Skin as thick as stone. Body armor. These spells have been added to the book... they had been written by his grandmother. How? This book was written after her death... after she jumped into the void. So how did she write...

No. One question at a time.

First, he needed to see what she wanted... no... needed him to see. Then maybe the second note... letter... would explain a few things to him. Or so he hoped.

Secrets, Lies and Betrayal
by: M.L. Ruscsak

CHAPTER 2: MAGMAS

Holding his Seer's Stone firmly in his narrowing fingers Magmas watched the boy who would steal his throne. Watch him lie almost helpless on his common narrow bed. His midnight blue blood dripping to floor below. Perhaps this time he would do the realm a favor and just die.

Then Myrddin moved. Damn child.

Seraphina had done her best to end the little beast. Even through the red hue of the stone, he could see the bones barely covered with blood and skin. Yet somehow the cursed child was still alive. Somehow the blasted child had survived every spell and incantation that his mother had said perfectly.

Secrets, Lies and Betrayal
by: M.L. Ruscsak

He survived even the beatings from the dark Fey, who had used the boy for their choice to strengthen their own merciless abilities.

Tossing the Seer's stone to the table Magmas paced the confines of these private rooms. Back and forth in front of the table. Such useless motion. Back and forth, each step stroking his fury. Each step radiating with new rage. He was a ruler Pallas, it should not be this hard to end a single Fey.

A single threat to all that the Fey really were.

He had tried so many things throughout the endless light cycles to end this abomination. He had given him books... laced with poisons... books that even he; The King, could not open without threat of death. Yet, the books that should have killed Myrddin the moment that he opened them somehow allowed for him... this forbidden nuisance... not only to open and read the long-outlawed book but the spells actually worked for him.

Flames of molten magma escaped from his fingers destroying most of the positions within the room. Destroying the table yet leaving the stone. As he thought back to the moment of learning that Myrddin had survived the gift that he had given him.

Of course, at the time he had been enraged that his plan to end the boy right then and there had failed. Angered that the boy had escaped death. But it had offered another

Secrets, Lies and Betrayal
by: M.L. Ruscsak

solution. Myrddin was young and naive. Too easy was for an outsider to gain his trust. Too easy for him the ruler of Pallas to offer him guidance that the boy soaked up.

In a few days it would be no different. Smear the boy's reputation. Find a reason for the people of his home star to completely abandon him... find a way...

Magmas retrieved the stone and brought it closer to his long haggard face to get a better look. Prim. He should have known she would have spelled something for the boy to find it. Damn her. She should have been his wife. She should have been his slave. Her powers, her gifts should have been his for the taking.

Damn her.

Yet...

Setting the stone back on the polished stone on one of the few remaining empty shelves, Magmas let a cruel a bitter smile twitched his chapped lips. The former creator had just given him a way to end her chosen heir. A way to end her entire line.

And this time he wouldn't fail. This time Myrddin would die.

Secrets, Lies and Betrayal
by: M.L. Ruscsak

Secrets, Lies and Betrayal
by: M.L. Ruscsak

CHAPTER 3: MYRDDIN

Myrddin waited until he was sure everyone… mainly his mother… were in their rooms for the night. Then and only then did he try the incantation for the invisibility, but didn't notice anything different until he passed a flat stone that reflected what passed before it. Instead of seeing himself or his black robe that he preferred to wear he only saw the wall behind him. Well, I guess it worked. He thought as he hurried down the corridors.

Passing several hallways, he finally stopped and pressed his hand on a solid wall. Not one that you could see through but completely solid. A hard push and he stepped back as it swung outward. Interesting.

He wondered which ancestor placed this wall here? Yet another question that he would like an answer to but one he doubted he ever would receive.

Secrets, Lies and Betrayal
by: M.L. Ruscsak

The steps within the door were damp, and the room smelled stale. Carefully he made his way to the bottom. There sleeping on the cold ground were his mother's pets. Naked males. One or two from Lunaista the rest had been given to her by other Star Cities. His mother had granted each a child. That child sent away as soon as it had been born. None of them were possible heirs to the throne, but rather would be raised in whatever Star City their sire had come from and one day either be chosen for the culling or live as a worker. Their life decided the moment of birth. Decided just by the color of their blood and the power each could wield.

Pushing the thought of his other siblings from his mind, Myrddin carefully continued through the stark room trying to find a door... or something that would lead him to where he needed to be. Finally, his hand passed through what should have been a solid wall. Cautiously he allowed himself to pass completely through.

The catacombs. He had heard about this place. The place where tribute boxes were held. The power contained in each feeding the star. Having no idea on how it works, he slid a single one out of its self.

Empty.

They all couldn't be empty. So, he opened another. A piece of flesh. As thin as paper but only two fingers wide. But the power that rose from it when he carefully touched

Secrets, Lies and Betrayal
by: M.L. Ruscsak

it. The power coursed through his veins energizing him... feeding him. Power. Untrained. Unused. Raw power. It was intoxicating. Carefully, he set the second box back on its shelf. The first now held at his side so that later he could examine it more closely.

He wanted to know its secrets. No, he needed to know them.

Carefully, he continued down the long dark corridor that he could now see curved and sloped downward. At the end, another door. This one stained blue. Such an odd color. Why would anyone want a door the color of dried royal Fey blood? Dried... blood. He pulled his hand away the moment he realized what it was.

His stomach turned inside him. The contents of his dinner threatening to escape his throat. Swallowing hard, he forced the door open. The hall of tribute. A small picture hung for each who had been a tribute. Their name etched into the frame. Nothing more. So many children. Long hair. Their eyes filled with joy, presuming excited they were going to be a tribute. Older men... his father's age some a bit older. Their eyes scared. One, he could see the tears already glazing the sun yellow eyes.

Yes, something was wrong here. Very wrong.

But what? Everything he had been told was that it was the sole job of the royal children to be offered as a

Secrets, Lies and Betrayal
by: M.L. Ruscsak

tribute. It had always been a secret as to what that meant exactly. No one would tell anyone what it meant. No one ever told the ones who would be tribute what it meant. Now? Finding all of the boxes… all of the pictures. Now he had to know.

A final door and he froze. A talking image stood before him.

"As the new royal Fey, I congratulate you. It is now time to sacrifice your tributes."

Sacrifice? What did it mean sacrificing?

Not knowing if the image would answer questions he asked, "Can you show me what I must do?"

On the platform, but a few feet away, another image. This one, a male. The one he had seen in the picture with tears in his eyes. He laid back on the table. Even from a distance Myrddin could see his pulse racing.

A woman appeared beside him.

A moment longer and he saw that it was his mother. A long knife in her hands. "Mother asked to make this quick. I would rather not." Then the knife slid down his leg. A paper-thin piece of flesh being removed.

In horror, he watched as the man… a man that must have been his grandfather… Watched as his mother started

Secrets, Lies and Betrayal
by: M.L. Ruscsak

to remove his flesh. Then a machine covered him. He didn't know if it was the machine or his grandfather screaming...

He turned then lost his meal. Before the machine lifted, he bolted from the room, tears streaking down his face. There was no way he was going to allow his sisters to be sacrificed. None.

There had to be another way. There had to be.

Surely Prim wouldn't have sent him there if there wasn't. She couldn't have been that cruel?

Then again? What did he know about her except she had taken her own life?

For two days Myrddin refusal even from... Refused to partake in any of royal duties. Refuse to bonus deals with the guards. All of which was a much better option than seeing a woman who would not only kill her own father but two of her children as well. But today was different. Today he couldn't hide. Today the ruler of Pallas would arrive.

Secrets, Lies and Betrayal
by: M.L. Ruscsak

Once Magmas arrived and be his only chance to get some answers for tonight would be too late.

Tonight, it would be the cure and dinner filled with most prominent Fey in all of Lunaista. Worry filled him about... oh what tonight would bring. Worry about what his mother may do. But, regardless of what his mother had planned for the entertainment for dinner... he needed to speak to Magmas the very moment that his coach landed.

That much decided Myrddin the hastily readied himself. The very second that he was dressed in his formal attire... a black vest and black knee-length kilt... he called it a kilt everyone else called it a skirt... and black sandals. He raced to where the carriage would land.

Then waited.

His eyes ever consonant watching the on goings in the city. His body always tense and rigid, preparing for any attack. You'd needless preparation to be sure, still he couldn't be too careful. as his eyes scanned the and the area he watched the citizens who were mulling about as usual. No-one spoke to him as his mother forbade this. That was fine. Today he didn't need friends. He didn't need anyone asking him what he was doing. He didn't need anything from those who lived on this star.

Catching movement from the Void, he saw the messengers coming in for the landing. Watched the coach bobble and sway as it grew closer. Watched as the size doubled, then doubled again. It was huge in comparison to the ones owned by his mother. Was so large in fact that it was being carried by a team of six messengers instead of the usual three. His stomach rolled thinking it was carrying tribute boxes. Boxes that carried the flesh of the recently killed.

Before the carriage could even stop the door flung open and Magmas stood his long red robe hanging loosely from his thinning body. "Myrddin, my boy. You look unwell. Come sit."

Bowing slightly, he hurried inside before he breathed out a sigh of relief at not seeing anything then a finally furnished travel coach. Breathed in relief at not seeing a single gold tribute box anywhere within the single room. "Thank you, my lord."

Magmas narrowed his eyes just a hair. Just enough to convey annoyance, but nothing more, "Come now. We are alone. No-one can hear you nor see you inside. And I do recall telling you several times to not call me lord. I have a name and I do like to hear it time and again."

"I would like to know about Primitiva." Myrddin blurted out before comprehending what Magmas was even saying. Blurted out words that had had spent days trying to form into a reasonable request.

Magmas smiled, "So you finally found her box." He leaned forward in his seat rocking the coach ever so slightly. "But before we speak about her I must have your word you never repeat what I am about to tell you. Not to a living soul. Not even to yourself in the dead of night."

Well, that could not be good. Not coming from this Fey… this King. Without hesitation Myrddin nodded once, "You have my word. Her name nor what we say here will ever escape my lips."

"Good then I will start at the beginning so you might understand." Magmas leaned back in his seat and closed his lava red eyes. Slowly laced his long boney fingers before finally speaking. "Long before I was the Lord over all of the Star Cities I was King of Osirus. Another his name was Azia was then Lord and master over all. Prim… that what she would later choose to be called… knew when she was being watched.

Much like you, she would close herself in a wall of mist so none could see her. No-one except me. It wasn't

Secrets, Lies and Betrayal
by: M.L. Ruscsak

until much later she told me flat out that she always knew when I was watching. I saw only what she wanted me to. Of course, at that time, I also wanted her as my mate. And my spying was a way to figure out how to make that happen." Magmas opened one eye to make sure Myrddin was paying attention before he continued.

Seeing that he had a captivated audience, he slowly leaned forward, "Then one day as I was watching her she dove into the void. Just before she did, I swear she looked at me. She knew something, but at the time I didn't understand what she was planning.

Enraged and hurt, I went to Azia. Looking back, I shouldn't have. I was a fool to trust him. A bigger fool for allowing what happen next."

Myrddin leaned back in his seat trying to remember the history of his own Star City. "You are speaking of the rule of Avyanna?"

Magmas nodded once, "In a way, yes. Avyanna was declared the daughter of Starlis. I knew better. She wasn't born, but rather created by Prim just few days before she leaped into the void. Azia raised her. In his eyes Starlis was weak. She couldn't control those who lived on this star. She didn't care for pain nor making those around her suffer. Still, he allowed her to rule until Avyanna was old enough to."

Secrets, Lies and Betrayal
by: M.L. Ruscsak

Myrddin leaned forward in awe, "I forget how old you really are."

Magmas waved his words off with a little flare, "Living in Pallas has some advantages. Now, should I continue?"

"Please?"

Closing his eyes once more Magmas spoke as those he was seeing everything that has happened. "Before she ascended Azia brought her to Osirus. He told her to test my boys. All three of them. The two that failed were tossed into the void. The other. Flint. He was my youngest. He wasn't allowed to be taken care of while Azia visited. I watched him die. To this day, I cannot go back Osiris."

For a moment, both were silent, then, Myrddin quietly said, "I'm sorry we don't have to continue. I had no right to pry."

"No, you have had much right to hear this as I do." Magmas paused for several long moments letting the memories come back to him. Finally, he spoke once again. His voice low and hushed. "My other two boys did not die in the void. Prim found them. I am grateful every day that she did. My eldest took one of my red orbs. It was what I used to see other Star Cities. Prim made it work so we could speak as need be.

Azia was already at this time looking to expand his reach. Until then, there were only about a thousand or so

Star Cities. And thousand more that none had explored yet. Because of Prim, the one that she took for her home was now glowing with Fey blood."

He could see things clearly now. See the corruptions that Magmas was speaking of even if he hadn't said the words. See the intent of Azia as the one who had wanted to rule all of the settled Star Cities. "And Azia wanted to conquer it."

"Exactly. He had just killed my child. The body wasn't even allowed to be taken to the catacombs. He too was tossed into the void. Betrayed, Angered and feeling reckless I reached out to the other Star Cities. Not to cause war, but so they understood what the Azia was now allowing.

It took years before he was ready to rage war. By then Avyanna was queen and Starlis went to live in Pallas. And I say live very loosely. When I found her, she was just a shell of what she had once been. She was placed in the catacombs while still alive. Her powers and abilities drained away a little more every day."

"And the war?"

Closing his eyes Magmas smiled bitterly, "Prim won, but at great cost to her. Aricia was already born by then. That was Avyanna's daughter. Born to a man who was her pet not her consort. But because of the war, she could not

Secrets, Lies and Betrayal
by: M.L. Ruscsak

send her away. I raised Aricia the best that I could, but Avyanna was killed. Prim took care of that herself.

Of course, that was after Avyanna killed all those who Prim loved. Both her consort and her first creations. After the war, the Star Cities started to revolt. They couldn't let Prim rule a place that didn't answer to Pallas. Nor did she want to rule Pallas and leave her home. She vanished after that.

I took over Pallas and have been slowly banning the cruelty as best that I can. Do too much, and the royal Fey threatens war. Do too little and innocent die. It is a constant battle."

Closing his eyes Myrddin reached into the waist of his kilt pulling out a piece of paper, "Prim was a seer?"

Magmas moved the curtain of the coach just enough to see the Fey scurry about darting from building to building. Just enough to remember that there had been a time when those in this Star City were revered for their abilities and their temperament. Lost in his own thoughts Magmas spoke more to himself than to his young ward. "Prim was a lot of things. Healer. Seer. Creator. There was nothing that the Fey could do that she could not do better. Why?"

Cautiously Myrddin held out the letter hoping for answers, "This was in the box?"

Secrets, Lies and Betrayal
by: M.L. Ruscsak

Taking the smooth parchment, carefully Magmas read it, "And you saw the truth?"

The gore from what he has seen caught in his throat. For a long moment, he could only sit there resisting the urge to lose his meal. After forcing the contents of his stomach back down, Myrddin finally whispered, "I did. Is there some other way?"

"There is. In fact, it works better I think, but the royal Fey are not so forthcoming to try it. One day, I hope, but not now."

Now to ask the question he needed and hope it wasn't a fool's dream. "How do I save my sisters?"

"Are you sure about this? There is no turning back once I tell you."

Myrddin nodded once in earnest, "I'm sure."

"Very well. One will have to stay behind. Knowing both of your sisters, I recommend the middle one. She may never forgive you for leaving her, but she will be of great help to me."

"Alright. If she can help end the slaughter of children, I will leave her here."

Pulling in the pocket of his robe, he held out a letter. "I have been carrying this around since the day you were born. I think it is time that you now read it."

Secrets, Lies and Betrayal
by: M.L. Ruscsak

"Have you?"

"No. Prim said it was for you. And after she helped to end the great war, she told me it was for you to read only. I dared not cross her. Not then nor now."

Why? Is she not dead? Or when you said vanished did you mean something else. Not that Myrddin could ask that. Not that he would even if it was acceptable. But think it? Oh yes, he was free to think anything that he pleased. Taking the letter ne nodded in what could be a bow. "Thank you. If you wouldn't mind may, I read this in my room?"

"Of course. I think I kept your mother waiting long enough." He patted Myrddin's knee. "Wait until I have left the main street before you exit."

"Why?"

Magmas looked over his shoulder and smiled, "My boy you do understand what people think is going on in here."

Puzzled, he shook his head.

Opening the door Magmas stood on the street and turned back to look at Myrddin, "Maybe it is best you don't."

"Magmas?"

"Let them think what they will. Soon it will not matter."

Secrets, Lies and Betrayal
by: M.L. Ruscsak

CHAPTER 4: MAGMAS

Seraphina paced her dark crystal throne room, glaring at the ruler of Pallas. Glaring at the man who had promised her power. "I have done as you asked, yet Myrddin still lives. He survives poison that can kill even the most powerful Fey. He has survived being burned by fire both natural and otherwise. Nothing I do seems to faze him more than a few moments." She paused, letting a demented gleeful smile twitch her lips, "Although those few moments of hearing his tormented screams are most pleasing... and the power that his blood gives me..."

Magmas lounge on the royal throne lazily listing to this queen both reeling from the distress that her ward was not yet dead. Listing to her boast about the power that just

Secrets, Lies and Betrayal
by: M.L. Ruscsak

the tiniest bit of Myrddin's blood had given her. How intoxicating it was to those who came in contact with it.

It was something that he wanted for himself. Something he needed to slow the progression of the wasteful disease that he had developed during the war. Or perhaps it was the same disease that led to the easy demise of the late Azia. Either way Myrddin was the key to his own salvation. The key to conquer the rest of the Star Cities. And the Key to end the threat that was Primitiva.

"No worries my dear. We will just play this out a bit longer then you will join me on Pallas and bare me an heir that is worthy of my name. We'll just have to see if your middle child can be trained properly to rule this star of if I shall father one for this little trove of power."

Glee lit Seraphina's bright violet eyes. "Baring children is not an easy task my lord, but for you I would happily bear more if that is what you think best."

Slowly he stood from the throne and with a serpent's grace stepped over to her his hand caressing her young thin face trailing down her neck. His fingers sliding the strap her shift off of her shoulder exposing her. He watched as the hunger danced in her eyes before lightly kissing her neck. "Just a little longer my dear. You are almost ripe enough. Even now I feel your powers growing. Powers that will nurture my child once I give it to you."

Secrets, Lies and Betrayal
by: M.L. Ruscsak

Too quickly he turned from her then hissed. Something or someone was watching him… he could feel it. "Now dress for dinner. I have a surprise for the boy. Then all too soon you and your daughter will join me on Pallas as a proxy of my choosing rules this star."

"Of course, my lord." Seraphina grabbed her shift from the floor not bothering to dress before leaving Magmas alone. Before summoning all of the requested guess to this dinner to play the game that would leave Myrddin feeling confident about leaving with the Lord of Pallas.

Alone once more Magmas stepped out onto one of the famed balconies of Lunaista. His lava red eyes trained on the midnight sky of the Void. He could feel eyes watching him. Could feel someone watching him even if the other stone had been lost just before the Great War.

Speaking to the sky he growled, "I can feel you watching my dear. I can feel you breathing on my neck." He

Secrets, Lies and Betrayal
by: M.L. Ruscsak

paused, "Jealous my dear that I found a little minx that wants to bear my children."

Laughing cold and bitter he smiled feeling the eyes with drawing.

"Soon you will learn why you should have joined me on Pallas. Soon I will have you all to myself."

Secrets, Lies and Betrayal
by: M.L. Ruscsak

CHAPTER 5: MYRDDIN

The moment Myrddin was back in his room, he sealed himself inside with his mist no longer trying to figure out what Magmas had meant. He could do without one more question that he needed an answer to. Quickly he unfolded the soft paper. It had a smell to it. One he could never find in this Star City. One that he doubted was on any for that matter. Then he read;

My darling grandson,

If Magmas had given you this letter, then you know the truth of the catacombs. We know how to change it, but it is yet too soon. Your first born will hold the answers.

Secrets, Lies and Betrayal
by: M.L. Ruscsak

I see her now in my dreams. She is strong and beautiful. Wise beyond her years. She is the queen that the Star Cities need. She is the queen that will once again make my home whole.

The woman you seek to be her mother has never been to the stars, for now, those things are forbidden. Fear not, you will know here the moment you meet. Your powers will eclipse hers but none the less she will be strong.

Both you and your daughter will be needed to rid the catacombs of the innocent blood. But I cannot tell you all there is. There still much that has yet to be decided.

Come to my star. As a whole, it has no name. It is splintered now into several different… what we call countries… You must seek out Alista. She is the granddaughter of Magmas. She is rude and spiteful yet fair. She rules what is now called Feyen. She does so with my approval.

She will take care of you as you should be taken care of. You have my word for that.

However, before you come to my star there are things you must do. And they must be done quickly or those who will seek to destroy you will. This is my only warning.

First, go the catacombs. I'm sorry I could not risk you doing this before. Each box is engraved with a symbol. Each symbol represents a power. Choose a minimum of three. More if you wish. Know this the power you will then possess will transfer to your first born. Choose wisely.

Secrets, Lies and Betrayal
by: M.L. Ruscsak

Second, anything you wish to bring with you must be able to carry both by incantations and in a bag that you can wear. Do not hinder your wings.

And lastly, once you take your sister. Run. Do not look back. Do not stop for anyone. Run.

-Prim

Wonderful. Just wonderful. He had to go back to the one place he didn't want to. He should leave now before the dinner. But...

He let out a long deep sign. No. She had faith in him. And he would not misplace that faith no matters the cost. However, he could...

"Brother? Mother is waiting."

Damn. Estare. If she was here then, it would be time for whatever his mother was planning. Except he was planning something too. And he would need Magmas' help. He just hoped the great lord of the Star Cities would be willing.

Secrets, Lies and Betrayal
by: M.L. Ruscsak

182

The royal dining hall was filled not with just their little family or Magmas… but with most of the citizens of Lunaista. Whatever was about to play out was going to be done to show the people how unworthy he was. That was fine it didn't matter after tonight he would no longer be here.

Raising his head, he met his mother's gaze. Chose not to address her, but their honored guest. "My lord, have you had a good visit?"

A twinkle of mischief glistened in Magmas' eye, "As always Queen Seraphina's taste in entertainment bores me. I grow tired of watching displays in cruelty. I have yet to see any Star City come up something truly original."

And there it was… The king of all of the Star Cities declaring there would be no display that involved blood… least not tonight. His mother did seem unpleased. In fact, she looked ready to let her temper sore. If she did, he would accent tonight and that she would never allow.

Taking a sip of his honeyed nectar Myrddin tipped his glass toward Magmas, "I'm sorry to hear that. Perhaps my little sister can show you her flying routine. Granted, it does just by a little girl, but it is mildly entertaining."

The citizens started to murmur around him. All approving of how he was handling the high king… their lord.

Secrets, Lies and Betrayal
by: M.L. Ruscsak

Magmas leaned back in his chair. "I would like that. It has been some time since I have seen a child gleefully play in the air." He turned to Queen Seraphina, "You wouldn't mind indulging me Lady Seraphina. Or did you have something else planned for this evening?"

She smiled so sweetly. Even managed to hide the anger in her voice, "Not at all my lord. But truly Estare is really a novice in flying. I'm sure watching the future ruler of our little Star City test his mantle would be far more entertaining."

"My dear, Myrddin has already been tested to my satisfaction. And that is the only one that matters. Now..." He paused to lock eyes with Myrddin once more. "... I have changed my mind. Those who are not of the royal house return to your homes I wish privacy while I dine."

No one protested as they filed out.

Once the room cleared Magmas raised his voice, "Myrddin my boy, I believe I asked you to gather some things for me. Do so now. I would like to leave after my meal."

He knew. Somehow Magmas knew. Bowing slightly, he replied, "Of course, my lord. Shall I place them in your carriage?"

Secrets, Lies and Betrayal
by: M.L. Ruscsak

"Yes, that will be fine. I also decided you and your youngest sister will accompany me back to Pallas. There are things there that may aid you for when you are king."

"Thank you, my lord. I will retrieve her now."

Secrets, Lies and Betrayal
by: M.L. Ruscsak

CHAPTER 6: MAGMAS

It was too easy to manipulate this boy. Too easy to get him to play right into his hands. Too easy to lead this boy to his certain demise. Did Prim really think that her line would be allowed to create some immortal creature? Did she really think after he, the great Magmas, would allow for it to happen after he had access to the entire library of Pallas?

Did she? Or did she hope to bare that child herself??

But that was a matter for another day. Right now, he needed to work up his once feared temper. A temper that kept fools from challenging him. A temper that was the reason for remaining the ruler of Pallas. Well, his temper wasn't all that kept him ruling the great Star City... but how

Secrets, Lies and Betrayal
by: M.L. Ruscsak

many actually knew it wasn't he who had slain the former Azia? How many knew his secrets?

Ah, but soon even they would be destroyed. Five insignificant stars. A few thousand Fey. Not much of an army. Not much of a threat. And all too soon even they would be destroyed. Just as soon as he figured out how to tap into the power of the golden tribute boxes.

Just as soon as he had the power of the long forgotten silent ones.

A deep breath and Magmas pushed away from the long crystal dining table. The once see through walls now covered and embedded with the ash that had coverall all of the Star Cities after the end of Azia. As to why no one had ever been able to guess, but it was enough to bring his temper to a boil.

Just remembering that fool. Just remembering it was because of him that his heir had been raised by the creature Primitiva. An heir that had turned from him and aligned himself with her. An heir that was now ruling one of those forbidden stars.

Bah.

His low chair crashed to the floor. His lava red eyes locking on the queen of this star. The queen who would be the key to birthing a true heir of Pallas. "I want every speck of this soot gone by next return. I grow tired of seeing it."

Secrets, Lies and Betrayal
by: M.L. Ruscsak

Exiting the palace Magmas watched as the scared and frightened Fey scurried away from him. Watched as a once feared race of dark Fey now cowered before him. No longer did children play in the street. No longer did grown men teach their offspring the art of battle.

No, that had been outlawed for many years before. Only those taken to the stars that now housed the massive army were allowed to be trained to fight. Their powers nurtured in the art of doing harm to their enemies. Those who showed weakness and compassion killed without a second thought. Sometimes if their power strong enough, they were given some honor and they would become tributes. The rest tossed into the void. Whatever happed to their bodies no one could say for certain?

But he knew without a second thought. The pull of Pallas would come to them and nothing more would remain.

Secrets, Lies and Betrayal
by: M.L. Ruscsak

Secrets, Lies and Betrayal
by: M.L. Ruscsak

CHAPTER 7: MYRDDIN

His heart pounded in his chest as he raced up to his small room. He didn't have time to think about what to take and what to leave behind. No time to neatly pack. Magmas would want to leave the very moment that he had finished his meal. Glancing only at his desk, Myrddin rushed over and pulled out all of his book unsure if he would be returning or not. Unsure if he would be permitted to take these books with him once he left. Leafing through the pages he found the incantation to create a bottomless sack out of the mist. A similar spell to the one that he used to make his desk. It would hold until he reached the carriage. Hold long enough for him to neatly stack the scores of books to show Magmas the care that he has taken to keep them safe.

Two straps of mist pulled over his shoulders

Secrets, Lies and Betrayal
by: M.L. Ruscsak

and he hurried down the long hallway to the nursery
wing. Every step the decor becoming more elegant. Gifts
from the other Star Cities proudly displayed. Fames of gold
and crystal. Wall hangings woven from the hair of a
Fey. Soft tusks velvet to the touch. One of mother's prized
possessions. Something he now worried had
been taken from a tribute before their lives were taken.

Not something he could prove. Not something he
would ever question. Still, it was a possibility. Just as it was
a possibility that every item that was displayed had come
from one tribute or another. Not to remember them by but
because they no longer had need of it.

Swinging into the nursery he saw Tenanye sleeping
in her cream-colored cradle. Her head of soft black curls
crowing her little head. So peaceful and innocent. How
could anyone ever wish to do her harm? How could her
mother want to destroy a child that she herself had given
life to?

Shaking the thought off, Myrddin carefully lifted her
into his arms. Then slowly wrapping his
black translucent wings around her. Softly he whispered,
"Just sleep, my little sister. Just sleep."

Secrets, Lies and Betrayal
by: M.L. Ruscsak

Softly rocking his sister, Myrddin paused as

Magmas yanked the door of the carriage open. Keeping his movements slow and steady he stopped altogether when Magmas hissed, "Your mother is a vile woman. I will be glad when she is no longer ruling. Perhaps serving the people of Pallas will do something for her temperament."

Finally taking a seat Myrddin winced. "Or she could try to sway them to revolt."

Closing the door Magmas fussily took a seat near the front of the carriage and furthest away from the neatly stacked books. "Doubtful. Those who live in Pallas have little tolerance for the like of her." Magmas took a deep breath, "You brought your books?"

Myrddin glanced down at his little sister pulling her

Secrets, Lies and Betrayal
by: M.L. Ruscsak

closer to his chest. "I did. As well as everything that belongs to my sister. Or at least the things she will need."

Leaning back in his seat Magmas gave a forced smile, "You will be returning in a fortnight. I trust Prim told you that you would need to do something before you left this little Star City?"

Nodding once Myrddin softly replied, "She told me that I would need to absorb the powers from at least three tributes boxes and to choose wisely."

"Ah. Then it is good that I am taking you to Pallas. The strongest are always sent there. There is a special room that I think you will find the powers that would be most beneficial. Take what you will. It matters not to me."

For more than a breath Myrddin didn't speak, but let himself absorb Magmas' words. "Magmas, why are you helping me? It's widely known that you have ordered the beatings of others before they ascend. So why spare me?"

Glancing out of the window, seeing the light of Lunaista fading into the void Magmas stared out for

Secrets, Lies and Betrayal
by: M.L. Ruscsak

several long minutes before responding, "My boy... Prim asked very little of me after the war. She swore my bloodline would always rule something within her kingdom. In exchange I was to make sure no harm, permanent harm would come to you. I promise to teach you what you would need, but never let the darkness seep into your heart. After seeing she not only saved my boys, but found matches for them that not fit them as men, but complemented their abilities... I would do anything for her. She kept them and their families safe during the war. Even when it looked like she... We... would lose, she still kept them safe."

"Thank you."

"Don't thank me. Thank her. If she had never found that star I would have lost all of my children and you would have been killed at birth. But enough about what if and back to the here and now. In exchange for giving you the powers of Pallas I ask one small thing from you. When the time is right, you must return. I do not care if you return to rule as you should, or only to help me end the suffering on all of the Star Cities that still use pain as entertainment. It makes no difference as to which. But you must return."

"You have my word. Prim said I was to have a

daughter, once she is of age to rule... whatever age that may be. I will return and assist in any way that I can."

Secrets, Lies and Betrayal
by: M.L. Ruscsak

CHAPTER 8: MAGMAS

The lights of Pallas slowly came into through the endless black Void. Across from him both Myrddin and the useless baby slept as the carriage swayed. The forbidden books… the cursed parchment… was once again stacked neatly in the far corner with an invisible web like netting keeping them from falling. Soon he would be rid of both. Soon the boy would feed the void along with the infant.

A deep breath and Magmas closed his lava red eyes. He needed to make this believable. Need to fool the boy by letting him think the powers of Pallas would respond to him. Oh yes, let the boy in the great tribute hall, touching the powers that would forever be just beyond his grips. Absorbing the powers of the greatest Fey in all of the Star

Secrets, Lies and Betrayal
by: M.L. Ruscsak

Cities just to have the powers turn on him and wither away before ever truly being accepted by his body.

Ha. It was a wonderful plan. A wonderful dream.

A dream to watch Prim suffer. A dream that still kept him protected should she ever show herself. But more importantly, one that would rid the realm of the boy who would bring death and war once again to their home.

The boy who would father Nisha. Father the Fey that would call forth the Silent Ones once again.

Secrets, Lies and Betrayal
by: M.L. Ruscsak

CHAPTER 9 MYRDDIN

The catacombs of Pallas were not what he had expected. The ones on Lunaista were dark and gloomy. Here? The floor was made of white and gold stones. The walls lined with the tribute boxes. Some silver, others gold. Some even made from black stone. And so many more colors that he could not yet describe. Each box set in its own place. The empty ones now stacked in a room all to themselves. The rest...

Glowing with power.

For a long moment Myrddin just stood in awe. Slowly he began to speak. "I know I should be appalled at this but..."

Magmas patted Myrddin's back almost in a fatherly gesture as he cut his young ward off, "The tributes are honored here. This is my doing. Now for business. The most

Secrets, Lies and Betrayal
by: M.L. Ruscsak

powerful are kept behind the far door. Each shelf holds a different ability. Those that held more than one ability are along the right wall."

Letting his eyes follow the long walls till finally settling on a gold ornate door with crystal shards that sparkled in the soft light of the room. "You're not coming…"

"My boy the less I know for a fact the happier I will be. I will be in the nursery with your sister when you're done. Then we will start to teach you about your new abilities. Know this each one you choose will be a natural one after today. I knew Prim for but a short time. But I think as her kin, you should choose the darker abilities. It is just a suggestion. For all I care, you can choose them all." Magmas turned the before leaving said, "Choose what you would like for your daughter. If Prim thinks it will be passed down to her then it will be."

Myrddin waited until he could no longer hear the footfalls of Magmas echoing down the hall. Waited until he could quell his nerves enough to move. He would be happy just ruling his little star and watching his sisters find worthy mates. This was not what he wanted, but he would need to make this work.

Pushing the golden door open he took a deep breath, then tried to allow his eyes to adjust to the light. A light brighter than anything he had ever seen before. Bright luminescent light filled the small room. Slowly he started to

Secrets, Lies and Betrayal
by: M.L. Ruscsak

make out the shapes of the boxes. Even slower where each shelf was and where it ended. Between six and two dozen boxes on each shelf. More than three dozen shelves filling the room.

How would he ever choose?

Magmas had told him to choose for his daughter. So... what would he wish for her to be?

Intelligent. Fast. A quick thinker. Strong.

All good qualities, but none were actual abilities.

Carefully, he removed a black box from itself. Shapeshifter. He had never heard of it before but...

The lid slid off and a thick piece of flesh lay in the bottom. Not thinking about what he was doing, he allowed his finger to lightly touch flesh. Power coursed through him just before every bone in his body snapped then reshaped. Just before the pain overtook him. Just before the power became his savior.

Not knowing how long he had laid on the floor, he peered into the box. Empty now. Gone was the flesh and with it, its power.

Leaving the box on the floor, he took another. This time, he didn't read it. It didn't matter, he had permission to choose one of each and right now... right at this very second. That sounded like the best advice that he could ever receive.

Secrets, Lies and Betrayal
by: M.L. Ruscsak

Secrets, Lies and Betrayal
by: M.L. Ruscsak

CHAPTER 10 MAGMAS

The boy was a damned fool. Did he not realize if Prim had left so much as a drop of blood her powers would have long ago been drained into the glory of Pallas?

Obviously not. Insolent fool.

No matter.

Even if the forsaken tributes responded, to the little fool, the powers would never transfer to anyone else. It wasn't possible. Couldn't be possible. Hadn't been possible since Pallas began to collect the tribute boxes and all of the glorious powers that were held within.

Bah.

Secrets, Lies and Betrayal
by: M.L. Ruscsak

He should have tossed the boy into the void the moment he had been born. It would have prevented all of the headaches. It would have…

… Forced Magnar's hand.

 And that was one Fey that he didn't want to cross. Not a second time. Not when those who served him were *the* most powerful Fey in all of the Star Cities. Not when the last time they had crossed paths with the famed creator had slipped into the Castle of Pallas. Not when he had been so silent, not a single alarm had sounded until after he had gone.

Damn abominations. Magmas could see why they had been outlawed so my light cycles ago.

Turning yet another corner, he took a deep breath not knowing how he came to this part of his own castle. How had he gotten to the nursery wing? How he had become to unhinge that he hadn't paid attention to where had been going.

Just something else to worry about later. Right now, …

Keeping up the appearances of being the gracious host too priority. Yes, playing with the infant who had barely learned to fly, yes, that sounded like a much better plan. Plus, should Myrddin survive opening those cursed boxes, then playing with the child would make sense. Of

Secrets, Lies and Betrayal
by: M.L. Ruscsak

course, if Myrddin died... then snapping the neck of this child would become all too easy.

Either way being in this room made complete sense.

Secrets, Lies and Betrayal
by: M.L. Ruscsak

Secrets, Lies and Betrayal
by: M.L. Ruscsak

CHAPTER 11: MYRDDIN

Making his way to the nursery he was only half aware of the people whispering behind his back. Only partly aware of the strange glances they were giving him. Barely aware of anything as he had to hold the smooth walls just to stand upright. So, he couldn't care what those around him were saying or doing.

And didn't care about anything until he saw Magmas playing some kind of game with his baby sister that had her laughing. It was a sight that warmed his heart. Slowly entering the room was glad that his vision had returned enough to take in this rare scene. "I rarely hear her laugh like that."

Secrets, Lies and Betrayal
by: M.L. Ruscsak

Magmas barely glanced up at first, then gasped as is eyes widened in shock, "Now I know what was taking you so long."

"I don't..." It was then he caught his reflection in a smooth reflective stone. He was nearly a foot taller than he had been. His dark brown hair now midnight black. Muscles that belonged to someone with great strength. If the size of them was any indication he could crush a person's skull with only one hand. Gasping Myrddin asked, "Did you know this would happen?"

"No. But it makes sense. Those who live here are more gifted, taller and have more muscle mass than any other Star City. Now, which boxes did you open?"

Suddenly turning shy Myrddin winced, "One of each."

The flickers of something ran across Magmas' face. There and gone before it could be identified. Still, he answered as gracious hosts. "Very well. I will find books for you for each of your new skills. But first, you need this one." Carefully he handed him a box. Silver with crystal inlays.

Myrddin ran his fingers of the Inlays. Such Fine craftsmanship of a simple box. Turning it over in his hands, he asked, "Prim made this?"

Secrets, Lies and Betrayal
by: M.L. Ruscsak

Magmas let a sly smile form as he nodded, "She did. I was told you are the only one who could open it."

Carefully, he slid the lid open with his thumbs. Looking into the box he couldn't help but to feel both awed and horrified at the same time. Fore not one, but ten different pieces of flesh. "Do you know what they are from?"

"Most of them I couldn't guess. But the large black one. If I had to bet is part of Prim's wing. The white from her beloved Shesha. He was a dragon. Marvelous creature. The others I can't tell you what but I can tell you they are probably something that you cannot find in any Star City and will be needed once you arrive at her home. If not you then your first born will."

There was something in Magmas' voice that warned caution. Something inside of himself that he couldn't place. It felt like a warning.

But why? Magmas had never harmed him. Never lied to him. So why ...

Ignoring the feeling his fingers lightly touched the thin pieces of flesh. Power greater than that of the golden boxed flowed through him. For only a heartbeat then...

... His world went black.

Secrets, Lies and Betrayal
by: M.L. Ruscsak

Secrets, Lies and Betrayal
by: M.L. Ruscsak

CHAPTER 12: MAGMAS

He had spent days with the boy. Each spell that should have ended his life barely caused more than a second of inconvenience. Each poison he drank had less effect than the spells.

DAMN HIM.

Why couldn't he just die? Why couldn't he show how weak that he truly was? Why?

This had to be Magnar's doing. It had to be.

Magmas paced the long, brightly lit hall. Muttering to himself. There had to be a way. There... had... to... be...

The markers. Prim had placed them so very long ago. Sometime after they had met at the tomb of the silent ones, but before the war. Messengers could see them. Little dots

Secrets, Lies and Betrayal
by: M.L. Ruscsak

leading away from Pallas. Leading away from any known Star City. They were weak now. Centuries old.

Yes... Yes, that could work.

Destroy the markers. Give the boy the vaguest of directions. Myrddin would die in the void. His body eventually pulled into a star and hopefully burned up before it met the ground. If not... ah well... someone could take it to a tribute hall and be done with it.

A cruel smile twitched at Magmas' lips. Yes, that could work.

CHAPTER 13. MYRDDIN

Myrddin took one look around at the empty street of Lunaista. His sister held firmly within his arms. Black mist keeping her from getting loose even if his arms should fail him. Tonight, would be the last time he would ever see this Star City. The last time that he would ever be known to have lived. His mother would strip his name from history if she could. Estare would one-day rule. With hope, she would be a good Queen. With Magmas guiding her she may even be kind and nothing like their mother. Only time would tell if that would be true.

A deep breath and he focused on the cobbled street before him. Concentrated on his heavy footfalls as he darted toward the high ledge that he could use to propel himself off if this star into the Great Void. One last deep breath and his dark dragon like wings were held tight to his body. His heart hammered within his chest.

He could do this. No, he had to do this. Prim had foreseen it. Magmas had faith in him. But more importantly, it was the only way both of his darling sisters could survive.

Turning back from the platform he took several steps away before turning back. His foot falls not running as fast as his legs could carry him. A single leap, a choking gasp from the bitterly cold air and he was hurled into the Void. Only a heartbeat to get his bearings. A breath, more to find the star that had been described.

Magmas had given him a vague location. Prim didn't give one at all. A bright blue star greater in size than even Pallas. That was his only instruction. White orbs surrounded him. Each a Star City. Narrowing his eyes, he looked closer at each of the orbs. Time was running out as the cold seeped into his marrow.

A moment of hesitation. A single moment of doubt that he couldn't do this. The doubt that he would die within the Void as so many others had. A moment of resolution and clarity... then...

... Just at the edge of his vision... Bright blue. A hue that he couldn't describe. So many Shades held within the one. Darks and lights blending into radiant light. The beauty of Pallas couldn't compare.

That had to be it. It had to be.

Sheer will and determination had him diving deeper into the Void. The strength that he had taken from the catacombs of Pallas have him the speed necessary to shoot though the darkness. His own heat keeping his baby sister warm as she pressed close to his bare chest.

Pride swelled inside of him. He was doing it. He was surviving the Void. He was...

Darkness started to cloud his vision. The Blue light becoming distant. Tenanye wiggled next to him. Her cries barely audible.

He had failed.

Secrets, Lies and Betrayal
by: M.L. Ruscsak

Secrets, Lies and Betrayal
by: M.L. Ruscsak

CHAPTER 14: KARNACK

Sitting in his private room deep within the Castle of Bone, Karnack stared at the jewel that had been trusted to his care so many Light cycles ago. A gem that was a great source of information. A gem that was both a privilege and a curse to possess. A gem that was simply known as the Seer's stone.

For as long as he could remember the gem had ways felt dull. The images, bleak and gritty. The on goings of the far away Star Cities not really his concern, but those who had been cast off to the Void...

Well, most were saved one way or another. Most had been brought here long after their bodies died. Only to be

Secrets, Lies and Betrayal
by: M.L. Ruscsak

reborn by one who still possessed the ability. But that wasn't his worry today.

No. he needn't worry about the Fallen Fey, who now dwelled among the dark stars. He need not worry about the boys who had grown up calling him uncle and had proven themselves in battle during the Great War. No all of that he could ponder later.

Today, however, he had a different worry. Today his stone... the Seer's Stone... it... it's power feeling more active today than it had in years. Something was stirring. Something. A single vision held with the stone. A Fey floating helplessly within the Void. The exact spot he could say for sure.

Shesha would know. The great dragon would know within a heartbeat. Would the Goddess, allow for her precious to travel from the Under Kingdom? Would she help this young Fey? Or would have to send word to Magnar?

Only one way to tell.

Grabbing his faded black cloak, he ran through the labyrinth of bones. Passing more flesh covered doors than he ever wished to see. The heart of the castle housed all of Prims first. Not living people that he had known, but their flesh and bones. Their blood coloring the walls and floor. This castle had meant to be a place to honor the dead. A

Secrets, Lies and Betrayal
by: M.L. Ruscsak

place to house what was left of them until the final battle. But the more years that passed the more horrifying this place had become.

The favorites were long gone. The First scattered within the realm of the living. Few of the honored had ever stepped foot within these walls. As the scribe of the goddess, he didn't have a choice. Oh, but how he wished he did.

How he wished he didn't have to be the one to intrude on her now.

Throwing open the only plain wood door, he quickly dropped to his knees as the siren's call filled the room. Not a true siren, but Prim screaming at the intrusion.

Secrets, Lies and Betrayal
by: M.L. Ruscsak

With the blaring sound and his eyes forced shut, he hadn't seen her but he still pleaded, "Goddess."

A long serpent's tail coiled around his thin, narrow throat as she hissed, "What is the meaning of this Karnack?"

He clawed at the scales that cut into his neck. Gasping out an answer as he did, "The boy... he is lost in the Void. Shesha... he needs Shesha."

The tail vanished as she stepped out from behind her throne. Her hand passing lovingly over the spikes that had once been her beloved dragon. Here he was forever frozen beside her. Her very first creation. Her most loyal pet and trusted friend. Her only friend that still stood by her protecting her from the prying eyes of Pallas. Protected her from the fool that she had helped rule the Star Cities.

Her dark violet eyes narrowed, "Are you telling me that my descendant is too weak to cross the Void?"

Not a question... oh no, not when said in that dark tone. Stammering to form words he carefully said, "Not weak my queen. If anything, his path was not marked as it should have been. If, that is, the case, then Magmas is to blame for this." There was more, but telling her now would not do the boy any good. If anything, she would destroy him and any chance for Nisha to be born.

Rage built in her eyes as her long black dragon wings grew until they dragged on the cold floor. Burning

Secrets, Lies and Betrayal
by: M.L. Ruscsak

black mist filled the curricular room. Bones rattled as something was coming alive. A loud hiss and thunderous clap just before the mist slowly dissipated. The throne of bones and spikes, no longer standing proud within the center of the room. No longer was Prim dressed in an old dress that was threadbare, but now dressed in something close to what she had worn years before the war. A narrow blue dress that sparkled within the soft light. Tiny stars dotted everywhere. Her fiery red hair finally combed and braided down her back.

Carefully, she bent down and allowed her little silver lizard to climb out onto her hand. His tail wrapping around her wrist and growing up her arm. A flick of his tongue was close to a loving kiss. "Ah, now my lovely. I need you to take Karnack to the Void. Make haste then return to me. I have much to prepare for."

Karnack watched as Shesha crawled up her arm, then down her dress. Stayed perfectly still as the great king of dragons climbed up his robes until Shesha came to rest on his shoulders. The hot breath that came with the flick of that long tongue was enough of a warning to leave. Bowing once he backed out of the door slamming shut before he even had taken a full step away from it.

Secrets, Lies and Betrayal
by: M.L. Ruscsak

Opening the Gate of the Under Kingdom to the realm of the living had never been very hard. Having the gate open where it was needed most, however... had never been an easy task. So, it was no surprise when the gate opened up in the middle of was now a vast wasteland. Years ago, before the war this had been an area overgrown in flora from the mind of their queen. A simple cottage housed in the center where Alec could rest while the Goddess tended to her garden and came up with new flowers and arrangements. A place that now housed a deadly dark Fey several feet beneath the sands.

Donny wouldn't harm him or even question the intrusion. The creatures that did his bidding, however, not

Secrets, Lies and Betrayal
by: M.L. Ruscsak

only would take offense, but could very well kill him before he called out for help.

Spreading his small wings Shesha glided down to the sand. His claws stretching out as he grew to the size of a small horse. A cloud of white smoke blooming from his nostrils. "We do not have time to dwell here. Where must we go so I may sleep."

Calling in the Seer's stone, he held it flat on the palm of his hand. The image of the body now lying limp in the void coming into view. "We must find this Fey."

A cloud of white smoke and Shesha doubled in size nearly six times. "I will take you."

Not much for words. Then again, when he had been, created Prim hadn't known the language of this land. Hadn't understood that most of what was spoken would be similar to her beloved Star City. Or perhaps she had hoped to put everything from her home behind her. Either way Shesha rarely spoke to any other then his queen.

With a deep breath, Karnack climbed up onto the great dragon's back positioning himself between two of the large protruding spikes. "Will this do?"

His answer was simply Shesha bolting toward the sky in a direct path to the star called Pallas.

Secrets, Lies and Betrayal
by: M.L. Ruscsak

Further into the sky, they ascended the darker it became. Bitter cold seeping into his body. Far colder than anything he had ever felt before.

How could anything survive out here? How had so many Fey come to their little blue star all of those years ago? Not a question that he could really answer. Nor a question that he would dare ask, but one that he could keep records with in journals to ponder later. Yes, that he could do and without breaking any promise to the goddess.

Patting the back of his ride he called out through clattering teeth, "Do you-you k-know where..."

Pumping his wings Shesha looked back over his shoulder, blowing hot air into the face of the queen's scribe, "You don't have Fey skin. You should not have come."

Secrets, Lies and Betrayal
by: M.L. Ruscsak

Fey skin? Another question without an answer. Perhaps he could ask Donny. Perhaps he would freeze to death before given the chance. Both were a possibility. But he was thankful for the blast of warm air. It was enough for him to think clearly for the moment. Just enough to form words that he didn't have time to speak, for he saw something floating just at the edge of his vision. "Over there."

"I smell him."

You what!?!? Smell... the damn beast could smell Fey? What else had been hidden from him in the years since becoming a scribe? No, best not to ask that question. Not when the beast might actually tell him something useful. Instead, he prayed that they weren't already too late.

Pulling the boy... no, not just the boy, but an infant as well... to the back of the great dragon king, he breathed out a sigh of relief. Both were alive. Frozen to the core and shivering. Neither could open their eyes for the frost that now covered their bodies. But both were alive. Another few moments and they very well could not have been.

Not that it would make much of a difference. Prim had the power to bring the dead back to life, had the power now to give them back everything that they had before death. If she would or not was yet to be seen. Her bringing back Shesha was merely an exercise done out of annoyance.

Secrets, Lies and Betrayal
by: M.L. Ruscsak

And hopefully the last time that she would have to so for a great many more years.

Secrets, Lies and Betrayal
by: M.L. Ruscsak

CHAPTER 15: MYRDDIN

Myrddin woke to the smell of dust that was clogging his throat. The feeling of being tied to some hard surface made his crust covered eyes open much faster than he had wished. Darkness surrounded him. Not a single light for as far as he could see. Not even enough break in the darkness to see what was coiled around him. Several deep breaths to calm himself.

He had failed. He had not made it to the blue orb where his ancestor had beckoned him to go. He was responsible for his sister's death. Anything that happened now was his own doing.

No, it wasn't. At least not yet. After all, he did have the powers of Pallas flowing through his veins. Many times more than any other royal Fey. A gift from Magmas. Calming thoughts and he called forth light to laminate the room. When his eyes opened, it wasn't the room that had lit up in a yellow hue but his own skin. Bright as a flame glowing in the city of Pallas. Enough to not only see, but hot enough to burn his bindings.

Cloth. He could see that now. Some kind of heavy cloth had bound his movements. The hard thing he had been lying on had been nothing more than the cold floor. Dirt. Or at least that is what he thought it was. A few places within the other Star Cities had places like this. Cells to hold the unworthy. Places that drained the powers from the Fey slowly until they died. What was left always fed the void.

Hope faded away. There was no door. Nothing that he could do would allow him to free himself.

Nothing...

The sound of rustling stones had him thinking of all of the terrible things that his mother had done to prisoners running through his mind. The memories of the screams that had been heard not only through the castle, but resonated throughout the city as well. His own fear paralyzed him.

Secrets, Lies and Betrayal
by: M.L. Ruscsak

"I see you finally awaken."

A dark voice. A shadow just beyond the reach of his light. Nothing more could he see., "Who are you?"

The Dark shape turned away from him moving away from the opening, "Donny. Come one I might as well feed you before taking you to Alista."

Alista. "Queen Alista?"

Slowly the shape turned back to him and drew closer, stepping into the light. Dark purple flames snuffing out the golden hue coming from Myrddin's skin. His dark robes showing a dragon's crest embroidered along the sleeves. The silver dragon appearing to take flight within the darkness of the flames as Donny crossed his arms. "Now, you being a descendant of my queen I am to give you certain privileges. Such as I won't kill you for intruding on my personal space. However, I never swore I wouldn't drain every ounce of power that you now have."

"Donavan, that is quite enough."

Another voice. This one old and crackling.

Donny turned sharply back to the door snapping at

the man who had entered the room,
"Damn you Karnack. You should have not brought this child here."

"You have been an uncle to all of Prim's favorites. I see no reason for you not to offer guidance to young Lord Myrddin. Unless you no longer believe in the goddess."

Purple flames erupted within the room. Scorching the walls and floor. Yet being absorbed into Myrddin's skin. It was the last thing he remembered before his world went completely dark.

What had happened after that Myrddin could only guess. He remembered, only the heat of the room and the deep purple hue of the flame. He didn't remember falling to the cold ground. Didn't remember being taken somewhere else. But he knew that he didn't walk into the elaborately

Secrets, Lies and Betrayal
by: M.L. Ruscsak

furnished room with more items in the room than he had words for. However, the bed was warm, the covers soft.

This was a bed worthy of any royal Fey. And for once he was laying it in not just dreaming that he could. He could drift here in this feeling forever.

Letting himself relax, he let his eyes close once more. Let himself trust that he was safe for only a moment. Would have laid there longer if a sound hadn't pulled him out of the slumber that he was just finding. The sound of a door opening heightened his awareness of the room.

"So, you have finally decided to wake."

He knew that voice. Old and unamused. "Karnack?"

Slowly Karnack shuffled over to the large bed and took a seat on the edge. "I'm glad that you remembered my name. Now, perhaps you would like to know where you are and perhaps see your sister?"

Slowly Myrddin struggled to sit up. "Tenanye? Is she well?"

Crossing his thin arms Karnack smiled. "Ah, so the child does have a name. Magmas and I have been discussing it."

He wanted to jump out of the bed. Might have if Karnack would have moved. Instead with surprise in his voice, he managed to ask, "Magmas? Of Pallas?"

Carefully Karnack placed his wrinkled hand on Myrddin's shoulder. "Although they share a name; the Magmas that I am referring to is the son of the other. But that can be explained shortly. For the moment a change of clothing has been set aside for you. The young guard outside of the door will bring you to the dining hall when you are ready."

Hope faded from his voice and his face, "I'm a prisoner then?"

"My boy, Queen Alista does not make prisoners out of those who are family. Nor did her father. The guard is here simply because he is trusted to keep you safe until we know what the blasted..." Karnack paused, then shook his head, "... I apologize my memory is far keener than my ability to hold my tongue. But soon enough we can discuss the great king of Pallas."

Getting to his feet Karnack stretched, moving a lot nimbler than Myrddin would have thought possible. Seeing the questions in his eyes Karnack smiled, "I am nearly four centuries old but I no longer age. My body was never meant to serve in battle, nor has it. But I am as nimble as I need to be."

Pulling the thick drapes open to the rain covered windows Karnack turned back. "You are in the Castle of Water. The weather here agrees with Alista more so than the other castles of Feyen. Now then. Once you have cleaned up and dressed a meal will be ready for you. "Almost reaching the door Karnack turned back, "My queen waited a long time for your arrival, but she has chosen to wait a while longer to be introduced."

"Your queen? What is her name?"

"She had many names my boy. Some are myth, others no more accurate as the stories told about her. When she wishes to be revealed she will be. It may be in your lifetime, but do so doubt it." With that Karnack eased out the door closing it tight behind him.

Puzzled Myrddin slipped out of the bed. His feet not touching solid ground, but... water... not water that he knew for his feet weren't getting wet, but water trapped under something that rippled under his steps. Curious, he knelt to feel the floor. His hand passing the invisible barrier to solid land. Something that he couldn't see nipping at his fingers. A quick jerk and he brought his hand from the barrier bright blue blood now dripping from the bite.

It was his own fault for being harmed. He was just lucky whatever was held within the fluid would forgive the intrusion. And was thankful that he had been given the warning.

Secrets, Lies and Betrayal
by: M.L. Ruscsak

Slipping the heavy black robe over the black tunic and black trousers that had been left, Myrddin opened the bedroom door to find what he recognized as a dark Fey standing before him. His instincts had always been correct when measuring the power of another Fey, but this one... Was either too light to hold any true ability or so dark that none could gage it. The thought alone terrified him. "Karnack said you would take me to the dining hall?"

The Man closed his midnight blue eyes and sighed, "If you are to survive here you will need to learn where not to trespass."

"I don't..."

"You are young and have traveled far to come here. Farther than most. But that doesn't excuse your lack of manners. Because of that I won't make a fuss about it this time."

Secrets, Lies and Betrayal
by: M.L. Ruscsak

Myrddin blinked unsure what to say... unsure what he had done wrong. "Can you tell me what I did wrong?"

Another sigh from the guard, "First you offended the MegMok Necros that lives within the water of the castle. You are damn lucky that it only took a sample of your blood rather than your life."

"Meg-Mok"

"MegMok Necros. Damn creatures. Invisible to the naked eyes and less distressing that way. If you manage to capture one and get it out of water... Well, imagine an eel with a single eye the flesh decaying from its scaled body. And the poison teeth are nothing to play with. Most are happy living in the castle being fed bits of table scraps from the kitchens, but the ones that live in the lake... you better be damned sure you have something on you repel them or you will most likely become dinner."

Myrddin closed his eyes and took a deep breath. He was being scolded for disturbing a creature that he couldn't see. How did that make sense? "Am I to surmise that I would be in trouble should I disturb these invisible creatures a second time?"

The young guard narrowed his dark eyes. "You misunderstand me. You can bother the MegMok all you desire. If you like pain and loss of blood that is on you. However, the captain of the guard would need to be made aware should any escape the barrier and start feeding on the inhabits here because you wish to be a fool."

Shit. Had this guard told him that he would be stripped of flesh it would have been one thing finding out the only reason he was even being told was because his action no matter how foolish would have consequences to another... "I doubt that will be necessary to tell your captain."

The guard turned and took but a single step," Names Claec. For the moment I'm tasked at looking after you Lord Myrddin."

"How do you know my name."

"My mother was from Tiresias. I trust you know that Star City?"

Of course, he had heard of it. Who in all of the Star Cities hadn't? "It was one of the Stars that was lost during the great war. Those who lived there were said to have the ability to foresee the further, but were unable to defend themselves."

In once quick movement Claec had Myrddin pressed to the wall, forcing him back into the water, allowing the MegMok to attack his back. A dark blade pressed against Myrddin's throat. "Is that the lies that is being spewed now?"

Secrets, Lies and Betrayal
by: M.L. Ruscsak

A hard shove and Myrddin was tossed to the ground with little more than a thought. His blue blood seeping from his back. The sound of snapping teeth being heard just below him. He didn't need to see the creatures to know they were trying to break the barrier. Didn't need to see them that they were becoming excited by the smell of his blood.

Reciting the incantation that he remembered, Myrddin carefully stopped the bleeding before sitting up. "Perhaps you would enlighten me to the truth, since I only know what had been passed down."

Glaring Claec hissed, "My mother and the other royal Fey foresaw the great war and wanted no part in it. Since they had no skill warriors, they had been left alone during the war.

Magmas after claiming Pallas as his own went to Tiresias and demanded that my mother be given to him. Her mother sent her and the rest of the royal Fey here. Tiresias was destroyed by Magmas to set an example.

My father's star Alois was another Star City destroyed by the jackal Magmas. Only their star was destroyed for not supplying the serpent with warriors to take on Magnar. My father barely escaped before the star itself was destroyed."

He was lying. He had to be. Yet the rage that was burning in those dark eyes... There were no signs of deception. No signs of smudging the truth. But if this were true...

"Claec, Enough."

Dark commanding voice. A body that stood, demanding instant recognition.

Not turning to the voice Claec instantly dropped to his knee, "My lord... I"

"I don't rule here boy. You can take this matter up with Alista after she meets with Myrddin. Now report to your father. I'm sure he will more than a few words to say about existing the MegMok."

All too quickly Claec disappeared out of the hall. Despite his speed he didn't look to be running. Yet...

Still seated on the ground Myrddin glanced up at the Fey who was now towering over him. A man in his prime yet still young enough to be trouble or cause trouble. A man who he could tell was another royal Fey. A man with more natural ability than what could be found in any one-Star City. "My lord?" It was acceptable wasn't it?

"I suspect you have questions? Perhaps you need to know who it is that could frighten a dark Fey without doing anything but entering a room."

The thought had crossed his mind. "Yes, sir?"

"You may call me Apollo. I believe you have been acquainted with my sire. Magmas lord and master of Pallas."

Relief washed through him. So finally, he was somewhere safe. Somewhere with Magmas' reach…

"And traitor to those who fought in the great war." Apollo paused scorching flames already encasing his massive arms. "But he is a discussion for another day. Right now, Alista is ready to greet you."

Slowly getting to his feet Myrddin took a shaky breath, "You call your sire a traitor. Is that something I will understand one day?"

"It's best if I'm not the one to explain that. Come, my niece is not one to be kept waiting. Neither is her father."

Secrets, Lies and Betrayal
by: M.L. Ruscsak

Secrets, Lies and Betrayal
by: M.L. Ruscsak

CHAPTER 16: ALISTA

Taking her seat at the head of the long table, she glanced to her right where her father lazily sipped on honied nectar. To her left Lord Griffith was putting words to parchment just to avoid glancing at anyone directly. Karnack sat the end of the table scores of books around him. What was held within those books she could only guess. But perhaps today she might have some form of an answer.

"Perhaps it would be helpful for me to understand why we are all here. Would one of you care to explain it to me?"

Secrets, Lies and Betrayal
by: M.L. Ruscsak

Magmas turned his head slightly to his daughter and smiled. "Pumpkin, you should know better than to ask questions."

He was right and she knew it. Still, she didn't like that her father came to her late last night telling her that she would be hosting not only him but her uncles as well. Told her that she would need Vasilissa to join her and she would need to bring both of her young daughters. No, she wasn't thrilled about any of this more so since she had been on the verge of some cold for most of the year. Each day draining her more. Each passing day aging her more than three.

Karnack glanced up from his books, "Flint will be here shortly. It appears Nicco is being more difficult than usual to locate."

How could he possibly know that…? Then she saw the shadow dancing next to him. A quick glance and one would assume it was nothing more than a true shadow being caused by the flickering of the candle. But if you really watched it…. Really paid attention to the size coupled with the way it moved.

A deep breath and she leaned forward, "As much as I enjoy having you all here, I will have some actual answers before anyone leaves."

Secrets, Lies and Betrayal
by: M.L. Ruscsak

The stained-glass doors of the meeting room eased open as Vasilissa stepped into the room. "Alista? You asked that I come, but you didn't mention that your uncles were joining us."

Easing back in her seat Alista tried to smile, "Magnar isn't here in case you were wondering."

"Of course not. Since we have already decided that his parlor tricks are of no match for my temper, I doubt he will come here unless need be." Crossing the large empty room, she pulled a chair out next to Griffith. "Grandfather? You look well."

"I look as I did a decade ago. I trust nothing has changed from your vision."

Vasilissa closed her eyes. "I see the place where the child will be housed but not near this star if that is what you are referring."

Griffith glance at her out of the corner of his eye, "We will disuses that after we settle today's little matter."

Magmas leaned back in his seat, "I hardly call the descendant of the goddess finally arriving as a little matter.

"You forget Magmas that it is your namesake that rules Pallas and is responsible for thousands of deaths. It is he who will be responsible for waking the Silent Ones. And it is he alone who is responsible for not allowing this

Secrets, Lies and Betrayal
by: M.L. Ruscsak

descendant to come here much sooner. It was your Sire who took control of that Star City by corrupting the current queen with stories of the power that she will never know."

Magmas leaned forward, "We are not here to discuss the traitor. We are here to welcome the descendants of the Goddess."

Griffith looked ready to say something, but a hand clamping down on his shoulder had him snapping around to see who dared touch him. A single wince followed by a shudder, "Nicco, always a pleasure."

Nicco glanced from one Royal Fey to the other, "I trust we won't be having any problems today?"

Alista watched in amazement as both great kings looked and sounded like two young boys caught doing something forbidden. Watched in amazement as both hung their heads unable to hold Nicco's gaze.

What was it about this man that could make both great warriors quiver with fear? She didn't know, but she hoped that one day someone would be kind enough to explain it.

Secrets, Lies and Betrayal
by: M.L. Ruscsak

CHAPTER 17: MYRDDIN

Watching Apollo opened the stained-glass door Myrddin sucked in a deep breath. He recognized Karnack who was seated that the long table, but the others? It didn't matter who they were. Not really. But the power that was circulating in that room… Even Pallas did have that feel. It hadn't felt ready to burst. This was power worthy of an alliance,

Slowly he took a single step into the room with so many eyes on him. At home no one had paid attention when he entered a room. At home it didn't matter if he came or went. Another deep breath. He wasn't at home anymore. He was however at the mercy of those in this room.

Secrets, Lies and Betrayal
by: M.L. Ruscsak

Karnack glanced over at him and gave a warm smile, "Come my boy sit. First, we have very important things to discuss then you can see your sister."

So that was the game. Bribery. Do as they wanted and see his sister. Yet he had no way of knowing if he would be able to keep her safe.

Taking the only open seat, he slowly sat next to the man who looked most like the Greta lord Magmas but he kept his eyes on the two women. After all it had been his experience that the Fey woman were much crueler when it came to pain. "Gentleman, Ladies?"

Taking a small breath Alista started to cough, "Damn cold." Noticing the worry in her father's eyes and the sharpness in Myrddin's she continued, "I'm fine. Now should we begin?" it wasn't what she wanted to do, but it did seem to break the tension about the room.

The man to Myrddin's left leaned forward. "I will the word of this counsel not to repeat what is said in this room until proper time."

In unison with the rest of the council agreed. With eyes watching him Myrddin finally swallowed, then said, "Agreed."

"Good, Karnack the introductions if you would."

Secrets, Lies and Betrayal
by: M.L. Ruscsak

"Ah, yes. At the head of the table is Queen Alista. To her left is Lord Griffith, Queen Vasilissa, Lord Nicco. Myself you have already been acquainted with. As well as Donny."

"For the record, I am not raising any children. And we will see if either have the ability that is worthy of me teaching anything as well."

Karnack took a deep breath, 'Very well Donavan, I will discuss your concerns with the goddess once I return to the library. I'm sure she will wish to address them."

Myrddin watched the two. Watched as Donny paled his bronze skin until he was nearly ash gray. Watched as a man who was clearly a threat sat back in his seat meekly.

Clearing his throat Karnack added, "Apollo you have met, His brother Flint, although a part of this counsel is tending to your sister."

Tilting his head in question Myrddin asked, "Tending? Do you not have maids to do things such as watch children?"

"Aye, we do. But for the moment Flint wanted to be somewhere else and there seemed like the reasonable place to be." Karnack paused, giving time for Myrddin to make his own conclusions before adding. "Lastly the man beside you. Lord Magmas."

"I was told that Prim only saved two of... um... Pallas' Lord Magmas' children?"

Griffith snorted. "There are days that I wished that she had. Yet she holds the gift of Necromancy."

"She holds many abilities. Many even she has not yet tested. However, "Karnack folded his hand over a thin book, "Lord Flint wasn't dead when he was found. Only slowly dying. But that my boy was before you came to this star and it will be the last time we discuss it."

Myrddin glanced down at the table feeling the words left unsaid. Anger from Griffith. Hate bordering rage building up for reason's unknown. Edginess from both Apollo and Magmas. Feelings of hate once their bloodline was revealed. Puzzlement from Alista. Vasilissa was more complicated she was bored and questioning the reason for her attendance. And Nicco... although he felt dangerous, he was silent sitting and watching him.

"Why does everyone in this room despise the ruler of Pallas."

"Narrowing his eyes Magmas soft spoke, "What did the traitor tell you about the great war?"

The softness couldn't hide his anger. Even if it did the steam rising from the cold table would have given it away. "Azia ruled the Star Cities his need for cruelty much worse than that now."

Secrets, Lies and Betrayal
by: M.L. Ruscsak

"Well, damn the bastard said something truthful."

Not Magmas nor anyone at the table. That voice came from the door just before a child's tired mew. Turning slowly, Myrddin didn't need the introduction to know the man that was holding his sister. After seeing his portrait in the hall of Pallas he didn't need an introduction at all, "I think perhaps I should continue my answer before I start asking the questions that I have."

Crossing the room and creating a seat out of air Flint smiled, "I think that would be best."

More than an hour later the room fell silent as Myrddin finished not only what he had been told about the great war but about the letters that Prim had left him.

"My sire has always the ability of tempering his words so that even a lie held some truth. I see he has not yet learned that will be his undoing."

Secrets, Lies and Betrayal
by: M.L. Ruscsak

"You plan of destroying him." Not a question, but a horrified thought.

Magmas sat back in his seat, "I think you need to understand what had really happened during the war." He paused and glanced around the room, "Does anyone disagree?"

Myrddin glanced around the room. Not a single man said a word. Not a single one even looked phased by the question. Then Slowly Griffith eased back in his seat. "None disagreed; however, you better not leave any detail out."

There was an "or else" that was left hanging in the room. What that might be Myrddin couldn't guess But Magmas gave a slight nod.

A breath more and Magmas sat his thick elbows on the table and squeezed the bridge of his nose His voice low and soft as he started speaking, "Since no-one in this room know for sure why prim ever left her own star I will not speculate. That being said I think it best if we kept this decision to the great war."

Watching both Queens shift in their seat a strange feeling came over Myrddin. He didn't know what was going to be said. But he had a feeling that these two-formable queens had been waiting for far too long to hear this story. To hear whatever that was needed to be said.

Secrets, Lies and Betrayal
by: M.L. Ruscsak

Nodding to Griffith Magmas finally continued, "Griffith is the last Heir of Pallas. The Last child alive that was sired by Azia. Or at least the last that we can verify for the moment. Vasilissa is his direct descendant. As you have already been made aware… Flint, Apollo and myself are the descendants… The only living descendants of the bastard that rules Pallas currently."

There was too much venom in the way this Magmas spoke of his namesake. Too much burning hatred that needed to be explained. "I understand the sediment of a child growing to despise a parent, but may I know what he has done since from what I have been told. He didn't raise you?"

The words flowed from Magmas' lips. Words that few would know and those who did were longtime residents of the Underkingdom. Yet even without knowing the words the bitter rage was enough to guess their meanings.

Flint winced, but spoke up. "I think I should continue for the moment. You see Myrddin we were all raised by Prim. And we all fought in the war. So, we understood not everything that was being seen by outsiders was in fact the truth. To them … to those who fought for the Star Cities and Azia …. They thought they were winning. They thought those of here were faltering. But in truth Prim… we were winning the war. Pushing the intruders into nicely made traps. Prior to the arrival Prim ordered Necromancers scattered through the realm to aid those who were… well….”

“The Necromancers gave back the lives of those fallen, allowing them to fight more. And also adding the effect that whatever had killed them to start would become little more than an inconvenience should the action be repeated.”

Flint looked at Karnack and sighed, “That I didn’t know, but it would have been appreciated long before now. Anyways… The stronger fighters of Pallas were being herded to two castles. The weaker were fighting in other places their rakes were unorganized and served no real purpose at the time.”

Magmas leaned forward, “I finish this. The less we discuss bout the war itself the happier I will be. The bastard Magmas had come here just hours before the first wave of Star City Fey arrives. Prim had just given birth not long before that. Still, he tried to play coy with her. He tried to earn her trust. We don’t know if she had sent Alec to the castle of Night before Magmas arrived or after. Nor do know what happen to her child.”

“Alec?”

“Hmm. Alec was Prim’s consort. Or that's what she said in public. But anyone who knew them. Who had spent a lifetime watching they knew better." Nicco leaned forward just a bit and smiled just enough to show the first row of sharp teeth. "Alec was my brother, so it's fitting that I try to explain. Something before we discuss the rest."

Since the rest of the Star City Fey all nodded in agreement Myrddin, inclined his head, "Please. I would like to know as much as possible."

"Alec was a pain in the ass and we had our share of disagreements. But he was still my brother. My equal he just didn't have the heart for my darker tendencies. Now your ancestor, Prim was a flirt. She didn't it mostly to see what Alec would do or not do. I doubt he ever figured out she did that when she was looking for an excuse to go have some time in her garden.

That was the only place that it was understood that While there they wouldn't be disturbed. And if they had to be disturbed… well Prim… had her ways so terrifying even the most steeled warriors wouldn't disturb her a second time."

"And Magmas…?"

Flint closed his eyes once more his own rage mixing with hurt. "The bastard tricked Alec. Prim had sent him to stay in the castle of Night. Despite how close it was to the final battle in had the best defenses. Somehow the bastard got Alec to leave and then turned him over to Azia. Alec was dead within moments. Or mostly dead. What kept him alive … it was to drag out the pain until Prim could watch him parish."

"I don't understand…" And he didn't. The Fey that he knew didn't have connections with their mates. It was simply a way to create new life. So, what he was hearing…

"Donny and Nicco taught all of the fallen Star City Fey how to use our skills. Both those that we knew and those that we didn't. But it was Alec, who took over being the father figure. He's the one that taught us right from wrong. He's the one that was there watching the smaller Fey learning to fly. He was the one that we all went to whenever a spell or incantation was proving more difficult. So, Magmas didn't just betray Prim that day he betrayed all of us."

"So, Prim tucked her consort away. Magmas tricked him and Alec died."

"No, Alec was torn apart in front of Prim the very moment she stood before Azia. There was nothing that Prim could do to save him. Nothing she could do to reach him before there was nothing left to save. It was I that moment Prims favorite creations who had no power or ability of their own sided with Azia. In blind rage she destroyed the castle of glass. The city that housed thousands. Many of whom were still inside their homes."

Secrets, Lies and Betrayal
by: M.L. Ruscsak

Magmas took a deep breath, "Just moments after everything was destroyed Magmas stood before Prim. We don't know what he said, but we do know it had something to do with her ruling Pallas as his bride."

Griffith slammed his fist down on the table, splashing water on everyone, "The damned fool thought Azia was dead. Thought Prim's loyalty was only to herself. He failed to understand that she had no wish to leave all that she had created. Prim warned magmas to leave and never to return. Vowed if he ever did anything to harm her blood line she would return and destroy him and all that stood in his wake. I arrived just as he flew away. Azia was just starting to claw his way out of the rubble. Prim had weakened him, but I finished what she started. The powers of Pallas were released from him and absorbed into me. So, the bastard rules a star that has no allegiance to him. And I have no desire to return."

Karnack cleared his throat, 'Boys that is the gist of it, but not the whole of his betrayal. What none of you understand is Prim marked the path to here from her home star and the ruler of Pallas snuffed them out. HE has been corrupting the queen of Lunaista with the promise of power for some time now. He has been trying to find a way to end lord Myrddin's life since the day he has been born.'

"I... no he has been..."

Secrets, Lies and Betrayal
by: M.L. Ruscsak

"The book he gave you. Book Prim had left in his care were poisoned. But he didn't understand that it was your ancestry that keeps you alive. Prim's daughter Avyanna was created from the mist. A creature such as that can't be destroyed. Her mate... Magnar is a creator the same as Prim but his abilities lean darker than hers."

"The box Magmas had. He said... he told me the flesh had been left for him by Prim."

"My dear boy, Prim left what you would need with her sister. No one else who lived with the Star Cities. She didn't trust anyone. However, she did warn Magmas what would happen should harm come to you. I fear the day when she finds out."

For a long time Myrddin sat there numb. "I gave my word that I would return to help the Star Cities be free of the torment they now face."

"And you will. You will but you will have years before that is needed. And in that time, you will see the difference of how your Star Cities are manipulated verses how they could be shown to live."

Secrets, Lies and Betrayal
by: M.L. Ruscsak

CHAPTER 18: MYRDDIN

Myrddin sat on his bed. A large soft bed with more covers than he had ever had. His sister was just across the hall playing with another infant about her own age. Happy squeals coming from both.

He should go watch her. He should explore the finely furnished room with solid floors and golden trim. At the very least he should glance out of his window to see the flora and fauna that littered the ground.

Yet he could do neither.

His mind was too full of the things that he had learned in the few days that he had been here. Prim had left him a single letter. She had never written a second. Lord Magmas had done that himself by mimicking her handwriting. The tribute box Prim had left, he had a second compartment held within. That...

Secrets, Lies and Betrayal
by: M.L. Ruscsak

Oh, that had a single token left for him by his grandmother. A single lock of her flaming red hair and all of the power that she could squeeze into that single lock.

He had touched out of curiosity. Had expected power not his own to take over his body as it had in Pallas instead. He was everything. In but a blink of his eyes, he had lived a lifetime seeing things through Prim's eyes. He had felt the love she had felt for Alec. The joy he had brought to her life. The pain that Magmas had caused her.

The torment that she still feels.

Oh, she was alive somewhere. She knew he was here. Knew he had taken what she had given him. Yet he somehow displeased her. He felt that too.

She was watching him. Waiting to pass judgment on him. Seeing if he was worthy of her power.

A tap on his door kept him from thinking about anything else. "Umm. It's open?"

Alista pushed the door open just enough to look into the room before opening it completely. "With all of the changes you are now facing I've decided to tell you this myself." She paused briefly. A series of cough that made her sound lie her lungs would be expelled shortly. "With my health now declining Elista will be ascending within the next weeks. She'll help you adjust to your surroundings and has already decided that you be the permanent liaison between both Feyen and Darke.”

“I barely know anything about this realm. Perhaps…”

“No, Vas. Decided it was suitable since she wants you being the one looking after her daughter when they are visiting. She trusts you so Elista trust you.”

Myrddin closed his eyes, “You aren’t sick Alista you have poison flowing in your veins. It’s old, but I don’t know how to anything about it.”

“Aye, I know. I have been fighting this since shortly of becoming queen.” Alista paused and offered a friendly smile, “So tell me who is it that is teaching you about poisons?”

“Nicco and Donny. Flint and Karnack have been going over every book in their library. Your father and Griffith have taken to teaching me everything they know about fighting. And Apollo is teaching me the skills that others can’t.”

“Oh, my. I guess I have forgotten how much of a taskmaster each of them can be. But I can offer this… They will only teach you what you need. So, learn well Lord Myrddin. Learn everything you can.”

Secrets, Lies and Betrayal
by: M.L. Ruscsak

Secrets, Lies and Betrayal
by: M.L. Ruscsak

CHAPTER 19: ADRIANNA

Eight years later

Stalking the halls of the Castle of Water, Adrianna let her fingers trail behind on the wall soaking in the gel like water. Feeling the cold that was no match from the chill that her sister had produced.

They were young. Less than eight Light cycles old. Yet, as princesses they were required to visit the other countries at least once a year. Learn whatever the royals could teach them.

In Celeste's case it had been the very basic of healing spells and fun incantations. Where her own training was in the darker of abilities. Incantations to both cause

Secrets, Lies and Betrayal
by: M.L. Ruscsak

considerable damage to a person, but also able to repair that damage. But only if she had been the one to cause it.

She wasn't a fighter. Didn't want to be a fighter. Yet… somehow the spells were keeping Celeste from causing real harm to her. Harm that she couldn't understand. Harm that she may never be able to understand. But worse of all harm that she couldn't tell a single living soul about.

Turning a corner, she bumped into the stomach of a taller youth. As she gazed up at him she fought hard to breath.

Myrddin.

She had heard stories about him and his dark power. Of course, she had seen him a time or two, but he had looked older. But being this close…. Breathing in his scented aurora. Spicy. Elusive. And just a hint of danger.

It was so appealing yet memorizing.

His voice soft yet filled with concern. "Princess?"

Her eyes drifted to his, "Lord Myrddin. I am sorry for bumping into you. I should be more careful where I walk."

Myrddin narrowed his eyes just a hair, then cursed with vivid clarity, "Come with me."

"I- "

Secrets, Lies and Betrayal
by: M.L. Ruscsak

Grabbing her hand, he began to pull her through more hallways than he could remember. Pulled her a door that she recognized as the entrance of the guard tower. "Stay here."

Unsure about what to do she didn't move. He was the permanent liaison between Feyen and Darke. A member of Queen Alista's household. If he had taken offense the it was up to her to make amends. Still, she didn't think involving the castle guards would be appropriate.

A breath more and Myrddin returned with two well-dressed Feyen men trailing behind. A heartbeat and she knew them both as personal guards of the royal family. And both men were usually hovering near where Myrddin was.

Hovering and always ready to make trouble. Or settle it. Yet today both men looked confused.

"Am I in trouble?"

"Are you..." Myrddin shook his head before kneeling before her, "Do you know that I am a seer?"

"A seer... OH.... Those who can glimpse into the future and predict a possible outcome."

Leaning on the door the tall blond-haired guard laughed, "I think you better ask her mother about this before you have all three of skinned alive."

"Not now, Blake." Then to Adrianna, "in my case I don't just see a possible outcome. I see several. Each path... each vision, leading to a new outcome. In your case I see only one solution to keep you safe."

Squaring her shoulder, she could feel her heart racing, 'I'm in danger? Even with the protection of the crown?"

"That protection won't keep you safe from those who already dwell within the castles."

Her eyes scanned the faces of the other men. Both worried yet approving of whatever Lord Myrddin had decided. They wouldn't stop him. Not if he meant to keep her safe. "What are you suggesting?"

Scanning the area, the other guard placed his hand on Myrddin's shoulder, "Not here. To many pass this corridor."

Slowly Myrddin stood keeping, her hand in his, "Claec? What do you see?"

"I see that I will be explaining this to one of two powerful queens before the day is through. But I know where we may go to have a moment of privacy before any detect what it is that you are planning."

Secrets, Lies and Betrayal
by: M.L. Ruscsak

They were deep under the castle of water. So deep that she could see the ocean life swimming past the translucent walls. Coral in its natural habitat glowing in an array of colors.

"It is beautiful down here."

Soothingly Blake rubbed her arms as he whispered, "You have my word that no harm will come to you."

"I don't...."

"Stop that Kairavi. You'll scare her." Slowly Myrddin came before her once more, "Adrianna, I swear once you are older to understand I will teach you this. But not yet. Not today."

"I will hold you to that."

Secrets, Lies and Betrayal
by: M.L. Ruscsak

Softly he laid his head on her chest. A moment of hesitation and he plunged his fingers deep inside of her pulling her heart out when he withdrew his hands. With his other hand, he did the same to himself.

Two hearts pumping next to each other. Both seeping with blue life blood and dark mist.

Taking the larger of the two, he sank it into her chest and gasped before accepting her own heart. Their powers… their abilities binding to one another. Blending until she couldn't be sure where her own powers began and his ended.

"How did… what did…"

Coughing Myrddin sat back on the floor, "The powers that I have will keep you safe. No poison will harm you. No matter how much blood loss you not be killed or render weak. It's the best that I can do right now. In a few years, in a few decades, I will be better prepared to keep you safe."

She didn't doubt his words. Couldn't doubt them. Not when she could feel his conviction beating in rhyme with his heart. A heart that now beat within her own chest.

Secrets, Lies and Betrayal
by: M.L. Ruscsak

EPILOGUE

Myrddin sat on the great throne of Feyen. His mind preoccupied with his own matters. On his own thoughts. That he didn't dare listen to those where standing before him. No, right now he wanted his mind to wonder. And wonder it did.

200 Years had passed since he had come to this star. Memories of his home mostly gone now. Memories of the pain that he had forced to endure was no longer things that kept him awake at night.

No, he had new troubles to do that.

His baby sister was almost ready to be betrothed to someone worthy of her ability and sharp temper. Almost ready to take her own place as part of Elista's court. But first he would need to find someone worthy of *her*.

Secrets, Lies and Betrayal
by: M.L. Ruscsak

Oh, Nicco had a suggestion or two. Only one of those suggestions he was willing to entertain as he had foreseen her being truly happy. But not yet. Not until he was sure. Not until he was sure that the man wouldn't turn on his dear sister wishing to have her powers for his own.

Neither he nor Nicco thought that was a possibility, but first, he would need to seek out Alista. Only a few knew where she now dwelled. Of them only he and Nicco had the authority to enter the place. But it was he who did so when he had constant worries that needed her ability to calm his nerves.

But that too could wait.

Elista was due to have her third child any day now and somehow, he had been put into the position of overseeing the entire Feyen Kingdom until she was once again ready to rule.

He was a royal Fey so ruling was in his nature. Or so she said.

Bah! He would much rather work on his own spells and incantation. Much rather create something that would terrorize those who sought to disturb him. Much rather take this time and spend with the princess of Darke while she was once again coming to the kingdom.

Secrets, Lies and Betrayal
by: M.L. Ruscsak

Damn her. Why couldn't her husband rule in her stead? Why couldn't her counsel whose job it was to oversee the kingdom rule it for a few days.

Why?

Because Elista thought it grand fun to irritate him. If he didn't think of her as a sister, he might find this annoying. But she was family and he did love her. Just not so much today.

Not when he was listening to strong Feyen men complain about trivial things that they in all reality could take care off with nothing more than a damn thought and a single drop of their natural abilities.

A deep breath and he pawed at the arm of the golden throne of Feyen. "You…."

The double doors of the throne room opened as a page rushed in, "The Queen has welcomed another daughter. Her name is Larna."

Secrets, Lies and Betrayal
by: M.L. Ruscsak

Secrets, Lies and Betrayal
by: M.L. Ruscsak

PART 3

LARNA PRINCESS OF FEYEN

Royal Lies, Family Secrets

and a Daughter's Betrayal

"My daughter has delivered yet another child. But I can her wrongness even before she takes her first breath. My dear friend Vasilissa will watch over my daughter's family while I am away. I just pray to the goddess that I will live long enough to watch my daughter's child ascend the throne of Feyen. I pray that the blood line does not end with her."

-The private journal of Alista former Queen of Feyen

Secrets, Lies and Betrayal
by: M.L. Ruscsak

Secrets, Lies and Betrayal
by: M.L. Ruscsak

Rain poured from the clouds above as lightning streaked the moonless midnight sky. The wind howled restlessly throughout the Castle of Water forcing cold water to pass the inviable barriers. This was an omen. It had to be. Or why else would the one calm night of the cold season suddenly turn into this massive, endless storm? How was this storm so powerful to displace scores of MegMoks?

No, this could be no ordinary storm. It couldn't be.

Oh, how those around the city feared this night. Fear the sky breaking open to another attack from unworldly Fey. Fear that the sins of Great war would come back to haunt them on this night.

They were the talking's of the old and descripted Fey. Men and yes woman who had stood witness to the Great War. Many who had been just small children back then. And many who knew more of the truth than others.

They knew that the war hadn't ended. Oh no it had yet to begin. The so called Great War had been nothing more than a few thousand Fey choosing sides. Choosing their victor. And both sides had lost.

Secrets, Lies and Betrayal
by: M.L. Ruscsak

Secrets, Lies and Betrayal
by: M.L. Ruscsak

CHAPTER 1: MYRDDIN

Myrddin glanced out of the tall glass window rain and sleet coving the darkness of the night. By rights he should be sleeping. He should be doing anything other than listing to this Feyen male ramble and plead for things that he could just well enough settle on his own.

Another bolt of lightning arched in the sky. Another bolt lighting up the sky mimicking yet another explosion.

After living in this place for less than two hundred light cycles he had never seen a storm such as this. He had never bore witness to any natural event that had caused every Fey... every living creature to take cover, hoping to be spared.

What was it that was putting so many brave warriors to bare their arms openly and look toward the sky? What didn't he yet know that would cause even the darkest of Fey

Secrets, Lies and Betrayal
by: M.L. Ruscsak

to sharpen their own skilled weapons? Weapons that had nothing to do with steel and everything to do with their trust of natures.

He didn't know, but as soon as this idiot left his sight, he would go and find the answer. That is if an answer could be found within the archives of the royal library. If not, he could and would drag one of his honorary uncles here and they could just as well explain it.

Not paying attention to the practitioner, Myrddin welcomed the chance at any intrusion. Welcomed the first sign of any reason to no longer be in this room when there were several more important matters that needed to be done.

Almost ready to dismiss the man… the large water crystal door slid open just enough for a worried page to enter.

Something about his demeanor didn't seem right. Something… "The queen? Is she well?" He spoke above the voice of the practitioner not caring if he offended the man or not.

At once all of those who had mulling about hoping to gain his ear, were suddenly looking toward the page that no one usually acknowledge. Most barely containing their rage at the interruption.

Secrets, Lies and Betrayal
by: M.L. Ruscsak

The page bowed just enough to show respect before approaching the dais. "Yes, Lord Myrddin. Queen Elista is well. She has finally given birth. The child will be called Larna. Tenth in line to the throne of Feyen."

Tenth? This was Elista's third child. Soo…

"Everyone out." When no-one moved… Myrddin growled loud enough for the water that held just below their feet to splash up… just enough for a few MegMok to escape from their home. "**NOW**."

It wasn't until every court currier, page and practitioner had left, that he finally let out a breath. Something wasn't right. And he had to find out what. The shadow fluttering below a candle gave him the means. He just hoped that Flint would be accommodating.

Carefully crossing the large empty room, he knelt before the shadow. "My friend. I need to speak to Lord Flint. Will you help me locate him?"

It was a long shot. Really, it was more than that. Flint had gone to some Star City to help prepare for something. The whole thing was much too vague to even guess. But Flint had said that could return should the need arise.

Naming this third born heir the tenth in line for the throne sounded wrong. It sounded that Flint would be needed to help deal with the reason behind Elista's declaration.

Secrets, Lies and Betrayal
by: M.L. Ruscsak

A loud yawn from behind him and a flutter of wings. "Nephew? It's much too late in any Star City to be dragged here by the means of a shadow."

Not Flint. Apollo. Not the uncle that he needed. In fact, unless it was a fight, this was the uncle that was the least helpful in most matters. "I was trying to contact Uncle Flint."

Oh, there was not a single drop of blood between them, but here was one of the few men... few people who knew his entire origin. And one of the few who had helped shape him into a man destined to rule.

Apollo waved it off as he yawned again, "Yes well. Even a shadow can make mistakes in the dark. Now, since I'm here, where were you seeking Flint? Perhaps I might settle whatever it is that has even you awake at this godforsaken hour."

Not likely be he answered as politely as he could. "Elista, gave birth to her third spawn."

Closing his eyes, Apollo carefully glided over to the throne of water and made himself comfortable. "We knew she would be giving birth sometime in the near future. So, is that the reason Queen Zarya is causing such a divine storm?"

Secrets, Lies and Betrayal
by: M.L. Ruscsak

What?!?! There was another queen? Another kingdom? When exactly was he going to be told about this? "Queen... I thought it was a natural storm."

Apollo waved it off "In short it is. Zarya is a water dwelling Fey. A fallen Fey in fact. Forgive an old man if I don't recall what star, that she once dwelled from."

"You're not old..." It was true, if you went by appearance Apollo only appeared to be a century old. Even if in truth he was more than three possible, even more than that.

"It's late. Tonight, I'm old. Come daybreak well see if I still feel the same."

Myrddin inclined his head to not only show respect, but to gesture for him to continue, "Of course, sir. Please continue."

Apollo rolled his eyes. Since he made the first old joke he couldn't grumble about Myrddin following his lead. "Zarya is... umm... Flint is much better explaining this. But... She is wedded to one of Nicco's son's. The mother of Sedna. Some think she is a mermaid when in reality she just prefers to look as one. In any case she gets riled up once and while and decides to test her abilities. Since few know for fact that she still dwells on this star..."

Oh, he could see it too well now. A Fey with great power that no-one knew about. The possibilities to cause both destruction and life. Sometime soon he would have to meet this Fey. Just not tonight. "Everyone sees a horrifying storm and nothing else."

"Exactly. Don't know what has her pissed off tonight... but I can bet it's her mate's doing. In any case, unless I'm asked personally to help calm her. I see no reason to step foot in that mess. The birth of my niece on the other hand..."

"Why would Elista name her the tenth in line of accession when she's the third born?" not exactly how he wanted to ask... when dealing with this Fey, direct questions yielded the best results.

For sever minutes Apollo didn't speak, didn't even blink. "Elista is a seer. Naturally gifted which you already know. I'm not one to question what a seer knows. And I will not question her choice... But between us... And I mean it boy. This stay between us. Alista named you as an heir. After Elista and her first three *chosen* heirs. If for any reason Kialen cannot rule, Feyen should go to you. Or to your bloodlines"

Kialen? Not a name that he knew. Least not yet. "Me but..."

"Alista decided it the moment you first met. Mag, seconded her decision. Only one or two of Elista's counsel

Secrets, Lies and Betrayal
by: M.L. Ruscsak

knows. Or will ever know. Lord Eros is not one of them, nor will he ever be."

Not surprising. Eros didn't care for any other than himself or the powers that other's may lend him to advance his own ambitions. But that was a different matter altogether. "So, tenth would mean..."

"You, your sister and any of your children would have to be eliminated before Larna could rule. With every birth, her place drops back. My niece doesn't want her having the throne. In time we might even find out why."

It was too much to think about. Too much to ponder this night. But would be something to keep in mind as Larna grew. No, he would never say anything about the line of accenting but then again, he didn't want to rule anything. He only wished to pursue his own endeavors and make sure the bastard who had tried to kill him, never set foot on this star again.

Secrets, Lies and Betrayal
by: M.L. Ruscsak

His head was spinning with new insight. How ... why had Alista wanted him named as an heir of Feyen? It didn't make sense. Unless....

No Magmas... Lord Magmas of Pallas... wasn't that much of a fool to think that he could bring the troubles of the Star Cities here to Feyen? Here to this great star.

No, he couldn't...

He wouldn't.

A chill went through him. The same chill of warning that he had had back on Pallas. Magmas was dangerous. He was hungry with power that wasn't his own. Starving for more. And he wouldn't stop until he had everything that he ever wanted.

Secrets, Lies and Betrayal
by: M.L. Ruscsak

CHAPTER 2: DIANDRA

Diandra fluttered just enough for her wings to hold her while she peered into the royal cradle of Feyen. Her golden blond hair falling around her as she peered down. Every royal child of the royal line had slept in the warm embrace of the gold inlay and gelled watered bedding. Yet this was the first royal to be kept in her own room just hours after her arrival.

Glancing back to her father, Diandra wrinkled her nose. "She smells and has more wrinkles than a troll slug."

Coming closer King Isdemus sat his crown on the small stand next to the door. Right now, he wished to be nothing more than the father for both of the small children. Peeking over at the sleeping newborn, he smiled, "I remember someone else who was full of wrinkles when she was born."

Her sapphire eyes widened as she gazed up at him, "Who papa. Who?"

Secrets, Lies and Betrayal
by: M.L. Ruscsak

He scratched his narrow chin, thinking back for a long moment. Then a slow smile touched his lips, "I think you grew into your skin quite well."

Slapping her father's arm playfully Diandra laughed, "Oh, papa. You're teasing."

Isdemus chuckled, "Come darling, I think your cousin Faerydae will be arriving soon."

With her sister forgotten she landed softly on the floor. "Faerydae? Really? Is she bringing presents? I love when she brings presents."

Faerydae was much too young to worry about presents or proper protocol. Her father on the other hand. "We'll just have to and find out." He let his hand down for his little girl to grip his finger. Neither worrying about the sleeping baby. Neither worrying about the reason her mother had placed this infant so far from the royal apartments. No, all that mattered now was the thought of presents and sharing the joyous news about the infant's arrival.

Secrets, Lies and Betrayal
by: M.L. Ruscsak

CHAPTER 3: MYRDDIN

Myrddin tapped on the Solaris door. Queen Elista had been hiding in here since just hours after giving birth. Hiding here instead of being with her newborn child. Hiding instead of allowing her body to rest after giving birth.

Some would think that she "the queen" just needed time to adjust to have a new baby within the castle. Some may even think that her distancing herself from the child was normal for any strong Fey. For any strong royal Fey.

He knew better. After all, he had been there within the hours of Elista giving birth both times before. He would be there when she had more children that she had already decided that she wanted. But there was something wrong with this child. This new born. He was damn well going to find out what.

Secrets, Lies and Betrayal
by: M.L. Ruscsak

Not hearing her answer, he slowly pushed the coral door open. Yet he didn't dare enter. Not yet. Not until she gave her permission. So, he waited until she turned from her window. A window that had the appearance of being a huge drop of water. Wet to the touch, but didn't moisten the air. "Elista?"

She hadn't yet turned to him, her royal blue house robe tied tight around her dragging on the floor. "I should have known you would be the one to seek me out when I ask for solitude."

Crossing his arms and leaning on the door frame, Myrddin leaned in feeling the bite of something dangerous still hanging in the air. Her acknowledgement of his presence wasn't enough to lower the protection spell. Least not yet.

Allowing his eye to follow the jagged curve of the frame he quietly said, "One day I would like to know about this spell that you have created here."

"If you truly wish to know ask my mother. It was she who developed it, I just added to it." Finally, she turned her face ash gray and sickly. Her eyes glazed from tears.

He didn't care if the spell was in place. Didn't care if he would be bleeding by the time he crossed the room. Something was wrong with Elista. Something was tearing her soul in a way that needed to be stopped.

Secrets, Lies and Betrayal
by: M.L. Ruscsak

Ten large steps and he held her in his arm. His dragon black wings folded around her taking the chill off of her skin. A few specks of blood already dripping to the floor. What had caused the now fresh wounds he couldn't say, for he hadn't felt them. Right now, that didn't matter. "Elista? What's wrong?"

"I carried my daughter in my stomach for months. Almost entire light cycle." She sniffled into his chest.

This he knew. He knew the joy that had lit her young face the day she had announced the welcomed addition that would bestow the kingdom. "I know."

"Then you must know Isdemus is not the father. He couldn't have been."

That he didn't know. Couldn't have known since he didn't ask questions that led to the knowledge of who was laying with whom. Unsure of what to say he only said, "Elista?"

"Oh, her father was killed… very slowly… so you…" She stiffened in his arms and sniffed the air, "Myrddin Devros, I swear you have rocks for brains. Coming in here with the spell still in place."

There it was the single switch from upset female to the queen. "It is my sworn duty to see that you are taken care of. I can't very well do that outside of this room, now can I?"

Secrets, Lies and Betrayal
by: M.L. Ruscsak

Elista balled her fist and plowed it into her shoulder. Not much of a punch since she was snuggling against him, but still enough to show some temper. "You are a pain in my ass and have been since you first came to Feyen. However, "She pulled away from him and recalled her spell... The gray hue that had lit the room fell as the spell lifted and the colors of the ocean floor reclaimed the area. "You do not deserve to bleed to death because you think that I need a hug."

"I wouldn't bleed to death. Just bleed. Beside the MegMok haven't had anything other than kitchen scraps for a while. I would think they would love to a few drops of blood to feast on."

Her eyes narrowed at him. "Only you would wish to feed them your blood."

Watching her shuffle over to the window seat he joined her knowing the rough coral texture of the wall would not be as comfortable as Elista made it look. "A proper couch and seating area in here would be more relaxing than the simple window seat."

She glances at him, puzzled. "You are really blind when you choose to be."

"I beg your pardon?"

A small gesture with her finger on the door tightly closed. A breath more and the windows began to leak water into the room. The floor began to bubble as the water... and the MegMok were let loose from the barriers.

"Elista?'

"Being completely surrounded by water helps me think. I can fill this space simply by closing the door. But if I were to go into the sea and cover myself..."

Even if she hadn't closed her eyes, he could have felt her longing to be within the water. But he could understand why she chose this room rather than doing what her heart longed for. "You would put every living thing that dwelled there in danger." Yes, he could see that now. Chuckling, he sat back against the wall. His feet now covered in the water and his robed completely soaked. "So, I guess no soft couch then."

It wasn't until the room was more than waist deep that Elista moved nor spoke. Getting to her feet, she slipped her robe off some covering made of plant life, covering things that only her husband should see. Lying in the water, she finally said, "Larna's father is dead, so you my over bearing pain in the ass brother can't be going and finding him just to see how many ways you can make him die."

Myrddin crossed his massive arms and glared at her. "Oh, I think we both know if there was a need I would do just that."

Secrets, Lies and Betrayal
by: M.L. Ruscsak

Not only would he but it was a possibility that he would force open the gate to the underkingdom once again. "He was fed very slowly to the MegMok. The last bit of him being fed to them just days before I delivered."

Oh shit. Elista wasn't one for cruelty. Wasn't one to make someone suffer, "He was..."?

"Uncle Karnack made sure he would be alive until the very last second that the MegMok dined on his flesh." She paused, letting her voice become dark, "At my request."

Clearing his throat, he very cautiously asked, "What exactly did he do to prick your fury?"

"He was a royal Fey. From where, I don't know. But not from here. I asked Vas To help identify him. Even she could not say where he dwelled from. But he wasn't born to this star."

"That's why she and her children were here?" he said it more to himself as the pieced began to slip into place.

"Partly. It was time for you to meet them. However, I do not recall giving my permission to give Addy your heart."

He had met Adrianna years before. Perhaps it was time to tell this queen about that meeting. "I still have a heart beating in my chest should anyone need to hear it." Myrddin paused, looking toward his feet, "Besides, that was

Secrets, Lies and Betrayal
by: M.L. Ruscsak

done the first time that I had met her. And that, my darling was well before you became queen."

It took only a moment for Elista to understand what he was saying. Only a moment to stand before him and wave her finger at him, "You... damn it... she is much too young...."

"She was much too young to be responsible for two hearts. That I will agree to. But..." Myrddin slipped off the bench and waded to the far end of the room. "You're a seer Elista. So, I hope you understand. There was something inside of me warning me of something should Addy not leave here with my heart. I discussed it with both Blake and Claec before doing so. And both men witnessed it. With both being of royal blood they combined what could and preformed a binding as well." Another breath and stood before her taking her small hands in his, "It was the only way to keep her safe."

"Very well. I will try to explain this to Vas. But I warn you now she is not to be trifled with when it comes to the protection of her children."

"I'll keep that in mind when I contact her about Larna."

She turned her head away from him, "Some things shouldn't be said Myrddin. And other things just as well forgotten."

Secrets, Lies and Betrayal
by: M.L. Ruscsak

"So, you have your daughter placed far away from you for the sins of her father?"

"Of course not. I would never condemn a child because of the father." She paused, "I placed her there because I can't destroy a child for events that I'm not sure will happen."

"Events that you can protect against?"

Once more her eyes narrowed into tiny slits. "I can and I have. As of her birth, she will only be able to learn any ability that I allow. The day will come that she will wish to learn the darker of the Feyen abilities. Between us we will decide what abilities that she will be allowed to nurture on her own. I just pray to the goddess that that will be enough."

As the water receded Elista stood before Myrddin. Her hand resting softly on his arm. Her eyes locking with his. "I need a promise. And I need this to be a blood oath."

In all of his years he had only heard of a blood oath being taken once. The reason had never been discussed. Nor would it be. But he understood the rules of such an oath. It could only be broken when one of them died, or the reason for the oath had run its course. "You don't need my blood to earn my silence, but I would give to you anyways."

It wasn't until they shared a single drop of blood that Elista said anything at all, "Should I die by the means of any. You must find a way to end Larna. She must not come into power. She cannot gain the gifts of the throne."

"Even if there is no other way but to completely destroy her. I promise she will never know the power of Feyen. Or that of her bloodline."

Elista looked at him a gave a grim smile. "I know you do not want the throne for yourself…"

"My first born has been prophesied long before I was even born. That said, I think someone who is destined to save the entire Fey race would make a wonderful queen of Feyen."

"When you figure out how she will rule you will have to share it with me."

"My darling sister, the only way my bloodline will ever rule this country would be over your death."

She patted his cheek and smiled, "And we both know the difference between "dead" and "**DEAD**"."

Yes, they did. And very few Fey today could claim to be able to give life to those who no longer could do so on their own. "Should you die at Larna's hand, I will see that your body is taken to the catacombs. Uncle Karnack will gather whatever is left from there."

Elista turned from him, "Not just me Myrddin, but my entire line. A place has already been made for us in the

Secrets, Lies and Betrayal
by: M.L. Ruscsak

Under Kingdom. We will stay there until it is time for your daughter to learn all that she need to know."

Myrddin turned another corner going deeper into the Castle of Water. The royal treasury was in the depths of the Castle. Hidden well below the whole of the Castle. All of royal treasures were hidden here. Oh, they weren't gold and jewels. Not even rare gems that could fashioned into jewelry. No, what was hidden in theses depths were far too dangerous to be seen by just any Fey. Much too dangerous for any including royal Fey.

Still, there was one thing that he was going to seek out. Just one…

"Halt. Who goes…"

Secrets, Lies and Betrayal
by: M.L. Ruscsak

He paused and narrowed his eyes. Now what was a light bearer doing down here? Much too young to have finished his training in war craft. Yet... "Now what did a young guard of the crown do you be placed down here?"

The staff that appeared in his hand was not that of a traditional light bearer. Not a staff that any born from this star could willfully create. No, the staff was made from the gold and Ivory of Barak. "I didn't realize a son of Barak resided in Feyen."

Lightning began to spark from the staff and it was lowered into position to strike. "You don't have permission to enter the vault."

Arrogant. Bah, all from that little star were. Yet they were all fierce warriors. Their staffs even have been told to kill even the darkest of dark Fey. None of that explained why one was here.

Slowly Myrddin took another step closer the bolt of lightning that discharged from the staff coming close enough for the heat to singe his dark blue robe.

A cough from behind him was the only reason that he didn't charge the young guard. "Aleron, lower the staff. Lord Myrddin has as much right to the contents of the vault as I do."

That deep voice. The deep rolling voice that hadn't been heard in far too many years... "Uncle Magmas?"

Secrets, Lies and Betrayal
by: M.L. Ruscsak

Gradually Aleron lowered the staff yet didn't vanish it. Not yet. "I have orders that none shall pass."

Slowly Magmas slid around Myrddin. Slowly approached the young guard, "My boy, I know the training that you have completed. And I know the natural skill that you possess. None of which will serve you any good should I pull the skeleton from your flesh."

This was not an idle threat. Not coming from this man. From this Fey.

It wasn't until the light bearer was far from the

vault that Myrddin dared to speak. "I didn't know a royal from the star of Barak was here."

"Not any royal, the sole heir. Magnar has just claimed the star as his own. That young man is the only one foolish enough to challenge the creator. Yet for the moment isn't willing to challenge me."

Myrddin kicked at the watery barrier, "Make sense. You have a certain name and bloodline."

Secrets, Lies and Betrayal
by: M.L. Ruscsak

Magmas narrowed his eyes but chose to ignore the statement, "Now why are you down here I wonder?"

Not so much a question as a demand to state his business. "Elista and I have both foreseen her demise. And the means that will cause it."

"Then it can be stopped."

With a single shake of his head, Myrddin whispered, "Delayed. Everything will happen in order that is meant to be, and Magmas, for the reason that I don't agree with, this must come about."

Reluctantly Magmas nodded, "Then let us go into the vault and you can tell me why."

The passing the thick barrier Myrddin couldn't help but to feel that he still had MegMok clinging to him. Couldn't help but to feel they were waiting for a reason not to make him their next meal. Yet for all of the feelings that

Secrets, Lies and Betrayal
by: M.L. Ruscsak

he was having, not a single one had actually attached themselves to him.

"What really protects this room?"

Was asked at the same time as, "Why is my granddaughter going to die?"

For a long moment they both assessed one another, measuring each other's natural abilities. Measuring each other's temper. Myrddin looked away first.

"Larna Is the child of another royal Fey. That Fey in question is beyond even my grasp, however, I believe that the ruler of Pallas sent him here."

Magmas turned slightly, "It wouldn't be the first time that he has used a child as a pawn in his sick game. I'm certain that it won't be the last."

"Uncle?"

"Faerydae. Are you aware that she isn't Apollo's daughter?"

Myrddin nodded once, "I'm aware that Apollo has only sired one child a boy. And that was shortly after the Great War." And he knew who that child was. Had always known but like today he would never admit that to anyone. Including Apollo.

Secrets, Lies and Betrayal
by: M.L. Ruscsak

"Faerydae is the daughter of Pallas. Born to a royal Fey they we have yet to Identify. She was tossed into the void by her mother. Retrieved by the traitor. Sent to live on a star that now houses Magnar and part of his army of creations. And taken in by Apollo before being handed over to his grandson. All before she was old enough to spread her wings and flutter for the first time." Apollo paused and turned from him, "Make no mistake she is not as sweet and innocent as she pretends to be. But she is trainable and is a suitable guard to watch over Adrianna."

There was more to that story, he could almost bet on it. Yet, he couldn't bring himself to ask. But he would ask, "How certain are you that she will not deceive my betrothed?"

"My boy, since we have met I have known two truths about you. One you are not naive though you pretend to be. And second, you will destroy anyone who wishes harm of your family. And that has included providing details about your home star so that Magnar could penetrate it quietly."

This was the first news that he had had in more years than not. Juts speaking of it now... how his heart longed to know about his sister. "And has he?"

"Your mother still rules, but for long. Your sister is ascending soon. And has already chosen a suitable mate."

Secrets, Lies and Betrayal
by: M.L. Ruscsak

There was something in the way Magmas said that. "One that Magnar chose?"

"See, you are learning quickly. Once they bind to one another, Estare will gain the ability to dream walk. We think that she will be able to reach Nisha once she is born."

"And if she can't?"

"There will still be ways to train your daughter in all that she will need to save the Star Cities." Magmas paused and drew closer to Myrddin, "That said, why did you need access to the vault?"

"The Black sword of the first. It will be used to slay the royal family of Feyen. I won't stop the event from happening, but I will buy Addy time to grow into the powers that she will need for the events that will follow."

"So, you mean to hide the cursed thing."

"Yes and no. It will be found at the proper moment. And only found by the little bitch that Elista has now given birth to. But, it won't be housed in plain sight. Not now." He paused, "This will hard for you watch. Perhaps you should stay among the stars until the time has passed."

"No, I have prepared for this for many years. It is why Faerydae's son will wed your daughter. It will keep the bloodlines whole."

"I'll see to it. Even if that is many years from now."

Secrets, Lies and Betrayal
by: M.L. Ruscsak

Cloaked in total darkness he sat the sword of the first deep within the great waterfall of the Castle of Water. None could see it from the surface. The MegMok will protect it from the water.

The moment that he left this cliff. The moment he took his hand off of the black crystal hilt the event that Elista had foreseen would come. Her death would not be stopped.

Perhaps delayed. Maybe for a short time.

His heart ached. As he was sure her grandfather's was.

It was for the greater good. He just had to remember that. He just had to remind himself that his daughter once she was old enough would have the ability to bring back the dead.

Death was only temporary.

Slowly his fingers withdrew from the hilt. The water crashing once more over the great cliff.

Secrets, Lies and Betrayal
by: M.L. Ruscsak

Secrets, Lies and Betrayal
by: M.L. Ruscsak

CHAPTER 4: LARNA

It was the eve of her fifth light cycle and her beloved mother was giving birth yet again. This should be her time. Hers. She should be the focus of everyone's attention. Diandra always had a week of celebrations for her birthday. Terza, didn't care for parties, but still a carnival was held in her honor.

But what did she get for her birthday? A new baby that had no more meaning to her than the older two that she already had. After all, she couldn't play dress up with it. Practice her flying with it.

No, all she could do was look at it and hope that it didn't cry or shit itself.

A tap on her darkly painted door only made her pout more. "Go away."

Secrets, Lies and Betrayal
by: M.L. Ruscsak

The door eased open to her so-called papa. She knew better. She knew they didn't share, a drop of blood in common. "Do want to see your new baby brother?"

A brother. Well, it could be worse, it could be another sister. "No, I don't want to see the little worm."

Isdemus laughed, "Worm is it? Well, I do suppose that is a better name than wrinkled troll slug."

At that she finally looked at him. But now instead of pouting she looked confused. She didn't much like to feel confused. "I never called him a troll slug."

"No, but your sister thought you were one. And your older sister thought her one. I am pleased that at least one of my girls could come up with a better name."

"You don't mind my calling him a worm or troll slug?"

Finally sitting on the edge of her bed, Isdemus kissed her head as he pulled her tight to him, "My darling, you are still but a little Fey. You speak honestly. You and your sisters. So why would I or anyone ever senor what you say when it comes to your own opinion. So, if you need to call your bother a worn then so be it. But you will not turn him into one."

Secrets, Lies and Betrayal
by: M.L. Ruscsak

She hadn't thought of that. Now she wished that she had... wished that she gone cast that spell before Isdemus had already banned her from doing so.

Yet...

Her sisters... surely, she could get one of them to as a birthday surprise.

"Now, since you are celebrating your birthday, your mother has granted you the privilege to go swim in her Solaris with the MegMok for the remainder of the day. She has also cast a spell so you can see the little darlings that you seem so fond of."

"Really? Really, I can go play with them?"

"You can on the condition that they all remain in the Solaris. I don't want to see a single one outside of their home."

She gave him a sideways glance and smiled oh so sweetly, "Yes papa."

Secrets, Lies and Betrayal
by: M.L. Ruscsak

Larna held one the slimy adult MegMok's close to her like a beloved teddy bear. "Who does he think that he is telling when he says I can't keep you with me. You love me, I know you do."

The MegMok snapped its teeth tighter contorting its body trying to slip away. It's only eye locked on her face, if it could have attacked it would have. As it was, it could only lay there helplessly in the child's embrace.

"You are the only one that understands me. I don't belong to this family, I really, really don't. Oh, how I wish that I could forever live among your kind and away from my bratty sisters."

Secrets, Lies and Betrayal
by: M.L. Ruscsak

"Maybe soon I can live here forever and ever and never have to listen to them again."

Secrets, Lies and Betrayal
by: M.L. Ruscsak

Secrets, Lies and Betrayal
by: M.L. Ruscsak

CHAPTER 5: MYRDDIN

He gave the nursery door a token tap before entering. Then stood there watching Elista rock her baby with the evening light streaming I through the pale blue glass. "It's good to see you with your offspring."

Elista glanced up at him with tired, haunted eyes. "Would you like to meet Kailen? He is the spitting image of his father."

Judging by the look in her eyes she wasn't talking about the baby that she held nestled in her arms, but the man that he could grow to become. "Has your vision changed?"

A deep sad sigh slipped from her lips. "I want it to so badly that it hurts. I want to see all of my children grown

Secrets, Lies and Betrayal
by: M.L. Ruscsak

into the Fey that they are meant to. Yet... I cannot be selfish. Their deaths will give the Under Kingdom, the power that your daughter will need to stop the great army that is planning our doom."

"You see her now? You see what is still veiled from me?"

She shook her head, then pulled her baby close to her. "I see the power that eclipses even that of Lord Magnar. I see companion in her that other will see as weakness. And see the power... Oh Myrddin, I can feel her power whenever I reach for the vision. She is the darkness and the light. She is all that is our star and even those that are too far away to see. I see all of it and yet I cannot tell you what she will look like. I cannot tell you if she will have your stiff deposition or her mother's flowing easy demeanor."

He nodded once, "What she looks like means nothing to me until I can hold her in my arms. Until the day that I can be with her to stand against those who only seek to destroy. But..." He turned his head slightly, "There may be a way to save your children."

She reached for his hand in earnest, "What do you suggest?"

"Magnar and I both possess the ability to create certain things. I'm not as skilled in it yet. But... I could use a few drops of their blood and create a being that would age and mimic them. The color of their blood would be different since they…"

Exactment lit her face and her voice, "Wouldn't be true royal Fey."

"But they would be alive and their powers would still feed the Under Kingdom."

"Could you do this for my husband and myself as well?"

"You are the Queen Elista. You are needed here."

Shaking her head, she stopped him, "Not so that I can leave, but so my children shall know their mother. And their father."

For a long moment he sat there. "I can. But not Larna. I will do nothing to bring her a full life."

"Then we are agreed. After her birth celebration you will gather what you need and my children will be housed with my grandfather on the star that now rules."

He didn't like it, but he understood it. For Elista to do what needed to be done, her children needed to be safe. Her blood lines would need to be protected. "I have one request."

She nodded once, "Of course you would."

Secrets, Lies and Betrayal
by: M.L. Ruscsak

"I would like for both Blake and Galeron to know about this."

For a long moment she just sat there too stunned for words, "You think there will come a time when one or both will need to know."

Myrddin turned from her to gaze out of her window. For a long time just watched as the water fell from the edges of the castle. "I think there will come a time when something happens that it will appear that I am the likely suspect. It would be prudent if others knew and were in positions to help should I need them."

"Very well. With that being the case I will talk to Vas about Celeste being betrothed to Blake. And to Uncle Apollo about betrothing Faerydae to Galeron. It would settle any problem that may show up after I am no longer here." Elista paused, then quietly added, "All of the royal decrees that I written or will write are housed in the sacred temples hidden beneath the castles. Should you ever need them."

Secrets, Lies and Betrayal
by: M.L. Ruscsak

CHAPTER 6: VASILISSA

Vasilissa sat back on the long over stuffed couch glaring at the child that she had known from birth. Her arms crossed in an un-queenly manner. And her long dark hair with strands of gold cascading down her back. Her eye narrowed just a bit with irritation. "Let me get this straight since I am clearly missing something..." She leaned forward just a hair, "You and Myrddin have both foresaw your death. You both know the cause of that death. And the best that you can come up with is making elaborate copies of your children and just buying time until Larna kills you." Her lips curled into a snarl, "Are you a fool?"

Elista raised her hands, chest high in surrender. Her mother had warned her that Vasilissa her aunt was fiercely

Secrets, Lies and Betrayal
by: M.L. Ruscsak

protective. But Vasilissa the Queen was a force not to be reckoned with. "Aunt Vas, please. I did not bring you here to discuss what I have already decided but to make sure you don't do anything to stop this."

Sitting back once again Vasilissa bit her tongue, but chose to say nothing.

"Before Nisha can be born, I will be needed in the Under Kingdom. Uncle Karnack has found a spell that will allow me to do that regardless of how much of my body is retrieved."

Frustrated, she snapped out of the seat. With anger she shoved the overstuffed winter blue chair across the wall with enough force to slam into the far wall. "So, you plan of doing nothing about the threat. A threat that you can kill right this second without anyone questioning you. A threat that could be fed to the MegMoks right here… right now."

Calming her breathing, Elista slowly let out a slow deep breath. "No, her death will be at the hands of the Queen. Not by me." Closing her sea blue eyes, she took a single breath, "Myrddin has the means to keep her alive until then."

Letting the mist seep from her body and covering the floor Vasilissa let herself feel all that was around her. Let herself listen to thinks that only she could hear. Finally

Secrets, Lies and Betrayal
by: M.L. Ruscsak

calling the black deadly mist back to her, she sighed, "Since I am assuming that your mother and grandfather both already know about this. I will concede not to kill the little darling the moment that she turns into such a ripe little bitch."

It was about as much of a concession that she was going to get. At least for now. "In the meantime, I am requesting that Blake be considered as a suitable betrothal for Celeste."

With a flick of her wrist a high back chair made of mist and water formed just feet away from where Elista sat in her own comfortable overstuffed chair. Just feet away from the Feyen Queen. Her face drew tight as she spoke through clenched teeth, "You understand that Celeste lust for Myrddin."

"I do. And I understand that Myrddin would feed her the Shades if she suggested a match. Trust me, my brother has no love for her only the will to tolerate her from time to time."

The words startled Vasilissa. From listening to Celeste, she had thought Myrddin would ask for a match well before he would consider Adrianna. Thinking back, she had found it odd that a dark Fey would want to bind to a Fey of Light... but now... A Star City Fey would never... "He wishes to be betrothed to Adrianna." Not a question but confirmation.

Secrets, Lies and Betrayal
by: M.L. Ruscsak

"He does. And you already know that he and your daughter have switched hearts."

Anger flashed in Vasilissa's eyes, "I know that she is much too young to have that kind of bond with anyone. However, seeing that Myrddin is who he is I can concede that it was in her best interest."

"Very well. Then it is decided That he will be betrothed to her after she apprentice's in my court."

Closing her dark eyes Vasilissa asked, "Is there a reason you don't want her sister to apprentice with you?"

"There is. And not one that I wish to discuss."

Vasilissa closed her eyes and pretended not to ponder those words. Ponder why one of her girls was favored over the other. And chose not ponder why Celeste now had the feel of those who dwelled deep within the marshlands.

No, she would not ponder it today, but later. Much later.

Secrets, Lies and Betrayal
by: M.L. Ruscsak

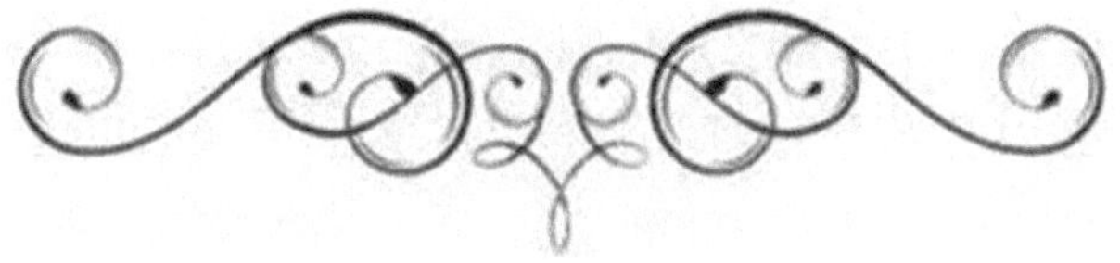

CHAPTER 7: CELESTE

Celeste very quietly made her way around the castle of water. No one would dare stop her. Not with her mother in residence. Besides, if she did, it wasn't like she would have to lie about her intentions. After all, she only wished to give her blessings to the birthday girl.

Turning yet another corner of coral and water trapped behind invisible barriers she finally she came to a stop. There only feet away was her little target. Her waist length blond hair dripping wet and her dress clinging to her. Forcing a friendly smile, she gave her best curtsy, "Princess Larna."

Larna paused before too cautiously approaching, "Since when does the heir of Lite curtsy to a Princess of Feyen?"

Secrets, Lies and Betrayal
by: M.L. Ruscsak

"It is your birthday." Straightening up and adjusting her long-pleated skirt she continued, "Besides, there is something that I wish to share with you. It is very important and very secretive. That is if I can trust you to keep a secret."

Narrowing her eyes Larna shrugged, "I keep many of the castle's secrets. I don't see the harm in holding one more."

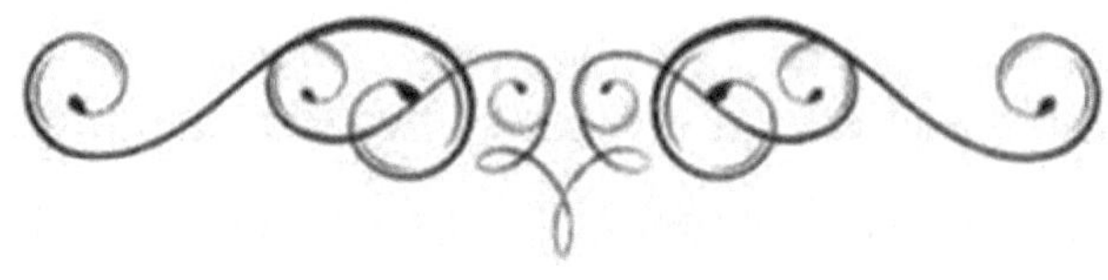

Going into the first private room that she could find Celeste pulled Larna inside and shut the door. "There I think this should be private enough."

Shrugging Larna shuffled over to the coral colored couch. Her short legs barely dangling over the sides. "No one comes in here. It's for unimportant guess who don't like the constant surroundings of water. It's really quite ridiculous if you think about it. I mean really this is the castle of water. One would think that you would be sounded by the element."

Secrets, Lies and Betrayal
by: M.L. Ruscsak

Looking around, she saw the room for the first time. Solid walls made with plaster and coral. Plain white furniture of white with gold trim. A single long couch worthy of any common Fey. Nothing remarkable in this room. Nothing that could catch fire, nor was worthy of any true royal. Deciding to play this coyly Celesta replied oh so sweetly, "You would but then you have those who are weakened by water. Such as those who draw their abilities from fire and lava."

Ignoring the statement Larna squared her shoulders, "What is the secret?"

Padding over to the couch Celeste sat near her young cousin then held out her thin hand. A red jewel forming within her palm. "Do you know what this is?"

"A red rock."

Of course, the little twerp would only see the rock and nothing else. Celeste thought, but managed not to say the words out loud. "Well, yes, but what kind of rock?"

Slowly Larna leaned I closer as swirling mist began to circulate within the stone, "OOO, how does it do that?"

"This is a Seer's Stone. It houses mystic abilities. And the deity that dwells inside sometimes is willing to share his vast knowledge with the holder."

"I want to see. Make him appear. Make him."

Secrets, Lies and Betrayal
by: M.L. Ruscsak

Just the reaction that she was hoping for. Greed was a part of Larna as was the desire to possess things that were completely out of her scope of natural abilities. "Well, I don't know. He does get very upset when people find out about him."

"I want to see. Make him appear. It's my birthday you have to."

"You have to promise never to tell another living soul about him."

Larna gazed deepened into the stone never looking back at Celeste, "I promise, now, where is he? Show me."

Making her smile Celeste drew the stone close to her face. "My lord, can you hear me?"

She knew that he could. Knew that he had been waiting for her to find the princess of Feyen. Knew that he was waiting until just the right time to show himself. Then ever so slowly the mist within the stone cleared and ...

"Ah, so there is a new Fey worthy of my help."

Startled Larna jumped back in her seat, then glanced up at Celeste, "He's so old. And wrinkly. Had he not grown into his skin yet? Or perhaps he's so old that he is growing out of it."

Secrets, Lies and Betrayal
by: M.L. Ruscsak

They both ignored her little outburst. After all, she was a child and children didn't always use caution with their words.

"I am, Magmas the great god of the stars. And who my dear might you be."

"I am Princess Larna."

Magmas smiled for but a moment. "Would you like for me to tell you your future my dear? Would like to know what the stars have in store for you?"

Clapping excitedly Larna bounced, "Yes. Yes, I would. Tell me. Tell. ME. Now."

"Very well…" closing his sunken in eyes Magmas cleared his throat, "I see you ruling all of Feyen. Your powers and natural abilities, bringing life back into the dyeing cities. And one day you will join me among the great gods and become my bride. But that won't be for many years yet. Not until the battle for your star has been fought and won. Then and only then will you join me on Pallas and join your powers with mine."

"I am to be the Queen of Feyen? But my sister…."

"Is weak. Her blood impure. When the time is right, you will know what to do."

Secrets, Lies and Betrayal
by: M.L. Ruscsak

It felt like hours that she had sat there listening to this dribble of conversations. Listened to a child try to earn favor with such a cherished and loved god. Still, she waited until the image of Magmas faded, then she snatched her precious stone away.

"I hope you found him as enchanting as I so." She leaned back, placing her stone into the fold of her skirt.

"I did." Larna paused and squared her shoulders, "One day I will be queen of Feyen. And all will cower before me."

Secrets, Lies and Betrayal
by: M.L. Ruscsak

CHAPTER 8: LARNA

10 years later

Larna slammed her chamber door close with a thunderous roar. How dare her mother dismiss her or the knowledge that she had. How dare she say that her powers were not strong enough to rule over citizens that could never be bound to her. How dare she think that Diandra would rule when there wasn't a single drop of royal blue blood held within her tiny veins.

Growling at herself, she used a gust of wind to slam her writing desk against the wall, leaving it nothing more than a pile of debris. Her temper... her dark, deadly temper flaring once more. Rage burning so deep inside of her that

Secrets, Lies and Betrayal
by: M.L. Ruscsak

she couldn't even feel the edges that might be smoothed out. Even if she could that was something that she would never let happen.

Not today. Not when the blasted crown princess of Darke had come back to the city. Not when the powers that should already be hers were muted and unable to be tapped into. Powers that the deity Magmas had told her that she should have. Abilities that someone had taken from her.

How dare her mother do this to her. It had to be her doing. It had to be.

Her dark wood bed caught a flame she grabbed for a single pillow to shed. Gleefully, she watched and the matching night stand caught a single ember. Soon her entire room would be ablaze. And if she could hold off the scores of guards the entire Castle of Earth would go with it.

Smoke caught in the back of her throat. Just a momentary inconvenience. No real harm could come to her. This she knew for a fact. Yet she watched as the flames grew. Fire danced around her now leaving nothing in the room untouched. Flinging her door open she stood silent as the flames warmed her back and exploded into the hall.

Tapestries being the first things that the flames kissed. The mud gray wall the second.

Secrets, Lies and Betrayal
by: M.L. Ruscsak

Cracks formed as the fire raced away from her tower room. Raced down the cold stone steps and into the royal apartments. It would consume everything before any knew of the threat, …

It would…

Reaching the bottom of the steps Larna paused, her heart racing in her chest. Staring back at her was the Crown Princess of Darke. Her raven black hair barley undone. A flicker of natural fire held dancing on the tip of her finger.

Nothing else was ablaze with anger. Nothing showing signs of smoke. Not a single singe of embers that had yet to be extinguished.

"Darling cousin, if you wish to burn your room then so be it. But really, trying to destroy the entire castle that has withstood so much dark fury… what are you ever thinking?"

She wanted to lunge at the brat… the whore… who would steal the man of her desire. Wanted to tear her limb from precious limb. And knew with great certainty that she would never get close enough to touch her.

Instead, she hissed, "You have no idea how hard it is to live here. To live knowing that you were born for greatness. And knowing your mother stole your abilities so that you will never reach it."

Secrets, Lies and Betrayal
by: M.L. Ruscsak

Taking a seat on the cream-colored sofa Adrianna patted the seat next to her, "Come sit with me Larna. Perhaps we shall reach a compromise. Perhaps not. But either way you need to give voice to your concerns or they will always consume you."

She didn't want to say anything to this Troll slug. This traitor to the Fey. This bringer of death. Yet... between the two of Vasilissa's children this was the one that held the ear of the Feyen counsel. This was a Fey that her mother would listen to. "Were you aware that my mother stole my natural powers the very moment that she gave me life."

Adrianna rolled her eyes and gave a half smile, "Elista did not steal your powers. She blocked those that would do harm to the Fey that dwell with your boarders. From where I sit, perhaps she should have blocked all of them giving you access to only one at a time until you not only mastered it but understood when not to use it."

That Bitch! How dare she suggest such a thing. How dare she...

"However, I can see your point of view." Adrianna continued, "So, I offer this..." She held out her hands palm side up, "Let me see your hands Larna. Let me see what your mother truly locked away. Let me see if this is a gift that you may earn back."

"And if she sealed it away forever?"

Secrets, Lies and Betrayal
by: M.L. Ruscsak

"I offer no promises. But I do not wish to be the one standing here each time that you decide to burn the castles to the ground. Traveling by shadow is no easy thing."

Traveling by Shadow!!! Only the great royals of the past could do such a thing. How was this worthless whore able to summon them? How was she able to use them for travel? How? How when even her twin could not. And Celeste had the ear of a great deity? It wasn't fair. It wasn't.

Hiding her rage, she slipped her hands into Adrianna's and felt the sense of calm surround her. Solace. A sense of being whole. Such a tranquil feeling. And not one of her own.

"Ah, I see now. Elista didn't take them, nor did she block them. She... I do not have words for what she did, but your bloodlines are the problem. Did you not know that Isdemus is not your sire?"

Larna had been watching since Adrianna closed her eyes and had started speaking. Now she just sat there all of her temper drained away. "I thought as much, but never..." It was a soft mumble. One that she hadn't realized that she had given voice to until Adrianna spoke.

"Your sire was not a kind man. Not a man worthy of royal blood. His powers... abilities were corrupted. Yet I cannot see how or by what. It's those abilities that have been locked away. Larna you can't tap into those abilities.

Secrets, Lies and Betrayal
by: M.L. Ruscsak

Not as learned one and certainly not as a natural one. They would not only destroy the Fey of this kingdom, but you as well."

Narrowing her eyes, she asked "What abilities were they?"

"It is a jumble. I'm sorry, but I cannot answer that." She sat back and sighed, "Larna please let this go. If you want to be a great Fey then be a great Fey. You do not need to be queen to do so. You have so much potential. So much passion you can truly do anything that you wish. Build anything you desire."

Quickly she got to her feet. And hissed, "You would rather my sister who does not bleed blue rule over the citizen of Feyen. Rather a child who bleeds purple mist control the armies of the Fey. How dare you. How dare any of you decide to allow a non-royal to rule when one stands before you."

"Oh, come now Larna we both know you are not the only royal Fey in all of Feyen. There are hundreds that bleed royal blue blood. Hundreds that have sworn a duty to protect your mother's bloodline. If she really felt the need one of them would simply wed one of your sisters insuring the bloodline would continue." Stretching her fingers Adrianna glanced down and lowered her voice, "It's been done in the past and I'm sure it will be done again. Now if you are done playing the hurt little princess I have lessons that I need to get to. And Larna…"

Bitch. Whoring bitch.

"… It wouldn't hurt you to sit in on some of those lessons. Perhaps learning to take care of those around you will do something for your temper. Or at least give you something to do with your time."

Storming from the royal apartments she snapped

at the first maid that she came across" Go clean the mess in my chamber. And don't make it look so cheery this time."

The maid curtsied before scurrying away, but the look on her face… How dare she give that look to a real royal Fey. Soon she would make that maid pay for that look.

Secrets, Lies and Betrayal
by: M.L. Ruscsak

That smirk. Soon she would make all of the servants understand who truly ruled this place.

Soon, but not today. No today she other plans.

Taking a deep breath, she slipped out of the main corridor of the royal apartments and began her long slow journey to her private work room.

Making her way to the sacred tunnels of the castles she carefully made sure no-one had foolishly followed her. Made sure none of those pesky shadows were going to tattle on her. Seeing that she was truly alone with not a single flicker out of place, she paused once a more just to double check. Then carefully pass through the solid rock

Secrets, Lies and Betrayal
by: M.L. Ruscsak

into the chamber that had been created long before the great war.

A chamber that she couldn't even guess what it had been. Since there were no doors nor windows. No way to enter unless able to pass through the stone. And there was only one other Fey in all of Feyen that could do that. And only he did so with the full acknowledgment of the royal house.

But she wasn't here to think about Myrddin. She was simply here to think.

This was her private spot. The single room within any of the castles that she could be herself. That she could create her own potions, practice her incantations, but most of all practice her natural Abilities. No-one knew about this room, no-one would ever...

At least not if she could help it.

A deep sigh and she closed her eyes, long ago Celeste had found the book for her. A book dark incantation spells to create life, potions to ensnare even the darkest of Fey. This had been a present for one of her birthday celebrations some years ago. This had been a present after Celeste had shown her the deity. The ruler of all of the stars.

If this Book had been given to Celeste by the deity or not she can say. But then again, it didn't matter. Now the only thing that mattered was the book itself. The binding

Secrets, Lies and Betrayal
by: M.L. Ruscsak

cursed, the pages poisoned. Both could and would kill a lesser Fey. Could kill any Fey Except a true royal.

Lazily to flip open the pages. There had to be a spell or something within the book. There had to be something to be rid of Adrianna. There had to be a way to force her mother to listen. There had to be a way to make Myrddin hers.

There just to be.

Scores of notes line the edges of the pages. Loose parchment scattered on the floor filled with incomplete spells of her own making.

There had to be away and somewhere within this room, she would find it.

Secrets, Lies and Betrayal
by: M.L. Ruscsak

Hours seemed to pass yet with no end in sight. She was nowhere closer to knowing the answers to her problems than she had been when he first entered the room. No closer to finding a way to be rid of the princess of Darke. And no closer to ruling Feyen.

Yet she knew there was an answer. There had to be.

There had to be some legend some spell, some creature that could help her with this. She just had to find it.

Of course, when she found it, she would still have to wait. Wait until at least her eighteenth year. But at least she would have an answer. And a plan.

Myrddin would already be over 200 years old as would Adrianna. Both would already be of age to rule. Both already skilled with their natural abilities.

However, when she wed Myrddin his powers would become hers. She could use him as the tool that she needed to rule over Feyen. She could use his dark abilities to force the lesser of Fey into submission. They would bow down to her as their queen. They would bind themselves with her or face death.

The royal Fey that still lives in Feyen would become her personal guards. Perhaps she would mate with them to see who would give her the most powerful of heirs. Or perhaps she would only allow for Myrddin to slip inside her bed.

But she had time to ponder that. After all it would be years if not decades before she would be required to produce an heir to the throne.

Closing her book, she called in another blank sheet of parchment and her writing quill.

Things that she needed to ask the deity. Things that she would need to know. Things that only he could explain were quickly jotted down.

She already knew that she would be his bride after the battle for this star was fought. Already knew that he wished for her to take a mate before then. She needed an heir to rule after her. One that her people would accept.

That she understood.

But there were other things that he had hinted. Queens who ruled with force were always the most coveted. Their powers the greatest. No-one betrayed them. None sought to destroy them. Those whom they ruled over would do anything for those queens fearing to appear unloyal. Fearing a fate worse than death.

She wanted... needed to know more about those queens. How they ruled. How powerful they were. How

Secrets, Lies and Betrayal
by: M.L. Ruscsak

they controlled those who had more natural abilities than they did.

Were they gracious lovers, or did they take only what they wanted from their mates? She needed to know more personal questions. Questions that a young daughter couldn't ask a mother. Questions that she would have asked any friend that had already been mated with another Fey... if she had any.

But she also needed to find out what he knew if anything, about a way to rid Feyen of its queen. And a way to ensnare Myrddin to wed her.

Then again... Celeste may see this as a betrayal since she lusted for the man just as much. No, not the man, but the power that he could give her child.

Perhaps a deal could be made. After all, she had a potion and incantation for that. Celeste could be given both as a way to beget with child. Another could raise the child as his own without ever knowing.

Yes, that would satisfy Celeste. And still leave her with the tool that she needed to rule over Feyen by force.

Secrets, Lies and Betrayal
by: M.L. Ruscsak

Secrets, Lies and Betrayal
by: M.L. Ruscsak

CHAPTER 9: CELESTE

As the great castle doors of the Castle of Earth opened Celeste stood proudly waiting for the herald to announce her. Waiting for the grand trumpets to sound and the banners of Lite to fall.

They should have the moment she had arrived. They did for Adrianna. Black petals of distant flowers fell from the sky whenever she visited this miserable city. For that matter the banners snapped in the wind the very second that the Princess of Darke announced she was coming for a visit.

Seeing not a single living soul within the castle waiting to greet her, Celeste huffed in. Blasted city. One day they would kneel before her. One day she would be worshiped as any true royal should be. One day she would have the ear of the Feyen counsel and Lord Eros.

Secrets, Lies and Betrayal
by: M.L. Ruscsak

She would just have to buy her time until that day. Just wait a bit longer until she had an ally within these hallowed halls. Just wait until…

… Her eyes drifted down the great hall to a thin woman approaching. Not a court member not when dressed in tight trousers and an even tighter bodice.

Then again…

As the woman approached, she could see who it was now…

"Larna?"

What had the girl done to herself? Her long golden hair was now cropped just above the neck. Her bodice filled out and being held together with nothing more than a gold winged serpent clasped between her breast. And her trousers… what was the Queen Elista thinking, allowing her to dress like…

… Like…

Well she didn't have any words to describe what Larna was dressed like but slut came to mind.

Larna twirled before her, "Do you like my new outfit? I persuaded my mother to allow me to wear it openly."

Persuade. A spell or incantation. How wonderful if it could work on such a powerful queen. Celeste's eyes lit up with glee, "Oh, it looks lovely on you. Perhaps we can talk privately about where you came up with the design?"

Not that she cared but the words didn't matter. Making the fools who lived in the castle believe that the princess of Lite actually had something of fashion to discuss with her cousin… did.

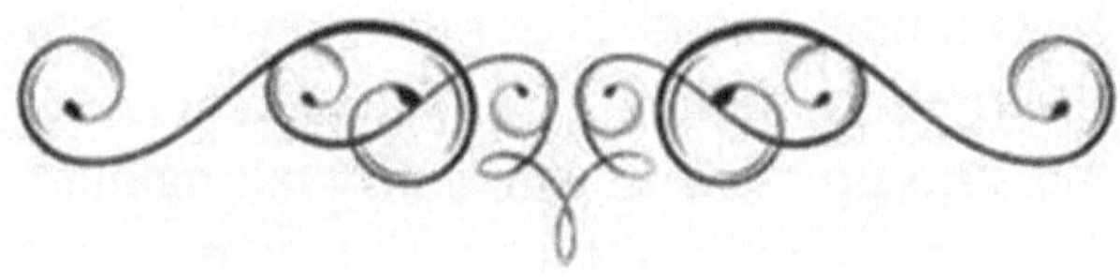

Well beneath the basement. Well beneath the castle strong hold was a warren of room that few knew about. Larna pulled her into an ornate room, donned from top to bottom with integrated patterns and polished stones.

Never had she been in this room. Never had she known about its existence. Surely, she would turn green with envy if her own castle… the castles of Lite… weren't all donned in jewels.

Still, how did this princess gain access to this room? Surly the gems were worth more than just mere decoration.

Secrets, Lies and Betrayal
by: M.L. Ruscsak

"This room is lovely? Did your mother chooses the gems for the wall accents?" Not that she really cared but that didn't matter. Not really.

Larna dropped drastically to the couch and placed her thin arm over her face, "My, mother lacks the ambition to decorate anything." She paused, "This room according to those that I can ask, is part of the original castle. The one that stood well before the Great War. I guess the Fey that dwelled here thought by placing rare stones into the wall none would think to mine the room and steal its treasure." Slowly Larna sat up her bossism nearly falling out of her bodice. "I plan on doing just that once I am queen. After all, what use is gems if they remain embedded in dirt?"

Celeste rolled her eyes, "Darling perhaps you should cover yourself. After all, there is none in this room that would take delight in your current wardrobe."

"Wha…" She glanced down. "Oh, drat. I simply must fix this so the clasp doesn't open every time I move. You wouldn't believe how many times the guards have been caught staring at a body that they will never touch."

The words were lightly said, but the twitch of Larna's lips said something else entirely. She was deliberately enticing the men of the castle. Trying to get her hooks imbedded in those who would assist her once she was crowned queen. And perhaps buy herself an ally.

Secrets, Lies and Betrayal
by: M.L. Ruscsak

Gracefully taking a seat next to Larna, Celeste smiled, "Our deity thinks it's time for you to be in passion of our little stone. Or at least for next few years. It appears he needs to groom you for the power that you have been denied."

Lara's eyes lit up with a delightful, greed filled fire. "Really? He really thinks that I will rule Feyen?"

"Darling, he doesn't think. He knows. And he will show you how."

Secrets, Lies and Betrayal
by: M.L. Ruscsak

Secrets, Lies and Betrayal
by: M.L. Ruscsak

CHAPTER 10: LARNA

She couldn't wait until she no longer was required to play the enchanted host for Celeste. Could barely contain her excitement at having time alone with the ruler of the stars. Still, she had to play nice through dinner. She had to sit through the solemn meal with her siblings... half siblings... Adrianna had confirmed that.

Then she had to sit through the evening entertainment. Some play that the school sage children who belonged to the city of Earth was putting on for their queen. It was really pitiful in her opinion. Who ever heard of an earth fairly dressing like a dark Fey trying to transform solid rock into a person.

Who ever heard of woodland nymphs wearing traditional coverings.

Secrets, Lies and Betrayal
by: M.L. Ruscsak

But this was a play, so it was understandable that the children would go against their normal upbringings and dress so commonly.

The red curtains drew closed and she stood. A searing looked from her mother and she sat once more. "I thought thyme were done" She said innocently

Elista squared her shoulders, "It was only the first act. Now sit, these children worked very hard to put on this production."

Her mother, despite keeping her voice low, was visibly upset. Or at the very least annoyed. Of course, if Adrianne wasn't here then the play would not have been a mandatory event.

Grumbling her folded her arms and resigned herself to sit for the remainder of this miserable attempt at entertainment.

Secrets, Lies and Betrayal
by: M.L. Ruscsak

Two minutes after the end of the play she raced through the castle halls. Raced to not her tower room. No, there were too many eyes there. But her private room. The one that only she had access to yes, that would work. That would be the perfect place to speak to the God of the stars. That would be a suitable place to ask all of the questions that she had burning within her chest.

Passing quickly through the wall, she fumbled to call in the flat red stone. After three tries there it sat in her hand. The cold turning to warm as it rested on her skin. Nervously... cautiously... she peered deep within the stone.

Her young voice shaking as she spoke, "My lord? Are you there?"

The red mist slowly withdrew to his face. Aging more every day. A face of a man who was old enough to be her grandfather. Yet despite his wrinkles and thinning hair, she found him attractive.

Perhaps it was the power that he was offing her. Riches that she couldn't even imagine. Or perhaps it was lust for a man that she couldn't yet touch.

But whatever it was....

... Oh, how she wanted it.

Secrets, Lies and Betrayal
by: M.L. Ruscsak

"Ah, so my little minx has finally grown up. How delightful."

Her pale lips tried to smile. Tried to hide the nerves that she was feeling. And the excitement. "I have so many questions my lord."

Magmas pulled away from the stone revealing more of the room. Elaborate wall hangings. Something dangling from the ceiling. Books lining the shelves. Coyly he folded his hands as he sat back in his seat, his translucent wings uncoiling just enough to appear bigger. "Then do ask my dear. I will hide nothing from you."

Secrets, Lies and Betrayal
by: M.L. Ruscsak

CHAPTER 11: KARNACK

Deep within the castle of bone Karnack sat at his old writing desk. A new journal set open just in front of him. The seer's stone delicately resting upon the table. The time was drawing near. Time was running out.

He could feel it. He could feel the threads of faith being weaved together. He could feel the secrets of the past coming unraveled. Yet he was powerless to stop it. Powerless to speak about what he saw.

Prim knew about the existence of the boy... of Myrddin. She knew he had found the bride that he was meant to wed in order to bare the prophesized daughter. Her dream coming to reality.

Secrets, Lies and Betrayal
by: M.L. Ruscsak

But with every step closer to the daughter of the darkness being born, it was too another step closer to a war that none may win.

His queen had chosen her pawns. Her knights. She had chosen to give power to a child that wasn't even born yet. A child that may want nothing to do with her war. Yet, Magmas had chosen his pawns as well. He had chosen the sister to Adrianna to entice Myrddin to her bed. An invention that was met with a short blade held near her throat.

Myrddin might have killed her if she had been anyone less than a crown princess. Yet, something told him if Celeste made another attempt Myrddin would do more than kill her. His temper could rarely be contained and his powers... ah all those inherited dark abilities that had come not only from his bloodlines, but also from those he had tapped into from the catacombs of Pallas... Oh, those abilities were seldom controlled.

This was by his own will.

Taking a deep sigh Karnack opened his eyes, trying to calm his nerves from his last report to the goddess. And it would be his last report that he would be allowed to give her.

Dipping his quill into the ink he flipped open to the first page. Fine parchment. Gold flakes held within the fibers. One day this journal would go to the Queen of the underkingdom. One day she would wear the crown of bone. And one day she holed the scepter of the dead. But right now, those things were entrusted into his care. Entrusted to look after until the queen held the power to rule over those who had been created by the goddess. Those who held power that the Fey could only dream of.

The tip of quill barely touched the page as a soft sounded on his plain wooded door. No need to look to see who was disturbing him. No need to wonder what she wanted. Barely glancing up from his work he asked, "Freya? What brings the famed general to knock once more upon my door?"

She was dressed in a long flowing skirt made of the finest of foliage that no longer grew. Her bodice barely covering her. "You spoke to the goddess." Not a question, yet not seeking confirmation either.

Carefully, he placed the quill back in its holder and turned to see her. "I gave my latest report to the goddess. And she left me with instruction."

As she gracefully drew closer her the vines that wrapped her arms dissolved into her honeyed skin. Her skirt turning to a pair of tight black leggings. And her bodice turning to a corset. She was prepared to fight if need be. Not good since she was looking at him like prey instead of a friend.

Secrets, Lies and Betrayal
by: M.L. Ruscsak

"My dear, what is spoken between the goddess and myself is private."

She stopped at the edge of his desk and sat on top of his papers. "I received a note from her today. Most peculiar since only you have seen or heard from her in far too long."

A note? The goddess penned a note? Peculiar ... no this was not peculiar this was ... well he didn't know what this was but it was not good. Not if Freya was here to discuss it.

Licking his lips, he tried to sound intrigued and friendly. Tried not to sound afraid. "And what did the goddess say?"

Leaning close to his ear, she growled, "That only King Magmas can give the order to send me to protect the child." She leaned back, "You wouldn't know anything about that... would you?"

Oh shit. Magmas had been fighting to liberate a handful of stars. Recently he had been wounded and was in hiding. And where he was hiding not even the Shadows could locate him. It was assumed he had been captured. Been assumed that the war was turning in favor of Pallas. Yet...

There was another message there.

If Prim had given an order... that...

Secrets, Lies and Betrayal
by: M.L. Ruscsak

"I'm sure Prim had her reasons. Perhaps in time will be privileged to find out what they were. "

He didn't see her move, but hear the whistle of the blade in the air. Heard it being stuck into the wood of his desk.

"One way or another I will be the personal guard of the child that rule the stars." Her voice raised, "You hear me scribe. Those who in power now have no idea how to protect a child with those powers. I do."

Yes, she did. And she knew how to bury any that tried to stop her. And that included King Magmas.

"I will convey your request to Magmas." As soon as he could be found.

The light in the sonances flickered once before being extinguished. The candle on his desk, his only source of light. The sound of wings rustling and cold air rushing at his skin juts before a hand yanked his shoulder.

Secrets, Lies and Betrayal
by: M.L. Ruscsak

His heart pounded in his cheats as he faced his attacker. No, not an attacker, "Apollo?"

His finger covered Karnack's lips, "Shhh. Some things are best said in the darkness."

And some things are better not said at all.

He nodded once and lowered his voice, "Tell me."

"Magmas holds the tomb of the silent ones. Do not contact him until the child is born. It's much too dangerous for those of Pallas to know he still lives."

"My boy, Pallas knows he lives. And I think his namesake is has already done damage to this star. But it is too soon to know for certain."

Apollo turned from him and let dark curses slip his lips. "When will you know?"

"When Nisha is old enough to rule."

Secrets, Lies and Betrayal
by: M.L. Ruscsak

CHAPTER 12: CELESTE

Looking at her map Celeste crossed of yet another room. Another useless room. Grrr.

Magmas had said the sword Larna would need was somewhere within the Castle of earth. It had to be. Only a true royal Fey could wield it. Only a true royal Fey could free it from its case.

But damn it. It wasn't anywhere within the great castle of Feyen. Not in any room including the damn treasury. So where could it have been moved to?

One of the lesser castles? Impossible.

Why in the name of Lite would anyone move something do important to any of them?

Turning a corner, she bumped into a warm body and… "Blake? What a surprise of bumping into you…"

His lightning blue eyes looked down at her, but he gave a friendly smile, "Looking for something, princess?"

Secrets, Lies and Betrayal
by: M.L. Ruscsak

"Oh, no... I..."

He reached down and collected her map, "You have been to this castle hundreds of times. So why do you need a map."

"I..." inspiration stuck her, "Oh... well... um... Larna sent me on a scavenger hunt of an item. She gave me the map. Of course, her instructions are a bit vague about what the item is so it is very possible that I have passed it a time or two."

His eyes narrowed just before a smile lit his face. "I happen to be a master at finding things. Why don't you tell me the clue and we might be able to see if you can retrieve it?"

It was risky, but... "A blade made of black. A hilt of the stars. Only the worthy can find it." She paused, "Larna is not very good at wording."

"No, she isn't. But then again, she doesn't pay much attention to lessons that she should be learning. However," Blake paused, "A blade of black sounds like the sword of Magma. It was said to be the sword wielded by King Magmas during the great war. It's not a toy princess. And not something that anyone can touch."

"Oh, I don't need to touch it only tell Larna where it is. That would-be surfactant for our little game."

Secrets, Lies and Betrayal
by: M.L. Ruscsak

"In that case you're looking in the wrong castle. It was moved from here a long time ago. As far as I know it's been missing for more than two decades."

"Wha…"

Blake laughed, "It seems your cousin sent you on a wild goose chase."

She watched him leave. Heard him choking back laughs. Son of a troll… what was her mother thinking betrothing her to him… a common guard. A worthless piece of flesh.

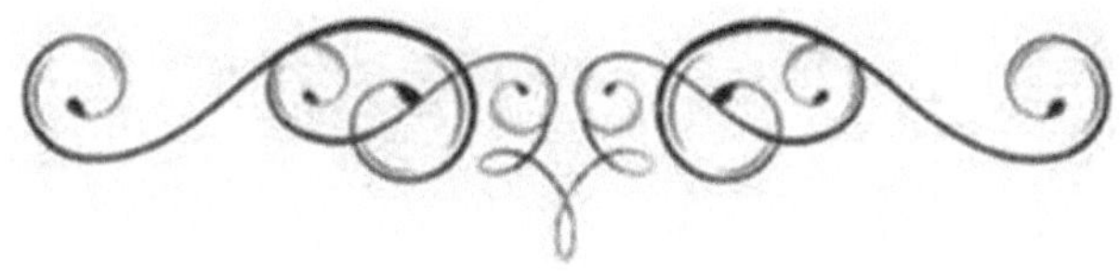

"What do you mean it's not here?" Larna wailed as she paced her newly finished tower room.

"According to the damn guard It has been missing since before your birth."

Suddenly Larna came to an abrupt stop. "It has to be in Feyen"

Secrets, Lies and Betrayal
by: M.L. Ruscsak

"Unless someone stole it. Yes, it should still be in Feyen. But where?'

Grabbing Celeste's arm, Larna pulled, "Come on. We'll go to my work room. I have a few maps there maybe if we combine our abilities, we can find it."

"And if you can't?"

"Then we'll think of something. In any case I start training with the guards in the morning to learn defensive maneuvers

In all of her years coming to the castle, she had never known that there were voids held in the lower parts of the castle. Rooms that only a few could penetrate. Rooms that required a great deal of ability to even find.

So how had Larna found these rooms? How had she gained the ability to pass through the solid walls with nothing more than a moment of inconvenience. Not only that, but how had she been able to bring the large onyx

Secrets, Lies and Betrayal
by: M.L. Ruscsak

desk in here or the golden chandelier. Or for that matter the dark wood shelves that lined the walls?

"This place… it…"

"Suits me. It's hidden in the shadows, unwanted. Underestimated. And yet it is the pillar that the castle rest on. A fitting place for me to hide all of my secrets don't you think?"

It was the perfect place to hide the Seer's stone. That they could agree on.

Sitting at her desk a large map of Feyen appeared. "Come here Celeste. Let us find the blasted sword. Even if it will take me years to retrieve it."

"Years?"

"I do not plan on touching the thing until the night that I need it. I'm no fool Celeste. If the sword is half as powerful as Magmas says I do not want it to be found before I plunge it into the heart of my mother. "

That made sense. "Very well, for this one task I will lend you my power in hopes of finding it."

Secrets, Lies and Betrayal
by: M.L. Ruscsak

Secrets, Lies and Betrayal
by: M.L. Ruscsak

CHAPTER 13: LARNA

Only three years had passed since Celeste had given her their secret stone. And only days since she had been ordered to give it back. At the time she had felt betrayed. Hurt. The god of the stars no longer wanted to communicate with her. But now she understood.

He needed her to concentrate on her task. He needed her to make sure Elista's bloodline ended with her.

Hidden away within the hidden chamber that she had found so many years before Larna looked down at her private journal. She had been keeping track of every spell that she had learned with thanks of both Myrddin and her deity. But tonight, her training was over. Tonight, she would put all of those dark spells to use.

Secrets, Lies and Betrayal
by: M.L. Ruscsak

Magmas wanted Elista killed tonight. And he was clear it had to be tonight. Adrianna was becoming too powerful. Myrddin to confidant in his abilities. Both needed to be stopped. Neither could be allowed to reign over Darke.

If she could force Myrddin into a binding ceremony than she could have him. Use him and his power to rule over Feyen. Force him into siring a child that Pallas could control. If not her then Celeste had to be the one to carry that child.

Taking a deep breath, she was ready.

Celeste had the potions to use should tonight fail. Should she be unable to force Myrddin into a binding. The tonic would make him ill, the inactions might be broken in time. But neither would interfere with granting her his seed.

Should it come to that? It wouldn't she, the only royal Fey of Elista's blood line, wouldn't let that happen. Not now. Not on the eve of her eightieth year.

Secrets, Lies and Betrayal
by: M.L. Ruscsak

She stood towering over her mother's body. Her black crystal sword plunged into the heart of the woman who had given her life. Holding her translucent black wings still, she glanced over her shoulder, her father's lifeless head on the floor, but a few feet away from where his body had fallen. He had been the last Feyen warrior to fall.

The last before her mother. At least there, she had found a worthy adversary to face. Well, at least until she too had faltered and died.   Such a simple mistake really. An unbalanced footing and her mother had lunged at her. And had fallen directly on the tip of the blade that she had been trying to avoid. A pity for sure since she had wanted all of the credit of slaying the queen.

A cruel smile formed on her dark crimson colored lips as she stood there silently watching her mother's blood started to pool around her lifeless body. Not the red lifeblood that most Fey had, oh no her mother's lifeblood

Secrets, Lies and Betrayal
by: M.L. Ruscsak

was midnight blue. An oddity unto itself. Watching the blood seeping out of her body, Larna could have spat on her mother's face for making her take this drastic measure. But, if she did it would ruin her plans, and that she wouldn't do no matter what the price. "You should have listened to me, mother. Now look at what has become of you. No longer will you be able to listen to anyone. A justice that serves you right for never hearing the truth that was set before your eyes."

A seer hardly. A true seer would have known about this long before now. A true seer would never have fallen on a blade when it could have been avoided all together.

Pulling her black crystal blade free from her mother's heart, she used it to cut the fabric of her golden gown. Methodically she made sure that the cuts on the fabric mirrored the cuts on her own skin. She had to make sure that the cuts were shallow enough to hinder her movements, but deep enough to look like she had escaped the slaughter. Escaping as the last surviving heir... the last of her mother's bloodline. And escaping as the only living Royal Fey in all of Feyen.

What had happened to the other royal Fey? The hundreds that had dwelled here just years before? She couldn't say. But they were no longer her responsibility. And the ones who still dwelled here... most were petty guards still climbing the ranks. Guards who would obey her.

Secrets, Lies and Betrayal
by: M.L. Ruscsak

Nevertheless, anyone who had seen anything was already bound to her. Their memories were whatever she decided that they would be. Right now, in this moment, she chose for all of them to believe that a hooded man had stormed into the castle coming from out of nowhere and slaughtering all that had stood in his way. A cloud a mist had hidden him until the very moment that he had killed his first victim.

Yes, that would do nicely. And as for the man... Oh well, she had planned for that as well. Myrddin was either going to marry her or every Feyen citizen would believe that he had been behind the massacre. After all, there wasn't a single person alive that didn't know how powerful he truly was nor how dangerous. Nor would any every question his motives. Power, greed, lust? It wouldn't matter what they chose to speculate, his very denials would only further their conviction in his guilt.

A cruel smile formed on her long, thin face. But she would offer him another solution. She would offer her hand in marriage, after all, he was exactly what she needed. A Feyen man with more natural ability and dark power than the whole royal family of Feyen. Or she should say the now *dead* royal family.

But tomorrow would be soon enough to work on that... Tonight on the other hand... She had to finish this. Sniffling until tears started to run hot down her face, she took a deep breath then took off in a terrified sprint down

Secrets, Lies and Betrayal
by: M.L. Ruscsak

the bloody castle halls. Her ripped gown collecting blood from the fallen guards as she ran. There wasn't anyone alive in this part of the castle or at least not anyone that would be of any use for her plan to work. So, screaming for help would do her no use at least not until she saw the light coming from the main gate... Then... and only then did she let out a shrill scream, "HELP! Help Me!"

She saw a single guard at the main gate and knew almost instantly who he was. A member of not just the royal guard, but also one that also served as an elite warrior. As there was never more than a dozen in that squad, she knew each of them fairly well. However, this one may be a problem for her.

Once she was crowned she might have to see to his death as well. No, better yet, to his execution. Not a far leap that he might have something to do with the murders. She would just have to see what played out.

The moment he turned to her, she knew two things. First off, he was scanning the area for trouble and secondly, he recognized her as a member of the royal family. In that breath, he partly ran and partly flew to meet her half way inside of the great hall. Just as he made it to her, she collapsed into his arms sobs running down her face as she gasped for air, "Princess... What..." He asked almost puzzled.

Secrets, Lies and Betrayal
by: M.L. Ruscsak

Catching her breath, she forced out, "A hooded intruder... My mother, you have to..." Clawing at his white and gold uniform she tried to push away. Tried to escape his strong grip that even if she had been truly trying she would find nearly impossible. "Please, you have to help my mother."

His sturdy grip finally failed as that was all he needed to hear. Larna watched only partly amazed as a single bolt of lightning flashed from his fingertips lighting the signal fire. Not a moment later more than a dozen armed guards stood surrounded them. All their eyes battle ready and scanning for the cause for the signal to be lit. Yet none moved for a minute waiting for the captain to join them.

A heart beats, then two and the armed guard who was holding her; the sobbing princess, took command. "We'll notify the captain later. The royal family is being attacked. The Queen is the first priority." Glancing down at her he continued, "Princess Larna please come with me. The guard tower will be safe. You have my word."

She had no doubt about that. After all, how would he ever know that it had been her that had killed her entire family? But even if he somehow did find out, after she was crowned not a soul would ever be able to do anything about it.

Secrets, Lies and Betrayal
by: M.L. Ruscsak

Secrets, Lies and Betrayal
by: M.L. Ruscsak

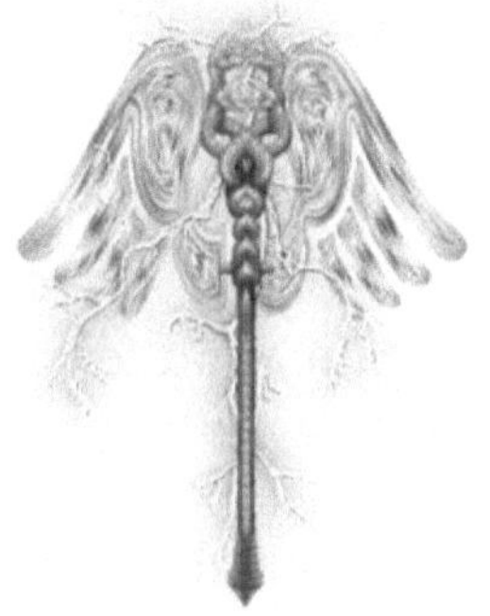

CHAPTER 14: GALERON

Time was of the essence. Every minute. Every second mattered... if there was a real emergency. If Larna was correct that some unknown intruder... some unknown Dark Fey had really penetrated the castle's stronghold. It had to be a lie. It had to be.

There was no sign of trouble until they reached the heart of the castle. No sign of struggle except the bloody footprints that the princess had left behind. Then a body. A young guard his name not yet known to all who worked the palace grounds... his body cut nearly in half. In an outcove, not but a few feet away another guard, Gavan, his throat slit from behind. Whoever had done this had to have stepped

Secrets, Lies and Betrayal
by: M.L. Ruscsak

through the wall behind him. A damn foolish thing to do unless one was trained. Even then, not many had the skill to do so without being trapped in the stone. Of those, none had been near the castle recently.

Except Myrddin. But he would have never attacked the royal family. Never would he attack from behind. No Myrddin for all of his ability and temper preferred to see the whites of his enemy's eyes before he stuck out. Yet...

No, he wouldn't think about that not yet. Not now.

Carefully with his golden wings now fluttering at full speed he flew down the corridors. His eyes seeing the bodies of his fallen comrades. Nothing about their deaths made sense. Unless all were asleep... *which was highly unlikely and completely impossible...* one of them should have called for help. One should have signaled for reinforcements or used mind-speech to call for help. Yet none did. And none seemed to have been fighting the unknown attacker. Not a weapon was drawn nor a spell cast. No whatever had happened here was not just a simple attacker. They had a purpose.

Galeron stopped just feet from the royal stronghold and fought not to become sick. Still he couldn't stop his hands from shaking violently. Kailen, the youngest prince laid partly in his room and partly in the hall. His purple blood sprayed over his door. Two doors down the heir had been torn apart in her bed. The protective shield around

Secrets, Lies and Betrayal
by: M.L. Ruscsak

her bed and room still fully intact. And covered in her flesh, her blood. The only thing that resembled her was her face that had been left untouched. The other three royal children killed so thoroughly that there was no reason to send them to the Under Kingdom... Not even as fodder for those who may still dwell there.

Slowly and carefully, he made his way to the queen's bedchamber. Made his way past corridors filled with blood. Alcoves holding more bodies of recently trained guards. Then he saw what he had feared... the king's headless body laid in the doorway. His hand still curled around the hilt of his golden sword. The sword itself broken cleanly in half. In impossible feat... yet someone had been able to do so. The amount of strength required to do that? So, few could have done that. And those who possessed that skill were now dead.

Pushing the double door open enough to pass without disturbing the body of the king, his eyes found the queen. Her body lifeless on the floor, her blue blood flowing around her seeping from wounds that were not visible. The blood itself pulling toward the head of the king. The last show of the blood oath they had taken.

For a moment, he swayed at now realizing the royal family had been wiped out. In a span of a breath his mind focused on the only two people in all of the Feyen that could have accomplished this without sounding the alarm... and by the gods, it wasn't Myrddin. Despite the attempt to

Secrets, Lies and Betrayal
by: M.L. Ruscsak

make it look like it had been... he knew better. The queen's window was open and there would be no time once dawn arrived... No time after his report had been made or when others found the bodies of the royal family. So, he dove from the window and flew over the city of Golden Sun and to the home of his friend

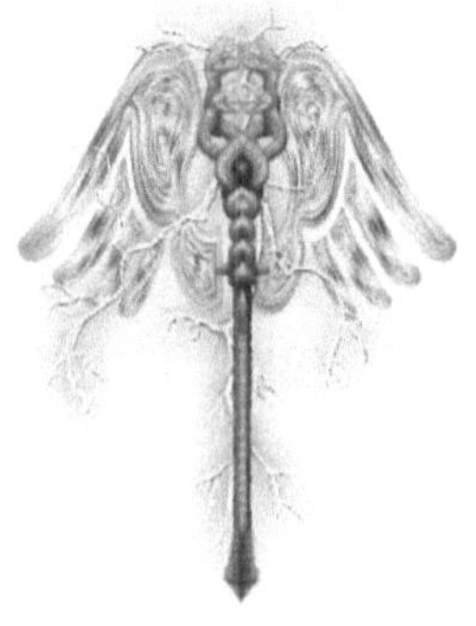

Landing in a back alleyway Galeron hurried down the several twists and turns of the inner city until he came to the door of his friend. Raising his fist, he pounded on the simple wooden door, "Myrddin open the damn door. Or I will break it down."

Secrets, Lies and Betrayal
by: M.L. Ruscsak

When it finally opened, it wasn't Myrddin but Princess Adrianna standing in front of him. Her long dark hair tussled from sleep. Her eye not yet open as she sleepily asked, "Galeron, what in the name of Darke is it?"

"We need to talk." Pushing past her, he saw Myrddin just tying the belt to his black robe. "It's started."

For a moment, Myrddin just stood there numb. Finally, he whispered, "Damn it. We should have had more time to prepare."

Closing the door Adrianna looked from her betrothed to her friend confused. Wiping her eyes to fully wake up she asked, "What's started?"

Myrddin shuffled over to his long dark couch and took a deep breath, "Addy you know you hold my heart."

Shuffling over to sit with Myrddin, Adrianna took his hand in hers then said, "Yes, and I know we will be married... So, what..." She looked deep into Galeron's eyes. There was a worry there in his voice but more than that, there was a burning rage in those eyes. "Queen Elista?"

"Murdered. And whoever did it made damn sure it looked like something Myrddin was capable of doing. Or at least, someone who had a strong natural ability in the dark arts."

Secrets, Lies and Betrayal
by: M.L. Ruscsak

Addy got up from the couch and turned away. She had only come here last year to learn some from the Feyen Queen how to rule true Fey. And she had. But she had also found scores of friends and the man who held her heart. More than that, she had been working on a treaty that would bind their houses together. A treaty that would fall apart if whoever now ruled didn't see the wisdom in it. "What's going to happen now?"

Myrddin sat back and snorted, "Princess Larna will become Queen. I'm sure all of the Feyen will be torn over it but not enough to do anything about it. At least not with some motivation."

Taking a breath, she spoke as the only person in the room with authority to speak the truth without fear of penalty. "As a Fey, her powers and abilities are yet untested. She will have some years yet before she matures enough to handle the gifts that she currently has let alone be able to handle those of her people without going mad."

A curt laugh then Myrddin growled, "She may be already?"

Addy raised an eyebrow in question, "Myrddin?"

"She's been learning the dark arts." Now both Addy and his friend stared right at him.

"What?" Both said nearly in unison.

Secrets, Lies and Betrayal
by: M.L. Ruscsak

"Larna asked if I could teach her. As one of only two people in all of the Feyen that was able, I consulted Queen Elista. After a very detailed conversation about what I was, willing to teach the little brat and listening to what the brat wanted to learn I agreed. As part of the agreement the queen gave her blessing to our union."

There was more but without breaking an oath to a queen that he knew as his sister. An oath that even with her death he won't break. Not unless he was forced to.

For a long time, no one spoke. Slowly Addy shuffled back over to her beloved, "We could leave tonight."

"No." For a moment, he just sat there. His eyes focusing on something far beyond his home. Finally getting up he took the few steps to his window and said, "Adrianna, I need for you to leave. Go to Draken and take my sister with you."

Jumping back with a start she growled, "Like hell I am. I am not letting her get away with this. Nor am I letting you take the fall for the likes of her."

In a deep growl, he snapped. His voice rattling his windows and making both his friend and lover jump. "*Adrianna* this is not up for debate." Slowly he came back to her and took her hand. Taking a deep breath, he needed to reason with her. He just hoped she listened just this once. "You will be the next queen of Darke. And I swear that I will

Secrets, Lies and Betrayal
by: M.L. Ruscsak

be married to you well before that ever happens. But, I need you to leave. Larna is in way over her head, and I'm the only one strong enough to put things to right. Or at least, make sure she is limited on options."

"Fine. I'll go and I'll even take Tenanye *and* Faerydae with me. After all, I'm sure Tenanye would love to see her betrothed. But I'll be damned if I leave here without both of you being blood bound to me."

"Now wait one second..."

"Don't you start with me Galeron. I don't know what game the little princess is playing. And frankly, I don't care. But I will not let her use either of you for pawns. Besides The only way that she can't bind you would be to be bound to someone stronger."

"She's right you know."

"Just because *your* future wife is right about something does not mean I have to like it." Galeron hisses as he paced the confines of the sitting room.

Narrowing her dark colored eyes, Adrianna spoke with all the authority of a queen, "No, but you're not stupid. So, what's it going to be Galeron... Be the captain of *my* guards and first chair on *my* council or serve her and never live long enough to become a father?"

Secrets, Lies and Betrayal
by: M.L. Ruscsak

CHAPTER 15: MYRDDIN

The sun was just starting to rise. Just starting to clear the gray skies of night into the bright, vibrant colors of the morning. The bell of the castle tolled in somber song. The citizens were already starting to mourn a queen who was admired and her children whom most knew. Morning the guards who had been lost in the attack on the royal family.

But that was the morning for those who lived within the city. For those who didn't yet understand what had really happened last night while they all slept. No, they didn't know, but he did. And he had sent word to those who would need to know. And he waited through the last moments of darkness. Waited until his day really started.

As the sunlight just started to reach his door, his morning started with armed castle guards pounding on his door. If he hadn't been warned last night Adrianna would have been here and naturally accused of the murders. Of

Secrets, Lies and Betrayal
by: M.L. Ruscsak

course, he had saved her from that... now to do what he could and hope it was enough. Slowly he opened the door and looked deep into the guard's sea green eyes, "I assume there is a reason you are trying to break my door in." His voice husky with lack of sleep yet it gave him the advantage of sounding annoyed and pissed.

Fear ran across the man's face. An Elf not a fairy judging by the lack of wings.

When he didn't say anything, he snapped, "Well, or would you like to waste my entire day?"

The guard shook himself from his stupor and forced out, "I... you're wanted at the castle for questioning."

"I see. Then let's get this over with. I'm already late for another important engagement." Not really, but being with Addy had taught him a thing or two. Such as being Feyen and the only dark anything outside Darke... he had the authority to be curt and difficult. More than that... once he married the future queen he could send all those who and offended him to the Under Kingdom... perhaps alive... perhaps not. Either way, it was entertaining to watch the door open and the dead standing far below the opening waiting to greet either their next meal or then newest comrades.

This was something Elista found amusing or annoying, depending on her mood. Remembering that it helped smooth out the sharper edges of his temper before he destroyed the city.

Stepping out if his home Myrddin looked around at the nearly two dozen armed guards. Fairy. Elf. Light bearers. Then his eyes darted to the chosen ride to the Castle. Not a fine carriage, but a trolley for trolls. Before he took another step, he used just a bit of simple craft... well simple, if you were a master of several kinds of craft... Black smoke, then a soft proof before a loud bang and a proper carriage stood before him. "If I'm going to the castle I will go in a style befitting my prestige. But certainly not in an ill-made troll trolley."

"Where is..."

He turned sharply to the young guard who had once again found his voice, "Where is who?"

"The Princess of Darke. We were told..."

"Hmp. The Lady had appointments elsewhere. I believe she left midday yesterday." That should be enough to keep Addy out of trouble. Then again, with her, he couldn't be too sure. After all, trouble seemed to follow Addy wherever she dared to travel. It was something her twin had been ready to point out several times within the past year.

Secrets, Lies and Betrayal
by: M.L. Ruscsak

At least he didn't need to worry about Celeste in all of this. Thankfully, she had left for the Spire some days ago to introduce some poor sap to her mother. Had left to formally introduce Blake to her mother rather than the queen that he knew.

Secrets, Lies and Betrayal
by: M.L. Ruscsak

CHAPTER 16: LARNA

Looking up from his book where he was trying to find anything useful Lord Eros tapped his book yet again and sighed. So many laws and traditions, but none for crowning a child after the loss of her family. But the funeral passages were very clear and needed to be taken care immediately, "Princess we must see to the funerals of..."

She had to play the distraught daughter who had lost her parents. The problem was that she was bored. Nor did she care what they did with the bodies. Burn them, bury them. Send what was left to the Under Kingdom. It made little difference to her either way. Of course, she couldn't

Secrets, Lies and Betrayal
by: M.L. Ruscsak

say that. However, she could sniffle once and fight back fake tears, "Oh, can the council, please...." She sniffled and turned her head, "I... I just can't."

Handing her his pocket square he patted her back soothingly, "Of course my dear. I should have considered... Perhaps the council should speak with Lord Devros."

"No..." Larna snapped and nearly left her seat. Nearly jumped off of the throne. Then, realizing her mistake, she started again as she calmly sat back, "No, I would like to see those who could have done this to m-my family."

The large golden doors of the throne room blew open and crashed into the walls behind them. Myrddin strode in his black robe that marked him as a High-born covered most of his natural muscle and actual size. They did nothing to mask the dark power that could be felt from his annoyance. Nor did it hide the black mist that dripped from his dragon like wings. "I assume there is a reason the castle guard has brought me here."

Jumping in front of the dais, Lord Eros hissed, "You will hold your tongue Lord Devros."

Narrowing his raven colored eyes, Myrddin stared at the first chair of the Feyen council, "As I am the ambassador of Darke and I demand answers Lord Eros. And I will have those answers or you can give them to my queen."

Secrets, Lies and Betrayal
by: M.L. Ruscsak

"Gentlemen, please, this a somber day." When that did nothing to get either man to back down Larna sniffled, "Please, I would like to speak to Lord Devros privately."

"I should think not..." Lord Eros protested.

Rising her voice Larna squared her shoulders. She would be damned if she let some Counselman dictate anything to her. "This is my will, Lord Eros. Now, please... I would think that m-my parents would like to be laid to rest."

"As you will princess." Turning back to Myrddin he whispered, "I will see you sent to the Under Kingdom for your crimes."

Once alone Myrddin circled the dais very slowly, "What's the game Larna?"

Her pale lips curled into a sinister smile, "Oh no game Myrddin. Just a proposition."

"Oh?" Slowly he came to stand before her, "Tell me, what it is you are expecting? Your future told, perhaps?"

She waved the gist off with an annoyed wave of her hand, "Oh, come now. We both know that is not a dark art Myrddin."

He shrugged, "Perhaps not. So, let's get on with it. What was so important for you to murder your family and try to blame me?"

How did he know? He didn't have the ability to foresee the future. And surely, he didn't hold the ability to for see the past. So how... Her eyes narrowed into tiny slits as she hissed, "Figured it out, did you. Should have known you would have a spy in the guards." She sat back on the throne, "No matter, I'll know *who* soon enough."

Putting one foot on the dais, he leaned toward her yet he didn't dare touch her, "Are you going to tell me why I'm here or should I guess?"

She couldn't let him see how she had unnerved him Couldn't let him see that she saw scared that he might actually kill her. Oh, no she couldn't do that, but she could force herself to sound calm and calculating. Yes, that she could do. "Oh, I guess I will tell you. You are going to marry me."

Like hell I am. It burned in his throat, but he managed to say is a swan song coo, "Am I? Now, why would I marry a child who has little in the way of natural ability? And nothing to offer in the way that I might find appealing."

If he wasn't towering over her, she would have bolted from the throne since she couldn't, she crossed her arms "I'm not a child. I am nearly two hundred years old.

Secrets, Lies and Betrayal
by: M.L. Ruscsak

And I have plenty natural ability." That was a lie. She had just turned eighteen light cycles last night. He might know that. Or she gambled that he didn't after all, no-one really paid attention to how old Royals really were unless it became necessary.

Turning away from her he started to the door, "You have not answered my question Larna. And your game is starting to bore me."

"Either marry me or you and Princess Adrianna will be held accountable for the murder of the royal family. And who ever warned you will join you for your death."

Having known how this would play out he wasn't fazed, yet he slowly turned from her. Just an act that he could perform for his little princess. "I will marry you on three conditions. As I do like the sound of being married to a queen." Although the only queen he would marry wasn't in this room. Or in this kingdom for that matter.

Larna mumbled, already too preoccupied with the power she would have once they wed, "Ambition suit you. Now, what are your terms?"

"Nothing much. First off, the royal family of Draken should be in attendance. Since My sister will be marrying the crown prince in the next year."

Greed lit her violet eyes, "Done."

Secrets, Lies and Betrayal
by: M.L. Ruscsak

"Secondly, you will declare that any child of mine will be your heir unless you have a child with someone else that holds your heart."

"Of course, your child would be my heir. What a silly thing to require."

Uh ha. We'll see about that. "And lastly, as is tradition you will give me your heart."

"Again, Myrddin that would have been said in the vows regardless. Now is there anything else?"

"No." He took a step up onto the dais and towered over her, "We will be married in three days."

"Three..." She gasped, already gazing into his eyes.

Smiling as her eyes locked with his, he allowed for them to blaze into a hypnotic blue haze, "You do not want your country without a queen any longer."

"No, I suppose I don't."

Secrets, Lies and Betrayal
by: M.L. Ruscsak

CHAPTER 17: ADRIANNA

"Addy, are you sure you want to be here? I mean my brother..."

Adrianna turned away from her friend and let herself see beyond the room... beyond what most saw. Looked well beyond the cream colored flowered walls and rows of high back chairs. Looked well beyond milk-white walls. Allowed herself a look back over the past three days in this room. Then whispered, "Myrddin knows what he is doing and I plan on being here to find out exactly what... That and I plan on strangling him the very moment that I can for making me witness this to start with."

Tenanye smiled as she watched her betrothed, Prince Craykren and her brother discuss something that

Secrets, Lies and Betrayal
by: M.L. Ruscsak

had both men playfully shoving each other. "I expected this for your wedding day, but..."

Signing Addy shook her head, "We should go separate them before this turns into a brawl. Besides, it will give me the excuses to speak to him and possibly finding out something useful." Or the reason to actually strangle him. After all, talking sounded good. Pulling him into the hall and ringing his neck for putting on this farce of a wedding... well, she was sure her family wouldn't mind.

The people of Feyen however...

No, she would do this with dignity. At least until she could very privately vent all of the frustrations that she currently had. Frustrations that had nothing to do with her upcoming coronation. And had everything to do with her betrothed marring another Royal Fey.

"Just be careful Addy. There are those here that think you are the one who killed the Queen."

Her sees scanned the room. Huddles of people. The ones that knew that she would have never harmed Elista were distressed yet speaking to her mother. Everyone else? If they realized that she could hear what they were saying about her... if they knew that she could feel their fear... well if they didn't they soon would.

Secrets, Lies and Betrayal
by: M.L. Ruscsak

Out of the side of her eye, he saw her mother's fist clenched. Oh, so soon the Feyen citizens would remember exactly how protective her mother was over her children. And they would all know what actually happened here just days prior.

But not yet. No, right now she just gave a friendly smile despite the anger and unease growing inside her. "Aye, I know. I can feel their uneasiness like prickles on my skin. But it helps that my mother and sister are here. They wouldn't dare cross Mum. She is already in a foul mood and I so doubt she will be able to control herself much longer."

Patting her friend's hand Tenanye smiled, "Your mother is always in a mood. But I agree with her if she should destroy this farce. However, no-one here would dare cross me either now that Craykren has given me a name that sounds more Draken. I doubt anything would be left of Feyen if they did."

Taking Tenanye's arm, she smiled, "Oh, you haven't told me, I simply must know what Cray decided on for his bride."

"Alyisope. It was his grandmother's name. I do like it, but I think those who have known me my whole life will continue to call me Tenanye." Stepping over to her betrothed Tenanye hissed, "Craykren, I do swear if you act like this on our wedding day I will refuse to marry you."

Secrets, Lies and Betrayal
by: M.L. Ruscsak

He spun around with the grace of a cat despite his large size. His armored scales looking like he belonged to a reptile race, but his horns... those were all bovine. Then again, he didn't bother to place a glamor spell on his black talons that he had for fingers or the long tail that held a poison stinger. "It is customary for battle before marrying."

"Yes, and you will do battle the night before our wedding. Not The day of. Do I make myself clear?"

He just turned to Myrddin and narrowed his gold reptilian eyes, "I should eat you."

Myrddin crossed his bare muscled arms, giving his friend time to consider the possibility of a real fight rather than the playful shoving. Then gave a twisted smile, "If you eat me who will continue to teach you to speak properly?"

"I should eat you for introducing me to... to... *sister*."

Pulling on Craykren's arm, she hissed, "Come over here before you cause trouble." As she pulled him away Adrianna could her hear mutter, "I swear, you are worse than your father. At least he can be reasoned with."

Adrianna smiled as she watched her friend walk away before turning back to Myrddin, "This all seemed to happen pretty quickly. That said... is there something I should know."

Secrets, Lies and Betrayal
by: M.L. Ruscsak

"Adrianna, my sweet you already know everything you need to. So, I ask you to please let this play out."

She looked him really looked at him. There was rage in his eyes. Rage that she hadn't seen before. And something else that she couldn't place. Didn't want to place. In all of her years of knowing him she had never felt threatened by him. But right here right now... she knew he would destroy the whole of the kingdom should he be pushed in any way. And that included any snippy remark made from her. "Because I trust you I will do as you ask. However, do not expect your sister to remain civil to Queen Larna after she marries Craykren."

Gone was the rage in his eyes, hidden now by amusement, "This *is* my sister we are talking about... I doubt she would remain civil with anyone I choose to marry." He smiled then touched her mind, *Besides you*

Returning the smile, she laughed, "I suppose you're right. She is never civil to anyone unless they can beat her in fighting. " A soft chime rang softly signaling the ceremony was to begin. Sighing, she asked, "Should I sit with my family or yours?"

"Addy, you are the princess of Darke. You must always sit according to your status. My sister has Cray to keep her from doing anything rash. At least for the moment."

Secrets, Lies and Betrayal
by: M.L. Ruscsak

At least he understood what she was asking. And why. "Fine. I'll try to keep Celeste from turning your bride into an ornate flower. But I make no promises. Both she and mother are in rare form today."

Secrets, Lies and Betrayal
by: M.L. Ruscsak

CHAPTER 18: MYRDDIN

Stepping over to the raised platform Myrddin took a deep steady breath. He promised Elista that he would end Larna's life should events take place that they had both foreseen. He had promised her that her bloodlines would not end with her.

Until now he had kept those promises. Diandra was housed safely on a distant star. One that had been fortified by Magnar and protected by the creatures that he created. She was happy and had even found a true royal Fey to win her heart and her trust.

Perhaps one day they would return to this star. Perhaps one day she would understand why she and her siblings had to be sent away. But not today. Not when he still had one threat to deal with. And not until his own daughter was old enough to rule over the stars as she was destined to do.

Secrets, Lies and Betrayal
by: M.L. Ruscsak

He gave a single nod to Lord Eros. They weren't friends. Nor did they try to be. Eros only believed in what he saw. Today he saw a man that would kill the entire royal family for his chance to claim the crown.

Fool.

But at least he understood something that Larna didn't. It would be he, and he alone that ruled over Feyen. His natural abilities… his reservoir of power and strength was so much greater than hers. He could never be bound to her. He could never be controlled by her. So, she would never rule.

She may hold the crown until the ceremony was completed, but not a moment after. No, she would be dead before any left this room.

This after all was the nature of a true Royal Fey. Of a Star City Fey. This was something embedded in his nature at all the time away from his home hadn't been able to erase. Nor could it ever be.

His eyes met Vasilissa's for only a moment. She was prepared to destroy the little bitch the moment the ceremony was completed. As a member of the high counsel she was well within her right to end any threat to the Fey. And that included killing another royal Fey in the name of protecting the star as a whole.

Secrets, Lies and Betrayal
by: M.L. Ruscsak

Craykren would second her decision. Nicco would appear by way of a Shadow at the very moment Larna's body fell to the floor.

Everything was in place. Everything...

... So why did his skin prickle in warning? Why were his senses heightened?

He had no answer, but a feeling in the pit of his stomach told that he would soon enough.

Secrets, Lies and Betrayal
by: M.L. Ruscsak

Secrets, Lies and Betrayal
by: M.L. Ruscsak

CHAPTER 19: ADRIANNA

Adrianna gracefully sat in a white high back chair next to her sister and took her hand, "What have you heard?"

Pulling a strand of golden hair behind her ear Celeste smiled, "Mother is beside herself. Don't expect her to be on her best behavior *if* Myrddin goes through with this farce of a wedding."

Looking slightly behind her, she watched as her mother stood rigidly near the back wall. Watched as those grief filled eyes narrowed in anger. "Mother is rarely on her

Secrets, Lies and Betrayal
by: M.L. Ruscsak

best behavior when surrounded by those who wish her family harm. And she is never on her best behavior when papa isn't around to soothe her."

"True. But she has never had to deal with a loss of a dear friend and children that she has known from birth."

Reaching out to her sister's mind, she decided to have the rest of this conversation privately. *And does mother know what happened that night?*

You know as well as I that she does. But without proof, she is powerless to do anything about it. Then again, that had never stopped her before when dealing with troublemakers.

Turning back to the door, Adrianna narrowed her eyes and watched the murderer slowly make her way down the aisle. Her dress looking more like something she should wear for the wedding night and not to the wedding itself. *I doubt she will get away with this.*

Celeste wrinkled her nose in distaste of the dress. Or lack of dress. *Does she realize that she looks ridiculous marrying a man who is twice her age and twice her height? Not to mention that thing that should be a dress... I swear her tailor elf forgot more than half of it.*

Adrianna rolled her eyes, *I doubt she cares about anything but the power that she thinks he can give her.*

Secrets, Lies and Betrayal
by: M.L. Ruscsak

Well, it should be interesting watching her learn that she may have bought his hand, but she will never have his heart nor his power.

Secrets, Lies and Betrayal
by: M.L. Ruscsak

Secrets, Lies and Betrayal
by: M.L. Ruscsak

CHAPTER 20: LARNA

Larna took the two steps up to the dais never looking at the guess who had shown to watch her become Queen of Feyen... but it was so lovely that the Queen of Lite and Darke had chosen to come but remain furthest from the festivities. Oh well... as long as the old hag didn't cause any trouble then she wouldn't need to have Myrddin dispose of her. Then again, it wouldn't be fun to rule all the countries that held Fey blood?

Tomorrow she would start planning on how to do just that... as of today...

Her voice filled with fake tears as she softly said, "Lord Eros, before we begin I would like to say something."

Secrets, Lies and Betrayal
by: M.L. Ruscsak

Bowing accordingly, he smiled, "Of course your grace."

Now she turned to her guest, "I know this is not what you all imagined for the succession of the Feyen line, but I do hope to make my mother proud."

The golden doors of the throne room creaked opened and an older woman slowly made her way to the dais. Even slower she removed her hood from her crimson cape. "As you have left us no choice child. Get on with it. I did not come all this way to watch you blabber on."

Her eyes widened in shock "Grandmother?!?"

The old queen leaned heavily on her crystal cane as she took a single step into the room, "What is it dear? Did you expect me to be long dead?"

"I..." She took a deep breath. Her grandmother hadn't been seen for nearly a century. Not since becoming ill with something that no Fey had ever been able to cure... and yet she was now standing before her. Silver in her hair sure, but not looking a bit unwell. Forcing herself to be calm, she took a deep breath, "I'm glad you could be here. Thank you."

"Well get on with it."

Secrets, Lies and Betrayal
by: M.L. Ruscsak

She had never met her grandmother and now was thankful for never speaking to a bitter old bat. "As I was saying before the dowry queen arrived, in breaking with the tradition of being wed before being crown I ask my first chair of the Feyen council to add this doctrine to my rein." She called in a signed piece of parchment and handed it to Lord Eros.

Taking the parchment, he began to unroll it. As he read, he stuttered, "Are you sure?"

"I Am."

"Very well, your grace. As this day, any child sired by Lord Devros will be named as heir to Feyen... Unless Queen Larna finds another man who can hold her heart."

Adrianna sat back and tried not to smile. She had known Myrddin for just over a year and he had taught her one thing above all else... always be precise when dealing with the Fey. More so when dealing with a Dark Fey, who would use every word to their own advantage.

Secrets, Lies and Betrayal
by: M.L. Ruscsak

CHAPTER 21: MYRDDIN

Larna stood to her full height now that she wore the silver crown of Feyen. Such a simple circlet, but the power that she could now tap into... what a marvelous feeling.

"My Queen, are you ready for the marriage vows?"

"You may proceed, Lord Eros."

"Very well." He took a deep breath and tried to smile, "Do you Queen Larna, daughter of Elista freely give this man, Lord Myrddin Devros every part of you. Your hand, your heart and all that you will make together?"

"I, Queen Larna freely give my heart to Lord Devros to have for all time."

Secrets, Lies and Betrayal
by: M.L. Ruscsak

Myrddin had been standing there quiet and not really paying attention to anything until this moment.... However, now that she had said what he had expected... He smiled and licked his wine-red lips, "Do you really give me your heart Queen Larna?"

"Yes, I give you my heart." It was then she realized her mistake as his hand reached deep into her chest pulling out her still beating heart.

He looked down at the black blood covering his hand, then called in a silver box. "I will keep your cold black heart. Since you have given it to me in trust. And in return, you shall live till someone who can hold your heart is able to give it back to you." Now he turned to the dowry Queen. "Queen Alista as you have ruled Feyen and being the one the one most capable please do so once more. It would seem your grandchild is but a shell of what she had hoped for."

Alista narrowed her old violet eyes, "Very well. My granddaughter will rule in name only and those in this room are forbidden to discuss what had become of her until my death."

"I think I can speak for all here when I say none shall speak a word."

Secrets, Lies and Betrayal
by: M.L. Ruscsak

Alista had ordered all of Larna's guess out of the castle. Their carriages had been brought around to the main entrance of the castle. When she had given that order Myrddin could not say for sure…

… Yet there, at the foot of the steps was the carriage of Darke with a team of marble white Pegasi waiting for them. The carriage of Lite only a few steps in front.

Adrianna's small hand wrapped around his as she asked, "Did you plan this?"

Helping Adrianna into a black coach he couldn't help but smile. "My sweet must you always ask things that you already know the answer to?"

She smoothed out her long black skirt before licking her lips and softly replying, "Maybe I want to hear you say what I already know."

Secrets, Lies and Betrayal
by: M.L. Ruscsak

Settling in next to her he smiled, "If you must know, I asked your mother to dispose of the queen once the vows were complete. But with the arrival of Queen Alista... I improvised. After all, she did just lose her entire family. It would be cruel for her to lose the last link to her daughter. At least, until she decides what to do with her." In time he may be able to tell his betrothed about the spell that he and Elista had cast so many years ago. Perhaps one day she would be able to understand that her cousins were all perfectly fine and completely safe.

The thought crossed his mind about telling her that Alista knew this day was coming. Perhaps...

No... no, he would say nothing. He had taken an oath and to him those words still meant something.

"How very kind of you." Looking over to the silver box that sat across from her, "And that..."

Ah, now that he could discuss.

"In a century or two, I will return it. Possibly return it. Or any child that we have may choose to. But nothing can destroy the box." *Or the contents within.*

Her eyes looked at the box almost memorized, "Enchanting."

Secrets, Lies and Betrayal
by: M.L. Ruscsak

"Yes, and if you're a good little apprentice I'll teach you how it works."

Sitting back, she crossed her arms smugly, "You assume I don't already."

Giving her a kiss, he smiled, "Incantation my dear, not power. And nothing that is close to your current abilities."

Secrets, Lies and Betrayal
by: M.L. Ruscsak

Secrets, Lies and Betrayal
by: M.L. Ruscsak

EPILOGUE

Larna gazed out of her parlor window. For more years than she could remember she had sat here unable to speak. Unable to do more than feed herself. Every need she had was someone else's to take care of.

Somehow it had gone wrong. She had been tricked. She had...

... Lost everything.

No longer was the queen of Feyen. Her crown stolen by her own Grandmother. Stolen by a queen that should long be dead. Her kingdom, her power gone. Used up.

Years trying to fight the spell that Myrddin had trapped her in had drained away any of her natural power

Secrets, Lies and Betrayal
by: M.L. Ruscsak

that he hadn't taken. The power that she had felt once the crown had been given to her... Alista had reclaimed.

A soft tap on the door.

Instinct said she should turn and face the intruder. But her body rarely responded to her command.

A soft leather hand petted her short hair. Fingers trailing down her neck. Then lip touching her throat. It might have pleased her she knew who this stranger was. Slowly he stood before her and smiled.

Such a handsome face. And those eyes. Gold eyes of a wolf. Of a hunter.

Slowly he knelt down before her. "Hello princess. I am Lord Edrich. I have been tasked with your care for the moment."

Edrich? All of her care was done by ladies... by...

Slowly he slipped her tunic off of her shoulders, and pressed his lips to hers. Pulling back, he whispered. "You failed Lord Magmas. However, he sent me here to help fix your mess. After I have my reward."

Reward... what...

Secrets, Lies and Betrayal
by: M.L. Ruscsak

His mouth covered hers and she received the first real kiss that she had had.

Hours later, after he was satisfied, he laughed as he dressed her once again. "Being half Fey I have ability to share my heart with you. You won't be able to control me. But you will be able to have some of your life back. At least until we can gain control of your heart."

She didn't understand what he was saying not until his heart beat in her chest. Then…

Slowly she brought her hand up and touched his young face. "My deity sent you?"

"He did. Now why don't we discuss a few things. Most importantly, how you will gain control of your kingdom and that of Darke."

Secrets, Lies and Betrayal
by: M.L. Ruscsak

Secrets, Lies and Betrayal
by: M.L. Ruscsak

Part 4

Teen Secrets and Buried Lies

NISHA PRINCESS OF DARKE QUEEN OF THE UNDER KINGDOM

"I can't help but to watch her. To watch this child that my queen had foreseen years before her birth. This child, who not only save the Star Cities but also save those who dwell here as well. I just pray that she be the answers to my silent prayers. The answer that will give the light back to the heart of my queen. And the one who will bring her out of this darkness."

-Private journal of Karnack; Scribe to the Goddess

Secrets, Lies and Betrayal
by: M.L. Ruscsak

They appeared by way of shadow. Appeared by stepping out of a darkness that had nothing to do with the time of night. But rather by form of travel known only to a select few. Adrianna was the first to gaze at her surroundings. The flicker of fire lighting the hollowed streets. Just enough light to give shape to those who had already fallen prey to whatever had caused this act of war...

This act of treason.

Myrddin was close behind her. His hand finding hers the moment that he had came to her side.

"Do you feel it?" She asked. Her eyes never wavering from the cobble streets. Or the crumbling houses.

"I do. Rage hangs think in the air. Thicker then the smoke and dust from the buildings."

Rage. Only a true royal Fey could put off this amount of rage. Only a true royal could cloud the air with this emotion and have it linger in the air like a bitter mist.

Adrianna glanced around at the streets of Night. Watched the building that days ago housed the promise of hopes and dreams. Houses that held the love of her people. Now...

... buildings crumbled around her. Fire both natural and not burned with a fury that few could create and less

Secrets, Lies and Betrayal
by: M.L. Ruscsak

could control. There were none who dwelled in Darke able to do this. Yet...

Myrddin gripped her hand his own rage filling the air. "Galeron you and Faerydae take the western streets. Myrddin and I will take those to the east. We will meet at the Castle."

His fingers curled tighter around hers. Screams echoed throughout the streets. "Addy? Maybe..."

"No. I'm Queen of this city... of this country it is up to me to end this."

A sideways glance and he let his fingers let go of her hand. Her choice was made. And so was his. "Go my pet I'll follow."

Galeron stayed only a heartbeat more as Faerydae disappeared down a lone alley. While their queen stormed off down another. "Myrddin?"

"We'll survive my friend. But... there will be death and pain."

"You're sure? Of course, you are..."

His eyes closed as a single tear slipped down his face as he kneeled down to a flicker near his feet, "Shadow my friend, go to my girl. Stay with her. Protect her. Do all that you can to keep her safe."

Secrets, Lies and Betrayal
by: M.L. Ruscsak

He didn't need to open his eyes to know who he had sent to Nisha. Didn't need to know anything. But knew his trusted friend would do anything to keep her safe.

Secrets, Lies and Betrayal
by: M.L. Ruscsak

Secrets, Lies and Betrayal
by: M.L. Ruscsak

CHAPTER 1: NISHA

The pale cream stone moaned as it shifted from its place. Fires blazed in the hearths. Windows crashed open with her fury. The maids and the court couriers scrambled to get out of her way. Only the guards still stood unfazed.

Fools. One day they would learn what her fury meant. One day they too would scurry from her sight. But she would allow them today to think that she was just a spoiled princess. Today she wouldn't against them. Today, she wouldn't lash out at those who had done her no harm.

Thirteen years ago, she had come here as nothing more than a babe. An orphan. Still, she was the Crown Princess of Darke. A royal Fey that even as an infant had been so powerful that a Shadow had bound itself to her. A shadow who was now hiding to escape her fury.

Secrets, Lies and Betrayal
by: M.L. Ruscsak

He recognized the danger. He recognized the fury, her rage that all others seemed to ignore. He understood what that rage could do to all that the castle housed.

Still she held her rage inside of her. For a moment longer, she would hold onto the hurt that cut deep. But only for a moment.

Storming through the Castle Sun-tear, Nisha held back her tears forcing them into a blind rage. Damn her aunt. Damn her to the bowls of the Under Kingdom.

How dare Celeste chastise her for being who and what she was born to be. How dare she compare her to a woman that she had never met. Compare her to a woman that had been her mother. How dare she even criticize the woman who was not here to defend herself.

A single tear rolled down her cheek as the memory of that night came to her young mind. Not her actual memory, but that of someone who had been there. The memory belonging to her Shadow.

The City was shrouded in darkness. Fires blazed in the City of Night. Buildings crumbled to the streets below. Citizen fought openly with one another in the streets. Some cowering in corners. Queen Adrianna along with her husband and Captain of the guards had rushed to the city from the Spire. They had stood tall assured that they could quell the uprising. Adrianna's hair fell around her and the staff of Darke Held firmly in her hands. She looked powerful, confident.

Perhaps too confident.

Queen Adrianna was lost that night, as was her father and so many others. The royal counsel was completely wiped out. The city and castle mostly destroyed. Leaving her the crown princess trapped in a kingdom not her own with an aunt that could barely stand the sight of her. An aunt that refused to allow her to learn about her darker abilities. An aunt that harbored ill feelings and blamed her for her own twin's death.

But today should have been different.

It should have been. But it wasn't...

Thundering up to her tower room Nisha slammed her light-colored bedroom door shut with the roaring slam. With tears streaking down her young face she threw herself onto her bed. Her raven colored hair falling wildly around her as she hit the soft bed.

She loved her aunt, she really did. But why couldn't she understand that a Fey that literally was the daughter of the darkness could never be a Light Fey? Why couldn't she understand that her dragon like wings were not some decorative design but her true wings?

Secrets, Lies and Betrayal
by: M.L. Ruscsak

Why? Surely Adrianna would have understood this, so why couldn't her twin?

This wasn't the first time that Aunt Celest had been brash with her, and it wouldn't be the last. But that didn't matter. What did matter was today was her thirteenth birthday. Yesterday Lilly had had a grand ball for hers. Had been doted upon and catered to from the very moment that the sun had come up until late into the night. So, was it too much to ask for a single person in all of Lite to smile and wish her... the crown princess of Darke... a single happy remark? Was it too much to ask for her aunt to even stop insisting for a single day that she... a dark Fey... learn healing craft?

Wiping the tears from her face Nisha sat up in her bed. Only a few more years and she could be rid of this place. Only a few more years and both Lilly and herself would be queens and they wouldn't be pitted up against each other by the current ruler of Lite.

Only a few more years. She would never survive it here if she continued to play by the rules of Lite. She wasn't meant to survive. Every day that passed it was becoming more and more apparent that she may never live long enough to become queen. Or at least not the queen that Darke needed her to be.

Closing her violet eyes, she ignored the footfalls coming up the stone steps. Ignored the sound of kitten

Secrets, Lies and Betrayal
by: M.L. Ruscsak

mewing. But she couldn't ignore the constant tapping on the door.

Tap.

Tap. Tap. Tap.

Tap. Tap. Tap. Tap. Tap. Tap.

Choking back her tears she allowed for a soft tendril of mist to open the door for her cousin. "You shouldn't be up here." Nisha sniffled once trying to dry her tears.

Slowly Lilly stepped but a single foot into the room. Her white silk dress skimming the golden tiles of the floor. Her golden wings fluttering slowly behind her. "I don't see anything a flame so I think it's safe. Besides, you promised me forever a while ago to go play in the forest."

"I also promised to turn you into a fat troll slug. Should I make good on that promise as well?" Nisha snapped back.

Lilly paused and considered the threat. "Oh, come now Nish, we both know you would never turn your favorite cousin into a troll slug."

She was right, but Nisha would never admit as much. "Why are you really up here Lil? Shouldn't you be healing something or learning how to draw power from the sun? Or some such ability that comes from being a Lite Fey?"

Secrets, Lies and Betrayal
by: M.L. Ruscsak

Slowly Lilly crept closer to the platform bed, her hands behind her back. "Well… I was thinking since you need cheering up today we could turn into butterflies and play with the pixies."

Wiping the last of her tears away Nisha gave a wobbled smile. "I'm not up playing with them today." She took a deep breath and slowly let it out. "But we could go play in the forest for a while. There is something I wish to show you and I think today would be as good of a time as any."

A wicked smile bloomed on Lilly's face, "So, we get to sneak out of the castle and have an adventure."

"Yes Lilly, we get to sneak out of the castle, however, we need to make sure no one comes looking for us. After all, I would never have you on the receiving end of your mother's temper."

Finally taking a seat next to her cousin, she wrapped her arm around her in a partial hug. Laying her head on Nisha's shoulder, she softly said, "She does love you Nisha. Mum just doesn't know how to teach you all of the things you will need in Darke. And sure, as the sun doesn't rise there, she doesn't want you to learn the things that lead to her sister's death."

Narrowing her eyes Nisha hissed, "My mother isn't dead Lilly. And sooner or later I will prove it." She paused just a moment to reign in her temper, "Now come on, I want to be in the forest before one of my forbidden powers destroys this castle."

Lilly rolled her sunlit eyes, "I hardly think you have that kind of ability. Then again, you are my cousin so it is a possibility." She was only teasing so why did Nisha look ready to expel all of her fury?

Secrets, Lies and Betrayal
by: M.L. Ruscsak

Secrets, Lies and Betrayal
by: M.L. Ruscsak

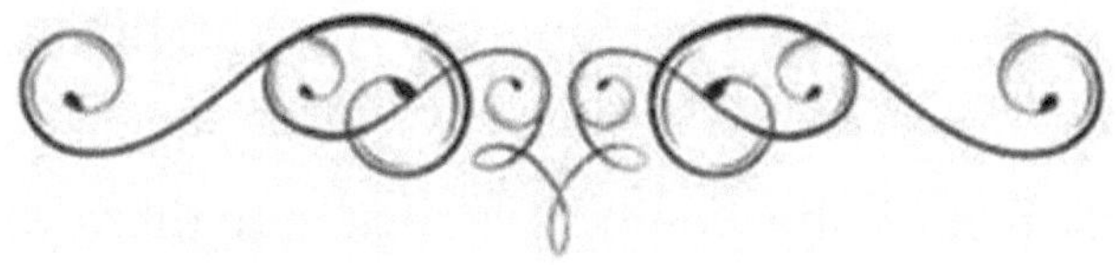

CHAPTER 2: CELESTE

Celeste slammed the golden door to her Solaris shut. Her fury growing with every breath. Nisha's powers grew every day. As was her temper. Insolent child how dare she question the person who had raised her? How dare she act superior to Lilly. How dare she go off and nurture abilities that she had no business in learning or even having.

How dare she!!!

It didn't matter that in natural power that Nisha was superior. Or would be once she grew into them. What did matter was that all of those beautifully deadly powers should belong to Lilly. But it was apparent in mere moments of their births which infant held all of those dark powers. Knew within a heartbeat that her sister Adrianna had given birth to the most powerful Fey in history.

A deep breath and she threw herself into her large overstuffed chair, allowing her long blonde hair to fall around her, she had tried so hard to destroy her sister long before they had been crowned queen. Tried to make every attempt appear as an accident. If she would have guessed

Secrets, Lies and Betrayal
by: M.L. Ruscsak

that it would take the royal family of the Marshland and Princess Larna of Feyen to complete the task....

... Oh, how she would have turned to them years, long before she had.

But Adrianna was another matter. Her death was so final nothing had been delivered to the under kingdom. Ah, but her prize... the key to all of Nisha's dark power... yes, that was something worthy of her. Too bad Myrddin still refused to submit. And until he did, he would stay a prisoner of the marshlands. If he didn't soon submit then he could perish in the dungeon of his own making.

She sat back, letting her long, narrow fingers massage her scalp trying to release the tension. There had to be a way to force Nisha to give up her powers. There had to be a way to take them. Even if that meant killing her and all of those that she cared for. Starting with her favorite guard.

Edgar. Yes ... the foolish oaf.

Slowly she let the idea form. Slowly she took in the golden light streaming in from the painted windows. Odd shapes appearing on the cold marble floor. Not shapes. Trolls. Yes, that would do nicely. And it would give her the access to the Under Kingdom. It would give her the ability to make sure that her own mother no longer interfered

Secrets, Lies and Betrayal
by: M.L. Ruscsak

with how Nisha was raised. It would make sure Vasilissa stayed right where she currently was residing.

Sitting back, Celeste smiled a cruel and bitter smile. She had been born the daughter of Lite. The queen of all things bright and cheery. Bah! If only her mother knew the truth. If only the old queen understood that she preferred the darkness that dwelled inside her. That she preferred to be anywhere the in this forsaken pit of boredom.

Secrets, Lies and Betrayal
by: M.L. Ruscsak

Secrets, Lies and Betrayal
by: M.L. Ruscsak

CHAPTER 3: NISHA

Reaching up into the spiral staircase to the highest point of the castle Nisha glanced over her shoulder. A single hesitation… Should she wait for her cousin or scare her witless? There was only one choice.

Lilly wanted an adventure. She wanted to see what she truly did when she was alone and not in the castle. Fine then she would scare her cousin witless today and hope she never asked for another adventure.

Still, looking back, she could see that Lilly was close enough to see but too far away to stop her. It would Do. Too quickly Nisha climbed onto the windows edge feeling the wind whipping at her dress. Letting the cold air blow her raved colored hair around her. But more importantly allowing the wind to seep through her now mist like wings.

Secrets, Lies and Betrayal
by: M.L. Ruscsak

Breathless Lilly called after her. "Nisha... What are you..."

One last look at Lilly and she dove from the window the currents tearing at her long black and blue dress. The feeling of a free falling more exciting than the last time her wings instantly transforming into their true form. Allowing her dragon like wings to open she slowed down before performing a somersault in the air and transforming into a large falcon beating its wings back to the tower window.

Lilly patted her cheat hoping to settle her heart. Hoping to catch her breath. Turning into fun little butterflies was one thing. Transforming into a falcon... that was another. "Nisha Devros, I swear you will be the death of me. Now I'm going to become a safe little butterfly and follow you."

Waiting until Lilly was comfortably settled into her favorite form of a blue fantasy butterfly and resting on the ledge of the window Nisha moved to appear to ready herself to fly from the castle, instead in one swift motion grabbed Lilly by the wings and disappeared into a fine black mist vanishing into the air itself.

Secrets, Lies and Betrayal
by: M.L. Ruscsak

Not a breath more and they both reappeared standing on the cliff overlooking the endless sea. Tall trees of gold and silver at their backs. The foamy waves of the Endless Sea several feet below them.

"What in the name of Darke was that? You could have killed me." Lilly snapped out before she even dared to glance around at her surroundings.

Nisha crept closer to the ledge memorized by the violence of the sea below. "No Lilly I wouldn't have. And it hurts to think that you would think that I would."

Rubbing her arms Lilly scowled, "You're not the one that will have bruises by morning."

Turning sharply Nisha crossed her arms, black, mist climbing up her back, "Damn it Lilly look around. You wanted an adventure. I gave you one. You wanted to see my thinking spot. I brought you. As a butterfly it would have taken days to reach this place. As a bird an hour or better.

Secrets, Lies and Betrayal
by: M.L. Ruscsak

Instead, I chose to travel in another form used by *my* people. And you still complain. What more do you want from me?" To quickly Nisha spun back to the sea hoping that Lilly wouldn't notice the sheen of tears already glazing her eyes.

"Oh, Nish... I'm sorry. You know I do not travel well by another's power. I'm just cranky." It was then she realized where they were. Not in Lite. Not in the forest near the castle. Oh no they were miles away in the country of Feyen. Near the border of the Griffiths. Standing on a ledge overlooking the endless sea and all of its beauty. "This is... Oh Nish do you know how much trouble you could be in if the queen of Feyen knew you were here?"

"Trouble? Alista is the one who showed me this spot. She's the one who taught me how to change trees of green and brown into crystal, silver, or gold. Damn it Lil, look around. Every tree, every flower and every blade of grass was created by *me*. To *my* liking. The sea foam platform, there on the horizon, I created so that I can spend time with the water dwellers. So that I can tag along on hunts. Or even ride a Kelpie. This is my place Lil, mine. No one cares if I learn about my dark abilities here. No one cares if I create something so terrifying that other Fey would be terrified. Alista encourages me. She knew my both my mother and father, she knows Grand'Mere. And frankly Lil, she knows me much better than anyone else, including you."

Secrets, Lies and Betrayal
by: M.L. Ruscsak

Slowly Lilly turned from her cousin and let her words sink in. True, they had grown up together. Being raised almost like sisters. And a sister *should* know her twin better than anyone else. The twin in question should not have to hide herself in another kingdom just to feel loved. "I wish you would have said this sooner. But neither of us can change time. So, I'm making a new rule between us. No secrets, ever. If you have to terrify me with all of the wonderful abilities that you have been nurturing on your own. So be it. If you have to practice those abilities you will teach me what you can and we will practice together. I will never be proficient in most of them, nor do I want to be but you will not learn them alone. And in turn I will teach you all of my abilities, knowing full well you never be proficient in most of them."

She didn't know what to ask, but Lilly no longer sounded terrified of being here. No If anything it sounded like she was going to do something that would benefit both of them. "Lilly?"

Turning back to Nisha, Lilly raised her head, "One day you will rule Darke. One day you need all of the abilities that you were born with. And one day we need each other as allies. So as of today, we start training. When we are here *we* will learn how you created all of this. And when we are in Lite..."

"I will try to learn the lighter spells."

Secrets, Lies and Betrayal
by: M.L. Ruscsak

Lilly nodded once. "So, since we are here. Terrify me. Show me your most terrifying form, then you can teach me how you did it."

Carefully, Slowly Nisha came to stand before her cousin. Not her normal slow, elegant movements. But those that were too similar to cat stalking its prey. Too close to a dangerous creature approaching it dinner. "I think it would be best if we were blood bound to one another first. Then I my dear cousin, I will happily become the things that belong only in nightmares."

Taking a deep, controlled breath, Lilly called in a short doubled bladed athame. The crystal hilt lightly held in her hand. Locking eyes with Nisha, Lilly asked, "Are you sure?"

"It's the only way to be certain that no matter what happens, we cannot be used against each other. The only way to ensure that our rule will be of our own making and decided by those will no longer have the right to rule."

Nisha was right, but it didn't make this any easier. No thinking about what Nisha was saying would only cause doubts about what needed to be done. To quickly Lilly pressed the tip of the blade to her finger. Just a single prick at the tip of her finger and bright blue blood swelled up covering the skin, "I, Lilly Kairavi, bind myself to you my cousin. From this day forth my powers and abilities cannot be used against you or those you love. With this single drop of blood, I bind myself to you, Nisha Devros, the daughter of darkness and rightful queen of Darke."

Taking Lilly's find Nisha let the single drop of blue blood touch her moist lips before taking the athame to her own finger. "I, Nisha Devros, bind myself to you my dear cousin. From this day forth my powers and abilities cannot be used against you or those you love. With this single drop of blood, I affirm this binding to you, Lilly Kairavi, the daughter of Light and the rightful ruler of Lite."

Light of blues and yellows engulfed both girls. Nisha's dark powers blending into Lilly. Lilly's light power blending seamlessly into Nisha. As the aura faded from them both the girls exchange a menacing smile. Lilly looked away first, "Your powers are much... stronger than I would have thought." There was something else that she would need to ponder later. Something in the words that Nisha had said. But That was later, right now she needed to understand what it was that she was seeing in her cousin's eyes.

With a yawn, Nisha retorted "Abilities my dear cousin not power. Power in itself means nothing for it only measures the strength of the ability being used."

"Well... abilities then. I think that is the only reason the binding worked so well. Because your natural abilities eclipse my own."

Secrets, Lies and Betrayal
by: M.L. Ruscsak

Nisha shrugged, "If you say so. Now I want to show you something."

"Oh, fine go, terrify me. Show me what it means to be the daughter of the darkness. Show me the depths of your abilities"

A twisted smile caressed Nisha's lips before she took off into a dead sprint toward the cliff propelling herself toward the sea only to let her body morph ten times her actual size Her arms and legs turning into giant dragon claws. No, not just her limbs, but her entire body.

Lilly stepped back. This was impossible. One could only turn into shapes that were real... and dragons... were not real. They were myth, legend. They were... well she didn't have the word for it, but watching Nisha change not just into one dragon form, but five before settling into a large silver form with a spiked tail and breathing black flames... she could no longer allow herself the fantasy of dragons no longer being just fantasy. Which begged the question if they hadn't been seen in scores of centuries... where they were actually living? The thought alone was terrifying. But as much as Nisha. Or at least not the moment.

Leisurely Nisha glided down and landed just before Lilly and bowed her head before silver smoke encased her leaving her once more in her true form. "Well? Did I terrify you?"

Secrets, Lies and Betrayal
by: M.L. Ruscsak

Lilly blinked once, then very slowly found the words that she wanted to say. "That... Nisha, you do realize dragons... they..." Her words failed her as she gazed into Nisha's eyes. She blinked once. There just a flicker of something just behind her eyes. Whatever it was... Lilly gulped air as she whispered, "How did you do that?"

Turning from Lilly, Nisha turned back to the sea. After several long moments she finally whispered, "Alista gave me some books. Some had been written by one of our ancestors. It told of a type of Fey that could create things, become whatever they chose. "

"I've never heard of this kind of Fey."

"According to the book Alista gave me, they are rare. So rare that only one is born for every million Fey." Nisha turned back to her cousin, "My wings, my true wings they mark me as a creator. Alista confirmed that much. What else she knows about those who can create is just speculation for one, hasn't lived here for several thousands of years."

Touching Nisha's shoulder Lilly whispered, "Mum doesn't know. Does she?"

"Grand'Mere doesn't know all of it, but she's the one who told me to speak to Alista. So, I think she understands enough."

Secrets, Lies and Betrayal
by: M.L. Ruscsak

For a long, breathless moment Lilly didn't speak. "I am amending our arrangement. While you work on your abilities, I will read the books Alista gave you. After all, we both know you hate to read anything that isn't a spell book. And I absorb the information that eventually you will need."

Creeping over the forest Nisha caressed the golden leaves of a tree. "We would need a place for you to work that would be protected encase any of my spells, incantations or abilities become destructive." She glanced over her shoulders, "It has happened you know. Then I had to rebuild everything that you see."

Oh, for the love of Lite. She did not need to hear that. "A small cabin would be sensible." Lilly agreed.

Turning back to her cousin Nisha shook her head. "Lilly don't you get it? I can create anything. Why would I want a small cabin when…"?

The ground beneath her feet rumbled, the sea began scaling the wall of the cliff blending into the dirt. The trees of crystal and gold melting into a colorful rainbow goo. The wind picked up howling through what was left of the trees. The waves began to crash loudly against the cliff wall.

Loose rocks tumbling into the water. Crashing into the sea.

Lilly scrabbled to get away from the edge, fearing the whole thing may collapse into the sea. While Nisha

Secrets, Lies and Betrayal
by: M.L. Ruscsak

hovered just a breath above the ground, her hands at her side palms pointed to the ground. Her head looking to the sky as the rain began to pour down just over her little spot.

Too terrified to watch what happened next, Lilly shut her eyes, listening to things crash and bang. Feeling the ground tremble beneath her. Then everything became still and terribly quiet. Slowly she opened just one eye, her body still gripping the trunk of a silver tree. With a gasp she lost her hold and fell back on the ground.

There, standing where the clearing on the cliff had been stood a tall domed structure. Crystal and gold. Water flowing from the top onto the ground, then somehow returning to the top once more. Then she saw Nisha standing in front of her work. Her hand balled into a fist and frowning at something.

Nervously she approached. Her wings, allowing her to flutter just above the ground. "Nisha? Don't you like your ... I'm not sure what to call this?"

"Rotunda, it means domed or rounded room. No, the structure is fine. I'm trying to figure out how the minnows got trapped within the glass, and how to free them without destroying the window itself. I'm thinking the bubble shapes that will be left after the fish are no longer there will be interesting."

Secrets, Lies and Betrayal
by: M.L. Ruscsak

"Oh, for the love of Lite. Let me. You trying to help living things will be distressing for the darlings."

Bowing slightly Nisha gestured with great flare for Lilly to help the fish.

Soft light sounded the windows Lilly pulled the trapped fish through the glass, leaving Nisha her fish shaped bubbles imbedded within the glass itself. Then ever so gently she places the now free minnows in the water surrounding the building. "There, they should be happy enough right there."

Following Lilly into their new secret room, Nisha smiled, "So have I terrified you enough for one day? Or should I continue my lessons?"

"You have both terrified me and taken my breath away. But I would like to see the books before we head back. If for nothing else but to memorize what I can about them so I can see if anything else may have been added to the library of our castle."

Using nothing more than her finger Nisha made a swirling motion calling up the ground to form both a table and two high back chairs. Leaving enough details within the soil and gold to resemble not only thick pillows, but also some intricate details that a cobbler might find to be of high craftsman's ship.

"Now, you're just showing off."

Secrets, Lies and Betrayal
by: M.L. Ruscsak

"No, Lil I wasn't. However, if I was I would have flattened everything you see here and put everything back as it was adding only the table and chairs. But I didn't see the reason to bother. Least not yet."

Shaking her head Lilly tried to smile, "The books please?"

Four thick leather-bound books appeared resting on the table along with a writing quill and blank parchment. "I will leave you to your work. I need to go see Queen Sedna. Her prize hippocampi should be having its calf any day now. And she promised I could name it."

Secrets, Lies and Betrayal
by: M.L. Ruscsak

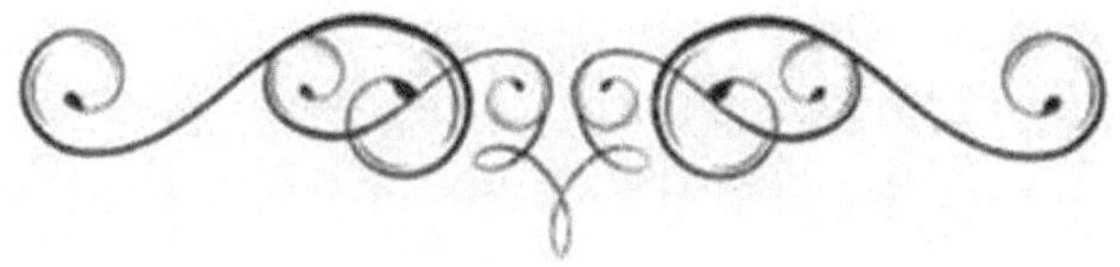

CHAPTER 4: CELESTE

The castle was eerily quiet. Neither Lilly nor Nisha were anywhere within the castle. Nor were they visiting the city just beyond the palace walls. Somehow, they had slipped out of the castle and the city without drawing the attention of those who dwelled here. Somehow, they had escaped the whole of Lite without sounding a single alarm.

Once they were found she would not only find out how they had gotten beyond her grasp, she would find out who had helped them escape the palace. And she would do what was allowed as the queen of Lite to prevent them from doing so again. Even if that meant stripping the person of all of their abilities and sending them to the Under Kingdom before they bled out.

After all, Lilly would tell her now that Nisha had finally taken her with her. So, she just had to wait until the little brat returned. It wouldn't' be long just a few hours. Lilly would wish to return before the sky turned gray. She would have the sense to return before the creatures that came out to feast at night started to stir.

Secrets, Lies and Betrayal
by: M.L. Ruscsak

Whereas Nisha could very well be gone well into the next day. But Lilly was smarter. More easily scared of the trolls. And very easily scared of being in trouble with her queen.

However, this did give her the time that she needed to carry out her other plan. Now... all she had to do was convince the guard...

... No, there was no need for that.

Celeste sat back on her throne. The gold just starting to melt at her finger tips. If it melted completely Those who lived within the palace would surely notice.

Getting to her feet, she reached out her hand, summoning a ball of dark light. Soft words slipped past her lips and spoken to the orb of light just before it vanished from her sight.

Carefully Celeste counted to herself very slowly. One... two... three...

Finally reaching ten, she summoned another spell. Her long simmering court dress vanished being replaced the one that she wore solely when there was trouble. For most they would consider it battle armor. Gold plated armor cover her chest, along crystal and gold chain mail skirt. She looked fearless and agitated. She looked ready for battle.

Secrets, Lies and Betrayal
by: M.L. Ruscsak

"Edgar!!!!" Her voice roared through the castle.

Heavy footfalls. Heavy enough for the hall and throne room to tremble as he raced to her. The two story double doors of light painted wood snapped open as Edgar came to an abrupt stop. His eyes scanning the throne room looking not to her the queen, but for that of the captain of the guards. A man who was not within the room. A man who if there was real trouble would be standing beside his queen. Slowly he stood to his full height. His broad shoulders, sliding back in the anticipation of trouble. Ina low voice Edgar slowly said, "My Queen?"

Turning sharply toward the south window Celeste stared out, "There is trouble near the farm lands. Those there are slow in gathering information. I doubt it would be more than someone of your stature can handle. But I will not stand here and not prepare for something more dire."

Some in the way she was holding herself made him twitch. Something... yet it was his duty to protect the crown. His duty to see that no harm came to Princess Nisha or to the princess of Lite. "I will handle whatever it may be. Rest assured my queen no harm shall come to the castle."

That she knew. Still, she gave a single nod dismissing him to his task.

Once his footfalls, no longer echoed within the castle, Celeste finally turned toward the door. The smile frozen on

Secrets, Lies and Betrayal
by: M.L. Ruscsak

her lips was one of the purest delight. Soon she would have exactly everything that she every desired. Soon she would have the leverage to force Nisha to give her powers to her the queen of Lite in exchange for the life of not only her trusted guard but that of her beloved grandmother.

Secrets, Lies and Betrayal
by: M.L. Ruscsak

CHAPTER 5: LILLY

Darkness was just creeping over the land when Lilly had given up on her reading or at least had given up reading for the night. Closing the thick leather covered book, she glanced up, "Nish, as much as find you creating those terrifying little creatures that I will never ask what you might use them for... I do think it's best if we return back to the Castle. Mum would surely raise the entire army should be not return before nightfall."

Nisha raised her head in question. Dark lightning flicking in her eyes. "Are you asking because you wish to return home or because you fear your mother's temper?"

Oh yes, there was defiantly more to Nisha's dislike for her mother than what she knew as truth. Closing her

Secrets, Lies and Betrayal
by: M.L. Ruscsak

eyes, Lilly breathed out very slowly, "Before I answer that I want an answer to a question that before today I would have never asked. A question that I don't want to ask now, but the simple truth that I am finding make it impossible to ignore any longer."

Slowly Nisha glided over the table and took a seat across from her cousin, "Oh, and what, pray tell, does my dearest cousin need answered that is so important that she can't even look at me?"

Not yet opening her eyes, Lilly shuttered, "You and mum. What are you not telling me?"

Nisha made a loud aspirated sound as her chair scraped against the hard floor. "A lot. Some of it Grand'Mere confirmed. Some of it I know from personal experience. And some... has been as of yet only speculation. Where would like me to begin?"

Oh Shit. She had expected Nisha to say something like "She hurts my feeling" not... well she didn't know what Nisha was saying, but she could feel the foreboding starting deep within her stomach. Still she answered "Start with what Grand'Mere knew then work up to what you think, but as of yet cannot prove."

For several long moments Nisha didn't speak as she petted the strange six-legged horse lizard creature that she had created. "Before deciding to seek answers within the underkingdom grand 'mere told me that when our mothers were younger that they were very competitive. If My mum learned something yours would try to master it. In the end both had mastered a handful of natural abilities before being the age to rule."

"There is nothing wrong with a little rivalry as long as it was meant to push each other to reach their potential."

"Maybe, but doesn't explain why your mother had tried several times to find out what could kill her twin."

Lilly let the word sink in. Slowly closed her eyes, trying to breath. "Are you saying that you think my mother... the woman who brought you here at her sister's request... had something to do with her... with the uprising."

"Grand 'mere thinks so. It's the reason that she really left to dwell in the under Kingdom. And Lil, I'm telling you right now, my mother might have asked her to bring me to Castle Sun tear but it was Alista who was to raise me. Tensions between both queens have been building since then. Sooner or later it's going to come to a head."

Lilly gave herself a mental shake, "Why would..."

"My father was part of her court. A part of her daughter's court and was still the liaison between Feyen and Darke. I have never been told much about him. Nor ever seen a single picture, but Alista confirmed it was he

Secrets, Lies and Betrayal
by: M.L. Ruscsak

that had the ear of both the Feyen council and the council of Darken. So, I highly doubt with that kind of power…"

Sitting back in her seat Lilly shook her head, "You're right the laws of Feyen are very clear. Should a council member perish in any untimely manner their offspring is raised within the court of Feyen. It was one of the first laws I remember reading about the rule of King Magmas. Grandfather made sure I memorized all of the laws created by him as well as those upheld by King Griffith."

Nisha sat back in her seat and folded her hands on the table, "So, are we deciding that your mother is hiding something?"

"I love mum. And I do not think she means you ill will. However, I will agree that something is amiss. And whatever it is, I do doubt that we will find out within the next five years."

"Very well then I won't confront her about it until I can verify the speculation."

It seemed that the darkness was being kind today. Or at least kind enough to allow her time to disprove this notion that her own mother had killed her twin. Or at least she hoped that would be what she found. Something in the pit of her stomach was telling her otherwise. Something that warned her that her grandmother already had some proof if she had never said anything to Nisha.

Secrets, Lies and Betrayal
by: M.L. Ruscsak

No, her grandmother would have had some proof before seeking permission to dwell within the Under Kingdom when she was still fully alive.

Shit. What had her done all those years ago? What could have made here take that kind of action against her own blood. And who was she going to have to tell in order to make this right?

Getting stiffly to her feet Lilly glanced out of the window. "I think it best if I review grandfather's notes and see if he knows of anything that we would need to know."

Grabbing Lilly's arm Nisha smiled, "Very well, my little bookworm. You go read in the Library. And I will figure out how we are truly related."

"Nisha! Our mothers were sisters. In fact, they were twins. How do you think we are related?"

"I don't know, but as I've been working all day I have been watching you. Measuring your abilities against my own. And for being the daughter of two Fey of Light you have abilities that reach into the darker. Almost equal to mine in some areas, but not as many natural abilities. It is most peculiar. Do you not agree?"

Shit. "Grand'Mere ruled both Lite and Darke ... it could be..."

Secrets, Lies and Betrayal
by: M.L. Ruscsak

"No, these abilities are not in your mother nor father. Abilities not even found in either of our grandparents. But I would like to think on it some more. After all, you do wish to be home before darkness falls and the trolls come out to play."

What was Nisha saying? Could she possibly think that they were sisters? How would that even be possible? No best not to ask that. Not when Nisha seems in the mood to answer questions. Not when those answers were leading to a war that no one wanted.

Secrets, Lies and Betrayal
by: M.L. Ruscsak

Shadows danced through the trees as the sun was still slowly setting. It would be dark soon. It would have been dark long before now if they were still in the colder months. So, it was fortunate that this was the season of flowers and new life. The one hundredth and twentieth day of the light cycle. Glancing at Lilly, Nisha smiled at her cousin who was patting her heart. "Happy now that we are back in your safe little kingdom?"

Lilly gave her a sly glance before sighing, "One day I will learn how it is you can travel with the ability of a shadow."

Secrets, Lies and Betrayal
by: M.L. Ruscsak

"Lilly darling, everyone knows shadows come from my country. Plus, one bound itself to me the night of the fire. So, it is quite possible it gave me that ability."

"Yes, well, I'm still waiting until we can prove that you have mastered it."

Nisha shook her head and smiled, "The ability that Shadow gave me wasn't just one. It was many. Alista, has already told me that I have mastered travel, and shadow speech. And I have been awarded pins for both."

"Shadow speech? I thought only a queen had the ability to listen to what is being said. And only if that person is bound to her?"

Looking thoughtful Nisha tilted her head slightly, "True, however, that only happens if the shadows wish to be helpful to the queen. Such as your mom, the shadows are not bound to her, but she plays it off as only the queen of Darke or Feyen has access to them. However, I know for a fact that even though David's mother is not the ruling queen, Shadows assist her whenever she needs. And Lil, you know as well as I, that none are blood bound to either her or King Craykren."

For several breaths Lilly stood there without speaking. "And do you think a shadow would be willing to assist me in the future?"

Secrets, Lies and Betrayal
by: M.L. Ruscsak

"Lil? Honestly, I don't know where you mind is most days. The shadows that live in the castle already assist you. Or have you not noticed that where you wish to be alone that no one is able reach you."

"I've always wondered… Never mind. We can discuss Shadows later. First, I want to have a large meal, then soak for ages in my bathing pool."

Linking arms with Lilly, Nisha began to lead her cousin out of the dense woods. "So, do you think that your mother has scoured the castle looking for us?"

"Mum? Probably. Daddy on the other hand, if he had a reason to look for me he would have found me anywhere. So, I don't think he was looking very hard."

"You know, it never dawned on me how different your parents really are. Uncle Blake leads by trusting those around him. Whereas your mother, trust no one."

"In any case, we can always say that there are a few good hiding places within the woods."

"Actually, there are several." A wicked smile bloomed on Nisha's face. "And of those a several are immune to others using their abilities to gain entrance or find those who are hiding within the pockets."

Taking their first step out the woods Lilly returned the smile, "How intriguing. I would like to explore those

Secrets, Lies and Betrayal
by: M.L. Ruscsak

areas sometime soon. I for no better reason than to find my own little spot."

"Of…" Turning her head sharply Nisha watched as a maid rushed toward her. As she drew closer, she could see the her flaming red hair coming loose from its thick braid. And her dress… light blue with the trim of gold… Only one maid wore a dress such as that… Only… what could have happened to tear Marigold's sky-blue dress to have it tattered and torn. Not to mention could have left those dark wet blotches all over it.

Panting as she reached them, Marigold didn't bother to curtsy. Didn't bother speaking to them as she was a maid, but spoke filled with distress "Lilly, thank the light I've found you. I- "

Narrowing her eyes Nisha sniffed the air, then hissed "Mari? What happened? You smell of blood."

Tears filled Marigolds ivy green eyes, "It's my father. He left the castle a bit before midday. Tolls attacked. I- I think it was trolls. The castle guard won't let him back in. They say the gate to the under kingdom will collect him. It's bad Lilly. Real bad. I-" Tears streaked her face, she was gasping air in her words as they tumbled out of her. "-I don't know what to do. Mum can't leave her work. Isn't allowed to leave the kitchens. I can't bring… I…" With light created by Lilly Marigold collapsed to her knees.

Taking Marigold's hand in her own Lilly let her light surround the maid giving her some comfort. The light stopping the thick sheen of tears before they could fall. Closing her eyes, Lilly could feel everything that Marigold was feeling. Could feel the distress that went far beyond the surface tears. Felt the grief that one would expect. But also felt something similar to betrayal. Such an odd feeling to have in this moment.

Grief at the loss of her father. Confusions that trolls would attack during the daylight hours. Betrayal that the castle guards not the queen would do anything to help. Helplessness that no healer would dare trouble themselves to help a single guard.

Yet, Marigold had been Nisha's maid, but she was also a friend. One of the few her cousin had. And one of the very few that came directly from Feyen. A friend that knew the danger and understood things far beyond those that a maid should know. "Show me. If there is something that can be done, it will be. Nish- "

"I'm coming with you."

Turning her head slightly to look at Nisha, Lilly took a breath and tried to reason with her, "You're not a healer."

"You're right, I'm not. But there may be something I can do. If nothing else I can make sure there are no more trolls lurking about."

Secrets, Lies and Betrayal
by: M.L. Ruscsak

Shit. She hadn't even thought about that. The thought of Nisha taking on a herd of troll was one that she wished that she hadn't thought about now. It was one of her more distressing memories of her cousin. And a secret that even David didn't know yet. A memory that she had to squash before Nisha picked up on the thought and misunderstood why she was thinking of that now. Swallowing hard Lilly finally found her voice, "Let's go."

Secrets, Lies and Betrayal
by: M.L. Ruscsak

CHAPTER 6: NISHA

It had only taken moments to fly to where Edger had laid bleeding. Only a moment to find the spot where the scent of blood would surely call to the creatures of the night. Yet... something about this was wrong. He wasn't in the forest, but near the village. Near a low wall that served no purpose.

Nisha's eyes scanned the area. Houses, cottages, and craftsman's huts all were within sight. Animals that were raised for slaughter grazing in the pasture unaware of any danger. It didn't feel right. Didn't look right.

Surely if there was danger lurking about the animals would cause a racket by now. Except they weren't.

Add to that, that Edger was nearly the same height as an ogre. Plus, he had the added muscle of a strong-arm Fey. A single troll rapid or not should have never gotten

Secrets, Lies and Betrayal
by: M.L. Ruscsak

close enough to hurt him. And certainly, should have never been able to cause all of the wounds that now laid openly bleeding all over the lush sweet grass.

Knowing Lilly was already doing what she could to help, Nisha moved only a few paces away from the spot where the guard had fallen. And he had fallen where he now laid for there was no signs of blood anywhere else. Not a drop on even a single blade of grass.

Yet...

Nisha sniffed the air breathing in deeply.

Trolls had a very nasty smell to them. One that was near the smell of rotted meat mixed other foul odors. Not to mentions they were loud and destroyed everything around them. So, no matter what Edger had managed to tell Marigold.... No matter what she had thought had happened, it wasn't a troll that has done it.

That being the case... what else could have...

"Nisha!!!" Lilly screamed, her voice full of tears and grief.

No need to turn around to know what had happened. No need to ask if her, trusted guard had taken his final breath. No, there was no reason to ask anything of Lilly... but she would be damned if she didn't find out what had happened to her guard... her friend... her loyal subject that

Secrets, Lies and Betrayal
by: M.L. Ruscsak

Queen Alista had so thoughtfully sent here personally just a few years ago.

Rage built inside her as she slowly turned and came back to the fallen guard's side. Something much worse than rage flowed within her veins as she knelt down next to his lifeless body. Lightly Nisha's fingers danced on his olive colored skin. Ever so slowly a purple mist begun to form around him and every blade of grass that held even the tiniest speck of his blood. Finally, the mist settled over her as well. Slowing her own breath, Nisha let her eyes close as she concentrated on the spell that she was creating. Not much of a spell really, but instinct as natural as breathing. One day she might have the time to teach this to Lilly but right now, her dear cousin would have to deal with not knowing.

Right now, she needed to give everything to do what only she could help her guard and get the answers that she so desperately needed.

Secrets, Lies and Betrayal
by: M.L. Ruscsak

Secrets, Lies and Betrayal
by: M.L. Ruscsak

CHAPTER 7: LILLY

Watching carefully Lilly pulled Marigold to her and sat back. Sat back gently rocking this strong Fey, who was crumbling before her. Sat back an awe as she watched Nisha not understanding what she was seeing. Not understanding what Nisha was doing, nor how.

Narrowing her eyes and opening herself up to feel around her, Lilly studied Nisha for a breath longer. Oh, it was a spell that her cousin was creating. A spell that once Nisha was no longer concentrating on it, nor still in a mood that even the dead would find terrifying, she would corner her into teaching.

Secrets, Lies and Betrayal
by: M.L. Ruscsak

After all Nisha had promised.

A moment longer and the light around both Edger and Nisha began to blend into different hues. A rainbow of dark colors. Black mist seeping into the guard's skin. Then... a tiny breath. Not far Nisha, but Edgar. How? Sure, there were stories... but...

Lilly gasped as she patted Marigold to look to her father. Both of them tense as the knowledge of Nisha was accomplishing settled in. True, there were stories... legends... myths even. All of them told at night about Fey, who had the power to grant life after death. Stories that put the elderly at ease when at the end of their own Life cycle. Stories to give comfort to those so that they could be granted entrance into the hollows of the underkingdom and granted time with loved ones passed.

But these were stories. None held truth. None...

Giving herself, a hard-mental shake, Lilly squared her shoulders. After today she had learned one thing. All of the stories had to be based on truth. They had to be. For the love of Darke there was Fey sitting right before her that had all of the abilities at none had seen in several lifetimes. All of the powers of everything that had been warned about. All of the powers that every Fey had always dreamed of but were too scared to even try.

Secrets, Lies and Betrayal
by: M.L. Ruscsak

May the light protect her because all of those powers now belonged to her cousin. Or perhaps they had always been there to begin with.

Terrified at her own, though Lilly concentrated on the guard. Forced herself to remain calm as if this kind of thing happened every day. Concentrated as Edgar's body slowly and painstakingly regained signs of life as the gate to the Under Kingdom opened not but a few feet from the four of them.

Somehow knowing that Nisha wasn't finished with her spell. Knowing that her cousin needed a few minutes longer doing whatever it was that only she could do… Lilly formed a shield of Light around her cousin, knowing that regardless of what Nisha may be doing to help her guard would also leave her vulnerable to an attack. Knowing that Nisha wouldn't be able to protect herself and finish the spell. And not knowing if Nisha's over protective shadow was somewhere close enough to protect her.

But she knew who wasn't here to protect them… Her kitty. Her precious, loving kitten who hid a deadly secret. Glancing at Marigold, who was good at a lot of things… all of them useful… and none of them useful for fighting Lilly quickly got to her feet. She had to do something… anything…

The ground was covered in twigs and small stones. Grabbing the largest of the stones she steadied herself and

Secrets, Lies and Betrayal
by: M.L. Ruscsak

took aim just as the gate fully formed before them. A gate that she could see now was made from the bones of the dead and some kind of gray and black swirling mist that filled the space between.

She had just enough time to glance back down, Nisha wasn't finished doing whatever that it was that she was doing to Edgar.

A single choice... and she threw the fist size rock and threw it as hard as she could into the mist hoping to strike whomever was coming through.

An older man in torn gray robes stepped from the mist tossing the rock back down on the ground. And not looking annoyed or even hurt. If he looked anything Lilly could say that he looked amused.

Lilly took in his features dusty blond hair just starting to show signs of graying. Long, narrow finger with manicured nails. He must have been handsome in his younger days. With a chiseled jaw line yet he didn't have the pointed ears common of all Fey. But she could ponder his race later, right now.... She screamed, "He's not dead. He doesn't belong to the Under Kingdom."

The man took a full step out of the gate and smiled. "Quite right my dear. But I'm here for the guard." He paused and waited for Nisha to finish her spell and turn her head just enough to see him. "My name is Karnack, and I have

Secrets, Lies and Betrayal
by: M.L. Ruscsak

been waiting a very long time for this moment. Princess Nisha? A moment if you will allow. Your guard will be in good hands of your cousin." He paused for just a breath, "Your kitty will be here monetarily, Princess Lilly."

Carefully Nisha got to her feet and nodded to Lilly, "I have your word that I will return to this place unharmed?"

"Nisha, no. He's…"

"Very much alive Lil. Shadow can taste the blood flowing in his veins and promises that he can be trusted."

Karnack smiled softly, "Your shadow is welcome to come as well. To ensure your safety, of course."

Stepping over to the man Nisha nodded. "I will come with you, but I will leave whenever I should choose."

"Princess, you misunderstand me. I have a gift that I have been entrusted to give you. After your show of recent abilities, I believe today would be a fitting day for you to receive that gift. If anything, you could consider it a birthday present."

Narrowing her eyes Nisha squared her shoulders and stepped through the misty gate.

Nodding to Lilly, Karnack turned back to follow the young princess. Stopping a not more than a step from the gate, he softly speaks. "The guard was attacked by one of your own to gain entrance to the Under Kingdom. Your cousin has completely healed him this time. I doubt she will a second. And Princess, be warned the gate doesn't always open for the dead. Only the worthy."

Secrets, Lies and Betrayal
by: M.L. Ruscsak

CHAPTER 8: NISHA

Stepping through the swirling mist, Nisha stumbled a step as she glanced around at the vast landscape. The stories told about this place... oh how wrong they were. Carefully, she took but a single step, Shadow to her right just beyond her fingertips. Her eyes watching the Fey... thousands of Fey wandering cobbled streets. Entering and exiting countless number of doors. No-one seemed in pain. No-one cared if they had gaping wounds that have long bled dry. None seeming to be filled with the daily suffering that every story had hinted to.

If anything, this place seemed more like the stories of where a fallen hero entered the under Kingdom. A place where he or she would be greeted by their ancestors before their powers, their abilities were slowly bled into the entire realm of the Living.

Secrets, Lies and Betrayal
by: M.L. Ruscsak

Still watching a small group of skeletons marched by, Nisha narrowed her eyes and took in all of the details that they could give her. The only sign of their race was their silver and gold armor that still bore the emblem of the great dragon. Still shone with pride of the victors of the great war. Even their spears still held an edge that the weapons fashioned today couldn't compare to. Yes, these skeletons belonged to the great king of Feyen. They had belonged to King Magmas.

Or possibly some king or queen before even him.

For several moments she stood there watching everything. Watching those who were of no known race that she had ever heard of speak cheerfully with those who appeared closer to the Feyen race. Watched as the Skeletons guards only glanced her way before moving on. Watched as those who dwelled here seemed to be doing in death what they had enjoyed in life.

"It's something, isn't it?"

The gate was behind her. Yet the voice... that deep, cultured voice that had sent a shiver down her spine had come from her left. Turning ever so slightly Nisha gasped before stumbling a step. Having been in the castle of Feyen she had seen paintings and sculptures of King Magmas. Who in all of Feyen hadn't seen his paintings? But he should look years older. Yet somehow, he was appearing at her side looking no older than her aunt. Somehow, she would ask him to teach this spell to her... if she could find the courage to do so.

With a small curtsy Nisha gave a wobbled smile, "Your majesty?"

Magmas raised a single eyebrow on his young face his wings hidden beneath his long dark robes. His lava red eyes narrowed just a bit before he crossed his massive arms over his dragon emblemed breastplate. A deep sigh escaped as he exhaled, "Darling, I haven't ruled for many light cycles. Nor am I planning to anytime soon." Turning to glance at the gate, he offered a bit more of an explanation as to his arrival, "When Karnack sent word that you were growing into your abilities, I offered my assistance in training you on how to be a royal Fey."

His what? The Great King of Feyen was offering... Without thinking Nisha blurted out, "Isn't that what my aunt should be doing?"

It was then Karnack stepped through the gate. Annoyance very apparent in his every step, "What she should be doing is nurturing your abilities. It is very apparent that she is has been doing everything within her power to suppress those abilities. Why I would never speculate."

Magmas pulled Nisha to his chest in an overprotective fatherly manor as he studied the queen's

Secrets, Lies and Betrayal
by: M.L. Ruscsak

scribe. Closing his wings slowly around her he gave her possibly the first real hug that she had ever received. "With her being Vasilissa's daughter it is a wonder. But that is a worry for another day. Today however is time for the daughter of the darkness to take her rightful place among the great royal Fey. Your abilities will be needed in the years to come, but understand me, myself and those of my bloodlines will do everything within our power to delay the trouble that was prophesied would begin shortly after your birth."

Gazing up at the man who she knew was a fierce fighter and loving father Nisha stepped back from his warm embrace. Later she could ponder why he still had blood flowing through his veins. Later she could worry about why he spoke as though he hadn't in some time. Right now, she needed to focus on what he said. Prophecy. He had said… Another step backwards and she   landed hard on a seat made completely of mist, "There is a prophecy about me? Why wasn't I told about it long before now?"

Both Karnack and Magmas exchanged worried looks. Words being spoken between them that only they could ever know. A loud disagreement that hopefully Nisha would never learn the truth behind. Finally coming before her, Magmas took a knee, then slipped her small hand into his. "There were only a few of us who ever know about it. Less now since the great war. Nisha, I can't betray the trust of

Secrets, Lies and Betrayal
by: M.L. Ruscsak

those who came before you, but I can tell you this. You will be a great Fey. A great queen worthy of so many."

Nisha nodded once in understanding, "I have no desire to make you betray the trust of someone that earned your respect." Seeing relief on the faces of both men she glanced up at Karnack "Is this why you brought me here? To meet The Great King of Feyen and to tell me about a prophesy?"

Karnack knelt before her a crown of bone appearing in his hands. Bowing his head, he held out the crown "No, I have come to offer this and the abilities that come with it."

For a long moment Nisha sat there unsure of what to do. Sat there as those who she had been watching not long ago were now drawing closer to her. The army of Skeletons now keeping the others back. Keeping the others from stepping too close to the gate or to her. Finally finding her voice she whispered, "The Under Kingdom has a ruler?"

Karnack's voice filled with sorrow, remembering the last time he had dared to enter her throne room. His heart aching at the truth. "She has been gone for too long. It was she who saw your birth and entrusted this crown to my care. To be given at a time that I deemed necessary and fitting. I think would do well for both."

Looking to Magmas, she nodded. "I do not know how to rule. Not here nor the country that I was meant to. But I

Secrets, Lies and Betrayal
by: M.L. Ruscsak

trust the father of Alista can teach me and not leave until I can rule completely on my own."

"I will remain here helping not only you as the queen of this place, but also tending to some personal matters that I fear will take far many more years than I have already seen in order to put to rest. In addition to my guidance I think it best if you also have some lessons with both Flint and Apollo. As well as Griffith if he can be persuaded,"

Griffith? Her grandfather? Well great… great grandfather. The man who killed the queen of Darke so his own granddaughter could rule, not one but two countries? That Griffith? Would it be polite to request that he be excluded? Then again… it was widely known that Magmas' abilities dwarfed in comparison to Lord Griffiths. "In that case, Karnack, I accept this responsibility on the condition you keep me informed on anything that needs my attention while I am in Lite. Also, I would like to know anything that can tell to me about the uprisings that took place in Darke. I have many questions and no answers in sight."

"Your terms are acceptable to the keepers of this realm." Carefully Karnack got to his feet and ever so slowly sat the scalloped bone crown upon Nisha's head. "I, the gatekeeper of the Under Kingdom bestow the crown of the dead and all of the abilities that comes with it. All of those who belong to this place are now blood bound to our new

Queen. Princess Nisha Devros of Darke, the new Queen of the under Kingdom."

Powers slammed into her. Dark light of purples, blues and black formed around her. The knowledge of the dead unlocking abilities that she had only read about. But that wasn't all she could hear them. Every voice. Every conversation. She could hear all of it in perfect clarity. Things that she needed to know. Things that she needed to recall was there with nothing more than a thought. Everything else... just an afterthought. As the light began to fade and she found solace in the powers and abilities of the dead, Nisha brought herself to ask, "Will those who I bind to me, hear or be able to use any of the abilities of the dead?"

"No, Nisha. No one but the queen can use abilities of those whom they rule, even if given your permission. It can't be done. However, if they have a natural ability similar to those you now rule it may be possible that it will be unlocked. Such as now you have every single one of your natural abilities that come from the dead... are now unlocked and you may find you will completely master them in little time."

"How deeply interesting."

Getting to his feet Magmas smiled, "You sound like your grandmother. I have yet to decide if that is a good thing."

Secrets, Lies and Betrayal
by: M.L. Ruscsak

"Do you speak to Grand'Mere often?"

For a long moment Magmas refrained from answering. For an even longer moment he pondered not answering at all. "I have not seen her recently, But I will tell you that when she was your age there was no one more formidable. Not even my darling Alista."

"Considering she her father was It's a wonder that she didn't destroy all of the castles of Lite before her abilities had been mastered."

"It's a wonder that Griffith didn't see which of his bloodline had the ability to truly rule Lite. But that is a matter for another day."

Karnack shrugged, "He wore the facade of a cranky old Fey because it suited him. He allowed for Enya to rule because he had no desire to. He's not much different from Flint. Now come. I wish to show our young queen the city that is not more than a few steps from here. And perhaps find her a guard that would be willing to return to Lite to watch over her."

"You should ask Freya. As the captain of my elite forces there are none here that I regard any higher. That and she is the daughter to both Mary and Uncle Donny. Her skills are not to be taken lightly."

"Uncle Donny? I don't believe Alista ever mentioned him."

Secrets, Lies and Betrayal
by: M.L. Ruscsak

It wasn't until Nisha had met with the handful of bystanders that Magmas even tried to answer, "Donavan was an honorary uncle. He helped to raise many displaced Fey. Those who had the temperament to learn darker abilities worked more closely with him and Nicco while others worked with Mary."

Letting her fingers caress the windowsill that she could now feel was bone, Nisha turned from the shop hoping that her act of curiosity wasn't looked at as disrespect. "Will you tell me about them? I do so love hearing about the ancestors."

"Perhaps one day. But right now, I think it would be best to get you back to your cousin." Magmas paused. "As queen you can grant access to any of the living that you wish. While here, they would be well protected and cared for."

Why was he telling her this?

Looking into his eyes she knew. Lilly. King Magmas was giving his consent for Lilly to be brought here

Secrets, Lies and Betrayal
by: M.L. Ruscsak

Secrets, Lies and Betrayal
by: M.L. Ruscsak

CHAPTER 9: MAGMAS

Magmas watched silently as Nisha slipped through the gate of the dead. Waited until Freya was mostly alone with him, "Freya?"

She turned slightly, his hand resting comfortably on the hilt if her short blade. Right now, she appeared to be nothing more than a Fey that controlled nature. Nothing more than a woodland nymph. That could change in the next breath. And Would change if her king, so willed it, "Your majesty?"

"I would never tell Nisha this… but do not trust those who dwell in Lite. And do not let one that you know who it is that is beside her."

Her eyes narrowed as she glanced over her shoulder, "The *Shade* and I will work together well. I see no reason to change the relationship that we had while in life." She

Secrets, Lies and Betrayal
by: M.L. Ruscsak

turned back to the gate and her eyes narrowing a bit more, "Should the need arise will I report to the Queen of the Under Kingdom or to you directly?"

"I trust your judgment. Take care not to harm the queen of Lite. Least not until I can prove her involvement in some matters. And then either I or Griffith will handle it."

Freya inclined her head ever so slightly. The vines that covered her arms, absorbing into her milky pale skin and a tight corset formed around her. Her long skirt transforming into skin tight leggings that wouldn't hinder her movement. "I see no reason for the living to know all of my secrets."

A shiver went through Magmas as she vanished into the gray swirling mist. "I trust her with my life, yet..."

Karnack laid his bony hand on Magmas' shoulder, "She still unnerves you."

Stilling looking at the gate, Magmas shuddered again, "There are only a few Fey living or not that can say that they can send a chill down my spine. Yet she does so with the ease of the like I have yet to name."

"Perhaps you shouldn't have dismissed her as a potential love interest."

Secrets, Lies and Betrayal
by: M.L. Ruscsak

Still gazing at the spot where the gate had been Magmas lowered his voice, "I asked Alec his opinion long before I had made my choice. He told me to ask Prim."

Nodding once with understanding, Karnack replied softly, "So, the choice was that of the goddess."

"No. The choice was mine. Prim said she had little use for the affairs of the heart. Which we both know was a flat out lie. But she did let me see how my life would be affected by either choice. Seeing Freya now... knowing that sliver of fear is still there. Even knowing that she is blood bound to me... that she could take joy in my pain. I didn't make a bad choice. And I would make the same again."

"My boy blood bound or not Freya would never take joy in your pain. Unless you stood in the way of her completing her mission. Then... well you know better than stop a Fey."

Magmas took a deep breath and sighed, "Perhaps I should contact Donny and let him know that his daughter is back in Lite. If anything, it would give Nisha another protector that says in the shadows."

"I sent a Shadow to tell him the moment that you suggested that she be the one to watch over Nisha. Not that she hadn't decided as much long before she was born. You simply gave me the means to please her without betraying Prim."

Secrets, Lies and Betrayal
by: M.L. Ruscsak

Magmas took a deep breath, "In that case, why don't we go find the more troublesome of my brothers and discuss the real reason we are here."

Heading toward the castle of bone Karnack let out a hard laugh, "You think I do not know why the sons of Magmas are on my doorstep. Why I have not one, but two dark Fey preparing for a battle that we all do not wish to see. I am old Magmas, but I am not so old that I have lost the abilities to see those beyond this realm. I know why you are here. But I do not think even you have the power to stop what is to come."

"No, we don't. But we do have the power to delay that war for a few more years. And hopefully by then we have found Myrddin and Nisha has grown into most of her powers."

Secrets, Lies and Betrayal
by: M.L. Ruscsak

CHAPTER 10: NISHA

Slipping back through the gate, Nisha felt as if it had been hours that she had spent with King Magmas. Hours spent touring a city that was now hers. A city filled with the dead and more than a few living. All of whom had offered immediately to be blood bound to her. All of whom that she had told that she would review the request for she hadn't been prepared for the crowing today.

And all of them saturated with so much power that she would have accepted if Magmas hadn't been standing right there.

The dead understood. The living? Well, if they understood or not Magmas would make sure that they did. The tone in his voice when one had thought to argue with her... coupled with words that she herself didn't know. The

Secrets, Lies and Betrayal
by: M.L. Ruscsak

person... creature... had back down its long-coiled tail taking far from her sight.

In a few days she would figure out how to blood bind all of those that wished to be bound to her. In a few days she would have the answers as to why some of the living were dwelling with the dead.

But that was in a few days.

Right now, she had other worries to deal with. One being, dealing with the person responsible for Edgar's injuries. The other, making damn sure that that person knew that although she, the princess of Darke, dwelled in Lite; she would be controlled by no one. Made sure all of Lite knew that she was no pawn to be played with.

Easing through the gate Nisha squared her shoulders and held her head high. She was the Queen of the Under Kingdom, The Crown Princess of Darke. King Magmas had faith in her abilities. The Royal Princes Flint and Apollo both not only had faith in her, but had bound themselves to her before disappearing into the city.

So, no matter what anyone else thought, no matter what they did. She and she alone now held the power to do as she pleased. She alone carried the abilities of both the dead and three of the most dangerous Fey that had ever been born.

Secrets, Lies and Betrayal
by: M.L. Ruscsak

Taking her first step from the gate Nisha glanced to her cousin who was now joined by her favorite kitty. A Draken knife tucked to her side. A knife that had been dipped in the poison of a Drakens venom.

"Lilly."

Lilly's eyes met hers only for a second. "David arrived moments after you…"

Narrowing her eyes, Nisha spoke more to the man who was hiding behind the shape of the cat than to the woman that she was gazing at. "I'm glad the *Cat* could be bothered to leave his comfy pillow and preform the job he swore to do."

Nisha didn't know if the arch of Lilly's back had been due to her tone or if she was reacting to another exiting the gate. Probably would never really know. Nor did it truly matter.

Freya, only she had changed her appearance. No longer dressed as a forest nymph, she looked… felt more like that of a dark Fey. Her long flowing dark hair was the only remanence of the nymph that she had met. Gone were the vines of foliage. Gone was the leaves that had covered her. In replace were clothes that could have been a second skin. Both the dark corset and black leggings flowing with her sinewy build. Neither would interfere should she need to fight. Neither were the common dress of Lite but that of the Feyen warriors long before the great war.

Lilly tried to smile as she finally rose from her seat. "Nisha? Do I dare ask who your friend is?"

Taking a few steps over to Edgar, Nisha peered down. Most of his injuries were now healed. Others would do so on their own. Turning yet again to walk away, she paused. Lilly needed an answer. David would demand one. "Lilly, Crown Princess of Lite, this is Freya, she now my personal guard. She and shadow will be looking after me until I return to Darke. In the meantime, Edgar needs to be taken back to the castle. If anyone asked you did the healing." Passing Lilly, she glanced over her shoulder, "Tomorrow will be soon enough to start testing our abilities. And Lil, as far as your mother is concerned, Freya came through the gate and protected us from something. Make it believable."

Stumbling forward Lilly rushed to reach her cousin. Joining Nisha, Lilly whispered, "You don't trust mum, do you?"

There were more questions there. Nisha could hear them. But she understood if Lilly put a voice to those concerns now, David would very well contact his father. If he did the very least both of them would be moved to a country not of Lite. At worst, it would mean war.

Secrets, Lies and Betrayal
by: M.L. Ruscsak

There was no need to cause that. Least not yet.

"I have no reason not to trust her. But Lilly, I'm telling you right now, something inside of me has been woken up and I will no longer tolerate being treated as less. I am the crown Princess of Darke. I am a royal Fey. But more importantly, I am the daughter of the darkness. It is about time your mother and all of Lite understands that."

Letting Nisha leave the empty farm area Lilly turned to Freya, "Well, I guess things are going to get interesting around the castle."

"Yes princess, you can safely say that." Pulling out her own knife, Freya studied it. "I have known the ongoing of your palace for many years. Be warned, I have a job to do and I will destroy any that interfere. Including your Draken."

Secrets, Lies and Betrayal
by: M.L. Ruscsak

Secrets, Lies and Betrayal
by: M.L. Ruscsak

CHAPTER 11: LILLY

For several long moments Lilly stood there. Never had she heard that tone in Nisha's voice. Never had she ever been threatened by a guard. A soft touch on her elbow…

She didn't have to say anything as David's tail wrapped protectively around her. Didn't need to say anything until those strong Draken arms enclosed around her. Leaning her head on his chest, Lilly softly asked, "Did the guard just threaten me."

"No." David arched his back slightly and nodded toward the direction both Nisha and her guard had taken, "She's Feyen, Lil. True Feyen. If I had to guess, and I am only

Secrets, Lies and Betrayal
by: M.L. Ruscsak

guessing. She was… is… some kind of dark Fey. One I hope never to cross and one I know my father will love to meet."

"You're going to contact him." Not a question but confirmation.

"Darling, Nisha's guard was attacked. I'm still waiting to hear by what. Your cousin is now protected by a Fey that if clothing is an indication, she died more than three thousand years ago. I think he needs to know. Don't you?"

Well, when put it that way… "I need to get Edgar back to the palace. It would be helpful if I didn't have to fight to get him back into the palace."

David closed his reptilian eyes, "Lilly, love, you are the crown princess of Lite. You are my betrothed. You should not ever need to fight to enter your own castle. Remind your guards of who you are. If that fails…" He shrugged, "I have yet to have a full meal since arriving. I do tend not to make meals out those who protect the castle, however, I am willing to bend that rule."

He wasn't joking. Drakens didn't joke about meals. Regardless of how discussing they made it sound. "I have five years to find you food that you won't have to kill yourself. I remind myself every day. And twice when you start talking about eating someone in front of me."

Secrets, Lies and Betrayal
by: M.L. Ruscsak

"Every castle keeps a herd of eatables in the pastors. My meals have already been found. And none of whom as you put are people. Now, let's get Edgar to the castle. I wish to hear everything once Nisha decided to be the crown princess that she is rather than the child that she is not."

Secrets, Lies and Betrayal
by: M.L. Ruscsak

Secrets, Lies and Betrayal
by: M.L. Ruscsak

CHAPTER 12: NISHA

This very morning the maids had rushed to get out her way. The castle carriers had made haste to hide behind closed doors. The guards at that time had not been fazed by her small show of temper. They had not been afraid of what the little spoiled princess would do. What she and her untrained abilities could do.

Now they were afraid. Very afraid.

Her long black dragon wing dragged on the floor behind her. The horned tips perched just above her crown. The royal circlet belonging to the Princess of Darke delicately placed around her head. Never had she worn it. Never had it left the royal treasury... until today.

How she had come by it... or who had given to her. Well, Shadows were notorious thieves. Why should the one that was bound to her be any different?

Secrets, Lies and Betrayal
by: M.L. Ruscsak

No even he... it... understood something that no one ever would. She a queen worthy of the respect of the Great Magmas. Her temper was one not to be dismissed. Controlled? Maybe. But never dismissed. And never underestimated.

Shadow understood this. Alista nurtured this temper. And it was well past time that those in Lite became afraid of it.

Every corridor looked the same now. A blinding gold light that was too quickly snuffed out by total darkness. Glass breaking as she passed. And guards... the ones who didn't think that she would dare harm them... fell to the ground twitching.

She wouldn't kill them. She refused to kill those who had done her no harm, but she would give them a warning. At least this time.

Turning the last of the mindless corridors she could see the wide hallway that lead to the throne room. She could see the interior doors still held open.

They wouldn't be for long. Not even if she had to seal them shut.

Entering the long hall that would lead to the throne room, she no longer gave warning to her temper. Didn't bother to make the hearths blaze with unnatural fire. No, the wind howling through the corridor was enough of a

Secrets, Lies and Betrayal
by: M.L. Ruscsak

warning to any that would be foolish enough to approach her. Those that were foolish… were now powerless to stop her.

The power held within the wind muted the abilities of those around her. Muted them to the point of completely, rendering them useless. The doors would be sealed shut until she passed safely from this hall. Sealed so tightly even a strong arm Fey would be powerless to open the door.

This was just a taste of her power. Just a taste of her true temper. She knew it would take much more to provoke her deepest rage. Much more than the few snippets that the dead had given her.

She just hoped that this would be the last warning that her aunt would need.

Secrets, Lies and Betrayal
by: M.L. Ruscsak

A strong gust of wind howled as the tall double doors of the throne room banged open, startling both the Queen of Lite and her husband. It only took a single heart beat for Blake to recover. A single breath, more for him to be ready to face whatever had caused the locked doors to open with that much fury. Judging by the way he faltered... the way he had taken a step back... he was not prepared to face the dark Fey who had strode into the room. He was not prepared to face the princess of Darke and all of her fury.

Nisha's eyes met his for only a moment. Just long enough to get a feel for his thoughts. Just long enough to know that he was seeking the reason for this display of temper.

As far as he knew there wasn't a single reason that could have proved her temper. Not a single mishap that could have provoked her into showing a glimpse of temper. Not a single...

A flicker of a thought when her eyes moved to the Queen, who was sitting too smugly on her throne.

Carefully she drew closer, making sure that her uncle saw her eyes. Made sure that he understood what was flickering just behind them.

Nisha knew that he understood the very moment that he swallowed hard and vanished his lighting staff. He wanted to hear what she had to say just as badly as he wanted no part in what happen after.

Halfway to the dais Nisha hissed, "There are matters we need to discuss."

Celeste leaned forward on her throne. "Nisha what is the meaning of this? You should be studying in your room after your short- "

"Enough aunt. You have hobbled me for far too long." Narrowing her eyes, she ignored the proper way for a princess to address a queen. Ignored her aunt's protest to remove the wings that she now openly wore. And ignored the guards that she could feel drawing closer to the throne room.

Raising her head high Nisha squared her shoulders to address her uncle. He would understand the threat much faster than this queen would. "My personal guard that was sent here by Queen Alista was injured today. The nature of those injuries is yet to be discovered in full. However, I know for fact that it was by no natural means that he was attacked. And I know for fact that regardless of what is said, the injuries were not done by no troll."

Drawing closer to Celeste, Nisha took in the fear that laid in her aunt's eyes. And knew the truth. She didn't need a spell to know who had used that incantation to harm her guard. She was looking at the bitch. "You should also be

Secrets, Lies and Betrayal
by: M.L. Ruscsak

fully aware... Edgar is now fully blood bound to me. Once I leave Lite, he and his family will join me in Darke. I have also added another guard to my personal protection."

Too quickly Celeste got to her feet slamming into the wall of power that separated her from Nisha. Separated her from any that may come to her aid. "If you think...."

The castle shook as lightning flashed within the room, shattering anything that had been made of glass including the crystal dome ceiling. The debris swirling around before neatly landing in the corner. "**SILENCE**!" She waited only a single heart beat before continuing. Only a heartbeat until she had regained control over rage once more. "I will remain in Lite until my eighteenth year. My proxy will continue to rule in my name as Grand'Mere has suggested. However, what abilities, I now learn is no longer up to **you** as I have found another royal Fey to oversee all of the things that I should be learning."

More than a hint of fear now laid in Celeste's eyes. More than just a hint of fear laid in her voice. "What royal Fey? I demand to know."

It wasn't Celeste, who Nisha watched now, it was Blake. Her uncle, yes, but more than that he was the captain of the guards for the country of Lite. He was a royal Fey was somehow connected to Queen Alista. And he was pissed. Oh, not at her, but at the queen whom he served.

Secrets, Lies and Betrayal
by: M.L. Ruscsak

Because of how Blake was holding himself the answer to Celeste's question came to her with ease. Not the truth, but not a lie either. "Queen Alista. It seems she understands me much better than you do." Turning to leave Nisha paused just before reaching the door. Just before she decided if she wished to scare the rest of the guards or let Blake deal with them. Seeing fear was reign dominate in their faces, she decided Blake could handle his guards'. At least today. "Uncle Blake please acquaint yourself with my newest guard, Freya. You may find her abilities to keep me safe far greater than your own." Another pause, then, "You should also know that she belongs to the Under Kingdom and answers only to the gatekeeper

Secrets, Lies and Betrayal
by: M.L. Ruscsak

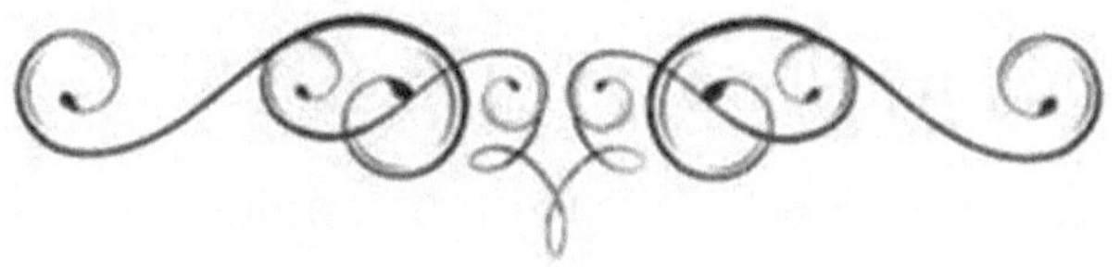

CHAPTER 13: CELESTE

Watching the doors slam shut behind Nisha, Celeste couldn't help but to jump. Could no longer hide the fear that she had. Long ago she had been promised power. She had been promised a place among the great Fey. Had been promised that her name would be as revered as that of King Magmas and Lord Griffith.

That power should have been hers. Not Adrianna's and certainly not Nisha's. There had to be a way to strip that insolent child of all that raw untrained abilities. All of that power. There had to be. Or at the very least transfer it to…

"What did you do?"

Blakes voice filled the empty room. Vibrated off the walls, loud enough to rattle the crystal that had been piled up in the corner. "I- I didn't do anything. Damn it Blake look around you Nisha…"

"Nisha is her father's daughter. She is not one for theatrics. Not one to prance around with the tiara of Darke.

Secrets, Lies and Betrayal
by: M.L. Ruscsak

And certainly not one to make demands. So, I will ask again... What. Did. You. Do."

She couldn't let him see her tremble. Couldn't dare to let him see how unnerved he was making her. And surely would not let him... her subordinate have the last word. "I didn't do anything. You know as well as I, that Nisha lacks the ability to control the few gifts that she has. It is quite possible that she has started to come unraveled."

Blake narrowed his eyes. He could sense a lie yet he couldn't call her out on it. "I- "

Something screamed in terror. It sounded like a siren or a harpy. Then again, it could have been the gargoyles. Looking at Blake tears of fear glazed her icy blue eyes, "Blake do something. You can't allow her...."

A cruel, bitter smile formed on his lips, "Darling, I did warn you." He towered over her, shaking his head then laughed at her own stupidity. "She is your sister's daughter. She is the daughter of Myrddin. You cannot suppress those powers. You cannot suppress that temperament. I have always done as you asked, but we both know the only reason that I am still here is for our daughter and that of my friend. Now if you'll excuse me, I would like to see Lilly and find out what happened to provoke this side of her cousin's nature before I deal with a guard that I can presume died in some battle."

Secrets, Lies and Betrayal
by: M.L. Ruscsak

"Blake… Come back here. I demand…"

He had reached the door before she had yelled after him. When she did, she understood her error, for his lighting staff appeared in his hand and was pointed at her heart. Lightning and fire danced in his eyes. Oh, she had seen him mad a few times, but this… this was a Fey, who had been trained not only with his own natural abilities but those of someone darker. His teacher had been Myrddin.

This was the first time in nearly two hundred years that she had even thought about what abilities he had. What temperament had laid dormant behind his quiet nature. This was the first time that he had looked at her as if she were the enemy that he would destroy.

For a long moment he just stood there with his staff pointed at her. A longer time clearly fighting the urge to end her. Still gripping the staff firmly in his hands, he snarled, "You don't demand anything of me Celeste. I'm not yours to control like some puppet nor will I ever be."

She didn't bother to stop him as he stormed from her sight. Nor could she send her guards' after him. No, she would have to find another way to deal with him. Right after she found a way to deal with Nisha.

Secrets, Lies and Betrayal
by: M.L. Ruscsak

Secrets, Lies and Betrayal
by: M.L. Ruscsak

CHAPTER 14: BLAKE

Under normal circumstances, he would have gone directly to Lilly. Any other day he would have her come to him and they could go into the meadow and work on one of her skills privately. Not today. Not when the temper that he had always managed to keep well-hidden had turned into this rage. Not when he could now clearly hear the gargoyles screaming for help.

Only one other Fey had ever terrorized the gargoyles. Nisha's father would have been proud that she has managed to make them scream in fright.

Turning a corner, He stopped just as a lovely woman pushed off the wall just before him. Leggings that accented her long legs. Shorts that moved with her body. Oh, and her corset. Celeste had never been the one to wear them, Addy had. It was probably the reason Celeste had banned them from all of Lite.

Secrets, Lies and Betrayal
by: M.L. Ruscsak

Which begged the question. "I don't believe that we've been introduced."

Her eyes scanned his body as she retook her position of leaning on the interior wall. "Your guards are poorly trained. Should the need arise they would be wiped out within a single volley. This castle's defenses have been mostly dismantled leaving you open for an attack." Looking out of the corner of her eye she asked, "So why should I allow the future queen of Darke to remain here?"

Oh shit. Nisha had said that she had a new guard. He had assumed that the guard had died in battle. If he could trust what he was seeing... trust that she knew about the castle's defenses... "Lady Freya I presume?"

"I have never been a lady of the court nor do I ever plan on it. But if you insist on formality, I was the general of the special forces during the time of the great war." She pushed off if the wall and took the two steps over to him. "Make no mistake, Captain Blake. I do not answer to you. I will not answer to the queen who rules this pitiful country. And do not count on me as an ally."

Oh, he would never consider her an ally... Unless... "Nisha should remain here to develop her abilities. It seems her aunt has a knack for bringing the more deadlier one to the surface."

Secrets, Lies and Betrayal
by: M.L. Ruscsak

"Very well. The princess shall remain here for the term of five years. On the condition that every defense, be put back in place."

He had no idea what she was talking about. Not a single mention of the castle defenses could be found in any written journal. "In that case, General, I'll leave that in your careful hands, seeing that I have no knowledge of such things."

If she was amused or not he couldn't tell, but she did leave without further comment.

Too many corridors. To many pail white doors that all looked the same. And too many prying eyes of every guard that he passed. There was only one reason that he ever came to Lilly's private room. Only one reason he would seek her out in the oldest part of the castle.

Secrets, Lies and Betrayal
by: M.L. Ruscsak

Nisha.

No matter what other drama or problems were in the castle, the only one that he ever sought his daughter out for… was to help deal with her cousin. For some unknown reason she seemed to be the only living person in all of Lite that that not only could handle Nisha, but could usually explain a thing or two about her cousin's temperament.

At the last white door at the end of the furthest tower Blake raised his fist to give a soft token tap. He only paused because Lilly was cursing… and his daughter never cursed. Never said one word in a fit of rage. It was enough of a reason to rush into the room.

A move that left him face to face with a prince of Darken. Know who this prince was wasn't as unsettling as knowing that he had been in the castle without him, the captain of the guard being informed… Not much he could do about that. But he could very calmly have a restrained conversation before contacting this boy's father. "Prince? It seems as though someone forgot to tell me that you are visiting with your betrothed."

Davkren narrowed his reptilian eyes as his long-pointed tail stayed carefully hidden behind his back. "I have been in the castle most of the past five years. I didn't announce my arrival, and then I didn't plan on doing so anytime soon. And after today I have even more reason to

Secrets, Lies and Betrayal
by: M.L. Ruscsak

stay unseen." He turned slightly and hissed, "And that was before Nisha made a blasted gargoyle cry."

Blake closed his sun kissed eyes and counted to ten twice.

Nisha making a gargoyle cry was something that could wait for a brief moment. A Draken being in the castle and more or less declaring this place unsafe... was something that could not be over looked. Not after what happen five years ago. Not after trolls had attacked both Lilly and Nisha while visiting the Darkens. And certainly not after Lilly was attacked and almost injured.

A flash of a memory. Lilly had come back not only betrothed after that... but had come home with a kitten. A kitten that had Darken eyes. And that meant at least one of this boy's parents knew their son was here.

That in itself was another warning. And one that he would take up with Craykren fairly soon.

"I'm not questioning your arrival, however, if you think it best to be unseen until Lilly's eightieth birthday the I whole hardly agreed. After I know what happened today to have a dark Fey now looking at this castle as a hostile battle ground."

Carefully Lilly took a deep breath, then sat on the edge of her bed. Her eyes down cast tot the floor so not to look at either of the men of her family. "Nisha showed me

Secrets, Lies and Betrayal
by: M.L. Ruscsak

her thinking spot today. Because I promised, I will not tell you anything about it. Not today or any day that follows."

Blake crossed his arms, "I know it's in Feyen. And I know Queen Alista has protection spell around it so Nisha won't be found while she's visiting."

"Nish didn't tell me that."

"Alista sent a message that at the time didn't make much sense. After the discussion I had with your cousin… I pieced it together. That said, I have no right to interfere with the on goings of another country. Nor does your mother. Even if she could Feyen is not a country I would dare question without a damn good cause."

Lilly nodded in understanding and relief. "When we came back, Marigold was waiting for me. Edgar had been attacked. After looking at all of the wounds I know two things. One someone targeted him, hoping to send him to the under Kingdom. And two, it wasn't a creature that attacked him. It was a single incantation. It seems very similar to the one Grand 'Mere used to end the hydra that threatened the town of Manicora."

So, Nisha's fears were just. "And do you know who could have used the spell?"

"I have my suspicions. However, the mother I lover wouldn't do something so careless nor ruthless. In any case, she best doesn't press Nisha."

Secrets, Lies and Betrayal
by: M.L. Ruscsak

Oh, his darling wife best not press anyone at this point. Not when he now had a Darken looking to this queen as a potential threat. Not when Nisha's shadow would probably be looking at the queen of Lite as a threat. And not when the Queen of Feyen would surely hear some form of this conversation, and reach her own conclusions.

"What else, so I need to know?"

"Nisha was invited to visit the under Kingdom. I don't know what happened there. Nor do I ever expect to. But I can feel the difference in Nisha. Her power... I can close my eyes and pinpoint all of the darkness that she is only now instead of just feeling a light pressure it's a deep void sucking everything into it. Her abilities in the dark arts, in things that I have only ever read about. They seem to eclipse everything now. Which is why, When I am eighteen I will become the queen of Lite. Mum would say one wrong thing and cause Nisha to destroy Lite and everyone in it. I on the other hand know how to work with her. It may buy enough time for Nish to gain full control over those abilities. If not I'm sure I can find something for her to do with them that won't destroy half of the realm."

Blake nodded once and slowly go to his feet, "I'll make the arrangements. Lilly, I don't know what your mother has been thinking these past years. *If* she had been thinking at all. But something died in her the night her twin was taken and it never fully healed."

Secrets, Lies and Betrayal
by: M.L. Ruscsak

"I know… but blaming Nisha and her abilities won't change things. If anything, it has only made things much worse. If you can, try to reason with Mum. With Grand'Mere now in the Under Kingdom I fear Nish feels like she no one. Well, no one but David and me."

Reaching for the door Blake nodded, "And David, I expect the only petting taking place in the room be done while you are a cat."

"Of course, sir. My mother would skin me alive if she thought otherwise."

"My boy, your mother is not the only Fey, who can deal with a hybrid Draken."

Secrets, Lies and Betrayal
by: M.L. Ruscsak

CHAPTER 15: CELESTE

The screaming from the gargoyles stopped. The guards were currently checking the rest of the castle for any other disturbances, so she had a few moments to slip into the Solaris. A few moments to plan her next move.

Celeste glanced behind her making sure not a soul was following her. Nothing out of place. Not a candle flickering unexpectedly. Nothing...

A flutter on the floor. Was that a shadow that belonged or that of the beast that was bound to Nisha?

Silently she approached as relief washed through her. Just a shadow from the candlelight. Just something that belonged. Relief washed through her as she tried to calm her nerves.

A deep breath and she patted her heart. If anyone found out her secrets she could be killed. Or worse...

Secrets, Lies and Betrayal
by: M.L. Ruscsak

Rushing back to the door, she slipped inside her long gold and white dress nearly catching on the frame as the stone door closed behind her.

She only had a few moments. Blake would find her in here. He always did. Always intruded on her private time. Perhaps she could spell a lock to keep him out. Not that they had ever worked for her before.

Damn insolent fool. She married him out of convenience. Married him because her mother had decided that they would be matched long before she was ready. But the choice to take him to her bed was hers. She needed him to cover a lie. So why couldn't he be what she needed? Why couldn't he be a silent mouth piece that wanted little more than to see her happy.

Why?

"Ahhhh!" She screamed to herself just to ease the tension that was building inside her.

Damn fool. Sooner or later she would have to be rid of him. But not yet. Lilly still needed him to complete her training... Then...

Yes, just as soon as Lilly was accomplished enough...

Crossing the room, Celeste let the thought of how Blake would die fill her mind. Opening her trinket box with the false bottom she smiled at allowing her lover

Secrets, Lies and Betrayal
by: M.L. Ruscsak

dismember her husband. Yes, that would be thrilling to watch.

Pushing the few odd shaped jewels out of the way she found what she needed. A small red cut stone with swirling mist. She had never known where it had come from but the deity that answered her calls…

… He had shown her what could be. He had shown her the way to rule not only this realm but another. The only thing that he had ever been wrong on had been what child of Myrddin would hold the key to power.

Holding the stone close to her lips, she whispered, "My Lord. Please I am in need…"

The swirling mist cleared for just a moment, "Ah my dear. Have you brought me good news?"

She ignored his question as she hurried to explain, "I need a way to strip Nisha of her abilities. A way to transfer them to another Fey worthy of all that she has been given."

Words flowed from his lips. Words that she didn't understand, but the viciousness of them…

"I have shown you the man that you needed to bed in order to carry the child of power. You waited too long to seduce him, then used a spell to slip into his bed to beget yourself with the child.

Secrets, Lies and Betrayal
by: M.L. Ruscsak

I show you the man who give you more power for your own taking yet he still is not blood bound to you."

"I've tried. I swear that I have. The binding does not work."

The Solaris door blew open as Blake strode in. He said nothing as he glared at her.

It was too late to hide the stone. Too late

Secrets, Lies and Betrayal
by: M.L. Ruscsak

CHAPTER 16: BLAKE

Blake flung out his hand using his own incantation to pull the stone from her grasp. "It's mine. You have no, right…" Celeste wailed a wall of power keeping her in place and far from her precious stone.

He glared down into the stone and shook his head. "Magmas, you damned old fool. I should have known you had something to do with the events as of late."

Magmas? King magmas. No. she had seen portraits of him and he was not the great Feyen king. Too stunted for words. Celeste stammered, "You know…"

"I know this worthless fool who rules by default and plays whatever tune suits him in that moment." Vanishing the stone Blake curled his fingers into a fist. "I know of the existence of two stones. So how did you come across a third."

Secrets, Lies and Betrayal
by: M.L. Ruscsak

That was none of his business. None. "I don't answer to you Blake Kairavi. I am the queen of Lite and…"

He was on her fast. Too fast for her to see him move. But she felt his fingers pressing into her throat. That he made sure of.

"You're right my dear, you are the queen of Lite. A queen who has been manipulated by another in hopes of creating a war. For that alone, I have the authority to kill you. However, I think it best if I go another direction."

Still keeping a tight grip on her throat Blake called over his shoulder, Shadow my dear friend some assistance if you would be so kind."

It wasn't a shadow who strode into the room, but a man created out of fine black mist and sharp deadly bone white teeth. "So, after years you have finally figured out who I am."

Not taking his eyes off of the Shade, Blake tried to smile. Tried to look calm and in control when in reality he knew that a single twitch and this Man… this Shade… would devour not only him but Celeste as well. "Actually, I knew that a Shade had taken residence in the castle the moment I was told that you bound yourself to Princess Nisha. I chose to keep to your secret since I know of nothing more protective or deadly then your race."

Secrets, Lies and Betrayal
by: M.L. Ruscsak

The man, dissipated into the air only to form, but a few feet from the Queen and her now captor. "I see. And why now do you wish for, my help, I wonder? Why shouldn't I just have a meal made from those standing before me? Why shouldn't I be rid of the bitch who would conspire to harm my queen?"

And that was the threat that he was afraid of. Keeping his breath steady he tried to answer as truthfully as he could. "If I can't bind this wrench to myself, then please for the love of Lite take her as your meal. However, if I trust what I know about the Great War and about the Ruler of Pallas then you will need my help."

Blake didn't see the Shade move. Didn't feel the slice on his hand, but his dark blue blood swelled up dripping to the ground. It would do for the moment. Prying Celeste's mouth open he forced several drops to flow down her throat. "I Blake Kairavi, bind you Celeste Trovos to me. Your powers are now mine to control. Your words, your body are mine. Gone are the days of your freedom. I will know your secrets and you will tell them freely."

Too quickly he bit her lip to draw her blood to affirm the binding. "With your blood I affirm this binding."

Power swelled inside of him as he shoved her to the ground. Her memories of every misdeed right there within his own mind.

Secrets, Lies and Betrayal
by: M.L. Ruscsak

Fourteen years ago. Not long before they had met. Celeste dressed in only that of a thin house robe. Her body barely covered. She passed a single mirror. It wasn't her reflection, but that of her sister's. Myrddin laid bound to some sort of bed. Sweat pulling from his skin.

Drugged. Feverish. Also, her doing.

Slowly she disrobed

He didn't need to know what had happened next. He knew some it himself Myrddin had been sick for days. It was why he had come here from Feyen. Adrianna had been beside herself with worry. Not understanding what her betrothed was telling her in his feverish Ramblings. At the time, neither had he.

It was all too clear now.

His friend had saw through the enchantment. He had known the truth yet…

"So was bedding your sisters betrothed your idea or that of the ruler of Pallas."

Celeste glanced down to the ground, unable to keep her thoughts or words silent, "I wanted power. It was a way to get it."

"I see. So, if I am correct, Lilly is the child of my friend." He should feel hurt. He should have felt anger and rage… yet. There was no shame in raising another's child.

Secrets, Lies and Betrayal
by: M.L. Ruscsak

At least not on his part. One day she would have to explain this to the children. It would be up to them if they forgave her. Lilly might in time. Nisha on the other hand…

He would need to find Vasilissa and discuss this with her before Nisha ever found out about this. If she didn't already.

Stepping back over to her, Blake knelt down, "As of today, you will rule in name only. And Celeste, your plan might have worked if Myrddin hadn't given Addy his heart within hours of meeting her. You remember that time, don't you? The first time your mother brought you to Feyen. The first time you were left alone with the first daughter of Elista."

A hesitant nod from Celeste was his only answer.

"Myrddin found Addy wandering the halls shortly after. Galeron and myself witnessed him exchanging hearts with your sister. You were barely eight, and ready Myrddin saw the potential in your sister and the corruption in you. It was some years after that when they became betrothed. Well, officially anyways. You my dear, never stood a chance of gaining his powers. Just as you never stood a chance at gaining mine."

Closing the Solaris door behind him Blake nodded to the shade, "Thank you."

"Is what you said about the traitor true? Is he trying to make war, yet again with this star?"

"I have no reason to lie to a Shade. And less reason to lie to someone of royal blood."

Turning from Blake, he softly said, "Blood hasn't run in my veins for far too long."

"True. But a single drop of Nisha's did something. It may be years before we find out what. But I intend to be there when you do."

"My name was Gwydion. I look forward to seeing you again ruler of Lite."

Blake didn't draw an easy breath until he was sure that the Shade had gone. Suspecting that one was in the castle was one thing. Knowing for fact was quite another. So, it wasn't for

Secrets, Lies and Betrayal
by: M.L. Ruscsak

several minutes his own heart slowed down enough to deal with all that now rested in his hands.

One thing was certain, he would have to contact his father and possibly his uncle.

Secrets, Lies and Betrayal
by: M.L. Ruscsak

Secrets, Lies and Betrayal
by: M.L. Ruscsak

CHAPTER 17: NISHA

Nisha sat on her platform bed that this morning had been covered in a pale pink floral cover. Bright ornate lilies. A cover that she had always hated but never complained about. Until now... The cover was no longer pink, but white with veins of smoke gray and black lines. Some thinker some thin others barely visible. But that didn't matter. What did matter was that she had created it. The natural wood wardrobe closet was now white with gold inlays. The floor matching the title of the Spire.

No matter what happened in the next five years. No matter what her aunt did or said she could no longer treat her as a burden. As something that she would rather not have living in her kingdom.

A soft tap on her now dark wood door.

Secrets, Lies and Betrayal
by: M.L. Ruscsak

Lilly. No need to use any ability to know that. She knew her cousin's token tap knock. "It's open Lil."

The door barely opened, "It is safe, isn't it? I heard... I'm sure what I heard, but..."

"The gargoyles who guard the castle were a little rumpled while I made this tower more to my liking."

Pushing the door all the way open Lilly stood with her hand on her hip, "Nisha! What did the gargoyles do to you for you to be rumpling them up?"

Nisha fell back on her bed with her eyes lightly closed, "Did you know the first time my father came here he made the gargoyles scream in terror. The way I see it me rumpling them is a warning to those who seem to think that I am anyone other than my father's daughter."

"Oh, for the love of Lite. I swear you will have me pulling out my hair by the time we are crowned queen."

With a Cheshire cat grin Nisha slowly sat up. "You mean by the time you are crowned queen? I on the other hand now rule the whole of the Under Kingdom."

With a hard thud Lilly plopped down onto the floor. "You're... Nisha that's not funny... That's..."

Calling in her crown and scepter she held both out to Lilly. "This stays between us until our eightieth year."

Secrets, Lies and Betrayal
by: M.L. Ruscsak

For a long moment Lilly didn't move, didn't dare breath. Finally, she whispered, "Yes, I think that would be best.

Secrets, Lies and Betrayal
by: M.L. Ruscsak

Secrets, Lies and Betrayal
by: M.L. Ruscsak

EPILOGUE

In thirteen years he had never bothered Nisha,

didn't want to bother her now. But he didn't feel like he had a choice. New rules would need to be made and agreed to keep not only her safe, but those who lived in Lite as well.

Pausing at the foot of the great tower that would lead to Nisha's undisputed territory, Blake hesitated. How much would he need to explain? How much would he be comfortable in telling? A flutter of a shadow darted behind him. The sound of boots scuffing the cold stone floor.

Too quickly he turned to face a man that he hadn't seen in too many years, "Flint?" It was him all dusty blond hair and thick muscles. But he looked tired... both mentally and physically.

Flint said nothing, just brought his finger to his dry lips and stepped back through the shadow. And disappeared once more.

A single glance up the steps. He could speak to Nisha later. Right now, whatever Flint needed was far more important.

Secrets, Lies and Betrayal
by: M.L. Ruscsak

Stepping out of the shadow Blake glanced around.

He wasn't in the castle. For that matter, he didn't think that he was no longer in Lite at all. The dirt floor and formed sand walls... he didn't know where he was but he knew where he wasn't.

"Blake come with me."

Flint's voice, but he couldn't see where it had come from. Couldn't see the man who voice warned caution. Letting his hands to guide him along the wall, he finally adjusted to the dimly lit room. Then he found his way from there. A long corridor hat led into what he assumed was a dining hall. A single long dark wood table and a dozen chairs. No ornate emblements. No hints of colors. Just smooth walls made of sand and dirt.

A handful of Fey.

Flint he recognized. As well as Magmas and Alista. It took a moment longer to place Vasilissa. Would have taken

Secrets, Lies and Betrayal
by: M.L. Ruscsak

him longer if she didn't narrow her eyes and look ready to rip his throat out. The others... Two Fey, and two... he didn't know the race but the one looked dangerous while the other felt like a benign, old clerk.

"Your majesties? Gentlemen?" He nodded to both groups hoping not offend anyone.

Magmas kicked a seat away from the table. "Have a seat Blake."

Swallowing hard, he obeyed. "Is this because I bound Celeste to me?"

The old clerk let out a pained laugh, "My boy all you did was save her life. And after what we discovered just moments ago, that may be a good thing."

"How is it good that my daughter killed her sister? Tell me Karnack because I would love to know."

Since she sounded on the edge of tears or hysterics, he took a deep breath to console her. But didn't because the other man spoke.

"I don't think your daughter dead. Nor do I think Lord Myrddin is either."

Magmas leaned forward, his elbows on the long dark wood table, "What do you know, Nicco?"

Secrets, Lies and Betrayal
by: M.L. Ruscsak

"Nothing for certain. Not yet. But the Shades that were in the City of Night have no knowledge of the Queen or any other's dying that night. By all accounts the Fey simply went to sleep, then vanished."

Getting quickly to her feet Vasilissa slammed her hands to the table, "How is that possible? That can't be…"

Looking at no one Blake whispered, "A few Star City Fey have the ability to do so."

"You think they are held within the Star Cities?" Magmas' voice sounding cautious and worried.

"No, that would be too far. But… Myrddin knew spells to hide a person's abilities. It's possible someone used his spell against him." He looked up noticing Flint next to him. Grabbing the man's hand, he allowed for the stone that he had taken from Celeste to materialize within his hand. "Celeste had this. I don't know how long she had it. Nor how it came to her… but the bastard who rules Pallas has been using her for his own means. And he knows that he has lost Lite."

Flint glanced down at the stone, "Donny, I think it's time you were introduced to Nisha."

The dark Fey leaned back in his seat. His chiseled jaw flexing with irritation. "I have never taken pride in raising warriors. But raising leaders? For what is to come, I

Secrets, Lies and Betrayal
by: M.L. Ruscsak

will teach her all that I know. And we will pray that it is enough."

So many things swarmed his mind. The great warriors of the Great War had come back to this Star City. They had come back to mold Nisha into the queen... the warrior that they all needed to survive. They had come back to hold off another war for as many Light Cycles that they needed to buy Nisha the time to learn... to grow.

But it wasn't until he was alone with Flint that he asked, "What was this?"

Flint paused, looking ahead at the plain dirt wall. His fingers running through his hair. "This is the counsel of the Fey. Nicco is the first Eostre his powers and strength are second to none. And he is the only thing that can destroy a Shade. Donny, has worked with every Star City Fey that has had dark abilities. Except you. That was at Myrddin's request."

Secrets, Lies and Betrayal
by: M.L. Ruscsak

Myrddin. Of course, he would want to oversee training of certain Fey himself. His ego didn't allow for him to yield to more experienced... well anything. Choosing not to vice that comment, Blake choose to ask instead, "How much if this should be told to Nisha?"

"Eventually she will know everything. Right now, she only needs to know what can be verified. That said, while she is in Lite, her care is in your hands. Make sure she understands that. Make sure she understands that you bound her aunt to you, because the alternative was convening the Feyen council to strip her of not only her title of queen but also her life."

Blake looked away, "Would Alista... would she have..."

"She was prepared to ask the Shade that dwells with your castle. In fact, between the two of us... she might have already."

The Shade that... "Was its name Gwydion?"

Worried now Flint narrowed his eyes as he asked, "Why do you ask?"

"Because he's the one who's bound to Nisha."

Flint sucked in a breath, "Shit." He turned and began to pace. After a few tense moments he returned to Blake, "As Nisha's uncle do what you can to help her. As a trained fighter, teach her everything that you know. In the meantime. Say nothing. We need to find out what he knows and why he chose to bind himself to Nisha."

He could have understood the power that she would one-day wield. But the way Flint had lost all color to his face... there had to be more to this story. So much more than what met the eye. And yet until Nisha became the queen of that, they all hoped for... he hoped never to find out what distressed this steeled warrior.

(To be continued in "The New Reign" a Lite and Darke Novel and the conclusion in "The Silent Wars")

Secrets, Lies and Betrayal
by: M.L. Ruscsak

Secrets, Lies and Betrayal
by: M.L. Ruscsak

About the Author

M. L. Ruscsak

In the summer of 2011, M.L. suffered not one but two strokes, two surgeries and fought to regain the ability to do what all those around her take for granted every day. She fought to relearn to communicate, to speak, to walk.

Most will never know the struggle that regaining lost abilities are. And she would never wish that on anyone. But for her she found a new strength that she never knew that she had.

Typing to communicate led to tuning her skills as story teller. And now her mind burst with stories to share, worlds yet to be discovered. And powers yet to be tested.

Living with her daughter, she continues to refine those skills and test new ones.

Stay up to date with her on
https://www.facebook.com/OfLiteAndDarke/

Secrets, Lies and Betrayal
by: M.L. Ruscsak

And as always Happy Reading

Secrets, Lies and Betrayal
by: M.L. Ruscsak